STORM IN SHANGHAI

BOOK ONE OF
THE MAGE FATHER SERIES

J. M. Bush

Milkman Publishing

Edited by Matt Rance @ Proof Professor

Author Photo by Chris Page @ Pages Pics

Cover Design by Christopher Granger @ Southern Fried Creative

Printed in the United States of America

First Printing, 2016

ISBN 978-0-9972842-0-1

Library of Congress Control Number: 2016901894

Milkman Publishing
914 El Dorado Drive
Dothan, AL 36303

www.eatplaywritetravel.com

To my wife Merissa, thank you for believing in me and allowing me to be a Stay-at-home-Dad and a full time writer. I will love you forever and ever and ever.

SHMILY

ACKNOWLEDGEMENTS

The list of people that helped me get this book out of my head and into print is extensive. First, my wife gave me time, love, and support while I wrote. My two boys, Lucas and Jonas, gave me hugs and sweet dance moves while I struggled to bring these characters to life. My mom, Janie Hinson, gave me love and support every day since I was born. My dad, John Bush has always stood behind me and supported my family's decision to live abroad, and for that I thank him. My elder brother, Jay Bush, is the reason I love fantasy novels so much, as he introduced them to me at a young age, starting with a copy of R.A. Salvatore's *The Crystal Shard*. My younger brother, Josh Bush motivated me to do something more with my life when he became the first of us Bush Boys to graduate from college. My sister, Tara Bush, revealed that our father once killed a bear when he was black, and I'll never forget it. Jaret Shank and Mike Herd helped drive my creativity through music while I wrote this book, and I'll be forever grateful for that. Chris Granger gave his time freely to create the beautiful cover for this book, and has been my steadfast homie since high school no matter the distance between us.

To all of the people that donated money to help me pay for proofreading, and to the beta readers, let me say... THANK YOU: Andy Best, Ivan Belcic, Elizabeth Carlino, Kali & Kam Mixon, Rachel Hawkins, Major Terry Miller & Nancy Miller – in honor of their son Quentin Miller (RIP), Laura & Nick Stakelum, Natalie Hughes, Candice & Sam Strickland, Meredith & Jeremiah Shari, Brandy Bass, Lee & Tara Parr, Rick & Sue Ann Lulling, Jason Bowman, E.J. Swider, Chelsea Weldon, Christalle Bodiford-Twomey, Jenni McKinney.

Storm in Shanghai

<u>ONE</u>
1990 AD
Turin, Italy

"Crowds are the worst place you can be right now, Jaret," Dad says without even looking at me.

"I know," I reply sullenly. Even though he keeps it locked up in a drawer, sometimes Dad forgets and leaves his Network tome on. I've seen the news; I know about the attacks. "But Dad, it's the FIFA World Cup!" I explain. "There's a match tomorrow at Stadio Delle Alpi. I need to be there. Seeing this match is super important to me."

"No way, kiddo," he says. "We're only in town to visit the Turin Hall of Storm Magic. It's something I've dreamed of doing my whole life, coming here and researching everything they have on Storm. They've got actual ancient Storm mages' handwritten thoughts and ideas, which might contain long-forgotten spells, Jaret! You know this is important to me, son."

"Fine, I get it, Dad. So, the stadium is probably not a safe place with the Maelstrom on the loose. What if we go and watch the Brazilian team at their public demo today?" I ask. "I just want to see them kick the ball around for a little bit. There won't be thousands of people there, just a few hundred."

He tilts his head, shakes it gently, and says, "That's probably worse, son. All of the Maelstrom attacks were on crowds in the hundreds, not thousands."

Again, he's right. I know it. It's always groups of a few hundred people who get – well, blown up. On the Network, it said no one knows why the Maelstrom is doing this, or who he or she is. No one knows much about it at all.

But everyone in the magical community is terrified.

"Dad, listen. We don't have to stay long. We don't even have to get out of the car. We can just pull up and watch from across the street. Please, I'm begging you. You're getting to do something that you've wanted to do for your whole life, and I've wanted to see something like this my whole life. It's only fair," I say, trying to reason with him.

"Calm down, Jaret. You're only ten years old," he says. "Your life hasn't been that long. And whoever told you life was fair, anyway?"

"But Daaaaaaaaad," I whine, "I promise it will be okay. Nothing will happen! The last attack was a long time ago. The Maelstrom is probably dead or something."

My dad looks at me with his lecturing face, but before he can lay into me with a full 15-minute talk about *blah blah blah*, I decide to use my secret weapon.

"I love you, Daddy. I just wanna do something cool together. Afterwards, we can go to the Hall of Storm, and I'll help you look up magic history. That way, if I can use magic when I get older, and if it's Storm, then I'll already be smart, like you." His lecturing face slips away, and a smile takes its place. *Bingo.*

"Okay, Jaret," my dad says. "We'll drive by the demonstration and stop for five minutes. *Only* five minutes. No getting out of the car, and we'll be across the street. Capeesh?"

"Really? Awesome! But don't try to speak Italian anymore, please. It's pretty embarrassing, Dad."

"Arrivederci, son," he replies, ignoring my groan.

We drive along the Italian back streets on our way to see the famous footballers in action, and Dad drones on about the magic history of this building, the famous mage who shaped this plaza, and the ancient spells holding that building in place. Don't care. Not interested.

"I'm ready to see something spectacular," I think to myself.

When we arrive, the demonstration is already in full swing, which is great because we don't have to waste any time listening to people talk. I get to watch the team live and in action for five whole minutes.

"Oh my gosh, Dad. Thank you so much! Seeing this demo is going to be the greatest thing I've ever done."

Dad leans his seat back, closes his eyes, and yawns. "No problem, kiddo. Enjoy the barbarism."

He hates reg sports for some reason. Go figure; the famous World Speedcasting Champion doesn't care about sports that regular people play. Of course, he doesn't mind when Speedcasting fans freak out on him like I'm doing for these athletes. It's not... **BAM!**

The sudden bang on the side of our car makes my heart stop, and my dad shoots to an upright position, a ball of Storm lightning hovering in his hand. Looking to see what caused the noise, I see it was only a soccer ball that flew out of the demo area, and slammed into my door... and... *and oh my God, one of the players is coming to get it*. I might die.

Tugging on the handle, desperate to interact with whichever player is coming our way, I can't seem to get the stupid door to open. My dad, one of the world's fastest casters, dismissed his ball of lightning and sealed the car door shut with Storm wind. He also charged the handle with a little bit of Storm lightning, it seems, because I get zapped as I grab it.

"Thanks, Dad. Really uncool," I say.

"Hey, listen up, pal. No getting out of the car was part of the deal," he smugly reminds me.

"Oh my *gosh*," I say, slumping down in my seat. "I never get to do anything! This sucks."

Dad looks over at me with The Eyebrow. The Eyebrow always means business and only shows up when I say or do something wrong. Realizing my stupidity, I attempt to tell him I'm sorry. But before I can apologize for saying *sucks*, a 'tap tap tap' on the front window interrupts our little stand-off.

"Holy crap," I mutter, "It's Jorginho."

Jorginho is the Brazilian team's right defender, and he's holding the ball that hit our car, and he's *talking* to us. The only problem is – we don't speak Portuguese.

"Dad, do something. This man is one of my heroes. I want to talk with him. Please," I beg through gritted teeth.

The World Speedcasting Champion, my father, rolls his eyes and twirls his hand around for fun; he's not a crammer, so his magic doesn't need hand gestures. All of a sudden, Jorginho's words change to English in my ears, and I hear, "...again, very sorry my ball hit your car. It appears to be okay."

I'm not sure if my dad did anything to affect the footballer's hearing with his Storm magic, so my only response is to smile awkwardly and give Jorginho two thumbs up.

The footballer smiles back and says, "Little boy, would you like to come closer and watch the demonstration?"

Oh dear. It's happening so soon. I'm actually dying.

"Daddy. Please. I'll never ask for anything ever again. Pretty please. I looooove yooooou," I say in my most pathetic-sounding begging voice.

But he only shakes his head and tells Jorginho, "Sinto muito, mas nós temos que sair. Obrigado por ser gentil com meu filho." (I am sorry, but we have to leave. Thank you for being kind to my son.)

"My life is officially over," I mutter.

Jorginho, seeing the look on my face, pulls out a marker, signs the ball, and hands it to me. Accepting the ball with both hands, I look back at my dad and grin.

"Scratch that," I say with a sudden change of heart. "I'm going to live forever, and today is the greatest day of my life."

Dad looks happily at me in the rear-view and says, "Come on. Sit up front and watch the rest of the demo with me, Janet."

Watch the rest of the demo? Today just can't get any better. I climb between the two front seats and sit in his lap. We spend the next 15 minutes watching the incredible show. Not once do I let go of the autographed ball. The demo ends and the Brazilian team load onto their bus and drive away. The fans all stick around to chat about the amazing spectacle they just witnessed.

I hug him and say, "Thanks for letting me stay to the end. It was so crazy awesome." He messes up my hair, kisses my head, like I'm still five.

"If you think it was that great, little man, what would you say if I let you drive the car?"

"Say what? You're going to let a 10-year-old drive? Mr. Never-Breaks-The-Rules?" I ask.

"Hey, I broke the rules once," he protests. "I let you find out about magic before you manifested any, didn't I? I could have gotten arrested by the MOP, or kicked out of the Mages Guild for that! So don't tell me I don't break the rules."

"Dad," I say, "you filed for permission to tell me, and Mom said it was only granted because you're a famous Speedcasting Champion."

"Alright, fine. I'm not breaking the rules this time either," he admits. "You can sit in the driver's seat, and I'll control the pedals and steering wheel with Storm. You see, Jaret, I can manipulate the air surrounding us…"

Before he can get going, I interrupt and say, "Dad, please don't turn something cool into a magic lesson? Please?" He just laughs and scoots over to the passenger seat in response. "This will be so much fun," I shout. "The regs are going to freak out. It's gonna be so hilarious!"

As we pull out of the parking space, I honk the horn at the crowd of fans still standing around talking, and wave goodbye to them. The looks on their faces are priceless. From behind the milling crowd, some laughing and pointing at the ten-year-old driving a car, while others merely look on with angry and disapproving scowls, I notice something strange. The brightest light I've ever seen floats down behind the crowd, beginning as a fist-sized ball and then expanding rapidly. The regs' surprised and laughing expressions suddenly change to fear and agony as the bright light engulfs them. And then everything goes black.

TWO
2015 AD
Shanghai, China

Dead silence. My eyes fly open, my heart is beating like a drum, and my mind is racing. Where the hell am I? What's going on?

"Calm down. Focus your thoughts," I whisper under my breath.

And that's when the sounds come crashing in like a tsunami. The water flowing, the heavy breathing, and the frantic wailing are the noises I instantly focus on.

"Oh no, it's happening again," I say through trembling lips as I look around wildly for any sign of danger.

"Honey, can you get the babies, please? I'm going to be late for work," my wife says from the bathroom.

"Oh, thank God… it was just another nightmare," I mumble sleepily, rubbing at my face to erase the bad dreams.

Head now clear of any nightmares, I assess the situation and find that Kelly's in the shower and the babies are awake crying for bottles and diaper changes.

"Get up. You can do this," I say to myself.

Once the twins are changed and happily sucking down imported milk from a box, I have a couple of minutes to handle my business in the bathroom. Kelly steps out of the shower as I brush my teeth, and as I watch her move I'm at a loss. It never ceases to amaze me how beautiful she is and that, for some reason, she agreed to marry me.

"Good morning, Mr. King," she says, winking coyly at me while covering up with a towel. No matter how much either of us wants to, there is no time for funny business, as usual. But that's par for the course when you have twin one-year-old boys.

"Good morning to you, pretty lady," I whisper. "I can't seem to remember your name, but you better book it. My wife will kill you if she finds you naked in our bathroom. She's a powerful businesswoman, you know; very well paid for doing who knows what at an international corporation."

Kelly hits me on the shoulder and giggles. "Jaret King, I will hurt you. So, what's on your agenda today, Mr. Stay-at-home-Dad?" she asks.

"The usual," I reply. "Shopping, mopping, and lopping off the heads of my enemies."

"I love you, honey, but you're very strange," Kelly says under her breath.

Well, she's right about that. Though, for all she knows, I'm only in charge of the shopping, cooking, cleaning, and taking care of the kids. But truthfully, the housekeeper/nanny does all of that while I take care of things at the office. If only I could tell Kelly about my real job, life would be a hell of a lot easier.

"I know I am, but what are you?" I say in my best imitation of my relatives back in Atlanta, deep Southern drawl and all. "I appreciate you being the breadwinner for our little tribe, though," I add, putting my hand on the small of her back. "I probably don't say it enough, but thank you. I love you, Kel."

My wife runs her hand down the side of my face sensually, making the hairs on the back of my neck stand up, and in a sultry voice she says, "Get some more face wash today: we're almost out."

She heads out of the bathroom to get dressed and ready for a long day of corporate negotiations, and calls over her shoulder with one last jab, "And trim your beard. It's getting too wild."

"Never!" I call back. Though she actually might have a point. I'm looking a little Duck Dynasty these days.

Not far behind my wife in leaving the bathroom, I grab the boys and get them dressed. Our twins, Luke and Han, just turned one a few months ago. Now that they are walking, they get into absolutely everything, and I mean everything. Climbing on and falling off of the couch, eating lint off of the floor, and digging in the garbage: just to name just a few. Hell, the other day Han took off his diaper and climbed our entertainment center to pee all over our flat-screen.

It's enough to drive a grown man crazy.

Kelly opens the door to leave, then bends over to pick up her purse and I can't help myself from sneaking a grab.

"After ten years of marriage, it still makes my heart flutter when you wear a short black skirt," I admit.

"You're not so bad yourself, Mr. King," she replies with a grin. "You don't look a day over 40."

"I'm only 35 and you know it, evil woman."

"Bye, dear. Have a good day with the boys. I love you," she says, kissing me on the mouth, even giving the old man a little tongue action. Nice.

Kelly then picks up the kids and kisses each one on the forehead while saying, "You boys act good for Daddy, okay?"

Heartbeat still elevated from the sexy kiss, I say, "I love you, too, babe. Have a great day at work. See you at 5:00."

Once she's gone, I glance down at my phone and see there is an hour or so before the ayi (what they call a housekeeper/nanny in China) arrives. So I put on some *Sesame Street* and let the boys eat Cheerios while watching Elmo talk about his favorite book, *Lucy the Lazy Lizard.*

While they're occupied, I check my email to see what's up with work today. If I'm lucky, I won't have to go into the office at all. I can just hang with my kids all day.

An email from one of my two bosses is at the top of my unread list. Stephen, the mage who sent me the email, is a sweaty jerk and I hate his guts. He seemed cool at first, honestly he did, but once I got to know him I found the guy to be a self-absorbed annoying know-it-all. Plus, you'd think that as a Canadian, Stephen might be super nice as they typically have that reputation. But no, he is just a pushy, egotistical douche.

He's also a control freak at heart, but Stephen and I have found a pretty decent work rhythm recently. Typically he will send me a list of things to check on and take care of for the day, or week. Sometimes that requires going in, and sometimes I can handle whatever it is from home. This email from him is unusual, though. It's not the usual fluff. It just says:

Jaret,

Please contact me immediately via the Network. We need to discuss something very important and it needs to be face-to-face.

Regards,
Stephen DuFrane
Head of MOP, East Asian Division

That sounds a little ominous, and I get the feeling that whatever he wants to talk about means I'll be in the field today. Shit. Sometimes it seems like there's never a moment's rest in Shanghai.

Stephen wants to talk via the Network, so I get my tome out of the locked drawer in my desk. Being a little bit of a social media junkie, I do like to use the Internet a good bit for email, Facebook, Twitter, and so on. But as often as possible, when the wife isn't around, at least, I use the Network. It's like a magical Internet, used in pretty much the same way, except that it's all done with spells.

Taking my Network book out, I place it on top of my desk. It has the look of a dusty old tome from some forgotten ancient library because, well, it is. I place my hand on the old book, release some of my magic into the book to activate it, and say, "Contact Stephen DuFrane, Head of MOP, East Asian Division."

His assistant's face projects in front of me, and she directs the call to his office. The next face that appears in the air above my desk looks supremely worried.

"Good morning, Stevie," I say in greeting. "I got your email. It sounds pretty serious. What's the emergency?"

"It's not good, Jaret. And don't call me Stevie. It's Stephen, and you know that. Please don't make me remind that you every time we speak. Now, I'm afraid we have quite a significant problem to deal with," he says in a strained voice. "The first item on your list is rather small. There are some freelance street magicians near Jing'an Temple that need to be reminded about the importance of discretion around regs. It should be rather easy to have that cleaned up, eh? You will delegate this to your team: no questions."

"Yeah, it'll be a piece of cake to wrap that up, Stephen. I'll send a couple of agents to sort it out," I say, annoyed that he feels the need to tell me how to do my job on a daily basis.

"Good. The other matter is not so simple, Jaret. One of China's most prominent crammers... I mean wizards, has gone missing," he says, making a very un-PC mistake.

Good thing Jenny Yu, his wizard counterpart, wasn't on the line with us. Calling a wizard a crammer in the workplace is akin to a... well, I can't make any comparisons without offending someone, so let's just say it's very bad.

Stephen continues, "Li Qiuan was supposed to give a talk yesterday about the differences between innate elemental mage spells and tome-based elemental wizard spells to a group of very excited young mages and their tutors."

"Yeah I've heard of him; he's supposed to be a real big shot. He is always on the local Network blogs," I say, recalling the name from several recent articles written by the man.

"Yes, well he never showed up for that lecture, and several of his friends found his villa wrecked. He has been missing ever since," he says. Stephen's voice suddenly becomes much more professional, as if someone is listening in. He clears his throat and adds, "This is very high-profile, so I need you to take the lead, Jaret. We have to show that we care as much about missing wizards as we would for mages, you understand. My counterpart for the WPS, Jenny Yu, will be watching how you handle this very carefully. It's a precarious spot you're in as a mage leading a dual division squad, you know. This needs to be handled professionally and, preferably, expediently."

This must be significant. He's pretty worked up about all of this, and Stephen never uses that many adverbs at once.

"Yes, sir," I say in my most obedient tone. "I will give this my full attention. Do we have any contact information on the friends that went looking for him, and do we know the last time he was seen?"

Stephen looks down at his notes and nods while saying, "Yes, yes. We have all of that. I'll send you everything in an email. Don't fuck this up, Jaret. People are watching."

He disconnects the Network call, his hovering face dissipates before my eyes, and I am left feeling a bit nervous. I've never had to handle a high-profile missing person case before. The detective work won't be a problem for my team; it's the damn politics that scare me.

One wrong move, and I'll be accused of giving preferential treatment to mages. I sure as shit don't need that in my file.

THREE
1000 AD
Kingdom of Croatia

"Poppa, it happened! I woke this morning and my arms were crackling with power! I have Storm magic!" the young boy exclaimed.

Yivan's father beamed with delight, "A Storm mage in the family! How blessed we truly are!"

Marko was a large Croatian man with powerfully muscled arms and long, black hair, who had access to the raw power of Fire and wielded it with incredible skill. His wife, Ema, a frail-looking woman with sallow and sunken features, was a very talented Water mage. They had both been hoping Yivan would manifest either Storm or Rock.

Marko had been afraid his son would either not manifest any magic, or take after his mother and gain access to Water. After all, he was skinny just like her and kept his hair trimmed short in her fashion. They resembled one another physically, so Marko thought it might have been so with magic as well. But now that Yivan had manifested Storm magic, Marko and Ema were ecstatic. Their hopes for complete command over the elemental forces of magic now rested on their daughter, Maeris.

Marko had high hopes for her. She was built strong like her father and had his same mane of long, black hair. But at eight years old, she still had a few years to go before her elemental manifestation. In fact, they were quite surprised to find Yivan had manifested his power so soon. The boy was only 14 years old, and most mages didn't mature magically until 16. This was a sign from God. Their family was chosen. Marko knew it.

"P… Poppa," the boy suddenly stammered, "I am… scared. I can feel it all over me. It… it hurts a little."

"Good. Good. That is splendid, my boy," Marko said reassuringly. "When a new mage is weak, he is unafraid. He cannot feel the magic coursing through his body. But when a mage's powers manifest and there is pain, this is good. It means that your magic will be powerful. That fear you feel is God whispering how mighty you will be one day. Listen to Poppa. He knows these things."

The young boy nodded in agreement, knowing to trust in his father. Marko had slain more people than any other mage they had met on their travels. He was wise in the ways of magic.

"Poppa, will you please teach me how to use Storm magic?" Yivan asked.

"I shall do my best, Yivan. But of this magic, I am not very knowledgeable," Marko admitted. "We will need to find someone skilled in Storm so that they may teach what you need to know. For the time being, just do what feels natural. But remember to never use your magic on your family. This is forbidden. If you wish to bring harm upon an ordinary man, then go ahead. But do not practice on us or other mages. Doing so might get you killed." Marko only laughed and tousled his hair at seeing the wide-eyed look on Yivan's face.

"Marko, do not tease the boy. He is excited! Today is his first day as a mage. It is a cause for celebration," Ema said.

"Do not tell me what to do, Ema. I am the leader of this family and will do as I please," Marko replied with a glare, his eyes glowing with Fire that licked out in tiny whips.

Ema bowed her head in submission and apologized, "I am sorry, my husband. Forgive me."

"However, my love, you are correct," Marko said, his voice becoming warm and friendly once more. "Today is a cause for celebration. Yivan, go wake your sister and give her the good news. Yesterday while scouting the area around our camp, I saw a large home not too far away. As best as I can tell, it is not inhabited by mages. We shall go forth and greet our neighbors. We shall bring them the gifts of Fire, Water, and Storm, and in return, they shall give us their lives."

Hours later the mage family sat in the courtyard of the large house and feasted on the food they had found within. The former homeowners' larder was full to the brim, and nothing would go to waste.

"Ha! This is a fine day, is it not, my boy?" Marko beamed. Yivan nodded vigorously, his mouth too full of grapes to say a word.

"You did very well today, Ema," Marko said to his wife, grasping her hands in his own. "How you made that woman drown from the inside was beautiful. When I saw the water rushing from her mouth and nose, I cried out with joy. When it poured out of her ears, how I laughed!"

"Thank you, my husband. You amazed us all today with your magic," Ema replied obediently. "I have never seen a man burned away layer by layer like that before. It was a work of art, my love."

"Yes. Yes, it was," Marko agreed. "Do not worry, Maeris. You will be able to join us in these moments one day when you have magic. Until then, my dear, you will have to continue to wait for us to clean out these homes. You see, children, if you are weak, then people will take what is yours because you do not deserve to keep it. You must be strong to hold onto what you want. This is why we roam the Earth. We take what regular and weak people have, and at the same time avoid keeping anything worth taking. This way, should a more powerful mage come upon us, we merely talk and trade spells instead of fighting to the death over material possessions. This is our way of life, and you must learn it. Especially now that you are a mage, Yivan!"

Marko leaped onto the table and created a column of fire that reached into the sky far above him, yelling, "MY SON IS A MAGE!"

Yivan smiled at this and felt warm all over. His parents were so wise and loving. He felt like the happiest child in all of Croatia. Eying the corpse of a woman his mother had drowned with Water magic, Yivan acted without thinking. He wanted to impress his father more than anything, so he reached out and shot a feeble but crackling bolt of Storm electricity into the body. It twitched, and Yivan smiled at his father proudly.

Until Marko's open palm caught him clean across the face. "Never use magic on the dead," Marko chided. "It's forbidden."

18

"I am sorry, Poppa. I did not know."

"Do not be sorry, Yivan. Be wise. Never do this again. The dead are to be left alone."

"Yes, Poppa. I will do as you say. May I ask a question?" Yivan said.

Marko threw his head back and laughed maniacally, his body still filled with the exuberance of the afternoon's carnage, and said, "Of course, my little Storm mage. What is it you wish to ask your poppa?"

Yivan seemed nervous. He was scared. Marko and Ema were so kind to him and Maeris. He did not want to make them angry, but he needed to speak his mind.

"Yivan, it is ok, my beautiful boy," Marko said lovingly. "You can only learn new things by asking and watching. So please, ask me."

Yivan looked up into his father's eyes and met Marko's happy gaze. The young mage tried to look confident and un-afraid as he asked, "Why do we kill regular people? I know they are weaker than us, and they don't deserve to keep what they have if they can't defend themselves. But why do we kill them, Poppa? Why not just take what we want and leave them alive?"

Marko rubbed his bearded chin, looked down at his inquis-itive son and said, "And why would you like to leave them alive, Yivan?"

"Because it feels wrong to stop them from living, Poppa," Yivan replied. "I imagine what it would be like if someone did that to my family. I would not like it."

Marko placed his hand on Yivan's shoulder and squeezed. "Ahh. I see, my son. First, let me say that no one is going to do that to us, Yivan. We follow a set of rules that all but guarantee no mage will want us dead. Second, we kill regular people be-cause we are here to take what they do not deserve. They are too weak, yes? Well, it is my opinion that they are so soft that they do not even deserve their lives, so we take them as well. Do you understand?"

Yivan nodded slightly and meekly answered, "Yes, Poppa. Thank you, Poppa."

"You are very welcome, my boy. Come let us continue our celebration," Marko said, kissing Yivan on the cheeks, and then roaring to the heavens, "My son is a mage! A Storm mage!"

Yivan ate with his family the rest of the afternoon, and even rejoiced with them. They sang songs together and his family took turns asking Yivan to create gusts of Storm wind or bolts of Storm lightning. Surprisingly, he did both quite easily. But through all of it, Yivan couldn't quite shake the feeling that his father, the wise and powerful Marko... was wrong.

"Killing is not right," Yivan thought to himself later. "If you don't want a man to do something to you, then why should you do it to someone else?"

Watching his family talk and laugh, surrounded by the bodies of the family who built the home they were soon to set on fire and leave behind, Yivan had a revelation.

"If Poppa is wrong about this," Yivan's thoughts raced on, "maybe he is wrong about everything else, too."

FOUR
2015 AD
Shanghai, China

My ayi, Lilly, arrived early this morning, which works out great. Now I'll have time to grab some street food before scooting over to the office. A couple of spicy vegetable baozi should hit the spot. The thick, white bread filled with a dollop of delicious pickled veggies and spices calls to me, and I must answer. Lilly receives my instructions for the day in Chinese, even though they are said in English, as a result of the same Water spell that I use for understanding the locals. She gives a thumbs-up in acknowledgement, and I can't help thinking that life as a reg must be really terrible. Imagine having to actually learn a new language. Ouch.

It's 8:45 am as I leave the apartment, and I have until 5:00 this evening before Kelly gets home from work. I like to be there when she gets home most days, or she might start to wonder where I am all the time. Telling her the truth would be easier; what I am and what I can do. It really sucks having to lie to my wife, but it's the rules; I'm not allowed to tell regs about magic. Period. Knowing that, you'd think I would have just married a fellow mage or maybe even a wizard. But you can't plan love. When it hits, it hits hard.

Standing in line to order some big, doughy dumplings filled with spicy, pickled greens, I see a pickpocket working his way down the street. He's sly and very talented at stealing. In the span of a few heartbeats, he's gotten three wallets out of purses and pockets. Now, it's not my jurisdiction, so to speak. The reg cops can handle this kind of stuff, you know? I'm not supposed to interfere with reg crime at all. Keeping our secret pretty much only requires patrolling the use of magic.

But I can't just watch this little ratty lowlife steal from innocent people. It's not in me to just turn the other cheek. The real question is how to stop him without giving myself away.

As he reaches into the next pocket, which happens to belong to quite a large and sturdy-looking foreigner, I create a flow of Water from his hand that drenches the large laowai's pocket and pants.

"What the hell," the big man says while spinning around to find the thief's hand still firmly wedged into his back pocket. The foreigner grabs the pickpocket by the arm and then yells, "Thief!"

Two locals rush over and grab the pickpocket's bag, and upon opening it find dozens of wallets inside. They start wailing on the thief, just enough to exact their own little justice before the cops arrive.

After a job well done, I turn back to the matter in hand; it's my turn at the baozi cart. I step up and order my breakfast through magically translated Mandarin, and the vendor gives me two baozi stuffed with spicy pickled vegetables while wearing a surprised look on his face.

I stride into the office at 9:10, satisfied in mind and body. It looks like any other generic office you might find in modern-day China – desks, plants, a water cooler, and a few of those lucky, waving cat statues. The map in the meeting room is the only object in the office that would make you take a second look.

A magically enhanced 3D map of Shanghai with which, by using the magic of the Network, we can track any large-scale magic use. Small, day-to-day magic won't show up, but great pulls on the Ether or destructive magic will show as a white dot. So honestly, we've never even seen it work.

I've always secretly hoped it would go off one day, just to have a story to tell. I know, I know. The saying "Be careful what you wish for" springs to mind. But I still often find myself staring at that map hoping for something to show up. What if it did? What would I do? I'm sure no matter what happens, we could handle it. Right? What could go wrong?

My agents have all arrived at the office before me, as usual. On the team, we have four casters and four crammers total. Casters are what everyone calls mages because we can just cast spells endlessly as long as we don't tire out. We wear the term with pride.

Crammers are what we call wizards because they have to study tomes all the time to cast spells. Once they use a spell, it is gone from their memory, and they have to learn it all over again. They also have to say words of magic and use intricate hand gestures, which looks really cheesy. Needless to say, the term can be used as an insult, which means a lot of wizards hate it.

The official name of my department is Mage Order and Protection, or MOP for short. It makes us sound like custodians. On the wizard side, though, they are known as Wizard Patrol Service or WPS. That sounds much more official, right?

Jenny Yu is the Head of WPS, East Asian Division, mirroring Stephen's position in the MOP. Our two divisions have been working together for years to keep magic a secret from the regs, but these dual division offices are a relatively new phenomenon.

Sometimes keeping our secret out of the public eye means stopping magic users from casting spells in the open, or abusing their powers to obtain wealth and respect amongst regs, and not very often it means keeping angry wizards or mages from fighting each other and killing innocents. Of course, there hasn't been any violent magical crime for about 25 years, since… well… the last Maelstrom attack in Turin, Italy, in 1990.

Both mage and wizard magic have their own distinct advantages and disadvantages, which is why I've grown to like running this dual division office. No matter what happens, we always have a solution; clever crammer traps and spells meant to affect large areas and multiple targets, or fast and powerful elemental caster magic that can do almost anything we want.

FIVE
1990 AD
Turin, Italy

Dead silence. My eyes fly open, my heart is beating like a drum, and I'm scared out of my mind. Where am I? What's going on?

And that's when the sounds come crashing in like a tidal wave: the water flowing, the heavy breathing and the frantic wailing are the noises I instantly focus on.

"Son! You're awake! Oh, thank God," my dad says breathlessly, with a hand over his heart.

"Daddy? Where are we?" I ask groggily, my body shivering. Everything seems covered in a fog, making it hard to remember much. "What happened? I'm scared…"

"Calm down, Jaret. Focus your thoughts," my dad says, giving his trademark advice. "We were in an accident, but you're okay, son."

There is a bandage covering my dad's forearm while his face is a mess of cuts. Why didn't he let a Water mage heal that? It's pretty simple from what I understand. They just direct the water in your blood…

"Jaret? You're starting to drift off again," my dad says, gently shaking me. "Focus on me. I want you to stay awake for a little while. Can you do that for me?"

Nodding clumsily, I look around to find that we're in a hospital. A reg hospital from the looks of it, as I see a nurse filling a pitcher of water from a tap. And in the bed next to mine, a man with half an arm, the end bandaged and stained red… is huffing and puffing his breath for some reason. Probably because it hurts. I bet it does. The rest of the room is scattered with curtains mostly hiding who is behind them, but they all sound hurt, too. Some people are yelling.

I look at my father and whimper, "Daddy, what's going on?"

"Calm down, sweet boy. Just focus on me," Dad reminds me in a smooth voice. "We were in an accident, do you remember it?"

"No. I just remember… I think I was driving the car?" I say, confused. "I can't drive. Was I really? It's all fuzzy in my head, Christopher."

Christopher King. That's my dad's name. Why did that just pop into my head? And did I just call him Christopher? I am in so much trouble if I did. But Dad just rubs my head and starts crying. Maybe I'm not in trouble. Maybe I'm dying.

"Daddy," I say with a shaky voice, "why are you sad? Am I ok?"

He smiles down at me, pinches my cheek, and says, "Yes, everything is ok, Jaret. I'm just so happy you're awake. Now, you were sitting in the driver's seat when we had the accident, but you weren't driving."

Then Daddy leans down and whispers in my ear, which tickles a little, "I was driving the car with magic, son."

He backs away from my ear but keeps rubbing my head. It's making me sleepy, so I let out a big yawn and say, "Daddy, you're hurt. Why don't you let a Water…"

He quickly cuts me off and says, "Shhhh, hush, Jaret. This is a reg hospital. We'll talk more about it later, ok? You just get some more sleep. I'll be right here beside you. I'm not going anywhere."

An angry voice loudly says to us, "It wasn't an accident, you know. It was a terrorist attack. I know it. I was in the army, man. I know a bomb when I see one explode. That's what this was. Terrorists." The man with the missing arm in the bed next to mine is staring at us with a crazy look on his face.

"Daddy…" I say, staring horrified at the angry man and his bloody, bandaged nub.

"It's ok, Jaret," Dad says, putting a hand firmly on my chest and smiling at me. He then tells the man, "Sir, please. You're frightening my son. I'm sorry about your injury, but please stay calm. Just focus on the fact that you're alive. Not many people in the crowd today can say that. You're one of the lucky few."

The man glances at me and his eyes change. He looks sad now, not angry. "Yeah, yeah. Ok, man. I'm… I'm sorry. It's just… I made it through Lebanon, Grenada, and the Persian Gulf without a scratch, you know?" His face suddenly changes back to the angry look he had before. Growing louder and more agitated than ever, he shouts, "And now some dirty, stinking terrorist has gone and blown my arm off and killed my wife and kids! How am I supposed to stay calm?! How am I expected to focus on anythi…" The scary man suddenly gasps for breath with wide eyes and drops to his pillow falls fast asleep.

"Daddy, what did you do to him?" I ask. "And what did he mean about terrorists and a bomb?"

"Don't worry, Jaret. He's okay," my dad says reassuringly. "I just helped him rest. He'll sleep for a little while. Don't tell Mommy that I used magic on a reg, okay?"

Daddy knows how to make me feel better. He winks at me with a grin and says, "That reg doesn't know what he's talking about, anyway. It wasn't a terrorist with a bomb, son… it was the Maelstrom. And thank God we weren't in the crowd, or else we probably wouldn't be here."

"Are they all dead, Daddy? Like the other attacks, the ones I saw on the Network?" I ask.

"I really wish you wouldn't use my Network book, son," he says. "How are you even turning it on? You don't have any magic yet."

"Well," I explain, "sometimes you leave it on."

"I have to remember to turn that thing off and lock it up in my bottom drawer. Anyway, no, not everyone is dead. There were a few people who survived, Jaret. But we were very lucky. From now on we have to avoid crowds, son. Just stay away from groups of people, do you hear me?" Dad says with a scratchy voice.

Too tired to answer, I just nod. As my eyes close, I can see the surprised look on the regs' faces as they watched a ten-year-old drive a car. It's hilarious. Then that scary light comes out of nowhere, and they all start to fly through the air, pieces of them hitting my window and making it shatter…

SIX
2015 AD
Shanghai, China

As I settle in to make a plan for the day, I see a note on my desk from Aurora that reads:

Hey, Laoban, can we chat when you get a chance?
Thanks, A.

Leaning out of my office, I spot my Second in Command at her desk already hard at work. "Aurora, I just saw your note. Come on in," I call out.

The Chinese woman entering my office is tall and slender, has a bob haircut, and a slightly flat nose; a beautiful woman, and more importantly, an amazing WPS agent. Her mother and father are both wizards, and they had her trained at a very young age. Aurora is one of the smartest people I have ever met, and according to her file she can hold about 140 spells within her mind at any given time. That's pretty impressive, as most crammers can only hold around 40 to 60. Her high level of intelligence is but one of the multiple reasons why I trust her to run things at the office most days while I keep in touch from my home. Not to mention the fact that she is a local, and so understands the situation in Shanghai much better than I do.

"How did you even know I would be in today and would see this note?" I ask.

Aurora smiles while pointing to her head, and says, "I'm very, very smart, remember? It's the only reason they let me work with a famously powerful mage like yourself."

I smirk at her silently in response; thankful she is always in good humor.

"Fine," she says, after a moment of not getting the chiding rebuke she expected from me, "I saw the reports, Laoban. When someone as well known as Li Qiuan goes missing, the boss is definitely coming in to deal with it. No way they'd trust a lowly crammer like me to handle something this big."

I can't help but laugh at that. Aurora has a great sense of humor about the strained relations between our guilds. If only the Councils felt the same way, things might not be so tense.

"Great. Since you have already seen the reports, I'm leaving it up to you to assign someone to handle the street magician problem in Jing'an."

Aurora scrunches her face up in thought for a second before saying, "I'd say we send Mian Mian and Rainbow."

Yes, she said Rainbow. Everyone in the office, other than me, is Chinese. Sometimes Chinese people will choose odd English names for themselves. Hey, it's better than a waiter that served me last week named Snail.

Mian Mian is a quiet, yet intense punk rock girl that comes from the MOP portion of our team. Also from the MOP side there is a half-Chinese guy named Jaysen, who has an Afro and speaks both perfect English and Chinese. Last of the mages, aside from yours truly, there is Liang. He's a very typical modern Chinese young man. All he wants is to get married and have a son, and he constantly talks about the value of family.

The WPS side of the team is also made up of one lady and two men. Rainbow is a very careful and sharp woman who always follows the rules. Some might call her nerdy. Tian Yi is a jester, always causing trouble around the office, but everyone loves him to death. And then there is Joyee. Mr. Nervous, all the time! He wears his backpack on his chest when out in public, so that no one can steal anything from behind him.

Dual division teams like mine are a relatively new thing, and are not common in the world. Most cities have one MOP office, and one WPS office. Because of the size of Shanghai, you would assume it would have multiple agencies, and in fact there used to be several of each. But recent budget cuts trimmed the fat and the High Councils both agreed that one dual division team would be sufficient, and I was selected to head the new team.

I think there are three other dual division squads in the world; one in NYC, one in Munich, and one in Johannesburg. Most of what we do here, and at all other MOP or WPS offices around the world, is based on tips provided by anonymous sources or from paid informants; all of which are magic users, of course. As with today, some local crammers joyously made a call to let us know what was going on in Jing'an. I could be angry with them for making the call. They only did it because they hate mages and want to see them in trouble. But honestly, that's how most of our work gets done. One side turns in the other, and the MOP or WPS make the problems go away.

"Good call, Aurora. Send one mage and one wizard. Two mages may be too lenient, and two wizards may be too harsh," I say with praise. "But why send the only two women on the squad other than yourself? Is it because you want them to be seen as just as capable as the men on the team? You don't have to worry about that, Aurora. I value everyone equally."

She looks away, folds her arms, and without looking at me says, "Is there anything wrong with my decision, Laoban?"

The word "Laoban" enters my ear, but the magic inside translates it into English as "boss." And of course, there isn't anything wrong with her picks. I probably would have chosen the same two people for the same reasons. The guys on the team still need reminders every once in a while that it's 2015 and women are equally as talented as the old boys' club, if not more so.

"Nope, absolutely brilliant choices," I say. "Go ahead and let them know to head out immediately, and tell them to check in with me as soon as they have the situation in hand."

Aurora mock salutes me, as she always does, and adds, "Yes, sir, Laoban, sir. And what are your instructions for the Li Qiuan situation?"

"Honestly," I say, "I need to have more information before I can make any calls on that. I'll read through everything and get back with you in about 30 minutes or so with my thoughts."

She nods and walks straight over to speak with Mian Mian and Rainbow. There is no wasting time with Aurora. She gets things done and does them well, which takes a lot of the pressure off of me. Look, I'm great at my job, but I don't really know China. So having a local as a Second in Command means that I have someone to rely on completely for advice and help. China isn't easy. I might enjoy the local magic very much, but adjusting to everyday life in here has been difficult for my family. Not speaking the local language was a huge obstacle in the beginning. Sure, I can cast a Water spell that affects my inner ear to receive human speech and interpret it into my native tongue, but I couldn't let Kelly know that. I had to pretend to struggle with fake classes for six months before I could start communicating in front of her. It's a lot easier now that I don't have to pretend, but the language is only one of the many layers of difficulty that Aurora helps with. For example, I have yet to figure out a way to read and write Chinese with magic. Anything on my desk in print has to go through Aurora.

Sipping on a large and glorious cup of coffee while reading the limited information on the Li Qiuan case, the realization hits me that I will need to get out there and question one of the witnesses for myself. Though, witness is probably too a strong word. Nobody actually saw anything other than a tossed villa. But as luck would have it, one of the people on the witness list lives really close to Jing'an Temple.

Looking out of my office, I see Mian Mian and Rainbow waiting for the elevator. Mian Mian is a short and skinny woman with a close cut Mohawk. She always has a little crooked smile on her face, like she knows something you don't. As per usual, she is wearing her typical business attire: leather jacket, torn jeans, and 14-eye oxblood Doc Marten boots.

Rainbow is a tall and slightly heavy woman, sporting a very popular bowl-style haircut and wearing her standard work attire: a well-cut business suit, pressed to perfection. Rainbow always appears as if she is thinking about very important things, so it would be better not to disturb her.

"Good morning, ladies," I say in greeting. "Would you two mind if I tag along? I need to interview someone in the Jing'an district. I'll watch you guys take down the street magicians, and get your field observation over with. Then you can drop me off. What do you say?"

As a mage, Mian Mian is pretty relaxed and laid-back, so she nods her head in agreement and says, "Sure, Bossman."

Rainbow, on the other hand, is a wizard through and through. Because they need to be reasonably intelligent to be talented at magic, wizards can sometimes come across as snooty, and often worry about following the rules to a T. She replies, "Yes, sir, it would be our pleasure to have you along with us."

"Alright then," I say. "Which one of you is driving?" I hate driving, and refuse to do it; I have ever since being ten years old.

But they are both accustomed to my stance on the subject, so Rainbow dangles a set of company car keys in the air, and say, "That would be me, sir. I have the best driving record in the office."

As we pull up to the corner where the magic show is reportedly performed, Rainbow finds a spot and parks the car. I look at my watch and see that it's 11 am. My instinct is to start issuing orders, but then remember to let my team handle everything. I am only an observer today. What could go wrong?

"You two do this, however you see fit. I am just here to watch," I say.

Mian Mian shrugs and walks away, casting glances around, looking for any sign of magic.

Rainbow looks down at her watch and presses a button as she says, "Thank you, sir. We should have this resolved in less than 25 minutes. We won't let you down."

With some time to kill, I think about practicing my dreadful Rock magic; pass the time and improve my skill with my least used school of magic. Kill two birds with one stone, you know? I mean, not actually *kill* any birds with a stone. Poor choice of words, I guess. Anyway, that's when I notice a bright flash of light and a big cheer from a crowd of onlookers. *Bingo.* I make my way closer to the source of the glow and find a large group of 30 to 40 people surrounding two men and one woman. Crowds have made me uneasy since I was a kid, so I just hang back, not wanting to get into the mix. Plus, I can see everything fine from back here, and observe my agents do what they do best.

The two men in the street magician troupe are creating lanterns of Fire and making them float in a circle around the woman. She is forming globes of Water and dousing the lights. Their rhythm is pretty impressive. Slowly, they increase the speed with which they cast, and the circle begins spinning faster and faster. It looks pretty cool, I must admit. I can see why the crowd comes every day to watch. There are a few hats on the ground already overflowing with the local currency. The tips are ample today, it seems.

One of the things I like about living in China is the way the locals cast their spells. Like these mages breaking the law, magic users here focus a lot of time on shaping their magic to appear what you might consider traditionally Chinese.
For instance, I might shoot a Fireball out of my palm while a Chinese mage might shoot a fire dragon out of hers; and that, my friends, is just plain awesome.

From the corner of my eye, I spot Mian Mian frowning, obviously pissed at these mages who are making our side look bad. On the opposite end of the audience, I see Rainbow intently watching the show, neither happy nor angry. But her hands… her hands are moving in intricate patterns and her lips are mouthing something.

"Oh crap," I mutter. She's casting a damn spell... in public. What in the hell is she thinking? Wondering if I have enough time to stop her or distract the regs, and how to do it without being seen, I let my connection to the Ether fill me with Fire magic on instinct. Before I can decide what to do with the magic filling me with warm power, the street magicians' fire lanterns and water globes all disappear. I look over at my two agents and see satisfaction written all over their faces.

Not too shabby, I have to admit. It was stupid of me not to have trusted them from the start. These agents are some of the best at what they do, after all. I motion for Mian Mian and Rainbow to close in on the mages so they can't run. They both nod back and move in.

"This is all going extremely well," I say to myself. And then, the brightest light I have seen in twenty-five years floats down from above. The light starts as a tiny ball and then erupts from behind where the magicians stand. Instictively, I cast a Rock spell to shield my body. And then everything goes black.

<u>SEVEN</u>
1004 AD
Bulgaria

Marko glared disapprovingly at his son Yivan, now 18 years old. The boy still commiserated over killing regular people. "Son, I have taught you this again and again," he said in an irritated voice. "If they wish to hold onto this food, these clothes, this wagon, these horses, and everything else inside of their homes, then people need to be strong. If they are weak, someone stronger will eventually take it all. Why not us? Why not our family?"

"And Father, as I have explained this to you many times," Yivan replies in an equally irritated voice, "I understand the value of strength. Do remember that I am the most powerful mage in this family. I hold the power of two schools of magic. You and Mother have but one. Maeris is still too young and has not yet manifested any magic. So I well know what it is to have great power."

Marko eyed his son darkly but did not protest. After all, what the powerful young mage said was true. Marko had never seen anyone wield Storm as well as Yivan, and a year after he manifested that mighty power Marko's son had discovered the ability to control Rock existed within his mind, as well. Already, Yivan's two schools of magic closed the elemental circle within Marko's family. Even if Maeris never manifested a single school of magic, they were still complete. It was wonderful, to be sure, except that Yivan had let the power go to his fool head. Now, he was outright disobeying his elders and refusing to kill. It was outrageous.

Yivan continued making his point to Marko and said, "I understand the way our lives work, Father. I agree that we shall take what is rightfully ours. It's our birthright. We have magic and they do not. What I cannot do is kill regular people without cause. If a man tries to harm us, then yes, I shall slay him. But if a man only wishes to defend his life and that of his family, why should I obliterate him? Should I not just force him away, or magically restrain him until we are gone?"

Marko put his face into his hands and held back the urge to strike his son. He was a man now, and past the age of physical discipline. Marko would need to use wisdom and patience to teach this young man why he must kill these ordinary people.

"I hear you, my son. I feel that it is my failure as a father that you think this way. I have not put it in terms that make sense to you. I apologize for this error," Marko said evenly.

"Marko, please let the boy think what he wishes. It makes no difference. He is not stopping us from killing these weak fools. He just does not want to do it himself," Ema foolishly contributed to their discussion.

Marko did not hold himself back from striking Ema. She was his wife, and would do as she was told. She would not contradict him in front of their children. "Quiet your tongue, Ema. I shall deal with this," Marko said darkly and he lashed out and struck her with the back of his large, calloused hand.

At the sight of her mother being hit, Maeris began wailing as she always did when Marko became violent with the family. It was hard for her to understand why Poppa would hit them.

Yivan bent down to lend her some comfort and explain, "Maeris, my darling. Do not be afraid. Poppa is not trying to hurt Mama. He is only reminding her that he is the head of our family and that she must obey him. Just as he has done to you, and even to me when I was younger. It will be okay, my little tiger."

"One day, when I'm a Storm mage like you," Maeris growled through her tears, "I'm going to blow Poppa up with magic. I hate him."

Yivan laughed in reply, but only because Marko was too far away to hear Maeris's dangerous words. "You must not talk like this, child. Poppa will unleash his anger on you if he hears it. Now, you go and play. I must say more to our father." Maeris wiped one last tear from her eye and then ran off to discover some kind of trouble as she most often did. Yivan approached Marko and asked, "Father, do you wish to continue our discussion?"

"Yes, my son," Marko responded. "I do. I am proud of the man you are becoming. You are powerful, and very few mages could best you in combat. Your life will be very simple, easy, and without the need to fear anyone. This is good. But let me explain to you why we can not let these normal weaklings live."

Marko sat down on a rock and gestured for Yivan to sit opposite from him. Once settled, he called forth strong connection to the Ether with Fire and created two separate flames.

"Look, my boy. This flame is our family, you see? And this one is a family of ordinary weaklings. They live in a house, they farm in the field, and they stay in the same place always. They have no magic," Marko gestured and explained. The flame that represented the family of mages moved closer to the one representing the ordinary family. A large portion of this flame broke off and joined the mage family fire, making it more substantial. "As you just saw, we took what we wanted from the weaklings. But in this case, we left this flame alive. We did not extinguish it. You see? What can this tiny flame do to us? Nothing. It is too small and too weak," Marko continued.

Suddenly, Marko conjured a hundred tiny fires, each one similar in size to the smaller, ordinary flame. They filled the air surrounding Yivan and his father as they sat on the stones. Yivan looked around and began to see where his father was going. "Now, if we continue in this way for a long time, what would happen? Could these individual flames cause us harm?" Marko asked.

"No, Father," Yivan smartly reasoned, "but if were they to join forces..."

At this, Marko silently commanded all 101 flames to combine, which formed a massive inferno that dwarfed the flame representing Yivan and his family. "Exactly, my son. Exactly," Marko said. "We can destroy a few. Maybe dozens. But can we stop hundreds of people, even ordinary men? All it takes is one arrow you don't see coming. You cannot stop all of the arrows, my son. No one can. So, we kill them and move on. Never staying in one place too long."

Yivan thoughtfully contemplated his father's lesson. It made sense. But it still felt wrong to the young mage, and so he said, "But Father, if we let them live, they may be scared of magic enough to never rise against us. They might be thankful for our mercy."

Marko forced the much bigger flame, representing all of the regular people, to descend upon the mage family flame and devour it. But before it could make contact, a large gust of Storm wind extinguished the inferno, leaving only the smaller mage flame untouched. Marko raised an eyebrow at his son, and Yivan only shrugged his shoulders. The two men, father and son, both threw back their heads and laughed together.

<u>EIGHT</u>
2015 AD
Shanghai, China

Dead silence. It always starts with dead silence. My eyes fly open, my heart is beating like a drum, and my mind is searching for answers. Where the hell am I, and what's going on?

"Calm down," I think. "Focus your thoughts."

A fire hydrant sprays a geyser of water into the air. Some man I don't recognize is lying on his stomach beside me, panting heavily. He's covered in blood. I can't tell if it's mine or his. All around me is chaos. I see people with missing limbs sprawled in the street, and random parts of what used to be people strewn all over. Blood is on the buildings, sidewalk, and road. It looks like a Pollock painting, but with the only color in the palette being arterial red. Screaming echoes from the few people still alive and not unconscious.

"Oh God, it's happening again," I whimper.

Looking around at the devastation, years of MOP experience kick in and the questions overrule the terror I feel. "Who? Who caused this?" I ask myself. It only takes a split second to find an answer. "The street magicians," I think. "They must have been the ones who did this." No one has used magic to kill people like this since I was a kid. We've had years and years of peace in our world, and now this... this destruction. Again?

The memories of Turin flash suddenly in my mind. It was 25 years ago... the last attack caused by the Maelstrom, a maniac showing up in random cities, finding large crowds of people, and blowing them to pieces with magic. There were mage and wizard casualties, too, but the number of regs that died was astounding.

The attacker came to be known on the Network as the Maelstrom, due to the belief that it was Storm magic being used to kill these innocent people, incredibly powerful Storm magic. After two years and ten attacks, it all suddenly stopped after the last attack in Turin. There was never any contact from the psychotic killer. Ever. Could this be the same thing? Could it be the same person? I'm praying that it's not.

"It has to be the street magicians," I tell myself again.

There were only about 30 people in this crowd. All of the Maelstrom attacks from 25 years ago resulted in at least 200 victims, but usually more. Several times, 500 people were killed in those attacks. The Maelstrom would never have attacked as small a group as today.

Scanning the area, I finally discover that the magicians were definitely not responsible. All three of them lay in tattered shreds right where they once stood performing incredible tricks. As I wipe someone's blood from my face, a disturbing question pops into my head, as I realize that I am standing alone. "Where the hell is my team?" I whisper.

Quickly searching the rubble and remains, I find one of them. Mian Mian looks dazed as she sits up amongst a pile of gore and bricks. There is a nasty cut running down the side of her face, but otherwise, she seems to be fine. Our eyes meet, and she mumbles, "I'm okay, Bossman."

"Where's Rainbow? I don't see her anywhere," I say, my voice frantic.

"She's probably fine, Bossman. I'll help you look."

"Yes, of course she is," I mumble to myself. Rainbow has to be fine. I'm responsible for her safety, after all. She works for me. Gazing around at the horror scattered across the road, I pray that she isn't a part of it. "Please be okay, Rainbow," I say under my breath.

Mian Mian and I start sifting through the bodies, looking for signs of our teammate. As I rapidly search, I feel a strange sensation pass over me. It's hard to explain, but it feels like the opposite of wind; a kind of suction almost, like something is pulling at me. My searching through the dead bodies for Rainbow continues despite that odd feeling. It is irrelevant. I need to find her and I need to do it now.

In my morbid investigation, I come across two bodies that look strangely different from the massacre around them. They are both missing body parts, like most of the other corpses, but their skin is desiccated and the faces are sunken in. I have never seen anything like this in my entire life.

I gesture to them and say, "Mian Mian, take a look at these bodies. What's wrong with them?"

"No clue, Bossman," she replies with wonder and disgust evident in her voice. All of a sudden, Mian Mian's head snaps around to look at something behind her. Her voice is full of troubled worry as she says, "Do you hear that, Jaret?"

"I do," I reply with a few curses. "Damn it. It's too soon. We need more time," I grumble.

"Sorry, Bossman. We don't have any more time."

The sound of sirens rings out in the air. The emergency services, police, fire crew, or hell…all of the above, are on their way. I don't know which, and I don't care. In fact, at this very moment, I don't care about much of anything because I found Rainbow at last…and she resembles the other two strangely dried-out corpses.

She's dead.

NINE
1995 AD
Sáo Paolo, Brazil

"Son, you can do this, just calm down and focus your thoughts," my dad says to reassure me.

"I don't know, this kid is already a two-time Champion Speedcaster. The fastest in all of the teenage rankings," I say back.

"Yes, but he only has Storm magic," my dad reminds me. "You've got Fire, Water, and Rock. Three schools of magic, son! What you're capable of… it's absolutely incredible. I still can't believe it."

"Yeah, but he's 17 and had his magic for two years," I complain. "I'm only 15, Dad. I've only had magic for a year."

He beams at me with that pleased expression again and says, "And see what you've already accomplished in that time, Jaret? Your magic is already faster and stronger than most adult mages. Your spell knowledge may be less, but your strength is so much greater. Now, calm down. Focus your thoughts."

"Calm down. Focus your thoughts," I repeat his instructions in my mind. The same ones he always gives me, and that somehow always seems to do the trick.

"Take a look out there Jaret. There are only three Stations instead of five," he says, gesturing to the field. "Only three. All you have to do is be faster than him in figuring out two of those problems. You only have to beat him twice, son. And you've got three schools of magic to choose from! This will be a cakewalk for you."

He's right. I'm ready for this. I may only know a handful of spells in Fire and Water, and only, like, two Rock spells... but I can do it. I can win this.

Faster than I think is even possible... the match is over.
It went so quick that most of what happened is just a blur in my mind. But hey, it is a sport called Speedcasting, right?

It's supposed to be fast.

My heart is beating like a drum, and my mind is racing. The host of the event walks over and starts interviewing me live on his Network show and I think to myself, "This can't be happening."

"We're here with the newest World Champion in Youth Speedcasting, Jaret King. Now, Jaret, can I call you Jaret?" he asks.

"You can call me Puddin' Pop if you want to," I awkwardly joke. "I'm on top of the world right now. I did it!"

Matthew Birge, the lead reporter from the number one news site on the Network, *Magicae est Potentia*, laughs at my stupid attempt at a joke. I'm so going to be famous. This is the best day of my life.

"Okay, okay, Jaret. Calm down," Matthew says, still chuckling. "Now, I'd like to go over today's match with you and hear some of your thoughts on how it went. How does that sound?"

I nod and say, "Sure."

Matthew goes on, saying, "At Station one, you and Connor were presented with a conjured Fire elemental. That seemed to be an easily manageable obstacle for the both of you. Tell me about it."

"What's there to tell?" I think to myself. "I crushed Connor by a few seconds. It wasn't even close." But if I said something like that on the Network, my mom would kill me.

So instead, I tell Matthew, "Well, I figured if we were met with a Fire obstacle, he would use Storm wind to try and put it out, since he only has access to Storm."

Matthew nods along, and says, "Yes, yes."

"Early on, I figured out that the grass surrounding all of the Stations contained a bit of Water inside of each blade. I pulled that Water out of the grass surrounding Station one, and... fizzle. The elemental went down, and since the Water didn't have to travel all the way from me, I was faster." The crowd roars applause at my answer. I could get used to this.

Matthew smiles and says, "We were all quite impressed when a rookie like yourself thought of such a clever tactic. Your Water spell made contact a full four seconds before Connor's Storm wind reached Station one."

I turn to the audience and throw my arms into the air. They go wild again. Dad looks over with a proud expression on his face and gives me a thumbs-up. I can feel my heartbeat in my toes.

"Now, the second obstacle was more of a challenge. You lost at Station two, Jaret. Can you tell us where you went wrong?" Matthew asks.

"Ugh," I want to say. "I could have had him there. I should have. I just... hesitated. Stupid Rock magic... it sucks. I hate it," I think to myself. "Well, I have access to three schools of magic, as you know, Matthew," I actually say, pausing to throw another wave at the audience, who all eat it up. "One of only 27 mages alive today that can cast three schools, if I'm not mistaken," I continue arrogantly. "And Rock is definitely the weakest of my three magics. I'm just not any good at it. So when I saw that giant boulder, I froze for a split second," I admit, owning up to my mistake. "Just long enough for his lightning bolt to connect."

"Now the final Station stumped both of you. It was a new obstacle that has never before been used in the Youth Speedcasting World Games: a live animal! Absolutely unheard of," the famous broadcaster says.

"Yes, Matthew. I was shocked and a little confused, as I'm guessing Connor was, too. Otherwise, he would never have tried to destroy that helpless dog. I still can't believe he would have killed it," I say, making sure to point out that my competitor wanted to murder a puppy. Sicko.

"Fortunately, young Jaret, you were the quicker competitor at Station three. I'm still not sure what went down there. It was several spells in rapid succession, was it not?" Matthew asks.

"Yeah. I needed to get the dog out of harm's way, so I used Rock first, as it was the last magic I had focused on. My father always tells me to calm down and focus my thoughts, but I didn't this time. I was still holding onto Rock. So I removed the earth beneath the dog. Connor's Storm lightning flew over the dog's head, and that's when I cast the second spell," I explain. "This time, I used Water and soaked the dog to protect it from my final spell."

"Incredible, young Jaret. My favorite part of the day was that last bit of magic. I just couldn't believe my eyes when I saw it," Matthew Birge gushes.

"I have no clue where the idea came from, Matthew. I guess I was just showing off. I'm good with Fire. So, I gave the shaggy dog a haircut by burning away all of its hair," I say while shrugging my shoulders. The crowd cheers raucously again at my recounting of the final Station.

With a pat on my back, Matthew wraps up his broadcast by saying, "Amazing, folks. Thanks to all the fans who came out today to watch the event live, and to all you magic users out there on the Network watching along with us, thanks for tuning in. As we sign off, take a look over at the sidelines to see who young Jaret's coach is."

The announcer gestures to my father, who turns in a slow circle and waves to the fans.

"That's right, ladies and gentlemen," Matthew says, "It's none other than the current Professional World Speedcasting Champ, Christopher King! He also just so happens to be our new Youth Champion's father, by the way! As they say – like father, like son. So let's all wish hearty congratulations to our new Youth Champ and best wishes for the future. For *Magicae est Potentia*, I'm Matthew Birge, and I'll spell ya later."

Dad walks over and wraps me in a crushing hug, which kinda hurts, and says, "I'm so proud of you, Jaret. Now we have two Speedcasting Champions in the family! More trophies for the mantle!"

"Yeah, I know. Thanks, Dad," I tell him, a little embarrassed.

His face still shining with pride again, he seems as happy as I've ever seen him. This might be a good time to ask him something... something I know he won't want to talk about.

"I was thinking about what you said before, Dad. About how having three schools of magic would give me an edge. It really did. Like, I actually felt I was better and faster than

Connor. Just imagine what I could do with all four schools of magic! There's a an old book I found in your study talks about it, and I think…"

Dad, suddenly growing solemn, interrupts me and says, "Son, you know that no one has ever been able to cast all four elemental magics; in fact, it's impossible as far as anyone knows. It's too much elemental power for one person to channel. It would probably cause you to explode or just…cease to be."

"That's just the current popular theory, Dad," I say. "The book I found in your study, along with a few sites on the Network, agrees that it's possible to have all four. The ancient text talks about the first mages, and how they initially found magic. It was by sensing it, Dad – by reaching out and taking it from the Ether. That sounds right up our alley!"

My father scowls, and says under his breath, "We escaped tragedy once already. Don't tempt fate again, son… please."

TEN
2015 AD
Shanghai, China

The sirens are getting closer. We can't stop moving now; it's time to get out of here.

"You grab these two," I say to Mian Mian, pointing at the two mummified corpses. "Put them in the trunk. We need to get them back to the office and figure out what happened." But she just stands there with tears streaming down her face, staring at Rainbow's still form. I grab her by the shoulders and say, "I know this hurts, Mian Mian, but we have to move right now." Still, she stands there motionless. I shake her violently and scream, "GO, MIAN MIAN! NOW!"

Finally, she stiffens up and nods, then levitates the two bodies into the trunk of the company car. There's no time for secrecy right now: we have to hurry. Besides, there isn't anyone left to be a witness to our magic. Rainbow deserves better, so I gather her in my arms and rush to the car as fast as I can. Gingerly placing her into the back seat, I cover her with my old bomber jacket. Still pretty disoriented, I get in and start the car's engine before I realize what I'm doing.

"Boss," Mian Mian gingerly asks, "are you going to drive?"

Realizing what I'm doing, my stomach suddenly drops as if I were on a roller coaster. Even in a situation like this I can't bear the thought of driving, so I tell her, "Uh, no. You do it, Mian Mian. Please."

Everyone in the office is used to the fact that I don't drive, but no one ever asks why. It's just as well; I don't like to talk about that day in Turin. I have a feeling today will end up being a close second to that in the worst memories ever category. As we peel off, I look back to get one last glance at the terrible scene. The sight causes horrible flashbacks, and my hands start to shake.

"Calm down," I think to myself. "Focus your thoughts."

This isn't the Maelstrom. Whoever that is died long ago, surely. This is different. There are far fewer corpses littering the street than there were in Turin.

One other difference between my memory and what I see behind me instantly catches my eye as the scene rapidly recedes. An unnatural green glow is coming from the top of a nearby one-story building. It's an odd sight. I've never seen magic create that sort of glowing light.

Curiosity makes me want to go back to check it out, but the reg cops and fire trucks pull around the corner and stop at the scene just as I hesitate. Emergency workers pour out of the vehicles to help try and save some of the victims. So instead of telling Mian Mian to stop, I turn around and slump down in my seat, leaving the unfortunately familiar carnage behind.

We pull into the parking garage at our office and sit there for a minute. Glancing down at my watch, I see that it's only 11:30. Only 30 minutes or so since dozens of people lost their lives, and I lost a friend. The first agent I have ever lost in the field. Not only that but also the first time in 25 years that something magical caused the deaths of regs. Was it magical, though? I can't be positive, but it all felt very familiar.

"What was that, Jaret? What happened?" Mian Mian asks, bringing me back to the present. Her voice is so different. It's always been soft with a hard edge, but now it sounds a little bit empty… and yet full of sadness. Her eyes overflow with tears of loss and sorrow.

"I don't know, Mian Mian," I answer. "I wish I could tell you. I'm going to find out, though."

We unload the bodies, including Rainbow's, and head inside. What we find confirms all of my suspicions that it was a magical attack. The office is alive with activity. A portion of the 3D map is glowing with a white dot. I don't even have to look closer to know that bright spot on the map is located in Jing'an, near the temple. Be careful what you wish for, right?

Mian Mian and I walk in with the three corpses and place them on the conference table in the map room. I remove my dad's old brown bomber jacket from Rainbow's body. Everyone stops their harried activities and stares at us, and then at the dead bodies on the table. Their faces change from confusion to fear in an instant.

"Team, gather around, right now," I say with an air of authority and calm.

They form a semicircle around Mian Mian, the three bodies on the table, and me. There are only seven of us left now, and my team starts to notice that Rainbow is not among them. All eyes focus on a familiar business suit worn by one of the strangely drained corpses on the table. The realization dawns on my team that Rainbow is gone. Wracking sobs mix with avoices denying the truth, as they embrace each other.

"This morning in Jing'an a crowd of regs was attacked," I explain somberly. "As you can see on the map, it seems that attack was magical in origin."

Gasps echo through the long room.

"I know," I continue. "It's been 25 years since the last time something like this happened. We don't currently know if it was intentional; it may have been an accident. I'm only calling it an attack for now, because… it reminded me of one from a long time ago. However, we still need more information. It's our job to figure out what happened."

I consider telling them about the strange sensation of being pulled towards something, and the ominous green glow I saw. But I don't.

"Rainbow and these other two bodies were among the dozens of dead, but they were the only three we saw that looked like this. If anyone has seen, read, or heard of anything like this before, now would be the time to say so," I say.

My team silently stares at the desiccated bodies on the table. The sunken eyes and skin drier than 1000-year-old papyrus would be an odd sight anywhere but in a museum. Seeing those features on people who were alive less than an hour ago is what really bothers me.

Tian Yi says, "Jaret, it looks like they were mummified. What happened to them?"

"I don't know," I reply. "There was a bright light and then an explosion. I woke up to find most of the crowd dead and in pieces. Mian Mian and I were okay because we both had magical protection. It seems Rainbow… wasn't fast enough."

This information is met with more silence and stares. Running my fingers through my hair, I let out a long sigh. This is harder than I thought it would be, but I have to keep going.

"Okay, time to get to work, people," I say. "I want everyone to scour the media and find out if we have to worry about secrecy on this. Do the regs suspect it was something strange? Or do they think it was a regular accident? Aurora, send anonymous tips to the media that it was a gas leak. Once we have that situation locked down, all of you check with everyone you can think of who might know why these bodies look this way. Be discreet with your questions. We don't want to alarm everyone with weird tales of explosions creating mummified dead bodies. I'll be in my office on a Network call with Stephen and Jenny."

My agents all look at me, expecting more from their leader. I'm not sure what to give them other than orders. Hope? Moral support? This is my first on-the-job tragedy, and I'm honestly lost for what more to do.

"I know this is tough," I tell them somberly. "It's tough for me, too. We will all have time to process this – with Rainbow's death – but right now I need my team to get us ahead of this situation. We can't afford to be behind right now. Do it for Rainbow."

At the mention of their dead teammate everyone rushes off to take care of business, and I finally feel free to let tears stream down my face. My hands continue to shake as I place one of them on the Network book on my desk.

Once the call connects with both Stephen and Jenny, their faces tell a story as much as mine does; they obviously know something is up, but at the sight of my reddened, tear-streaked grimace, my bosses realize it is worse than they anticipated.

Jenny starts off by saying, "Stephen and I were just on the line discussing a large, destructive spell that went off in Jing'an. Can you tell us anything more about it, Jaret? Was it the street magicians we had reports of?"

I take a deep breath to gather myself before starting. They are not going to like what I am about to say. "Yes and no. I was there and witnessed everything. It was a magical attack on regs," I answer.

As I explain what happened in Jing'an step by step, their eyes go from concern to disbelief. However, when I mention Rainbow's death, and the way her body and the other two seemed dried out, Stephen and Jenny's faces reveal something else entirely. They glance at each other, recognition written all over their features.

In an angry voice I grumble, "You two may be in charge here, and I respect that. But if you know anything about this, tell me right now. One of my agents is dead, and I intend to find out why. I am going to put whoever did this away forever, or maybe just burn them to a crisp. I haven't quite decided which."

They glance at one another again. Stephen rubs his stubbly chin as he says, "One more question before we say anything else, Jaret. Were you able to interview anyone concerning Li Qiuan's disappearance before this happened?"

Un-fucking-believable.

They are still worried about one missing famous wizard after this tragedy? Politicians are all morons. Can't they see the political ramifications are far worse in a magical attack on regs than for one single famous missing wizard?

Even angrier, I say, "No. I did not. I was busy being blown up along with about 30 regs, two other MOP/WPS agents, and several street magicians."

Jenny, the more level-headed of the two, explains. "We have reason to believe that these two cases could be connected, Jaret. They may even have been caused by the same person."

Excited for a lead and a target to point my anger at, I unleash a stream of unfiltered thoughts on Jenny. "Who is it? What do you know? I swear if you two are holding back on me after I lost a member of my team, I will fry you both. No offense."

Stephen jumps in and says, "Jaret, we don't know who it is. All we know is that after I had talked to you today, Li Qiuan's body was found in an abandoned warehouse about three blocks from the site of the... accident this morning."

Accident? Is he fucking kidding?

I growl through gritted teeth, "Don't you dare call it an accident. We both know this was something more. Show some damn respect for the dead."

His round, sweaty face goes red with anger and his beady eyes pop open to their full extent as he struggles to keep his wormy mouth shut.

Seeing his struggle, I add, "And there's more you aren't telling me, isn't there?"

Stephen doesn't say a word but gestures to Jenny, who adds in a stern tone, "Yes, Jaret. There's more. But you must calm down. Being angry won't help any of us. Do you want to help us figure this out or not?"

She's right, of course. Being angry isn't going to accomplish anything. I need to take my father's sage advice.

"Calm down." I think to myself. "Focus your thoughts."

As my heart rate slows and my breathing evens out, Stephen confirms my suspicions and says, "There is more, Jaret, and you won't like it. Li Qiuan's body was found with six other dead wizards in that warehouse... and every single one of them appeared dried out or mummified."

My heart stops beating for an instant, as I begin to comprehend what is going on. Jenny continues where Stephen left off by saying, "Stephen and I received the report around 10:30 this morning that these bodies had been found. We were waiting until you returned to the office to go over it with you."

Thinking over the events of the day a thought suddenly hits me and I say, "Stephen, Jenny, will y'all hang on for just a minute? I'll be right back." Poking my head out of the office, I yell, "Aurora! Get in here!"

She runs from her desk quicker than usual and says, "Yeah, Laoban? How's it going in there? How can I help?"

Impatiently I ask, "Have you finished leaking those anonymous tips yet?"

She nods, reciting her list and ticking them off with a finger. "Yeah, I got all the major expat magazines, the local newspapers, all the big websites in town, both foreign and domestic, even CCTV. I told them I lived around the corner from the explosion, and that I smelled rotten eggs all morning in the area. I also told them that right before the blast, a man threw a lit cigarette into the sewer across from the magicians. Every news source said it was probably a gas leak explosion caused by the cigarette. They bought it, Laoban."

"Good job," I say curtly. "Can you work on trying to identify the other two bodies for me, Aurora? I want to know if they are wizards, too."

She looks at me in surprise and replies, "Already done, Laoban… and yeah, they're both wizards. How did you know?"

Damn. That is not what I was hoping to hear. "Lucky guess," I mutter. "Get me all the info on those two that you can, and pull Rainbow's file for me, as well. I'll fill you in later."

At the mention of Rainbow's name, Aurora begs with pleading eyes, "Please, Jaret, I don't want to go through her file right now. I don't think I can…"

Snapping at my closest ally in the office, I say, "Get it together, Aurora! This is the job and I need your help. Seven more dead and dried-out wizards were found. That's ten, in case you weren't counting. Something crazy is going on. Do this for me without questions, right now."

Looking ashamed, she hurries off without another word and I step back into my office with fresh determination. Glaring at the two faces floating above my desk, I say, "I just verified that the two corpses found at the scene with my agent were also wizards."

"Really?" Jenny replies while sounding suspiciously unsurprised.

"You don't say," Stephen says, also unconvincing in his shock, and then adds, "I was afraid of that. Jenny, tell him the other part."

"There's more?" I ask. "What in the hell is going on here?"

Jenny takes a deep breath before hitting me with the truth, finally. "Jaret, we fear that wizards are being targeted, just as you now suspect. Earlier, Stephen and I put it out in the Network, asking about mummified bodies of dead wizards. We were shut down immediately by both guilds. Any information about dried-out dead wizard corpses is completely blocked on the Network right now."

Information never gets blocked on the Network. Sure, sometimes it is heavily edited but never entirely blocked. At least that I know of.

"Blocked?" I ask. "That could only happen if both High Councils agreed the subject matter was dangerous enough to threaten the peace treaty."

Stephen wipes his sweaty brow with a cloth and adds, "Yes, Jaret, that's right. Both High Councils have deemed this line of inquiry to be off-limits. They have since informed us that the cases are to be worked as separate, and forget about the dried-out corpses. Can you do that?"

How in the hell are we supposed to ignore this entirely relevant information and still solve the case?

"You guys are kidding me, right?" I ask incredulously. "There is literally no way I can do this without looking into what caused those bodies to dry out."

Jenny and Stephen glance slyly at each other. Just before disconnecting the Network call, Stephen looks straight into my eyes and whispers, "Good. I had hoped you would say that."

ELEVEN
1008 AD
Alexandria, Egypt

"You should turn around and go back the way you came. What you will find in this country is madness and hatred of our people. What you will find here is death," the feeble old mage said to Marko.

The man held no actual power. Should Marko wish it, he could end this old fool's sad life in the blink of an eye. But he had nothing worth killing for, and so Marko would let him live… for now.

"Oh, is that so?" Marko retorted. "And what, old man, would kill us? Are there mages stronger than me in this country?" To emphasize his point, Marko used one of his favorite spells to show off. He engulfed himself in flames to the point where all you could see of him were his eyes, which blazed as red as the Fire that leaped out and around the elderly Egyptian mage.

"Or more powerful than my wife?" Marko asked. On cue, Ema created a globe of Water that engulfed the wizened old mage, with space in its center just big enough for him to stay dry. She then froze it solid with a thought, sending icicles creeping out dangerously close to the man's face, before it all melted away, receding into the sand.

"Or my children, whom both command multiple elemental magics?" Marko then said.

Yivan heaved an enormous sigh and rolled his eyes. His father had taught him that an impressive show such as this was a good way to ward off any attacks from hidden threats. This old man, after all, could be just the bait to a much larger trap. If there were dangerous people in hiding nearby they would think twice about attacking his family, if they only knew how powerful Marko and his family were. So, Yivan played his part, loath though he was to do so.

Maeris, on the other hand, reveled in using magic. Now that she had matured and manifested her elemental powers, she was becoming much more powerful than the rest of her family, and being able to wield three types of magic was very rare indeed.

Yivan conjured a boulder as big as a house from the ground and sliced it cleanly in half with a purple bolt of Storm lightning from his hand. Simultaneously, Maeris summoned a looming Fire elemental with the face of a nightmare. The young girl then created a whip made of frozen Water that roiled internally with the power of a maelstrom. She lashed out with her creation, which crackled with blue Storm lightning that combined with the ice to form frozen bolts of magical energy. They flew forth and annihilated the Fire elemental with such force that it resulted in a gust of wind knocking the old man off of his feet. The elderly mage slowly stood up and dusted the sand off his clothes. The terror and amazement in his eyes were plain for all to see.

"Now you have witnessed a taste of our power, and you know my family is not afraid of anyone, old man," Marko said with pride in his voice. They were truly unstoppable in his eyes.

"Infinite pardons to you and your family. I meant no offense; I swear it. I only thought if you left now, you could use the same boat that brought you here. Please, let me live and I will tell you of the troubles this land faces," the terrified old man pleaded.

Marko went from calm bravado to furious rage in an instant, and roared at the gray and withered old mage, "Did you not see our strength, old fool? I care not for whatever troubles this land. Soon it shall be my family and I that trouble the pathetic people here. No mages would dare attack us."

"Yes, you are very right, my powerful friend. Mages would never attempt such suicide as to challenge your intimidating family. It is the wizards you need to fear," the stranger added hesitantly.

Ema, Yivan, and Maeris all looked at each other in confusion hearing this strange new word. Marko held onto his angry tirade and bravado, but also secretly wondered at the man's words.

"We fear NO ONE," Marko growled into the man's wrinkled face. In his anger, Marko raised a hand and let loose a spray of flames that engulfed the old mage. He burned to ash with such haste; the man never had a chance to scream.

Yivan looked from the dusty remnants of the feeble old fool and back to Marko with annoyance. Why must his father be so brash and foolhardy? The man could have told them more information.

"Father," Yivan spoke softly, "about what the old man said; what is this word... what is a wizard?"

"Yivan, my son. I do not know. The old mage was past his prime. His mind was no longer sharp. Let us not worry about his pathetic warning. If danger wishes to find us, we shall welcome it with destruction," Marko replied.

Yivan feared that his father was becoming too reckless. After Maeris's magical manifestation last year, her three points of contact with the elemental Ether arising at the same time, Marko had become drunk on his family's potential. Yivan's father was beginning to ignore many of his own rules for safety. They never paused to observe and consider anymore.

These days it went like this: find a target, attack them, kill them, and take everything. It was always the same. There was never any compassion or mercy to be found, and Yivan was worried about the burning trail his family was leaving in their wake. It would not go unnoticed.

Yivan tried to reason with Marko. "Father, we must be cautious as you taught me to be. We move too far, too fast, and take too many risks along the way. I fear for our safety."

Marko dismissed Yivan's worry with a wave of his hand and said, "Your sister alone could rid us of any threats, and she barely knows any spells. The ones she does know are so powerful that they could kill a dozen mages in an instant!"

"Perhaps, Father," Yivan said. "But what of the lesson you taught me before? What of the flames that joined forces to defeat our own? We leave a scar in our wake; one easily followed. It would be wise for us to lay low. Take a season off and try to live peacefully for a change."

"You worry too much, my boy. We will be fine," Marko reassured his fretful son.

A month into this new land, keeping out of cities and staying in the wilderness, as they had always done, had proven fruitless. Marko's little tribe found this country was devoid of everything, save for sand. They had encountered no other mages in their travels during this month, and very few ordinary people. Those people, of course, Marko and his family destroyed utterly and took everything they had.

Maeris was becoming quite adept at painfully killing a person very slowly. She enjoyed watching them suffer. Yivan was not pleased with his father's violent influence on Maeris, nor the fact that she was now Marko's favorite. Her cold demeanor and extreme power had Marko all but worshipping the young girl.

One afternoon, Yivan questioned his sister about her destructive path. "Maeris, my dear. Why do you listen to him so much? Why do you let his words affect your actions?"

As usual, Maeris was bored with this subject. She merely shrugged, and created flame after flame with her powerful Fire magic. Each one she destroyed with her Storm and Water-fueled whip. Marko had said it was good practice.

"Yivan, we must listen to Poppa," Maeris chided her brother. "He is the head of our family. It is our duty to do as we are told. You know this, big brother."

Maeris then conjured five bonfires as tall as a man and just as fast cut them down with her whip. Yivan was in awe of his sister's magic. Her ability was exceptional, far greater than Yivan or their parents, in fact. He only wished that Maeris had more compassion in her heart, or at the very least, some more foresight. Their path was clear to see, and he was genuinely terrified that it would not end well if his family didn't change.

A sudden and unknown voice intruded on their conversation and said, "You should listen to this mage, little girl."

As he spoke the words, a strange man stepped out of no-where right in front of them. His sudden appearance startled Maeris so much that she released her ice whip, which disappeared the moment it left her hands. Yivan, not being caught off guard so easily, held the man to the ground by encasing his feet in solid Rock. The young mage had purple lightning raging up and down both arms as he pointed at the stranger in their midst.

"I do not know if you mean us harm, but know this," Yivan said menacingly. "If you attempt to cast any magic at all, I will melt the flesh from your bones. You may speak, but only to tell me what you are doing in our camp, and where you came from."

The strange man, obviously not ready for Yivan's speed and power, looked stunned. He was apparently expecting easy targets this day. How unlucky for him that he chose this family to prey on.

"My name is Khalid, boy," the stranger replied, trying to maintain control of the conversation. "I am a wizard. And you will have to kill me, filthy mage, for I will tell you nothing, except to say…" He paused and rolled his eyes to meet Yivan's with a horrible glare.

"…we are coming for you."

TWELVE
2015 AD
Shanghai, China

I spend the rest of the afternoon researching local historians from both guilds and find a few of each worth speaking with about this strange phenomenon of dried-out wizard bodies. It's now just past 3:00 pm, and despite the tragedy of this morning, I still need to keep my family life separate. On the way home, I stop at FamilyMart to grab a couple of drinkable yogurts for the boys.

As I open the door, Han sees me and waddles over with the biggest smile on his face, his brother Luke closely following behind. Lilly fills me in on how the day went, and I barely listen. Not in the mood to chat, I send her home early, as all I want to do is play with my kids and try to forget about this morning for a little while.

By the time Kelly gets home I have dinner ready. Fried chicken, broccoli, and rolls. Three things I know everyone in the family will eat.

"Thanks for making dinner, honey. How was your day?"

"It was a disaster," I tell her, for once being totally honest.

She takes it as a joke and doesn't follow up with another question, thankfully. That is one less lie I will have to tell her.

"How about yours, pretty lady?" I ask in return.

As Kelly goes over her day, I zone out and stare at my wife. She has the cutest freckles all over, and her dark red hair is almost brown. She is perfect in every way. I watch the boys as they eat/play with their dinner. Luke puts ketchup on every bite of food. Han shovels anything nearby into his mouth, hoping it's edible, but not really caring either way.

Just like every single day, I consider just telling Kelly about magic. It would be easy. I could just say, "Hey, baby, magic is real and I'm a cop that polices magic users." Then I'd do some impressive display of magic, and ta-da! No more lies. The only problem is that if I did, I would be fired from my job, and kicked out of the Mages Guild. I would basically be excommunicated from magical society.

The most important law we have in our world is to not let regs know about magic. As a cop, I can't break that law no matter how much I want to tell her.

We finish dinner and play a few games. Truthfully, my mind is still elsewhere the entire time. I can't stop thinking about that feeling of being… I don't know… pulled is the best way to describe it. And the green glow I saw on top of that building. What was it? The more I think about it all, the more questions I have.

We put the kids to bed for the night, then sit on the couch with a few beers and watch *Chopped* together. After a while, we sleepily drift to the bedroom together. It's been a long day for her, and an even longer day for me. I kiss my beautiful wife goodnight and fall asleep before I hit the bed.

Suddenly, my eyes open to find blood and body parts everywhere, and a green glow radiates from all around the area. I look over to see if Kelly is okay, but she's not there.

To my left Mian Mian is crying crimson tears. To my right is Rainbow…she's begging me to help her. They both look so terrified, but I can't move. I can't help.

I see Rainbow begin to drain away, and her skin starts to dry out then shrink inwards, tightening to her frame. A sound similar to a gentle gust of wind fills my ears, and I feel a tugging at my core that pulls me forward… towards something dark.

Dead silence. My eyes fly open, my heart is pounding, and my mind is racing. I take a deep breath and find my center. "Calm down," I whisper, my voice trembling. "Focus your thoughts." Opening my painfully tired eyes, I see that it's 7 am already, and realize it was all a dream. "7 am?" I groan groggily, "Shit… I overslept."

I rip the sheets off in a hurry to get the morning ritual going. But as it turns out, my wonderful wife got up and started the routine for me. The kids are already eating breakfast, and she is getting dressed in the living room.

"Honey, I'm really sorry I slept in. I guess I forgot to set my alarm," I apologize.

Kelly waves my apology away with a smile and says, "Don't worry about it. Even stay-at-home dads are allowed to be late for work every once in a while. And your alarm did go off; you just slept right through it, love. I got started without you because you didn't sleep very well last night. You kept tossing and turning, even moaning in your sleep. Is everything ok, Jaret?"

"NO. Everything is most definitely not ok," I think to myself, wishing I could tell her. But instead, I say, "Yeah, babe. I'm fine. Must have been all of that fried chicken I ate."

Kelly laughs and pats my stomach. "Maybe two pieces will be enough next time, big guy," she says, winking at me as she walks away.

"Hey, woman, don't tell me how to live my life," I say and chase her down the hall, planting a kiss on her before going to check on the kids.

Later, after Kelly is gone for the day and Lilly has arrived to take care of Luke and Han, I immediately head to the office. There too much to do today and not enough time to get it done. Everyone is already hard at work when I arrive at the office. Sometimes I feel like my team should resent me more for not being there all the time, but they always say not to worry about it, that they all understand.

Aurora sees me coming, meets me in my office and says, "All three of the deceased have been taken to the Hall of the Dead for a full autopsy and burial preparation. The other two wizards' names are Sun Xiaoying and Sharon Qi. They are the friends who made the anonymous call regarding the mage street magicians."

Aurora is on top of things, as usual, this morning.

"Well, I guess it makes sense that they would be there," I reply. "Have you talked to their families yet?"

Aurora turns away from me, crosses her arms over her chest, and mumbles, "Yes, Laoban. And I also… I made the call to Rainbow's parents."

Damn. "I'm sorry, Aurora," I say. "I should have been the one to make that call. It was my responsibility, not yours "

She gazes past me, holding back tears, and says, "Don't worry about it, Laoban. They speak almost no English, and don't really trust foreigners. Even though you could have used a spell to communicate, for them to hear this news from another Chinese person is better. It's easier for them."

"Ok, if you say so, Aurora. I'm still sorry that I dropped the ball. Thank you for everything. I mean it. I might be a bit of a jerk sometimes, but I would be entirely lost in this country without your help."

The smile that lightly touches her lips before retreating into hiding shows that she isn't as tough as she wants me to believe.

One more reason we work so well together.

"So, Laoban, will you be interviewing all of the historians today?" she asks.

"Yeah. I've asked the four I think will be the most helpful to come in today. I'd like for you to sit in with me on all of them. I'll need your local knowledge, as well as the rest of the information in that giant brain of yours," I reply. "Go get some work done, and I'll let you know when they arrive."

She nods and heads back to her desk. Now, it is time for some coffee and brainstorming on what questions to ask the historians. I have no clue where to begin. I could ask, "Know anything about mummies?" Of course they do. Or I could lead with, "Ever seen a wizard get dried out like a raisin?" Of course they haven't. Maybe I could try, "Do you know who the Maelstrom is?" Let's face it; they are probably all going to think I'm insane.

After interviewing three out of the four historians, it turns out none of them believes I'm crazy at all. I, however, am highly suspicious of their sanity at this point.

The first three interviews went smoothly, but we got nothing useful out of them. The historians were all interested in the sensation I felt, of being pulled towards something unknown. Hearing this particular detail pissed Aurora off because I still hadn't told her about that or the green glow.

The historians, though, were just as clueless about what the weird sensation was. That didn't stop them from offering infinite hypotheses on the subject, however. The first one said, "Perhaps it was a Storm spell using the power of wind to create suction to pick pockets." The second one said, "Maybe it was the inhalation of a magical giant beast slumbering nearby."

Seriously?

The third one said, "It could have been a temporary change in gravity caused by some unusual wizard spell."

While none of these were completely out of the realm of possibility – well, except the second one – they didn't quite feel right. But out of respect for the historians, I nodded my head and thanked them for their insight just the same. All three of them agreed that the green glow was either my imagination or just a light on top of the building with a green bulb. But I know that wasn't right either. It was unquestionably caused by some kind of magic.

I have higher hopes for the wizard historian currently walking into my office. I'm not ageist, but I have found that people of a certain age are usually crazy or know just about everything. At least that's my experience with the extremely elderly among the magical population. And this woman is *ancient.*

As she gingerly eases into the chair opposite Aurora and myself, I see the old Chinese woman cringe with pain. Using a Water spell, I change the cushion so that it feels like one of those old waterbeds, in an attempt make Mrs. Chang more comfortable.

She smiles at me with genuine appreciation and says, "Thank you, young man. I find that even sitting down at this age can be quite uncomfortable."

Already I like Mrs. Chang. Her smile is warm and genuine, and her eyes show an intensely sharp intellect hidden beneath all of those wrinkles.

"It's my pleasure, Mrs. Chang," I say. "Thank you for agreeing to come in today and talk to us. I don't know if you are aware of the events from yesterday morning, but there was an incident that may or may not have been a magical attack on regs in Jing'an."

Mrs. Chang's eyes widen with shock and she quickly replies, "What kind of attack, young man?"

Her sudden and intense interest is a good sign for my investigation. I say, "An explosion," carefully watching her eyes and facial expression, "possibly as a result of Storm magic, but we're not sure just yet. That's why we asked you to come in. We'd like to give you the details of what happened, and see if it reminds you of anything that you may have studied from the past." The old wizard looks nervous, but motions for me to continue. "Obviously, the attack reminds us of those carried out by the Maelstrom 25 years ago," I say. "Although yesterday's attack was on a much smaller scale. In the aftermath, we noticed something very different from the Maelstrom attacks in the past."

Looking wary but curious, Mrs. Chang leans closer, her interest piqued. Academics always want to test their ability in making connections between the past and current events. And that is exactly what I'm hoping she can do for me. I begin to explain the strange sensation I felt, the unusual condition of the three bodies, and the green glow that I saw on top of the adjacent building. But before I can finish, the ancient wizard historian is hurriedly standing to leave.

"Whoa, wait a minute Mrs. Chang. What's the matter? Where are you going?" I say, attempting to halt her progress. She looks back at me with terror in her rheumy eyes and stutters, "I…I'm sorry. I cannot help you… other than to say… it is time to flee China, Mr. King. Good day."

Bingo. This lady knows something. I harden the door into a solid sheet of Rock, hard as steel, just before she reaches the only way in or out of my office.

"I'm sorry, ma'am. I can't let you leave. This is an ongoing investigation, and one of our agents died in the attack yesterday. I need every single bit of information that you have on this, and I need it now," I say sternly, slamming my hand down on the desk for emphasis.

Mrs. Chang, meanwhile, whips her left hand out and traces an elaborate pattern in the air while mumbling an incantation. The Rock-shielded door shatters into a million tiny shards, all of which instantly evaporate before hitting anything to cause further damage.

Holy shit. I gotta admit: she's a badass.

The ancient historian glares at me with unbridled fury and says through gritted teeth, "Don't you ever try to keep me locked up again, Mr. King. I will not be chained... I will not be held captive."

This response is way more intense than I expected, so I backtrack a little and calmly apologize. "I'm really sorry, Mrs. Chang. Please forgive me and please sit back down. Help us. We're desperate." I say, and gesture to the chair with a pleading look.

She hesitates, glances at the doorway (which is now doorless thanks to her), and then sits down, immediately saying, "The three dried-out bodies you found were wizards, weren't they? I'm also bet that they are not the only bodies you've found in that condition recently."

Aurora's look of shock matches my own, and we both say, "How do you know that?"

Mrs. Chang breathes a long sigh as her body gives a brief shudder. I notice her hands are now trembling consistently.

She says, "I don't know much about it, but I'll tell you what I do know." Closing her eyes, Mrs. Chang settles into the still soft Water-imbued chair and continues, "27 years ago, I was not a historian. I was in my nineties at the time and held a very prominent position in the guild. I cannot tell you what position that was, but suffice it to say, I was privy to all kinds of information blocked on the Network."

That catches my attention and reminds me of the conversation I had yesterday with Stephen and Jenny.

Mrs. Chang goes on, saying, "You mentioned earlier the famous terrorist attacks that spanned those two terrible years. Well, I was in charge of one of the investigations that surrounded these attacks. I'm sure that I don't need to go into detail about how terrible it all was."

"No, Mrs. Chang. You don't," I say.

"I see. So you understand, don't you? Were you there?" she asks.

I nod my head and admit for the first time since coming to work in this office that I had been present at the Maelstrom's final attack 25 years ago. "Yes, ma'am. I was in Turin." Aurora places a hand on my arm and looks at me with sympathetic eyes.

"What I am about to tell you is something that most people do not know," Mrs. Chang says. "Each time there was an attack by the Maelstrom, the authorities found dozens of wizards among the dead."

Snorting, I curtly reply, "Come on, Mrs. Chang, that's common knowledge. There were mage casualties, too. It's not a big secret. I was ten at the time and knew it back then."

She gives me a dark look and snaps, "Do not interrupt me, young man. I can still take my leave, if you wish?"

"No, ma'am," I say. "I'm sorry. It won't happen again."

Aurora nudges me and hisses, "Show some damn respect, Laoban. She's old enough to be your grandma's grandma!"

Mrs. Chang smiles politely at Aurora and then says, "Yes there were mage casualties as well, Mr. King. But the mages were not dried out and mummified, were they? Well, the dozens of wizards I mentioned were found in such a state." She pauses and gives me a knowing yet sad smile.

"I don't believe it; that was never mentioned before by the media. Why would the guilds keep it a secret?" I say.

"Most likely it was at the orders of both High Councils. They seem to be hiding something, and have been for years," Mrs. Chang replies.

"Are you telling me that every Maelstrom attack, all ten over the course of two years, had wizard victims that were dried out like this, and no one ever heard about it?" I ask.

Mrs. Chang locks eyes with me and replies, "Have you disclosed any information to the magical public about the condition of the wizard bodies you found yesterday, Mr. King? No, you have not. And why? Because doing so would cause panic in the wizard community. If they knew that some strange force was killing hundreds of people at a time, but in truth targeting only the wizards, there would be confusion and chaos. Without more information, it would have been unwise to let those facts out back then, just as it is now."

Damn. She's right. "Okay, so what else should I know, Mrs. Chang?" I ask. "What about that green light? And what about the strange pulling sensation?"

She looks down, averting her eyes, and says, "If I knew, young man, I would tell you. We had a few reports back then about a green glow, but not many. Only one survivor ever mentioned the feeling you described, of being tugged at. So we just assumed it was a strange coincidence. As you well know, we never figured out who or what the Maelstrom was, or why it was doing such horrible things. But if it is starting up again, all wizards are at risk. Every single one in the world."

I can't tell if she is being completely honest or not, but I have to trust her at this point. Mrs. Chang has given me more to go on than anyone else.

Concluding the interview, I tell her, "Thank you, Mrs. Chang. If you can think of anything else that would be helpful or anyone else that might know more, please give us a call." I give her my business card and offer a hand to assist her in standing up.

She shakily accepts and makes her way to my now door-less entryway. Turning around, she looks right at Aurora and pleads, "Dear, please be careful. If you feel that odd sensation Mr. King mentioned... run. If you see a green glow, get away as fast as you can. And Mr. King?"

"Please, ma'am, just call me Jaret."

"Ok, dear," Mrs. Chang smiles as she replies. "I think you need to talk to an old acquaintance of mine, Jaret. He is much older than I am and has been studying the Maelstrom's attacks for 27 years. He has become quite obsessed with the monster, in fact. He followed me to China when I retired because... well... he's in love with me." A grin spreads on my face, but before I can joke about the possibility of there being some steamy backstory to go along with this mysterious person, Mrs. Chang raises a hand and cuts me off. "But the feeling is not, and never has been, mutual," she says strongly, brooking no argument from me.

Another lead is something I desperately need. "Who is he?"

She frowns, looking away, and says, "His name is Herod."

THIRTEEN
1998 AD
Atlanta, Georgia

"Tendrils of magic? What the hell is this book talking about?" I mumble while reading the book I had found in my dad's study years ago.

My mage tutor looks at me like I set his shoes on fire again, which I hadn't done in at least a week, and says, "Jaret, your father explicitly said that you were not to read any more of this book. It's all foolish nonsense anyway. We cannot change our connection to the elemental Ether, and we cannot form new connections, either. It's beyond our control. Some might say it's random while others would call it destiny. Either way, everyone everywhere knows that you cannot take magic for your own whenever you please."

"The wizards did," I snidely reply. "They had no magic, Lee. None. But they found a way, didn't they? They figured out a way to access the Ether; or some Ether, at least. I don't think theirs is elemental, but whatever. It's the same concept."

We've been having this same argument for years, ever since my dad told me to forget about the possibility of wielding all four elemental magics. But my father and Lee are both wrong. And lame. I know it's possible to somehow reach into the Ether and take more magic. I just need time to figure it out. Lee, who has been my tutor since I came of age and manifested three schools of magic, strongly disagrees.

"Jaret, can we please let it die?" Lee begs. "This is our last lesson together ever, and I don't want to waste it arguing about something that is impossible to prove."

"Fine, dude. Just get on with it," I grudgingly agree.

Lee straightens his bow tie and continues yammering on about how to create a protective barrier. "You could use Rock to harden your entire body against harm," he reminds me. "It's been known to save mages from dying in all types of horrible accidents. Train wrecks, falling off skyscrapers, explosions…"

Yadda, yadda, yadda is all I hear. All I want to know right now is what this dusty old book means about tendrils of magic? I still don't get it. I've done everything the ancient text in the book said to do.

Organize your different access points to the elemental Ether in separate parts of your mind. Check.

Next, practice quickly switching between these access points so that you become intimately aware of their location. Check. I mean, I am still the World Champion in Youth Speedcasting primarily thanks to my dad's advice and the tips in this book.

Now reach out tendrils of your magic to search for and find a like kind. Never opposites, as the reaction can be explosive. Once again, I try to form a tendril of magic but can't make it work.

Lee brings me out of my reverie by shouting, "Jaret, are you even listening to me? This is crucial information. Rock armor could one day save your life, you know? Please listen, Jaret."

"Yes, Lee." I drone in reply. "Look, I mastered Rock protection spells months ago." Showing off, I put a Rock-based magical barrier all over my body. It works flawlessly.

Well, except for one slight mistake.

The barrier is supposed to be microscopic, invisible to the naked eye. Thinner than paper and harder than steel, if I remember correctly. By accident, mine ends up a good bit thicker. Like… really thick. I end up looking like the Thing from Fantastic Four, only dark brown and without neat blue panties.

"No, Jaret. That is much too thick." Lee says, exasperated as usual. "Regs would see that. It would be too obvious! It has to be so much thinner. Why don't you…?"

Interrupting him, I shout, "Okay, I get it! I messed up, Lee," and throw my arms out wide in frustration. One of my huge, Rock-encased hands accidentally connects with Lee's chest. He flies across the room, and slams into the wall, leaving cracks in the cinder blocks.

"Oh man. Oh shit, Lee! I'm sorry, dude," I say worriedly. Dismissing the barrier, I rush over to check on him. He's breathing, thankfully, but Lee is knocked out cold and my dad is going to be here any minute.

I am so freaking dead.

"Wake up man, wake up," I beg while shaking Lee by his shirt. I try slapping his face a few times like in the movies, but it does nothing. When this kind of thing does happen in the movies, how do they always wake people up?

Thinking about it for a minute, I hear the faucet dripping noisily from behind me and get an idea. I pull some Water from the tap, hovering the globule just above Lee's head with a thought. It comes splashing down right onto his face and… nothing. When I say nothing, I mean it. Nothing happens.

In the driveway, I hear a car pulling in. Lee and I are in a little room off of the back of the house built specifically for spell practice. Dad won't come straight here, so I've got a few minutes to try and fix this. Pacing the room, my mind racing, I try to think of a solution. My dad's constant advice to me over the years drifts through my memories.

"Calm down. Focus your thoughts," his voice whispers in my mind.

As if I were about to start a Speedcasting match, I clear my head and do exactly what my father always tells me to do. My heartbeat slows to a calm rhythm. Utter silence fills my thoughts. I focus on finding a solution.

And that's when I feel it for the first time. An invisible tendril of my magic reaches out from the inside of my mind with no physical presence in this plane for anyone to witness. The tendril exists only in the elemental Ether, I'm guessing.

Not exactly knowing what to do with it, I reach out for Lee with this odd rope of Water magic. If I touch him with it, he might wake up. It's my best guess at this point.

As the tendril approaches his unconscious body, I become aware of his access to the elemental Ether. I can actually sense the connection, which resembles an umbilical cord made of Fire. My tendril of Water reaches out and makes contact. Too late, I recall what the old text said about opposing powers touching.

As contact is made between our two magical essences inside the elemental Ether, the opposing forces of his Fire and my Water cause an explosive reaction here on Earth. I am thrown all the way to the other side of the practice room, and Lee flies into the air to connect solidly with the ceiling before crashing back to the floor.

My body feels as if it is on fire. The pain is intense and that's just the magical trauma. In the physical realm, my back is killing me from hitting the solid cinder block wall. Both of our bodies and clothes are soaked and steaming, almost as if we took a hot shower fully clothed and then ran out into the snow.

"Oh my God," a voice says as the door to the spell room opens. My father walks in and surveys the damage in his spell studio, well aware that something strange has apparently just happened. A moan comes from the direction of Lee's steaming body.

"Thank God," I mumble, "he's alive."

"Jaret! Lee!" my father exclaims. "What on Earth happened?"

Lee sits up and shakes the stars from circling his head, clearing his thoughts. My tutor glares at me from his seat on the floor and says, "Yeah, what the hell happened, Jaret?"

I look from my dad to Lee and lie, "I have no idea. But I promise never to do it again."

My father's features fall from fear to disapproval and disappointment as he notices the ancient book on the table. "What did you do, Jaret?" he asks.

"It's not what you think, Dad. I made a mistake," I admit, but before I can explain, he snatches the old book from the table and storms out of the practice room in a fury.

I go to follow him so that I can explain, but Lee clears his throat and says, "Leave him be, Jaret. You can talk to your father later. Right now, we're going to work on that Rock barrier so this never happens again."

"Ok, Lee," I say, ashamed of myself. "Sorry about what happened." I hate disappointing Lee, but ever more so I hate disappointing my dad. The guy is my freaking hero. I just wish he understood what I was trying to do.

"Don't worry about it, Jaret. As a mage tutor, I'm used to being hurt on the job by young mages," Lee says with a pained grin. "Now let's see if we can thin that Rock barrier out."

Glad he isn't pissed at me, I nod and say, "Ok, sure thing, Lee. But man, imagine how useful that kind of Rock armor would be if I ever got into a fistfight," I say, trying to lighten the mood.

"Jaret, we're mages," he says. "We don't get into fistfights."

FOURTEEN
2015 AD
Shanghai, China

After giving us the address of Herod's shop in the Minhang District, Mrs. Chang leaves the office as fast as her frail form will take her.

Aurora scowls and says, "Laoban, shouldn't we tell the rest of the team about the green glow and the sensation you felt? That could be significant, especially now that we know they are connected to the Maelstrom's initial attacks."

Chewing my lip, I make the call I don't want to make. "No. For the moment, we're going to keep this at our level, Aurora," I say. "They don't need to know just yet."

She looks unsure but nods her head anyway, refraining from saying what's on her mind.

I check my watch and see that it's already 2:45. "I gotta take off soon, Aurora. I'm going to research Herod on the Network tonight. I need you to interview the witnesses who found Li Qiuan's villa trashed. I never got a chance to do it yesterday, and they might know something we don't. I doubt it, but you never know."

"Absolutely, Laoban. Anything to get my mind off of... Rainbow. Want me to hit all of them today?"

"Yeah, if you can that would be amazing," I reply. "It could give us a new lead. Anything would be helpful at this point." Aurora clicks her heels together and gives me her trademark mock salute before sprinting out of my office.

A few minutes later, as I hop on my scooter in front of our building to head home, I notice a fellow laowai sitting on a bench a few feet away. It's a rare sight in this neighborhood as there aren't many foreigners out this way. Curious and wondering if it's someone familiar, I take a closer look. I find that he is not only a complete stranger, but also pissed off and seething with a shitty attitude. He might, in fact, be the angriest person I've ever seen. If he were a Fire mage, he'd be literally steaming with rage while glaring angrily at everyone who passes by.

The man's long, black hair hangs loose, covering his face while his sleeveless shirt reveals skull tattoos adorning his heavily muscled arms. As an MOP officer with keen detective skills, all of this information leads me to the conclusion he could kick my ass in a fistfight, has an extensive collection of leather garments, and hates Top 40s radio hits.

I've had a long couple of days dealing with all that has happened, and even I don't feel as angry as this guy looks. Even though it's none of my business, I decide to try and help the man. I walk over and sit down beside the big metalhead and say, "Hey, man, cheer up. Whatever has you feeling this way, it can't be that bad."

The intense stare now focused in my direction is a little intimidating, and then the asshole gives me the finger.

Well, I was raised to kill them with kindness, so I smile back and say, "Sorry man, I was just trying to make you feel better. We all have rough days in China. Take it easy," then I get up and wave goodbye.

Who knows, maybe my good attitude will rub off on him. Sometimes that's all it takes. I wish someone would drop some sunshine on me every once in a while. This dude probably doesn't have to lie to his family every day to keep a huge secret from them like I do. So, actually, whatever put him in a bad mood can't be as bad as what I am dealing with.

Before scooting away, I get the feeling he is still staring me down. I turn around to tell him, "Look, man," but the bench is empty. "How can a guy that big move so fast?" I wonder aloud.

Turning back to face the road, I find the skulking metalhead standing directly in front of my scooter with his massive, muscled arms crossed over his chest, and contempt in those dark eyes.

He stares down at me with hatred and says, "You should mind your own business." Before I think of some witty comeback, he spins around and stalks away. Maybe I should mind my own damn business. For a second, I thought he was going to punch me right in the face.

Later that night, I wake from a very similar dream as the evening before. Except this time, Mrs. Chang was there warning Aurora to stay away from the strange green glow. But once again, I couldn't move a single muscle as I watched the scene play out. Both wizards started to dry out and shrink in on themselves, their faces in total agony.

I must have called out, because Kelly is awake and looking at me with a furrowed brow. "Bad dream?" she asks sleepily.

If only it were just a dream, instead of an actual possibility. "Yeah, babe. You and the kids were eating dinner and… you all hated my cooking. It was terrifying," I say to ease her mind.

She slaps me on the arm and says, "Go back to sleep, beardo."

Yeah, right; as if I'll be able to sleep anymore tonight. Once Kelly falls back asleep, I quietly creep out to the computer room. After locking the door, I get out the old dusty Network book hidden in a locked drawer.

The Network really is an amazing bit of magic. The Wizards Guild created the spell that links these books together centuries ago. It functions a lot like the regs' Internet, but we've had the Network for hundreds of years. In fact, there's an urban legend that the inspiration for the World Wide Web came from some money-hungry wizard who cashed in on the idea and sold it for a fortune.

The Network is a system of spell tomes that are connected to a central archive. The books sold to wizards are just like the rest of their tomes, endless recharges of a spell they have to learn each time they want to cast it. Network books for mages are slightly different, I guess. I don't really understand how it works other than you release a little bit of magic, any school of magic, into the book and say what you need.

If I want to contact someone that has a Network book, I just say his or her name. If I need to check the news, I just ask for news on the date I'm curious about. If I want to research something or someone…

"Archives," I say to the Network book. Once connected to the almost infinite amount of stored magical files, I look up Herod by saying, "Herod. Wizard. Shanghai."

Without delay, all the scrolls, books, documents, and so forth linked to a wizard named Herod relating to Shanghai are projected in front of me to read as I wish. Luckily, there is only one wizard named Herod in Shanghai.

For the second time today, I read up on this man. When Mrs. Chang said that he was older than her, I was assuming he was like 150 or 160, but I was a little off. Herod is currently 279 years old. Now that is ancient. It's not uncommon for wizards to magically lengthen their lifespan to keep death at arm's length for as long as possible. The longest it has ever worked was on a wizard named Nathaniel "Breezy" Clayton, who lived to be 304 years old.

Mages typically don't go for that kind of stuff. First of all, it's a wizard spell and we're a relatively independent group of people. Mages, however, do sometimes allow wizard spells cast on them: hell, I've done it plenty of times. So it's not just the wizard magic that puts mages off from extending our lives.

We also couldn't marry regular people, only other magic users, if we increased our lifespan. Since our guild forbids us from telling regs about magic, it would be hard to explain how I never aged while Kelly grew older and older. But, despite all that, it's not entirely unheard of for some mages to live for around 140 years.

I scan another document, this one concerning one of Herod's research projects that were shut down about 50 years ago. All the information detailing his research was redacted, although there is still mention of his dismissal from the Library of Discovery, where wizards research and create new spells. That is something to ask him about when we meet.

Here is an article on Herod from about 70 years ago. Not a very nice piece on him, either. Written by a colleague at the Library of Discovery, the article critiques some of Herod's more unpopular theories, several of which were removed from the file. I'll try and remember to ask about those when we talk.

The author of the article had this to say, "Herod is a weakling of a wizard. His spell capacity is embarrassingly small while his spell power is laughable. I have no idea why he is taken seriously as a researcher."

That is not something to ask him about when we meet.

I read for a while longer and realize it's almost time for the family to rise and shine, up and at 'em. I need to put on some coffee and start making breakfast. Just as I am about to close the Network book, one more projected scroll catches my eye: a medical report from the magical division at a local hospital in Shanghai detailing Herod's recent visit due to a chronic and continuing condition.

It seems that Herod, the old-timer, is dying. His life-extending spell is fading and, despite the efforts of the best Chinese healers, won't keep him alive much longer than a few weeks at most. The worst part of this report is that it's already two weeks old.

"Shit," I say. "I hope he's not dead yet. I need his help." Only one way to find out, I guess; I'll have to stick to the plan, and head over to his shop this morning. What could go wrong?

FIFTEEN
1008 AD
Alexandria, Egypt

"…We are coming for you."

Those words chilled Yivan to his bones, and he hesitated for just a moment. The wizard, still bound to the Earth by a Rock spell, began saying strange words and moving his hands in odd, geometrical patterns.

Yivan had never seen anything like it before and had no idea what the man was doing. The wizard concluded his spell-casting and flung both hands outward towards the young and dangerous mage before him. Yivan was caught by surprise when he flew a dozen feet backward, his chest having been struck by a spray of sharp spears.

Though small, the spikes penetrated Yivan's clothes and even stuck into his skin slightly. Luckily, he had enacted a barrier of Storm wind on himself when the strange man had appeared, but the wizard's spell had been strong enough to punch through, because Yivan felt blood trickling down his body.

Using more Storm wind, Yivan removed the spikes from his chest and flung them outward to disappear into the desert sands. "So," Yivan thought in wonder, "this wizard can use magic."

A fight it would be, then.

By the time Yivan was done removing the tiny spikes from his chest, the wizard had freed himself from the Rock bonds that had once held him to the Earth.

"Why are you after my family, Khalid the wizard?" Yivan said, circling to the left.

Khalid circled to the right with an amused look on his tanned features and said, "Your family? I could not care less for you or your family, mage."

"Lies!" Yivan spat. "You said the wizards are coming for us."

The wizard threw his head back and laughed sadistically, then moved his right hand in a circle while reciting a few more of those odd sounding words. A scimitar made of bright light appeared in the wizard's dark hands.

As he twirled it around to test its heft, Khalid said, "Mage-boy, you have a high opinion of yourself and your kin. We wizards are not after just you. We are after all of the mages. Too long have your kind tormented the land and destroyed everything ordinary men hold dear, but no more. For we have discovered our own power."

The wizard leaped forward to slash at Yivan's still bleeding chest with his blade of pure light and magic. Yivan was ready, though, and conjured a wall of Storm wind in front of him to deflect the blow. The blade tore right through it as if nothing were there. A typical blade would have been caught in the Storm barrier, but this scimitar of light was no ordinary sword.

Yivan saw the blade slicing towards his heart and knew he did not have time to stop it from penetrating his chest. This was the end, then. Yivan would never get to fully develop his power. He would never get to take a wife and share his life with her. He would never have children.

It was almost a relief.

Just before the magical sword could connect with Yivan's heart, his little and yet powerful sister intervened. Maeris extended her palm, sending a thin string of Fire out to wrap around Khalid's hand; the one who held the magical scimitar. Once wrapped tightly, she pulled the fiery thread back towards her.

Khalid the wizard's hand came off, and the sword of light dissipated immediately. The burning strand of Fire had sealed the wound. He would not bleed to death, but his agony was immense. Falling to his knees in the sand, the wizard stared at his missing appendage and unleashed a torrent of pained howls into the empty desert.

Khalid then roared, "YOU VILE LITTLE CREATURE! WE WILL TAKE EVERYTHING FROM YOU AS YOU HAVE TAKEN FROM COUNTLESS REGULAR PEOPLE! YOU WILL PAY FOR THIS, I SWEAR IT BY…"

The wizard suddenly fell silent and passed out in the sand. Brother and sister turned to find their father, shirtless and heavily muscled, glaring at the unconscious wizard. A braid made of real Fire held Marko's long, black hair back. It neither burned him nor seemed to offer any discomfort at all. The fire tattoos on his chest moved with the power of actual Fire.

"Father, did you kill him?" Yivan asked cautiously.

"No," Marko replied darkly. "Bind this fool, children. We must know more of what he said."

So, Yivan thought, Marko had heard the wizard. But had he seen his son almost die? Yivan wondered how far his father would have let it continue if his sister had not intervened.

Maeris began to affix bindings of Storm wind to the wizard. Yivan placed larger and more elastic Storm wind bonds on top of those, in case Khalid was able to break free of the first set. Ema, the most adept at coercing information from a captive, woke the sleeping wizard with a dousing of cold Water. Khalid shrieked in shock at the frigid temperature of the magically summoned Water, and at the realization that he was outnumbered four to one.

"Father, how much did you see of our encounter with this man?" Yivan quietly asked.

"From the moment the fool stepped out of the Ether, my son. I was proud of how you handled yourself. Do not feel shame for the failure of your barriers. This is a new type of magic. I've never seen anything like it before, and so we must be careful moving forward. Things are changing, my son, and not for the better, I fear," Marko said.

Maeris said, "How did I do, Poppa?"

"Maeris, you did well, my child," Marko said with praise. "I, too, noticed that his hands were used in creating these strange spells. The removal of one of them should make him easier to control. Well done."

Maeris only shrugged and said, "I just wanted to cut his hand off, Poppa."

Marko tousled her long, black hair and said, "The instinct was there. You did well." Maeris knocked her father's hand away, and sat down, waiting with anticipation to watch what would become of this wizard that foolishly attacked her family.

"Now then, fool, tell us more about your people. Who are these wizards? How is it that you have this strange new magic?" Ema said, walking around the disabled magic user.

Khalid spat on the ground, struggling against the Storm bonds holding him tight and said, "Your time is over, mage. Our time is only just beginning. Soon, we will rid the world of your stench. The end of all mages is soon to be at hand, I promise you that."

"It is good that you are willing to talk," Ema said as she stroked his wet face with one of her long, slender fingers. "Talk will be good for you, my friend. You see I can make your final moments – or days – more painful and horrible than you can possibly imagine. Or you can tell me everything right now, and I will kill you very quickly. No pain. The choice is up to you, wizard."

Khalid looked defiantly into Ema's sunken eyes and made his choice. Two very long days later, Khalid the wizard finally died. Horribly. Pieces of the man would later be found miles away. Those two dreadful days were filled with screams that could only be the result of torture, the sounds of flesh being torn and repeatedly regenerated by Ema's Water magic, and eventually with the sounds of Khalid begging for mercy.

"So, we go to this city. Cairo, he named it. We will visit the compound he spoke of, where the wizards perform their studies," Marko told his family.

"Father, that sounds like a risky plan. Why don't we just leave this land and return to Croatia? There were lands we completely bypassed on the way. We could stop there and roam the countryside, living as we did before. There is no need to risk our lives on this foolish errand," Yivan reasoned.

Marko looked darkly at his disrespectful son and silently begged God for answers. Why was Yivan so weak and yet so powerful? Why would he not see reason, and adhere to the set of laws that Marko had carved out for their family? Not for the first time, Marko wished that it had been himself blessed with two connections to the elemental Ether, and not his son.

"It is too late to go back, Yivan. The rebellion has begun. These ordinary men have learned magic. It is unnatural. If we do not do something now, it will only get worse. We must take the fight to them in their homes while they lie in their beds, dreaming of new ways to use our magic. Did you not hear that dog admit how they are learning our magic?"

"I did, Poppa. I heard him," Maeris said. "They are capturing mages, like us, and doing... what did he say?"

Yivan placed a hand on his sister and pulled her closer. She was still acting like her father more and more every day. Maeris was even beginning to form large muscles on her arms from working with that whip so often.

"He called them experiments, sister," Yivan explained. "Khalid said that they found out how to access another conduit of magical energy, a second Ether, through..."

"Go on, Yivan. Say it." Marko barked. "Through dissecting mages. Cutting our people to pieces and studying us from the inside. And you expect me, the leader of our family, to let this stand? No. We go to Cairo and we kill every wizard we find there, and along the way."

"But Father, we don't know what we will find there! They could have an army, possibly with hundreds of thousands of ordinary men. If that is so, how can we possibly defeat them?" Yivan asked.

Marko took Yivan's smooth-shaven head into his strong hands and stared into his son's eyes. He smiled and kissed Yivan on the forehead before saying, "If that is the case, my beautiful boy, we will not win. We will all die. But our family will die with such a fight. A real demonstration of power and destruction like the world has never known. We shall be a Storm in the desert. We shall kill so many of them, my dear son. So very many."

Maeris smiled at the thought. After all, the young girl felt as if she *was* a Storm in the desert. She even looked forward to meeting more wizards. Well, meeting and killing them, that is.

SIXTEEN
2015 AD
Shanghai, China

Skipping the office today, I head straight to the Minhang District to talk with Herod. On the way, I call Aurora's cell, but it goes straight to voicemail. I leave her a message detailing my schedule and ask her to get all the information together from her interviews with the Li Qiuan witnesses for me to review this afternoon.

Since driving is not really an option, and a taxi to Minhang would take forever, the Metro is the most sensible option. Besides, riding the train relaxes me somehow. Maybe it's the gentle sway of the train or the elbow-to-elbow contact with hundreds of strangers. That may sound strange, but being part of a minority group in a foreign country combined with being part of a hidden magical society can leave you feeling lonely sometimes. It's hard to feel lonely on the Metro during the morning rush hour.

After arriving at the right stop and leaving the station, I see a vendor selling jidan bing, which is a kind of eggy Chinese breakfast burrito. It's one of my favorite all-time foods, after living here for a year and eating them on an almost daily basis.

Munching on that and chugging some warm soymilk, I notice a shop that has a sign in both English and Chinese that reads: *"Ancient Chinese Medicine and Magical Supplies"*

"Magical supplies?" I grumble through my breakfast filled maw. I should bust him for that, but I've got more important shit to worry about right now.

The door is open, so I walk right in. I didn't call ahead in case Herod didn't really want to talk to me. An unexpected face-to-face will force him to open up a little more than a scheduled interview. The badge and title of Lead Agent at a dual division MOP and WPS office carry a good bit of clout in our circles.

Seated behind the counter and reading a local newspaper is a little Scottish man wearing a kilt. His hair is red but fading to grey, and his skin is a bit wrinkled. However, he doesn't look a day over 55, much less his actual age of 279. I was kind of expecting a dusty old geezer, to be honest.

Before looking up, the elderly ginger welcomes me to the store in Mandarin, "Huanying guanglin." His accent is perfect. The Scot sounds like a local, and that wasn't even magically reproduced Chinese. That was the real deal.

"Good morning. Are you Herod, the wizard?" I ask.

Herod looks up, surprised to hear English spoken back to him, not to mention a reference to his actual identity. I guess not many laowai or real magicians frequent his establishment.

"Aye, that I am," he replies with a smile. "And who are you, might I inquire?" His Scottish accent is thick when speaking English, but his kindness feels genuine.

"My name's Jaret King, and I head up the MOP and WPS office here in Shanghai. I spoke with a friend of yours yesterday who referred me to you. A nice lady by the name of Mrs. Chang?"

A lecherous grin spreads on his weathered old face, then he offers a bawdy wink and says, "Och, aye. A beauty, that one. Been tryin' to bed her for years, ye ken?" His laughter fills the room, and I can't help but chuckle along as he continues. "But eh, she won't have me. I cannae understand it. I'm thinkin' that it must be the kilt," he says, raising his traditional Scottish garment to a level that almost reveals his religion. "She's seen too much of me, if ye get my meanin', and not been much impressed."

He guffaws again, even louder, and I join him. I think I'm going to like this old guy.

"But eh, what can I do for ye, laddy?" Herod asks.

Looking around at the large windows in the shop, and the dozens of locals walking by, I say, "Is there a… ah, a more private place where we can speak? This is concerning a subject matter that regs should not be privy to. I'd hate for one to walk in and overhear us."

Herod walks over to his door and flips the open sign to closed, and lowers the blinds on his windows. He then raises a hand, traces some geometric patterns in the air, and says a few words of power. Instantly we are no longer in his shop, but instead in what looks like a medieval alchemy lab. The dark room is filled with glass bottles containing odd concoctions, strange things floating in jars, and an actual bubbling cauldron. I half-expect a cackling witch to walk up and start stirring while telling me about toils and troubles.

"This is…quaint. Where are we, Herod?" I ask.

He chuckles while looking around at the embarrassingly stereotypical magical dungeon and explains, "This is where I make all the ridiculous ancient Chinese potions that I sell. I don't go for that traditional Chinese medicine nonsense. No, I corner the market in 'magical' potions in the area. Of course, no one with a lick of magic would buy the bastards because they haven't the slightest bit of magic in them. And I made it look like a frickin' castle dungeon down here because now and then I bring a customer down for a peek at the trash I'm brewin' and charge them extra for the privilege!"

"So we're just below the shop then?" I say, mildly annoyed. "Why didn't we just take the damn stairs?"

His lips pursed tightly, Herod says, "I don't have the energy to do that verra much anymore. Gettin' too damned old, ye ken. But anyway, we're here and alone. What is it ye're wantin' to talk about?"

"Well, I hear that you're very knowledgeable about the Maelstrom," I say to the old Scot.

"Aye, that I am, laddy. Probably better than anyone alive, save for the Maelstrom him or herself, that is."

"Herself? You think it's a woman?" I say.

"Well, I cannae say. I dunnae ken. No one does, lad. But it could just as likely be a woman as a man. And why not? That sly fox Mrs. Chang can hold her own in a spellfight. Don't ye doubt it," Herod replies with a wistful gleam in his sparkling eyes.

"Oh, I don't. My office is freshly doorless thanks to her," I mumble with mock irritation.

Herod laughs his larger-than-life guffaw, slaps a knee, and says, "Did she do that now? Blasted your door off. Isn't that just like her?"

Smiling at the memory of the feisty old wizard, I sit down on a stool and grow more solemn, holding Herod's gaze with my own.

"There was an attack in Jing'an yesterday, Herod. To all intents and purposes, it matches the Maelstrom's MO," I say.

Intrigued, Herod leans in, eyes wide with curiosity and whispers, "In what way, laddy? Tell me everything and leave out nothing."

I tell Herod about the attack, the odd sensation I felt and the green glow from the rooftop, and the peculiar condition of the corpses we've found. Then I recount what Mrs. Chang said yesterday about the connection to the Maelstrom's terrorist attacks from the past.

Afterwards, without saying a word, I just look at Herod. This is a good tactic to get people talking. Don't ask them anything; just say what you know, look right at them, and wait. Eventually, they'll either say something funny to break the silence, or offer up everything they know. So, Herod and I sit in silence for a few moments staring at each other. Then the old wizard opens his mouth to say something. *Bingo.*

"Aye, laddy," he says. "That's a familiar-sounding tale ye've told. One I had hoped never to hear again for the rest of my days. Which, to be honest with ye, is not that long away." Staying silent, I continue to watch him intently. Herod hesitates only slightly, before saying, "Tell me Jaret, what do ye know about wizards when they pass on from this life? You know... when we die?"

What an odd question. But, it's definitely leading our conversation in the right direction. Dead wizards are at the forefront of my thoughts these days, unfortunately.

I reply, "Well, as much as I know about mages or regs when they pass away. We die, we get prepared for burial, we get buried, and people mourn. Are you talking about whether there is an afterlife or something?"

Herod grimaces and shakes his head as he scoffs, "No, no, no, nothing like that. Ye see, I've always wondered what happens to the spells we wizards hold inside of us after we die. You casters just tap into the elemental Ether and cast it at will, ye lucky bastards. Us wizards have a rougher time of it, as ye well know."

"Yes, I'm aware of how wizard magic works," I say.

He points a finger angrily in my direction and adds, "But do ye know that when we hold those spells inside of us, we're actually holding the entire sum of magical energy used to cast them as well? We can't tap into the Ether as you mages do, so we have to create these tomes and cast the spells directly into ourselves via the bloody books, only so that they can later be directed as we please. It's a damned dangerous way to use magic, lad! Though we've managed to make it as safe as we can over the past thousand years. But what happens when we die, eh, matey? Where does that magical energy go?"

"No clue. I've never really thought about it to be completely honest with you, Herod," I say.

He nods and sighs, "Aye, not many have. And those that do are often told to stay away from that particular train of thought. Now, I'll be truthful with ye and say that I've never had much skill with magic."

"I don't know, Herod," I tell him. "That teleport spell was pretty good."

"Thank you for thinkin' it was a decent spot of magic, Jaret. But it was not verra strong. It was only to pop us downstairs. A wee bairn could do that by accident, ye ken. No, I've always been more of a researcher. I love readin' old spell tomes and histories; tracin' back the origins of what it is we do."

"My father did, too. He was obsessed with Storm history. I got a little into magic history myself at one point, but... it didn't work out so well for me," I admit.

"I can understand that, big man," Herod commiserates. "It didn't work out so well for me either. You see, long ago when I started to wonder about the unspent magical energy and what happens to it when we die, I worked for our High Council. Before my career went tits up, I was able to do a bit of research. As it turns out, from what I can gather, nothing happens to that residual power. It stays within the wizard that dies. At that point, it's just unspent magical energy, and no longer a Fireball or teleport spell. Do ye understand, lad?"

"It sounds a bit loony and out there, but I think I see what you mean," I reply. Herod pours himself a glass of water and is about to go on with his story when my phone abruptly rings. I look down to see Jaysen's name displayed on the screen. Holding a finger up I say, "Hang on a second, Herod. It's one of the mage agents on my team. I have to take this."

As I do so, Herod begins mixing some foul-smelling brown liquid with an odd looking powder from a container labeled POWDERED PANDA PARTS. I honestly hope that label is just for show.

I answer the phone, "Hey, Jaysen, what's up?"

His voice trembles, sounding terrified as he responds, "Jaret, I need your help. She's gone. He took her. I tried to stop him, but... but I couldn't. I don't know what to do. Please, Jaret. You have to help me, please."

"Whoa, slow down, Jaysen," I say calmly. "Start from the beginning. Tell me everything and leave out nothing."

"Okay...okay. So, Aurora went to interview the witnesses from the Li Qiuan case like you asked her to do yesterday, but she couldn't find any of them, and no one knows where they are. She came back to the office, and we all were thinking the worst because – you know – they're all wizards. We felt like it was only a matter of time until we found their dried-out corpses like..."

"Rainbow. Yeah, I know. Keep going," I urge him.

His voice still trembling, Jaysen takes a deep breath and then says, "Well, this morning we got an anonymous tip through the Network that the missing witnesses were all kidnapped, and being held in a warehouse near the Expo site in Pudong. Aurora asked me to tag along, which was great, you know? I mean, I don't really get to work with her that often, and she's... so amazing, Jaret. She really is the most talented person on our team, no offense. So, I really just wanted to impress her, you know?"

"Jaysen, stay on track, pal," I say. "You said someone took her. Did you mean, Aurora? Where is Aurora, Jaysen?" I ask tensely, my pulse quickening.

Jaysen sniffles and his voice grows thicker as he goes on, "We drove to the warehouse mentioned in the tip, but when we arrived all Aurora and I found was a bunch of chains connected to a central pole. There were signs that people had been held captive there, Jaret. It was disturbing. I enhanced my hearing to see if anyone was still in the building. Aurora... she changed. I've never seen her look like that, Jaret. She was furious, and kept saying things like, 'How could anyone treat human beings like this?' She cast a barrier spell, then enhanced her speed and took off running. When she was on the other side of the building, I heard her shouting for someone to stop and stay where they were. Then I heard the rush of a spell… and an explosion."

Jaysen stops to catch his breath, and I say, "Oh my God. What happened next, Jaysen?"

"I ran as fast as I could and prepared some Storm lightning for whoever was fighting with her. I came around the corner and saw a tall figure in a black cloak. I couldn't see the face, it was covered by a black mask. Aurora was casting something, but before it could go off the figure in black threw a Fireball at her. It was fast. I've never seen a wizard cast anything that fast. He was as fast as you, Jaret."

"Maybe he was a mage, Jaysen. There is no way a wizard can cast a Fireball faster than I can. It's impossible."

"Well, after the Fireball hit her dead center in the chest, it knocked her back like ten feet. Her barrier spell held, but she was out cold. I threw a bolt of Storm lightning at the figure. I thought I had the element of surprise. But it just arced right over him. He had a barrier around himself, too, but way stronger than any I've ever seen. He looked in my direction and said an incantation and did some wizard stuff with his hands. That's how I know he's a crammer."

"Ok, so he's a wizard. A really fast crammer," I concede. "What happened next, Jaysen?"

"Next? I'm stuck to the ceiling, and she is floating over into his arms. I'm completely immobile, but I focus on the figure and press down on him with Storm wind to slow him down long enough for Aurora to wake up, or for the spell he used on me to wear off," Jaysen says.

"That was quick thinking, Jaysen," I offer. "Did it work?"

"I guess, for a second the figure did slow down, but as soon as Aurora came within reach, the crammer flung her into the back of a van with more people inside, lying unconscious."

"Probably the missing wizards," I guess.

"Yeah. Well, then the crazy wizard hopped into the van and released the spell holding me to the ceiling. I had to slow my fall, and by the time I hit the ground he had turned the warehouse into an inferno. I ran to where the van had driven out and was struck by a bolt of lightning right in the legs. They both started twitching uncontrollably and hurt like you wouldn't believe, Jaret. If he had hit my chest or head, I'd be dead. As soon as I could, I called you. So, tell me what I am supposed to do now."

"Listen, you may be in shock, Jaysen," I say, worried about his state of mind. "Get back to the office immediately, and I'll meet you there." Herod is still busying himself with his potions and looks up at me as I walk over. "I'm very sorry, Herod," I say, "but I have to take off. Something major has just come up. I'd like to continue this conversation later, though. Your insights could be crucial to my investigation. Can you meet me anytime today or tomorrow? I won't be able to make it back out to Minhang, but maybe we could meet in Xuhui?"

His features looking troubled, Herod smiles wanly and admits, "Aye, I overheard some of yer friend's story on the phone. Sorry to eavesdrop, lad, but these old ears still hear everything. It seems ye have a lot to deal with, and I'm sorry to say that it is probably all connected to what I have to tell ye. How about we meet tonight at a pub I know in Xuhui. 9 pm good for ye?"

"Fine, but don't be late," I tell him sternly. "If it is all connected, then I am going to need your help more than ever." I ask him to text me the address to the pub, and then I am on my way to figure out where Aurora has been taken and why.

SEVENTEEN
2000 AD
Hoi An, Vietnam

"I still don't understand why you're going to college," my dad says, repeating his opinion on the subject for the millionth time this week. "It's a waste of time, son."

"You know, you may be the first father in history to give their child that advice, Dad," I say.

"Not at all. My dad told me that college was for regs," he says proudly. "Mages should study magic. It's all we need. We can easily manipulate their world, Jaret. We have no need to learn academic reg subjects."

I love the guy, seriously, I do. He's my damn hero and all, but my dad is so stubborn. "I want to work for Mage Order and Protection, Dad," I begin to explain for the hundredth time. "I want to protect the regs and the magical community from harm. That doesn't mean I'll neglect my magic studies. I'm still going to study new spells and develop my power; it's necessary to be a good agent. But I feel like a degree in Criminal Psychology will give me an advantage."

"Son, MOP doesn't care about a piece of paper from a reg college. They care about skill, and that you have plenty of. It's genetic," he says with a smile and tousles my hair as if I'm still ten.

"I don't mean an advantage in being hired, Dad. I know that I'm going to work for MOP. They'd be crazy not to hire me," I say. "I meant an advantage against criminals once I am an agent. You know, understand how the bad guys think?"

He just shakes his head as he hands me my Speedcasting gear; all the essential uniform pieces for professional matches. It might look silly but it's tradition and, to be honest, I think it does help me cast a little bit faster. The helmet, though, I could do without.

"Why did they add the mask again?" I ask my dad. "No one was wearing them in the old photos from when you first started."

"Well, there was an accident. Some competitors lost their lives, and both Councils decided that stricter safety measures needed to be added to the professional league. The obstacles are more dangerous, and the spells are more powerful. It makes sense to me," he explains, shrugging his shoulders.

"I guess it's just hard to see out of the dang thing sometimes," I complain.

Dad takes a cloth and cleans the viewfinder of my helmet for me. "That's because your visor is filthy. It needs to be crystal-clear, Jaret, especially today. This is a big match. The most difficult opponent you've ever faced. It's going to be tough and you're going to need every advantage you can get."

"Like having three schools of magic? I remember once you said that was a pretty significant advantage," I say, half-joking.

"Yeah, just don't let it trip you up like it almost did with your first Championship. You need to have a clear head out there, kiddo. No hesitation, okay? Just think and act in one fluid motion." Dad says in his lecturing voice.

He always believes in me, though, no matter how much he lectures. My dad, the World Speedcasting Champion, thinks I can beat anyone, regardless of what the circumstances are. I don't know why he thinks I'm so unique. I'm only doing what he's taught me.

"I know, Dad. I need to stay calm and focus. Right?"

He grins broadly and pulls me in for a hug, and softly says, "Exactly. Now, put on the rest of your suit. It's almost time."

After I pull on the skintight bodysuit, fingerless gloves, and light shoes, I begin to slip on the carbon fiber plates to protect vital areas in case of… I don't know what. Explosions and flying debris, I guess.

Dad examines me from top to bottom, gives a thumbs-up in approval, and asks, "Ready, son?"

"As I'll ever be, Dad," I respond.

"Remember, no hesitation out there. This won't be easy for you," he says with a wink and a jokingly smug expression.

As I look at him, all of my tension falls away. He's trained me. My dad has taught me how to win. I just have to go out there and do everything he's prepared me for my whole life, and then I'll have my first Professional Speedcasting Championship.

"Let's do this," I say.

We walk out of the tent and are greeted by the roar of thousands of mages. A few hundred wizards are in attendance, too, but really Speedcasting is a mage thing, and so not a lot of crammers ever attend. This is like our Super Bowl, and I'm playing in it.

110

My dad already has his helmet on, so I slip mine on, and we stand side-by-side as the announcer, Matthew Birge, introduces us to the crowd. "Mages and wizards! Ladies and gentlemen! Fans here in Hoi An, Vietnam, and our viewers around the globe via the Network... It's time to begin our main and final event!"

The crowd goes bananas.

"This is a most unusual and yet historic Championship match. I am, as you all know, Matthew Birge, and I have covered every Speedcasting Championship for the past ten years. Before that, I was a rather mediocre competitor myself. I have been a fan of the sport my entire life. You could call me a student of Speedcasting. But never before in our long history has there been a match like this!"

Getting the crowd pumped up for an event is Matthew's specialty. It's even working on me. My heart is beating faster than it should. My palms are sweating. The visor of my helmet is starting to fog over from my heavy breathing.
I think I might puke.

"An epic battle will soon take place between the current defending Professional World Speedcasting Champion, the amazing Christopher King..."

The audience roars so loud that I can't even hear my heart pounding in my throat anymore. I still might puke.

"And the challenger... his SON! JARET KING!"

If the audience went mental for my father, they are now past the point of mere insanity. The stadium fills with so much noise, I am actually afraid that the regs are going to somehow hear it beyond the magical barrier constructed around this ancient place. I take my helmet off and gasp for air. If I puke in there, it's going to ruin my chances of beating my dad today.

My father takes his helmet off as well and starts waving to the gathered fans in the stands. "Jaret, listen to me," I hear him whisper. "Calm down. Focus your thoughts."

I attempt to steady my breathing, and then lock eyes with my father, giving him the slightest tilt of my head.

"You can do this, son. I believe in you," he assures me. "But I'm not going easy on you. You'll have to rip this victory out of my hands. I like to win, you know."

I take a few more deep breaths and focus. My access points to the elemental Ether are lined up and situated in my mind the way I like them. I slow my heart a little and my breathing finally evens out.

"You're going down, old man," I warn him, an impish grin crossing my features. "I got this in the bag."

He laughs, slips on his helmet, and I hear his muffled voice say, "We'll see about that."

Two Stations into the match, and so far all my wildest dreams are completely out of reach. My father is crushing me. He wasn't kidding about not going easy on me. One more Station victory and Dad stays Champion. He basically murdered me at Stations one and two.

The blazing inferno at Station one should have been easy for me. I tried the same trick I had done years ago against Connor. The Water from the grass had no effect on these flames, however. Sure, I was faster than him, but my dad noticed the metal container swinging gently in the breeze above the flames. He went for that instead of the Fire, rightfully guessing its purpose. The chemical concoction inside was the only way with which to extinguish the blaze. He won there.

Station two was closer, but I still got creamed. A school bus was about to fall off the top of a tall tower onto a child below. I hurled a massive boulder at the back of the bus, hoping to change its trajectory while readying a second stone in case I needed additional adjustments as the bus fell. Dad, once again, outsmarted me.

He hit the gas tank of the bus with a lightning bolt. The resulting explosion evaporated the bus and saved the child, which turned out to be an illusion anyway.

"Son, you're faster than me. But you're only looking at the obstacles; you're not reading them," Dad says to me on the way to Station three. "Read the situation before casting. Calm down and focus your thoughts, or *I've* got this in the bag. Do you even want to win? Do you want to be the Champ? If so, then challenge me, son! Show me what you've got!"

Station three is either my chance to get back into the game, or the last Station of the match. The buzzer goes off, and the obstacle is revealed. Or, rather, it should have been revealed – but nothing is there. I scan the field and look for something – anything – but it's useless. Whatever they planned must not have worked.

I look over at my dad and he seems just as bewildered and confused as I do. I shrug and put my hands in the air, ready to give up. My father raises a hand to shade his eyes and keeps scanning. He wants this win.

That's when I see it - a hummingbird hovers dead center of Station three, not flying outside of the Station boundaries. And just like with the dog against Connor, I know what to do. Dad probably does, too.

As fast as possible, I encase the bird inside a ball of solid Rock, and as it begins to plummet down to Earth I wrap layer after layer of ice around that. Dad's gust of Storm wind blows the tumbling ice rock into the audience, who scatters. His lightning reaches out and shreds the ice layers off all at once.

I can't let him win this Station, or it's all over. A long, thin spear of Rock shoots out of the ground and attaches itself to the ball. Before a second bolt of Dad's Storm lightning can break open the Rock encasing the hummingbird, the spear of Rock retreats into the ground at my command, pulling the ball with it. As it reaches the ground, the buzzer goes off and I release the bird.

Time's up; I win Station three, and the crowd goes wild and starts chanting my name. "JARET! JARET! JARET! JARET!"

Dad slaps me on the back, and grinning ear to ear says, "Not bad, son! I've never seen anything like that before. Brilliant piece of magic, Jaret. I thought for sure once I blew it away, you'd be lost for a way to get the Rock ball back. Well done. You've earned those cheers!"

Station four is a walk in the park after the confidence boost from Station three. Four was a six-foot-tall nesting doll, with each layer made of increasingly harder substances to destroy. In all, there ended up being ten layers, but we didn't know how many there were in the beginning. When I saw the nesting doll, and recognized the obstacle from past events, I knew that I would have to be faster and destroy more layers than my dad to win.

After blasting through the first three layers all by myself, Dad finally got his first point on the fourth layer. When the fifth one showed through, I thought it was wood and tried to burn it. But it was actually papier-mâché', and the glue was still wet. The flame wouldn't catch. Dad soaked it with Storm rain and then used his wind to shred layer five into pieces.

114

I got the next four after the papier-mâché', and then the final layer was made of diamond. I would have crushed it, but Dad surprised me with a gust of wind again and charged the diamond layer with enough Storm electricity to power NYC for a month. It crumbled to dust and revealed no remaining obstacles. That didn't matter though, because I won Station four by scoring seven to three on the nesting doll.

Station five was different, though. The match planners tried to play a joke all in good fun, but it didn't work out the way they thought. Station five was just a framed picture of my mother. No barriers, no tricks. The first competitor to annihilate the photo would win Station five. Mom was there in the audience and gasped when she saw the cruel joke.

There really was only one option. My father and I stared at the framed photo until the buzzer went off, neither of us ever casting a spell. Either of us could have won the game, and the Championship, with one simple spell. But instead, the match ended in a tie; my father having won Station one and two, and me with wins at Station three and four. You'd think after all that build-up, all that training, and all the preparations that I would be pissed about a tie, but honestly, I couldn't be happier about it.

Dad embraces me and says, "What an amazing match, son! I can't believe what they did at Station five. I'm going to talk to the match planners about that. I'm proud of you for not taking the easy win in the end, Jaret. Very proud. I don't think my old ticker could have endured a loss like that."

"Oh stop it, old man. Your heart's been fine for ages. I'm glad it was a draw, too, though," I say with a sly wink. "I know how much you hate to lose, Dad."

Mom runs out onto the field and hugs the both of us. Standing here in the field of the World Speedcasting Championship, having just tied with my world-famous father, is the best moment of my life so far.

"Ladies and gentlemen! Mages and Wizards!" Matthew Birge's voice calls out, echoing through the game field and audience stands. "The judges have a final ruling. Due to Station five being a draw, they have decided to use the results of Station 4 to determine the winner. Both contestants did win two Stations, which would leave us with a tie. However, at Station 4 there were ten obstacles. And since Jaret eliminated seven of those ten..." The fans erupt with noise and lose all control. The sound of their roaring cheer is deafening. "...WE HAVE A NEW PROFESSIONAL SPEEDCASTING WORLD CHAMPION... JARET... KIIIIIIIIING!"

The judges all rush over and shake my hand. They present me with a trophy and we pose on the game field for what seems a million photos. I feel dizzy, and don't know which camera to look at or what to say when asked about the win. I'm lost. My dad should be here to help with this stuff.

I answer some questions, not knowing what is coming out of my mouth. My vision starts to go black around the edges and I sit down on the grass. My breathing is uneven and hard to catch. There's a shooting pain in my left arm. Is this a heart attack?

People crowd around and fire more questions at me. "No, I'm not ok," I say. "Yes, I want some water," I reply. "Please, get away from me," I beg the reporters.

"Give the boy some space, for God's sake. He's a World Champion," Matthew Birge growls, shooing everyone away and helping me to my feet. He supports my weight and helps walk me back to the prep tent.

"Where are my parents, Mr. Birge?" I ask.

"I don't know, kid. They'll come find you in your tent soon enough. Great job out there today. You're one hell of a talented mage, young man, and faster than lightning. Literally!"

Off to my left, I notice some kind of commotion and glance over to find a crowd of people surrounding something on the ground. Everyone seems to be freaking out about whatever it is. A gap opens in between some of the fans. I see my father lying on the ground clutching his chest. My mother is kneeling beside him screaming something unintelligible as tears pour out of her eyes.

EIGHTEEN
2015 AD
Shanghai, China

The office is silent. Everyone is staring at a small glowing white dot on the 3D map of Shanghai. The pinging illumination is in Pudong, near the Expo site. It's where two of my agents had a run-in with a mysterious crammer dressed all in black. It's where Aurora was taken from.

I storm into the conference room and slam my hand onto the table. Even though my entire body is covered in a cold sweat, and even though my heart hurts like there is a spear stuck through it, my face shows no sign of it. "Okay, tell me we know something," I say. "Tell me anything."

They all remain silent except for Mian Mian, who says, "We don't know anything, Bossman."

"Alright then," I say, "starting right now someone will be monitoring that map around the clock. Any spells cast in this city big enough to show up will point us to our killer, which will lead us to Aurora. Jaysen, is there anything you can remember that might help us find this crammer: his license plate number, the color of the van, or which way it was headed? Any details could be vital to tracking the lunatic down."

Jaysen looks down and covers his face with both hands, his body visibly shaking.

"So, that's a no, then?" I say. Based on the looks of disapproval from everyone else, I sense my response is too harsh, but I don't have time to play nice. "Look, we're down to six people, and I'll be honest with you: it's not enough. But it's gonna have to be. Right now, we are all the hope she has of staying alive. Joyee and Mian Mian, you two are on call to investigate any activity on the map. Liang and Tian Yi, you two monitor that map non-stop. Take shifts if you have to; one watches while the other rests. Jaysen, you grab a nap right now. You're coming with me later tonight to meet up with Herod in Xuhui. He says this is all connected, and we're going to find out what he knows." Everyone better be on their game, because I feel like we're on the crest of a giant wave that it is about to come crashing down all over Shanghai.

I head home for a few hours to see the boys. Luckily, Kelly has a meeting out of town until tomorrow, and so I ask Lilly to stay the night and watch the kids. She's done this for us before whenever Kelly and I want a weekend getaway or a date night, so she's happy to help tonight.

Lilly cooks dinner for us all while I play with the boys, and read them some books. After we eat, I watch the clock like a hawk. I don't want to leave them too soon because I feel guilty, but one of my friends is out there right now scared and alone with some…thing.

I decide to leave a little early, and apologize to Lilly, who tells me to go and not to worry. She's got the boys' routine memorized, so I'm good to go. When I arrive back in the office, everything is basically the same. Nothing new has shown on the map since this afternoon's incident in the warehouse, and no calls have come in with any helpful tips.

I find Jaysen sitting at his desk and checking the news on the Network. "Jaret, you better take a look at this," he says with a nervous edge to his voice.

The article he shows me is from a leading Network source about crime in the magical world. The writer is anonymous but calls himself "Merlin Brando: The Godfather of Magic."

The article is titled "Where Have They Gone?" and, as I scan it, the blood freezes in my veins. Merlin Brando has written about the missing wizards case we're working, and not only does he know specific details about all of the wizards we know are missing, but he also has listed 30 additional people we didn't know were missing. I should hire this guy: he already knows more than we do.

"Jaret, this is bigger than we thought, isn't it?" Jaysen says, his voice uneasy.

I can't lie to him. "It looks that way, Jaysen, and I have a feeling it's going to get a lot worse… and very soon. Come on, let's get outta here; maybe talking to Herod will help us out somehow. You're driving."

At about 6 pm we pull up to the Glasgow Foe, a Scottish-style pub in Shanghai that specializes in traditional Scottish whisky, ales, and some brews targeted specifically at the magical clientele. They have, for example, the Dancing Arse: a straight whisky containing a spell, which causes the person to dance uncontrollably for a full minute. It's a very popular drink with the young expat mages and wizards. Magical cocktails, such as the Dancing Arse, are reserved for a secret room in the back, accessible only through the use of a lightning spell cast at a special painting on the wall.

I can't use Storm, but you can have the bar staff let you in if you show them some real magic. Or, if you're a wizard, you can learn the proper spell from a tome behind the bar.

Luckily, I have Jaysen with me, and his only school of magic is Storm. We walk right up to the painting and I say, "Be discreet." Regs are always trying to find out how to enter the private room, even though they are told such a place doesn't exist.

Looking around to ensure our privacy, Jaysen casts the smallest lightning bolt I've ever seen. Heading into the private "magic users only" part of the pub, we find it relatively empty tonight, but Herod is in a booth at the very back.

Seeing us enter, the old Scot waves his arms like a crazy person and shouts, "Hallo! I see ye've brought along a drinking companion, eh? Good! You boys will need to switch off to keep up wi' me!" He downs a whisky and calls for another.

For a man who may only have weeks, or less, left to live, Herod is not taking it easy on the hooch. Jaysen and I, on the other hand, have work to do, so we only order a couple of ales.

"Ok, big man, where were we?" Herod says much too loudly, "Och, that's right; unspent magical spells in dead wizards!"

"Keep your voice down, laowai," Jaysen snarls, looking over both shoulders. "People will think Jaret and I are as insane as you."

"Keep quiet, ye numpty," Herod says to Jaysen, and then directs his attention to me and adds, "As I was sayin' to ye earlier; when a wizard dies, their unspent magical energy continues to reside in the corpse forever. Now, I want ye to think on that for a wee minute. Imagine all the wizards that have ever died, and all the spells they never cast before their death. All of that magical energy still resides within their bones. It's a bit much, is it not?"

"Yeah, that's crazy," I say. "But Herod, what does this have to do with my case?"

He looks sadly into his empty whisky glass and beckons for another after burping hot fumes that smell of a distillery.

Herod then says, "Eh, everything, laddy – everything. Ye see, I was involved in creating new spells at the Library of Discovery, long ago. Did ye know that?"

"Yeah, I did, and you were fired," I say gruffly. "I couldn't find out why, though, because all of the documents were edited."

Herod shakes his head, lets out a laugh, and slurs, "Those bastards are scared of anythin' that isn't in the rule books. Aye, I was researching the very idea we are speaking of now. Unspent... spells. Management seemed to... think the idea insane. I thought perhaps we could find a way to use this residual... what's it? Oh yeah... magical energy. Redirect it somehow, ye ken. But before I could really get going with my research... I got the sack."

"Makes sense to me. A crazy old man wants to dig up dead wizards and use their unspent spells for a power source? I'd fire him, too," I snap, as I begin to realize this is all a waste of time. Aurora is out there somewhere with a murderer, and we're stuck in here with the town drunk. I pound my fist on the table and shout, "Why did Mrs. Chang tell me to talk to you about this? We're not interested in unspent spells in dead wizards, Herod. We're looking into yesterday's attack. Tell me about that strange sensation, or the glowing green light I saw, or how about we discuss desiccated wizard corpses!"

Jaysen once again looks around to see if anyone is listening and says, "Keep it down, boss. These people might hear us."

Herod sets down his emptied glass and looks at Jaysen with contempt. "Ye're the... numpty's numpty, laddy. Now shut it!"

He then puts his unfocused eyes on me and says, "Come now, lad. Have ye not put it all together yet? Think. Dead wizards… dried out because… maybe something is being pulled out of them perhaps? Ye've felt it, have ye not?"

I fold my arms over my chest and look down my nose at this old, drunken loon. "So, what you're telling me is that someone has figured out how to harvest the magical energy of unspent spells from dead wizards?" I ask.

"Aye," Herod says, and almost pukes in the process. "But not someone, matey boy. The… Maelstrom… and he's… back at it again."

Jaysen scoffs at Herod and says, "You're joking, right? You're saying that someone is actually doing this? That the strange pulling sensation Jaret felt is magical energy being sucked out of dead wizards? And that it's the same person responsible for a bunch of terrorist attacks 25 years ago? It's impossible."

Herod smirks, and orders another whisky. This wizard is going to be drunk past the point of consciousness very soon if he's not careful. In fact, his eyes begin to close and then shoot wide open. He does this several times before he manages to say, "Is it then, big man? Is it…indeed impossible? No, it's not. I've…seen it with my own two…eyes, so I cannae say… it's impossible."

"Whoa, whoa, whoa. Hold the phone. You've seen it?" I say, almost ready to get up and leave. "When and where? Don't lie to me, Herod. My friend's life is at stake."

Herod's eyes regain some focus at the mention of Aurora's predicament, and so clears his throat to say, "It was about 26 years ago was when I saw it. I was… in Barcelona during the Maelstrom's attack there. I was too far away from the… explosion to be hurt, ye ken, but I ran to help as soon as it happened.

Back then all magic users were walking the blade's edge. We were terrified of being found out because of these attacks… and also being blamed for them if we were discovered. For fuck's sake, we were scared about being killed, as well. So, when I heard the… explosion, I instantly knew what it was, no question. When I saw the devastation… laddy, I cannot begin to describe what I saw."

"You don't need to, Herod. I was in Turin a year later when the Maelstrom attacked," I admit. "And I was there yesterday. If it is the Maelstrom again, which I'm starting to believe, then I've seen its handiwork twice."

Herod tilts his head and nods with watery eyes, before tossing back another shot of whisky, and says, "As the smoke cleared… and the survivors began to flee – the ones that could, anyway – I felt something strange pulling at me. Like the suction from a drain, pulling the water down into it. I looked to my right… and there stood a man with a black cloak and a mask that covered his face."

Jaysen visibly tenses up at the mention of the figure in black, the sweat returning profusely to his forehead while he wrings his shaking hands.

Herod, oblivious to Jaysen's nervous reaction, continues his painful recollection of past events. "The man in black… raised his hand and a green glow came from his whole body. I looked down and there lay a corpse… it was missing… a leg. As I watched with my own eyes, the body began to… shrink in on itself… as if drying out like… raisins in the sun. When I looked up… the figure in the cloak was gone. Vanished. I looked about… everywhere… looking for any sign of him… and found the fiend clear on the other side of the carnage. He was doing the same spell on another body."

Leaning forward, now finally interested in what Herod has to say, I ask, "What does it want with unspent spell energy, Herod? Why do this?"

"I dunnae ken, Carrot... Jaret. Whatever the fuck yer name is. Now... afterward is when I met Mrs. Chang for the first time. She was working... an investigation into these attacks. A real high up... in the Wizards Guild, she was. Interviewed me. I told the bonnie lass... what I had seen. She was rather open about the fact that they had already found dried-out bodies of wizards at every... Maelstrom attack. Now, it was... at this point that I gave her my suspicions. I told her what I had been working on at the Library of Discovery and... how it had gotten me sacked. She did not think... me a lunatic. No... she believed old Herod."

"You know, Mrs. Chang could have told me all of this, or most of it, at least, and saved me some time," I say with a sigh.

"Ahh, but lad...she didn't want you...to say she was crazy. Vanity...she's...bonny, though..." Herod mutters while looking at the table.

"The thing is, Herod. I think I believe you, too," I say. Jaysen rolls his eyes and slams an open palm onto the table in frustration, as I had done earlier.

The loud bang causes the old Scot's eyes to shoot open, and he says, "No! I didn't! I swear it..."

Jaysen gestures to the old drunk and says, "Come on, Jaret. Herod is crazy."

"No, Jaysen. Well, yeah, maybe he is. But I'm buying what he's selling. Doesn't it make sense to you? All the evidence is pointing to the Maelstrom being active again," I say.

"But why, Jaret? Why now?" Jaysen asks me. Not knowing the answer, I deflect to the Scot.

"Herod, you think the Maelstrom is back. Is it starting all over again? Or is this something new and different?"

He orders another whisky, and his words begin to slur much worse as Herod says, "As to tha', Carrot the Jaret, I do think... he is back. And let me tell you why... After that day, all I wanted was to prove my theory right. So I could be... re...re...reinstart...hired back at the Library of Discovery. To tell those bastards... they were wrong about me! But I didnae... know how. The only way I could think of... was to find out... who this terrorist was... stop him... and get him to confess... his crimes."

My jaw hits the floor. Jaysen smirks as if to say, I told you so. I say, "Herod, you felt that was a safe thing to do as an admittedly weak wizard? No offense."

Herod grins and spills some whisky onto the bar and says, "Tone naken, lad; tone naken. It's true that I'm not... verra useful with speels...spells? But as I told ye... I am one hell of a research man...dingo... I was aimin'... to find him through, what do ye call it? Detective-ing. Using my connection... with Mrs. Chang... and the inside information that bonny lass was giving me... the only bloody thing she ever gave me, I might add... I began to form a theory. I know who he is and why he is... doing this. Ye see..." Herod releases a sour and noxious belch, closes his eyes, and passes out on the table completely asleep.

"You have got to be kidding me," I moan.

Jaysen and I load Herod into the back of the company car and head back to the office. It's only 7:30 pm and I do not intend on letting this little Scot out of my sight until I hear the rest of his story.

"He said he knows who the man in black is, Jaret," Jaysen says. "What are we going to do?"

"We're gonna pump him full of the strongest coffee I can find, use magic, and stay up all damn night if need be. Aurora is out there somewhere with a madman who sucks the spell power out of dead wizards. Supposedly. Even if that is all a bunch of bullshit, she is still missing and the guy who took her does seem to match the description of the Maelstrom. And if he is back at it, Aurora is as good as dead if we don't find her soon," I say all at once, in a rush.

"Yeah," he says, "but what are we going to do?"

"What are we going to do?" I echo Jaysen. "We're going to get some fucking answers."

NINETEEN
1009 AD
Alexandria, Egypt

Maeris stood apart from the gathering of mages her father had assembled. She didn't care what any of those fools had to say; all she wanted was to fight. It's all Maeris ever wanted anymore. Her control over Storm had surpassed even her brother's, and her spell knowledge was far greater than anyone else in the family. Yivan spent his time arguing with Father about their family's safety. Maeris spent her time practicing magic and learning new ways to kill.

She learned Fire spells from her father, Water spells from her mother, and Yivan showed her Storm. But the one she liked the most, the ones Maeris used to inflict the most pain and suffering, were the spells she had created herself. Like her StormWater whip, or the string of Fire she had used to sever Khalid's hand. Maeris practiced with that whip so much that the muscles in her arms had become defined and quite large. Maeris was even physically stronger than her older brother.

She loved Yivan, but he wasted his time talking when he should be honing his magical skills. They were going to attack the wizards' compound soon, the Wizards Guild they called themselves, and no amount of chatter would sway Marko's mind on the matter.

Maeris conjured a small Storm cloud to pour rain over a little bundle of sticks she had set on the ground. The rain came forth and soaked the sticks, rendering them useless for burning, until they dried out, at least. She then added a tendril of Fire magic, imbuing each droplet with the power to burn. Everywhere a raindrop landed, Fire immediately caught and burned with a fierce intensity. The young mage had been perfecting this spell for months and finally had it ready to her liking. It would destroy hundreds of wizards, if not more, once her family reached Cairo.

"Let them have an army, as Yivan is afraid of," Maeris thought aloud. She was afraid of nothing. Not even death.

Marko looked out at the twelve mages spread out before him, including his wife and son. Maeris was out practicing her spells again, which was fine with Marko. He didn't need a child's opinion on these matters, and the more she practiced her magic, the more powerful she would become. Marko liked that thought very much.

"You are the only mages in this godforsaken land that have responded to our call for help," Marko said to the gathered crowd. "The Wizards Guild is hunting down mages for their sadistic and unnatural studies. They violate the very laws of magic by accessing the Ether intentionally."

"How can they do this??" an elderly mage with a familiar face asked Marko. "How is it these ordinary men can do such a thing?"

Marko, of course, knew the mage speaking to him, despite the fact that the old man was pretending to not know Marko. The fool chose to not use a proper name, and instead always asked to be called the Healer. His skill with Water tripled that of Marko's wife, Ema, though. The Healer could be a fearsome enemy to the wizards indeed, if only he would use deadly Water magic. But the old mage refused. He would only use his magic to heal others. Still, that would be quite useful in the war to come. Marko was actually rather glad to see him, though he would never admit it.

"Healer, I do not fully understand how it is the wizards have or use their magic, and I do not care," Marko replied with a smirk. "I was only told that once they take a mage into their compound, that mage never comes back out. They dare to murder our people, and if we don't stop them, we could all be next."

Yivan could hold his tongue no longer and said, "Father, they act only in rebellion and retaliation to the way we have treated their kind since the dawn of man. We have always murdered ordinary men, and taken whatever we desire from those less powerful than ourselves. Perhaps we should speak with these wizards. They have magic now. So be it. We can work alongside them, and come to an understanding. If they don't kill us, we won't kill them."

Marko stared furiously at his son and fumed, "Shut your impudent mouth, Yivan. I will not hear this kind of talk."

"The boy has a valid point," the Healer chimed in. "We mages started this. By the actions of mages everywhere... robbing, killing and stealing... we have forced regular people into this drastic action. Mages are to blame. Perhaps a more peaceful resolution can be found."

Marko took a deep breath, put his hands over his face, and stated flatly, "None of you, not even my own family, will be forced to come with me. But I am going to Cairo. I am leaving tomorrow morning. Alone, I should reach the compound within a week. Were any Storm mages to accompany me, they could speed our travel to only four days. The wizards will eventually come for us all, so why should we wait? Let us come to them first."

Marko stalked moodily away to sit in solitude. He desired the serenity of being alone with his own thoughts. The rest of the mages milled about and discussed who was going and who was not. Yivan had no desire to hear what any of them had to say. He retreated into his own tent and struggled with a difficult decision. Ema had nothing to add, as usual. She did what her husband commanded of her, as was her duty. He said they would go, so Ema would go. She walked out on the open sands and watched her amazing daughter develop powerful new spells.

"If only Yivan would take his duty as seriously as does his sister," she thought to herself. "Well done, my daughter," Ema said aloud, love and praise filling her voice. "The ball of frozen Water with exploding shards is truly a wonder. Have you considered letting it fall from above? The spray of ice spears would rain down upon the wizards, affecting a wider area, creating more dead wizards, yes?"

Maeris considered this idea for a moment. If she combined it with Fire or Storm... it could be truly devastating. "Thank you, Momma," she said. "It is an excellent idea. I shall work on that later." The young mage took her mother's hand and they sat down together, Ema cradling her daughter's head in her lap. Sitting like this, they watched the sun go down before going to fetch food for the family.

Marko sat in his tent preparing his pack for the journey to Cairo, muttering to himself all the while, "Fools. If they all stay behind, then I will die alone. So be it. I will not let this offense stand unchallenged. These so-called wizards will not steal our magic. They will not rob us of our power. It is an outrage! How can the others not see this?" A rustling outside caught Marko's attention, and he readied a ball of Fire, just in case.

His son pushed into the tent and drew back in surprise as he saw Marko's hand engulfed in Fire, pointing right at Yivan's face. "Father?" he said weakly.

Marko visibly relaxed, released the flames back into the Ether and said, "Have you come to say goodbye then, son?"

Yivan's eyes grew wide and his mouth fell open, unable to speak, other than to mumble, "How...?".

"I'm not a fool, Yivan," Marko told his son. "I knew that once I said you were not bound to accompany me, you would be the first to accept the offer. You and the Healer claim it is not weakness, this desire for peace, but it is. It is a weakness, Yivan. One day, you will learn this. They will come for you and take everything you hold dear. On that day, you will wish that you had listened to your poppa."

"Father, please reconsider, I beg you," Yivan pleaded with Marko. "It could work another way, we just have to try."

"NO!" his father growled angrily. "You will speak no more on this, my son. I love you with all of my heart, but a damned child will not treat me as if I know nothing. You may think yourself a man, and you even look the part, but your actions are those of a child. I will not make you go with me. But I will not have you try and dissuade me, either. Goodnight, Yivan. Please leave my tent."

Yivan stumbled back out into the approaching night. The temperature was dropping, and a chill worked its way down his entire body. He couldn't shake the feeling that maybe he was wrong and his father was actually right. Was Yivan making a mistake by disobeying his father's wishes? Or was his family going off to their deaths? Should he go with them anyway and

132

die alongside his family? Too many questions filled his mind. So Yivan wandered off to see if there were any answers inside of his wineskin. He would drain several skins that night in search of answers, though he would find none.

TWENTY
2015 AD
Shanghai, China

Jaysen and I unload the inebriated Scottish wizard from the company car. Herod starts to sing a song about, "a lass that is gone" then hiccups and falls back asleep. Nothing seems to be happening in the office at the moment; everything is still and quiet. So we toss Herod onto a couch in the lounge.

"Make some coffee, Jaysen," I say forcefully. "Make it potent as hell, thick as mud, and make enough for all three of us."

He lets out a big yawn and says, "You got it, Boss. Anything else?"

"Yeah," I say, pointing to the snoring lump on the couch. "Pray that we can get him awake and talking again. Time is running out."

The map room is deserted as I enter, which pisses me off even more. No one is watching the map.

"What the hell, guys?" I say under my breath. "I gave them specific instructions to monitor this damn map non-stop."

I slam my fist down on the table and scream, "FUCK!" As my hand connects with the solid tabletop, and I wince in slight pain, my eyes focus on the 3D magical projection on the wall: the map of Shanghai. That's when I notice something different in the room. Something new. A new white dot is glowing on the map.

The two previous white dots are still there, but the intensity of their light is fading due to the passage of time. This new shining illumination is bright and fresh. My blood runs cold through my veins instantly as I notice the location.

Minhang District. Herod's potion shop.

I call Mian Mian's cell, and she answers on the first ring. "Boss, there has been another incident. Joyee and I are headed that way now." Thankfully, someone is actually doing their job like I told them.

"Yeah," I say slowly, "I'm looking at the map right now. At Herod's shop in Minhang, huh? What do you make of that?"

"Joyee thinks it's a trap, but he thinks everything is a trap, even the escalators at Metro stops. I'm reserving judgment for when we arrive, Bossman."

"Where are Liang and Tian Yi?" I ask. "I told them to watch the map non-stop, but no one is here."

Static comes from the line, and I hear, "Did you say… ang and Tian… ot there?"

"Mian Mian," I shout into the phone, as if that will help with the shitty Chinese cell connection, "you're breaking up!"

"…there…er we left, Jaret. They…should be…"

"Ok, let me worry about it, Mian Mian. Keep me in the loop, if you can. Call me back as soon as you get to Herod's place, and tell me what you find."

"Sure…ing, Bossman. Tal…ou soon."

The call disconnects and I look around the conference room a little more. I'm getting a weird vibe from the empty office, and notice a few things out of place: a piece of paper on the floor, a coffee cup spilled on Tian Yi's desk, and an overturned chair on the opposite side of the conference table. My pulse doubles at the sight.

In the lounge, Jaysen is sitting down with his head on the table, waiting for the coffee to finish brewing. Herod is still out like a light.

"Hey, wake up. Stay alert and keep an eye out for anything weird," I whisper in Jaysen's ear. "I'm gonna look around a bit." Jaysen arches a brow but sits up fast at the sight of my troubled expression and says, "Want me to help, Jaret?"

Looking over at the couch and its drunken inhabitant, I say, "No, I want you to keep a watch on the office and Herod. I don't want him waking up and taking off."

Ten minutes later, after searching the entire office from top to bottom, and finding nothing else out of the ordinary, I'm stumped. Where the hell are Liang and Tian Yi?

In the lounge, I grab a coffee and say, "I've checked every single place in our office I can think to look, Jaysen. There's still no sign of Liang or Tian Yi other than a few things out of place. I've got a bad feeling, though. Something is wrong here."

"Did you check the bathrooms?" Jaysen asks. "Maybe they're both in there. They had Sichuan hotpot for lunch, you know."

I walk over and push open the door to the men's room. Empty. No signs of a struggle, nothing out of place. Pushing the door to the ladies' room open a little, I say, "Anyone in here?"

Jaysen laughs from the lounge and says, "There aren't any women in the office right now, boss. Just go in."

"Better safe than sorry," I reply. "I don't need a lawsuit in addition to everything else that is going on." Suddenly, from the inside of the ladies' restroom, I hear a groan and a pained voice calling out for help. I throw the door open and rush in.

Blood is everywhere.

The dried-out corpse of Tian Yi lies crookedly on the floor, his face forever frozen in a mask of pain, his body in several pieces. Hearing the groan again, I turn to find Liang wedged behind the door. He's hurt badly, but thankfully still breathing, at least for the moment.

"Liang!" I cry out, kneeling beside him in a pool of his blood. "What happened? Who did this?"

His answer is quiet and staggered, "Jaret...you came. I knew... you would."

"What happened, Liang?" I ask again, trying not to let him see the tears rolling down my cheeks.

"... Mian Mian and Joyee... they left. Tian Yi... pacing the... map room... we heard a noise... in ladies' room."

As he talks, I examine his wounds and see that they are severe. Below the knees, his legs are a mess of splintered bone and pulp. No way will he ever walk again, if he even lives. Even serious healing spells can't fix something this mangled. His blood loss is worrying me. I'm amazed he's still conscious.

"Liang, wait. Let me help you first," I say, trying to formulate a plan on how to save his life. I'm a detective, not a healer, though. "You can tell me all of this later when you're all healed up. You need to save your strength."

"No...just listen... everyone was gone...we...thought it was our imagin...ation. Tian Yi...heard a noise...again and went to...check it out...I followed...heard a pop... rushed in.. felt...a strange...p...pulling...saw...tall...figure...in...black...cloak glowing... green...he...crushed... my legs."

His suddenly breathing becomes more ragged and Liang's eyes open a little wider. "I wish I knew a fucking healing spell!" I scream and try to stem the rapid flow of blood with a Water spell. If I can stop the bleeding, maybe I can save his life.

"Don't... Jaret...it's too late. Please... tell my brother... I'm sorry... for being a pain when... kids. Tell him... always looked up to him. Tell my mother... I wish I... more kind... to her."

My throat closes so tight that I can barely make air pass through it, and words are even harder. My eyes burn with sadness. I cradle Liang's head and whisper, "We can save you. I can save you. Let me stop the bleeding and take you to the hospital. Let's go, Liang. Let's go. I'm going to carry you."

His sightless eyes look up and blood trickles from his open mouth as he says, "No... but... you can... save... everyone... else..." Liang's body tenses for an instant, and he stares at something I can't see while reaching out his arms. As his eyes begin to glaze over, and his muscles start to relax, he whispers one last warning, "... figure in black...said... Herod...is..."

And then he goes limp and leaves me alone in the bathroom, covered in blood. Sitting on the tile floor, holding Liang's empty shell of a body, I fill with a rage that I have never felt before and hiss, "You will pay for this. Man in black... Maelstrom...whatever you are."

Three of my friends and teammates are dead, and a third is missing. My life is falling apart around me.

"No more," I mutter, and kick the bathroom door open, running madly to stand beside Herod's sleeping body.

Jaysen's mouth gapes open as he notices my bloodstained clothes. He tries to say something, but I don't let him get a single word out. "Pour coffee. Now," I say with a cold and threatening voice. I grab a hold of Herod's shirt and shake the shit out of him, while screaming, "WAKE UP!"

When he doesn't right away, I immediately begin slapping his face, punctuating each hit with the same repeated words, "WAKE. UP. WAKE. UP."

Soon, Herod's hands come up reflexively to block my attacks, and his bloodshot eyes shoot open. The little Scot's mouth trickling a line of crimson, he shouts, "What in the bloody hell are ya on about, lad?"

I step back to give the old wizard a look that promises endless pain and say, "Two of my team members are on the way to your shop right now, Herod. Some kind of destructive magic was recently cast there, and another two members of my team are dead, in this office. A person wearing a black cloak and mask killed them. Oh, and the Maelstrom left a message with my dying friend. Do you know what that message was, Herod? DO YOU?"

Cowering, covering his face with both hands, Herod answers, "No, laddy, I haven't a Scooby... a clue, I haven't a clue!"

I lower myself into his face and violently growl through gnashed teeth, "He said your name, Herod. The Maelstrom used your name." In a very sinister whisper, I add, "Now why would he do that? And why would there be destructive magic going off at your shop?"

The old Scot's terrified eyes look from side to side in search of escape as he sputters, "Honestly, Jaret, lad. I'm tellin' ya the truth. I dunnae know!"

Flames erupt over my entire body and I look Herod dead in the eye to say, "If I find out that you're lying to me, you'll wish for death. I am not messing around, Herod. I will end you."

Nodding shakily, he replies, "I promise, big man. I would nae lie to you."

The flames flowing like a burning ocean all over my body suddenly extinguish. I look calmly over at Jaysen and say, "Make that coffee to-go. We're heading to Minhang right now. You're driving."

On the way, I call Mian Mian back, but there's no answer. That has me sweating and swearing like a sailor. I leave her a voicemail that says, "Mian Mian, if you get this, do not go into Herod's shop. Just wait for me. Call back as soon as you can."

Herod sits in the back seat sipping gingerly at the hot coffee in his hands, attempting to sober up. Looking back at him, deciding whether or not to trust the peculiar little man, I tell my agent, "Drive like their lives depend on it, Jaysen. Because they probably do."

He slams the gas, hitting ludicrous speeds, and hot coffee spills down the front of Herod's shirt, which causes him to scream, "Aye, ya bastard! Don't get us killed before we die!"

I glare into the back seat, fire rimming my eyes, and the almost 300-year-old wizard closes his mouth like a scolded child in elementary school.

A half-hour later, screeching to a halt in front of Herod's shop, we find the entire front of his once lovely neighborhood magical potion shop is now a gaping hole. The windows are all shattered, the walls are crumbling, and nothing that was inside is recognizable.

"Mother of Mercy, what happened to my bleedin' shop?" Herod whispers with what seems like sincere dismay.

Across the street, an empty company car is parked crookedly, half on the sidewalk. Joyee and Mian Mian must already be in the basement of the shop as the only thing visible in the rubble of the store is the stairs leading downward.

140

"Jaysen, you stay here and watch out for the Mael...the man in black," I say, putting my hand on his shoulder and making direct eye contact. "If you see him, do not fight him. Run away. Run and find me ASAP. Ok?"

"I'm scared, Jaret," he admits.

"I am, too, Jaysen, but we have to squash that. Neither of us can afford to be scared right now. We need to be in control," I say. Thinking of my father, I add, "Calm down and focus your thoughts. We'll get through this together."

"Yes, sir," Jaysen says, his eyes beaming a little and his voice steadier than before. "Go save them."

Grabbing the old, kilt-wearing wizard, I say, "You're coming with me, *laddy*."

Herod goes first down the stairs with no say-so in the matter. My phone shows the time is only 9 pm. My, how time crawls when your friends are dying. Down in the bowels of Herod's mock alchemist laboratory, everything looks exactly as it did earlier in the day. No real damage to the place, and no dead bodies strewn about. That's a good start. The problem is, my two agents are also absent from the scene. Where are Mian Mian and Joyee?

"They've got to be down here somewhere, Herod," I say, shoving him against the table containing the cauldron, which is no longer bubbling. "Are there any rooms other than this main one?"

"Yes, lad," he says, agreeing rapidly. "There's a secret door in the back where I keep all of my valuables. Go have a look."

"Show me," I say. As we near the back wall, I can just make out the very faint line of a hidden door, and ask, "How do I open it?" Herod grins, whispers into my ear, and then winks lewdly before stepping back. "Now is not the time for jokes, Herod," I tell the old pervert.

"I'm sorry, lad, it's true," he says while stepping back and raising his hands in a defensive posture. "I never planned on having to open it under such grave circumstances."

Breathing a deep sigh, I step up to the wall and say, "Mrs. Chang's tits." The door slides upwards, and I realize that I cannot imagine any way in which Mian Mian and Joyee could accidentally stumble upon that phrase to open the hidden entryway. Something about this feels wrong.

Bending down to get a look at what's behind the door before stepping in, I feel a shove from behind, and fall to the ground inside the hidden room.

Herod recites an incantation and says, "Sorry, laddy. Truly, I am." The door then slams shut with an ominous red glow.

TWENTY-ONE
2000 AD
Atlanta, Georgia

He looks different. People always say that about their loved ones after they die, I know. But he does. Dad looks different.

"Why, Mom? Why did he have to die? It's not fair," I say, choking back a sob.

My mother pulls my head to her chest, trying to hold it together, and says, "Life can be like that, Jaret. We don't always get to know what's going to happen next. Surprises, miracles, and tragedies all get an equal shot. He loved you, son. He loved you more than anything else in his life. He talked to me about you when you were at school, asleep, or just in the other room. You were his pride and joy. He told everyone he met about his son, the Champion."

Tired of holding back and pretending to have our shit together, my mother - Cynthia King - and I sit down on a bench and let it go. Together, we let it all go.

People come by to say their condolences, but realize this moment is a private one and walk away without interrupting. We are letting each other release our anguish, sorrow, and loss without having someone tell us they are sorry or it will be ok. My mother and I both want to empty ourselves of all sadness, and be held while we do so.

After a few minutes, we head into the room where his body is. Everyone is waiting for us to arrive. I step up to the podium as my mother takes her seat.

"My father, Christopher King, was the greatest man I have ever known," I begin, attempting to convey exactly how this all feels by giving my dad's eulogy. "He taught me how to be a genuine person. He taught me how to be a mage. My tutor, Mr. Lee Parr," I say gesturing to Lee, happy to see him, "was a great help to me in magic theory, history, and in the application of many aspects of elemental magic. But Dad was my real teacher. He showed me how to be fast but thoughtful, and he taught me the benefits of a calm mind."

I take a sip of water to wet my throat and continue. "Some of you may not know this, but my father pulled me from a wrecked car in the aftermath of the Maelstrom's attack on Turin in 1990 - ten years ago this month, in fact. He never lost his cool in front of me during all of that. He kept it together in the most stressful and terrifying situation imaginable. He saved my life like he was a superhero."

The room is silent except for the muffled sounds of weeping, and the occasional cough. Everyone is watching me; feeling sorry for me. How am I supposed to go on? My throat closes almost completely and I can barely breathe through it, much less talk. I try to swallow, but the saliva gets caught. I sip some more water and do what my father always taught me to do. Even now, in death, he still tells me what I need to hear, his ethereal voice seeming to whisper in my ear, "Calm down. Focus your thoughts."

"Dad, I'm going to miss you so much," I say with tears falling freely. "I can't imagine living the rest of my life without your advice, without your reassurances that everything will be okay, and without your support. But I will, somehow. I promise you now that Mom and I will be alright. She's always been smarter than you anyway, we all know that."

My father's gathered friends and family laugh. Good. Dad wouldn't want us moping around and crying all day.

"And I will dedicate my life to protecting people the way you protected me. I will do something worthwhile, Dad. I know you wanted me to be a Speedcaster, but that's done now," I say, announcing my retirement for the first time to anyone, even my mother. People gasp and make hushed conversation for a brief moment before I continue.

"From now on," I add, "I have one goal: to become the lead agent of an MOP office and make a difference in our world. So everyone, please join with me. Loved ones, friends, and family, do my father and me a favor."

Speaking the long-practiced words with confidence, yet weighed down with unbearable sadness, I say, "First, I want you all to calm down. Next, I want you to focus your thoughts. And finally, stand and say one last farewell to Christopher King. My father. My hero."

Later, I sit in the hall sipping a cup of coffee. Everyone has finished saying goodbye in their own way; a gentle touch to his face, a lean in and hug, a kiss on the forehead, a grasping of his hand, and some leaving behind a token of their relationship with Dad.

"That was a beautiful eulogy, Jaret. Your father is looking down on you right now and could not be prouder," my favorite aunt says, pulling me in for a kiss on the cheek.

"Thank you, Aunt Janie. I'm glad you're here," I tell her.

"Atlanta isn't that far away from me, you know. Even down in Alabama, we have MOP offices. You should consider moving down and taking a job there. I know the local head MOP agent very well. We went to school together," she says.

"Really? Wow… thank you," I say, completely taken aback. "I just might take you up on that, after college that is."

"Ok, dear. You take your time and call me when you're ready. I love you very much," Aunt Janie says with a hug.

"I love you, too, Aunt Janie," I say, holding her tight. "And thank you again."

"No, my boy, thank you. You made my brother and me proud today. Take care, and call soon, dear," she says, walking away.

While getting a refill on my coffee, my friend from college, E.J., offers his own brand of condolences by saying, "Want some whisky for that coffee? Irish funerals usually have a good bit of alcohol involved."

"My family isn't Irish, E.J.," I remind him.

"No one has to know that," he whispers jokingly, then adds, "Seriously, though. You doing ok?"

"Yeah. It's just strange that he's gone," I confess. "It's even weirder to have a room full of mage family members here to say goodbye, and know that I have to do it all over again for the reg family members soon."

E.J. sighs and says, "You casters are crazy, man. The Mage High Council is so weird. You guys should tell your family about magic, like us wizards. What's the big deal?"

"Yeah, well wizards can teach family members how to use magic, E.J., and then they won't be regs anymore. We can't: mages are born, not made."

"They could always learn to be wizards, Jaret. Then they wouldn't be regs and you'd only have to have one service. See? I should go into government. I'm a genius."

E.J. always cheers me up. We've been friends since freshman year at college. They put us together since we were the only two magic users in the freshman class that year. It's always good to have magic users in leadership positions who can look out for young mages and wizards like that.

He stands up and offers me one of his giant hands. I take it and he yanks me up with barbarian strength. At 6'7", E.J. is officially the tallest person I know. Walking beside him at school always makes me feel like a child.

"I gotta get going, man," he says. "Unless you need me to stay for the reg service?"

"No, it's cool," I tell him. "You can jet."

"I'm sorry about your dad, Jaret. I'll see you back at school, brother," E.J. says and wraps me in a bear-hug that crushes the wind from my lungs.

"Oof… thanks, man," I say breathlessly. "And, hey, thanks for coming. It's nice to have someone here I'm not blood-related to, you know? I'll catch you later."

As he walks away from me, E.J. passes by my Aunt Janie. Thinking about what she said earlier, a smile spreads across my face. I don't have any classes this summer. I could get a jump-start on my law enforcement career. Maybe I should get an internship at her friend's office.

"Aunt Janie? Can I ask about this MOP friend of yours?"

TWENTY-TWO
2015 AD
Shanghai, China

"That little bastard," I say to myself. Then, pounding on the magically sealed door, I scream, "Open up, Herod! Let me out of here!"

But there's no answer from outside, and it's pitch-black in here, other than the soft red glow from the door. I create a floating flame that hovers at chest level. Looking through the gloom, I see cages lining the walls of this massive room. Each one has a pillow and a length of chain inside. How charming, Herod.

"Is that little Scottish fucker behind all of this?" I wonder aloud. "Is *he* the Maelstrom?"

Although things are bad right now, and this situation is way past serious, I can't help but laugh at the thought of that drunken little idiot being the most powerful and deadly magician the world has ever known. "No way is that possible," I mutter while searching for a way to escape this dungeon.

The red glow coming from the door indicates a magical barrier and, usually, this type of spell is hard to break, but not impossible. I hurl everything I can think of at the protected door: a huge boulder, a Fireball, Cone of Cold... all of which does nothing. The barrier is too robust, which tells me Herod did not make this layer of protection. He may have activated it, but there is no way he put this powerful spell into place with his low level of magic.

So, the question remains – who did? It might as well be the Maelstrom for all I know. There is no use in making guesses right now. My dad's voice floats through my mind as it often does when I'm confronted with a difficult problem.

"Calm down," I tell myself. "Focus your thoughts."

Luckily, Lilly will stay with the boys until I get home, and she knows how to take care of them. Kelly won't be home until noon tomorrow. That gives me about 14 hours to get out of here.

All of a sudden, my train of thought is interrupted by a noise from the dark recesses of this chamber. Cautiously, I make my way to the back of the massive underground warehouse. No one would ever guess that Herod's small shop was sitting on top of a dungeon this expansive. It must stretch the entire length of the neighborhood.

Following the occasional clanging noise, I realize it's the sound of metal tapping on metal. And it seems purposeful as if someone – or something – was deliberately tapping out a rhythm. "I may not be alone in here, after all," I say to the rats scurrying along the walls.

As I peer into the gloom approaching the back wall of this dungeon, my eyes focus in the low light, and relief surges through me. All the way down this long row of cages, I can see three of them are occupied. Mian Mian is fast asleep in one. Joyee is lying with his back to the others, knocking his head against the back wall. And in the last cage, clanking her chains together, is Aurora. Grinning from ear to ear, I clear my throat, and sternly say, "You're all fired."

Joyee and Aurora instantly focus on me. Aurora's immediate reaction is joyful and full of hope while Joyee only moans sorrowfully. "Great," he says. "Now we'll never get out of here. There is no one left to rescue us. We're all as good as dead."

The lack of confidence and ease in which he gives up will be documented in his performance review. If we live through this ordeal and I'm able to write it, that is.

"Hey, don't give up just yet," I say. "Jaysen is still outside. He might be able to get us out of here."

Mian Mian still hasn't stirred awake, which worries me a little. Rattling the cage doesn't wake her. Grabbing her shirt through the bars and shaking her doesn't work, either.

"Don't bother," Joyee says in a defeated tone.

"Why is Mian Mian not waking up?" I ask.

"Spell sleep, Laoban." Aurora informs me. "The man in black is keeping her that way so she can't wake up and break us out of these cages with magic."

Looking at the two wizards sitting shackled in their cages, I ask in a puzzled voice, "Then why don't you two cast some crammer jammers and break out of there yourselves?"

They both look away, ashamed, not wanting to look me in the eye. Joyee says, "We can't, Jaret. We have no spells left. He forced us to use all of them."

"Yeah, Laoban, we have nothing left," Aurora agrees, adding, "and as you can see there are no tomes here. Our tanks are running on empty."

"Wait," I say, still lost, "how did he force you to run out of spells?" Even in the dim light, I think I can see both of their faces turn red with embarrassment.

"It shouldn't have worked," Joyee mutters.

150

Aurora agrees with him and says, "Yeah, we were stupid. When I woke up in this dungeon, Joyee was beside me. Mian Mian was already asleep in a cage nearby. I was so excited to see them… I wasn't thinking clearly. When the man in black started taunting us, Joyee and I just reacted. The only thought in my mind was that I needed to use all of my stored magic to stop this man. We both started throwing spells at him, one after another."

Joyee nods and says, "I felt compelled as well. But he dodged some, reflected some, and blocked others with a powerful barrier spell. It was all part of his plan, Jaret. He tricked us."

"At the time, Laoban, I just thought he was a coward," Aurora shamefully admits. "But after a while, Joyee and I ran out of spells, and the man in black laughed at us. Now here we are in these cages, chained like animals."

Joyee mutters, "I'm sorry I let you down, Jaret."

"Don't you dare apologize to me, Joyee. Neither of you did anything wrong. We weren't trained to handle this. Stop street magicians, break up fights, cover up incidents where regs saw magic. But stopping a violent maniac that uses magic to kill? It's completely new territory for all of us."

Both of their embarrassed expressions fade somewhat. I can't believe they think I'd be disappointed in their bravery.

"Why would I blame you?" I say, grinning. "Hell, I'm in here, too, you know? Why don't we wake up Sleeping Beauty over there, and find a way to get out of here."

"How, Jaret?" Joyee asks.

"Yeah, we don't know what spell he used," Aurora says. "We have no way to break it without endangering her."

"Well, I'll just have to tread carefully and try a few different tactics," I say with a shrug.

First, I slowly raise her body temperature and then quickly cool her down, thinking maybe the shock will wake her up. It doesn't work. Next, I try something basic but familiar. I conjure a globe of cold Water over her face and let it fall. She sputters in her sleep, gasping for air, but doesn't wake up.

"It's not working, Laoban," Aurora says.

"Yeah, I told you not to bother," Joyee adds.

"If you guys have any ideas, just chime in. Otherwise, shut it." I say, annoyed.

Aurora says, "I have no ideas that could help you, Laoban. I don't understand how that simple caster magic works. I'm an intellectual. There is no guesswork with my spells."

"What spells?" I remind her. "You don't have any right now."

"I have no idea how to wake her up, either, Jaret. I'm sorry. I thought your trick with the Water would work," Joyee says, "It always does in the movies."

His words pluck a chord in my mind, and a memory floats to the surface. "This is just like that time with my mage tutor, Lee," I say. "The Water didn't work with him either, but..." I trail off, remembering what it is I have to do.

I take a deep breath and do as my father always used to tell me. "Calm down," I think. "Focus your thoughts."

The compartments of my mind where I keep all three of my access points to the elemental Ether suddenly become crystal-clear to me. I once said that I would never do this again. Guess I was lying.

Focused solely on Mian Mian's sleeping form, the magical energy flowing through her comes instantly into focus. Fire magic burns white-hot within this talented mage, connected to the Ether by a large, braided cord. An invisible tendril of Water magic reaches out from my magical essence. There is no physical form to it; the tendril exists only in the elemental realm. Remembering the last time I did this, I brace myself for the violent reaction sure to follow. Opposite forces have that effect on each other, as I recall.

I extend the tendril of Water magic, and the moment it makes contact with Mian Mian's Fire energy, I shoot across the room, banging my head against an empty cage as I crash to the floor. My body is drenched and steaming as if I took a hot shower in my clothes and then ran outside into the snow. Mian Mian appears the same way, and then her eyes fly open.

She looks around dazed and mumbles, "What the hell was that?" Noticing that we are both steaming like a sauna, Mian Mian raises her arms to examine her wet clothes.

"That was something I had hoped to never try again," I say. "Welcome back to the land of captivity and consciousness, Mian Mian."

We bust the two wizards out of their cages and shackles, then sit down to have a talk. There's some news they need to hear. "I have some bad news to tell you all."

"What is it, Laoban?" Aurora asks with trepidation. All three of my agents stare at me, not ready to hear what it is I have to tell them, and fearing the worst.

"Liang… and Tian Yi…are dead," I say with difficulty. Joyee begins whimpering softly, and Mian Mian offers him some comfort with an embrace, her own teardrops leaving tracks on her dirty face. I let them have a few minutes to process this new loss. Aurora only stares at the floor, lips pressed tightly against her teeth.

"I know it seems like we're losing," I tell her. "And to be fair, we are. Three of our own have been murdered, and we're locked away here in this sick dungeon, captured like rats. But Jaysen is still out there. He'll find us. I believe in him."

"Me, too, Laoban," Aurora says with a smile, her eyes brimming with moisture. "He's… good. He'll find us."

Joyee can't stop crying, but finds the courage to ask, "Why us, Jaret? I mean, what did we do to deserve all of this? Why are we being targeted? Why are we even still alive?"

"I don't know, Joyee," I answer truthfully. "It's all very confusing to me, too. Herod is apparently working for the man in the black cloak, who may or may not be the Maelstrom."

"Laoban, if that is the case, how can we trust anything Herod told us about the Maelstrom and his attacks?" Aurora reasons. "The reclaiming of spell energy from dead wizards, that could all be made up lies, right?"

"Only time will tell, Aurora," I reply. "Right now, let's focus our energy on getting out of here."

The four of us explore the entire massive warehouse inch by inch for a couple of hours to find… nothing. It's the same all over: cages, chains, and darkness. There are two doors, both with the telltale red glow of a magical barrier. One is the front door where I was shoved in, and the other is in the back, probably where the three of them were brought in.

Mian Mian and I take turns trying to blast down the rear door, but with the same type of barrier spell on it, we are equally effective in bringing it down as I was with the front door.

"Alright, we all need some rest," I declare as our search for another way out, and our efforts to escape have both proved ineffectual. "It's late. Mian Mian, you recently had a long spell sleep so you can have the first watch."

"No argument here, Bossman," she says, settling against the wall and keeping her eyes on all paths coming our way.

The rest of us settle down, and Joyee falls immediately asleep. Aurora takes several minutes longer, but her soft snores soon fill the space around us. I feel better seeing them with me once again, and now peacefully sleeping away the horrors of the day. They deserve some rest.

Mian Mian finds me still awake and catches my eye. Jabbing a finger in my direction she says, "You're not any good to us exhausted, Bossman. Get some sleep. I swear to wake you up if I hear or see anything; even if it's just with my screams of pain or death rattle, you'll be forewarned, at least."

"Thanks, that's very reassuring, Mian Mian," I groan. But she's right: I do need some sleep. I calm myself and find a peaceful center. Breathing steady, eyelids shut… everything goes black.

My eyes fly open to find that I'm back in the ladies' room. Only now there's even more blood than before, and the cause of it is resting at my feet. My entire team is dead.

Kelly is there, too. She stands in tattered clothes, alive and helplessly searching for something. She suddenly stares right at me and says, "Why did you do it, Jaret? Why did you lie to us all these years? Why did you kill all of those people? WHY?"

Her final shout wakes me from my nightmare with a gasp. I notice that Aurora has traded places with Mian Mian, and is now on watch.

"How long have I been out?" I ask her.

Aurora shrugs and says, "Three hours or so. I slept for an hour and woke up about two hours ago. It's hard to tell time in here, and they took our phones, so…"

I cut her off, realizing how stupid I am, and say, "Holy shit, they didn't grab my phone! I still have it!"

Aurora slaps my arm and chides, "Why the hell didn't you think of that earlier, Laoban?"

Grimacing at the sting she left behind, I take out my phone. "No bars," I say, deflated. "Fuck. But it's 3:00 am, by the way. My kids will be up in a few hours, probably wondering where I am."

"They're only a year old Laoban. They probably don't even know who you are or that you're gone," Aurora says.

"Shut up, crammer," I reply. "Lilly's used to taking care of them, but she's going to be worried about me. I need to get home before Kelly does or she is going to freak out."

A sudden noise catches my attention, and I'm hit with a sense of déjà vu. This time, though, the sound is coming from near the front door. Aurora and I both take at a sprint to find the front door is rising.

"Go back and wake Mian Mian," I say firmly. "You're out of spells and I don't want you getting hurt. Tell her to get here now and be ready to fight for her life." Aurora runs back without a word. Ahead of me, standing in the doorway, is a tall figure in a black cloak. A hood covers his face.

"Finally," I growl angrily, "I get to meet this bastard."

TWENTY-THREE
1009 AD
Cairo, Egypt

Yivan's bloodshot eyes popped open, and his head ached with the pain of too much wine from the night before. He cast his gaze around the campsite to find it had changed since he passed out hours ago. It was now empty.

It seemed that all the mages had followed Marko on this suicidal march to Cairo, after all. Yivan was the only person left. His family had abandoned him. In the distance, Yivan saw movement. He shaded his eyes against the harsh sunlight, to better discern what approached.

"Maybe everyone didn't leave me," he said aloud. The lone figure walked towards Yivan from the barren desert. "Father?" Yivan called out hopefully.

"No, I am afraid not, boy," the Healer said. "But it is good you are finally awake. I was worried that soon I would have to use opposing forces to bring you out of that drunken sleep. Here, drink this."

Yivan took the offered jug and drank deeply of the cold water. Where the old Water mage had found cold water, Yivan did not know.

"Good, is it?" the Healer asked. "Clean and pure water, pulled directly from the clouds in the sky."

Yivan frowned at the pounding drum residing in his mind and said, "What did you mean by opposing forces, Healer?"

"Oh, never mind that right now, young one. How are you feeling?" the old mage said.

"Not well. I am sorry to ask it, Healer, but could you please do something about this pain in my head?" Yivan begged.

The old Water mage laughed deeply and said, "Of course, of course. Too much wine will do that to a man. Here, this should help you to feel better." A chilling energy rushed throughout Yivan's body, and he instantly felt energized. He no longer had a headache, and it seemed as if he could run in the hot desert for hours without tiring.

"That was… impressive, old mage," Yivan admitted. "My mother does not have this type of strength with her healing."

The old mage scoffed, rolled his eyes, and said, "No, she wouldn't, boy. You and your family worry more about the ability to kill than the skill it takes to help others. If more of our kind tried to make this world a better place for everyone, and not just mages, we wouldn't be in this trouble with the Wizards Guild."

"Is that truly why they are doing this, Healer?" the young mage asked.

"They resent us," the Healer said. "We have abused them and taken what is rightfully theirs since the dawn of civilization. How would you feel if someone were to take everything you hold dear, kill your family, and then leave you alone?"

"I… I would be devastated," Yivan quietly answered.

"Exactly. That is how the wizards found the motivation to discover magic for themselves. We did this. We drove them this far. Mages must now face the consequences."

"How long ago did the others leave, Healer?" Yivan asked, scanning the horizon for signs of his family.

The old Water mage looked at the sun, tilted his head, and replied, "About five hours ago. Do you wish to catch up with them, young man?"

Yivan stood and dusted the sand from his clothing. He looked in the direction of Cairo, and said, "I will catch up with them, but I do not wish to."

The old Water mage stood as well, and used Water magic in a very fine spray to rid his body and clothes of sand, leaving him cooled, clean, and dry. Yivan felt foolish for using his hands.

"If you do not wish to go, then do not," the Healer scolded. "Are you so eager to die, boy? Why chase certain death? If you are smart, you will go the other way. Find a place to live peacefully and pretend to be a regular man. You may just live to be my age."

"I will not abandon my family, Healer. I will go to them and speak with my father again. I will stop them from making this foolish mistake."

The Healer spread his hands out wide while motioning to the empty campsite and said, "And why not abandon them, eh? They abandoned you."

Yivan placed a hand on the Healer's arm, held his gaze and said, "Just because they have done wrong does not mean that I should do so as well. Thank you for your help, Healer. I hope you find the peaceful life you wish for."

The old man laughed and said, "I will not have a calm and quiet life, Yivan. I am going to die in Cairo, along with the rest of your family. But I will die trying to save as many lives as I can. I am the Healer. It is what I do. Besides, my son has need of me there."

"It is settled then," Yivan agreed. "You and I will leave now, together. We will need to be quick, though. They already have quite a lead on us. Will you be able to travel fast, Healer?"

The old mage cast a Water spell, cleansing his blood and organs as he had done with Yivan to remove the hangover. The Healer suddenly felt much younger and more invigorated. "Yes, Yivan. I will not slow you down. I promise," he said.

"Good. Let us make haste then," the younger mage said. As the Healer refilled two waterskins with cold liquid from the clouds far above, Yivan hardened their bodies against the spray of desert sand with Rock magic and quickened their steps with Storm wind. Before they covered their mouths for the long and silent run, Yivan curiously asked, "Healer, which mage is your son?"

The old mage wrapped a cloth around his face, leaving only a small slit for his eyes, and then mumbled, "Marko. Your father."

Four days later, Yivan and his grandfather found the Wizards Guild compound in Cairo. They arrived under the cover of night and kept to the shadows to assess how dangerous the situation truly was. Their observations proved beneficial, as the results were not good.

The wizards did have an army as Yivan had feared: 10,000 ordinary men armed with spears, javelins, and bows and arrows – all distance weapons. This army was purpose-built to attack one person, or small group of people, from a distance. It was an army built to fight mages. And they were camped right outside the Wizards Guild compound.

Yivan ventured out disguised as a beggar in rags to obtain any information he could. In his probing, he discovered no mention of an attack by mages. Which meant that his family and the other mages were still alive. Yivan also uncovered the name of this uncommon army; it was a strange name in a strange language.

"Rego," a drunken soldier had told him. "It is Latin and means 'to govern.' Our job is to capture mages for the wizards to study. But our duty is also to keep the wizards in their place so that they do not become as the mages have always been – murderous and power-hungry. Ordinary men shall rule the world, not magical monstrosities, and we will do so with the Rego Army to lead us."

"So, the wizards were not in charge here," Yivan thought to himself. It was the Rego Army, the ordinary men, who ran the show. Yivan found this quite interesting. He found his grandfather waiting for him in the desert, not far from the wizard compound.

"Well, boy?" he asked in hushed tones, "Have our people attacked yet? Are they slain?"

"No, grandfather. They have not yet come," Yivan said in reply. "Perhaps we passed them in the desert without knowing it. Should we go back and search?"

"No, boy. They will be here all too soon. If we are lucky, we can catch them before it starts and talk your father out of this idiocy."

Yivan looked out into the dark night, hoping to catch a glimpse of his family. He saw nothing but stars in the sky... But he and the Healer both felt the rumble beneath their feet.
A loud and trembling explosion rocked the Earth, causing the sand to shift and slide under the soles of their sandals. Yivan whirled in search of the source and found it on the far side of

the Wizards Guild compound. The wall farthest from the Rego Army sported a new hole, blackened at the edges with crumbling stone strewn all over the nearby sands.

Even from this distance, Yivan and the Healer could make out the solid form of Marko leading the charge, his long, black hair held back by a band of pure Fire. Marko's large, muscular body was shirtless, revealing the flame tattoos covering his chest to be once again filled with real Fire as he called upon the elemental Ether. Jets of flame leaped from Marko's hands to engulf the many wizards pouring from the breach in their wall.

"We have to get down there, grandfather," Yivan said. The old Water mage nodded, deep in thought, and said, "How? There will soon be an entire army between us and the other mages. Look, the Regos are on the move, grandson."

Yivan saw the 10,000 man army beginning to march on his father's position, and started to panic. The young mage took a deep breath to steady his breathing. He calmed his mind and focused his thoughts. In desperation, Yivan pulled as much Storm magic as he dared from the Ether. A great sandstorm rose in the desert, and headed straight for the Rego Army, covering them in a thick, cloudy haze. The soldiers would not be able to see far, as the burning sands filled their eyes. Breathing, too, would be difficult as it flew into their mouths and noses.

"That should buy us some time, grandfather," Yivan said proudly.

Taking a cue from his brilliant grandson, the old Water mage called forth a river from deep beneath the sands. The Water rose to their feet and quickly whisked them closer to the battle so they could join their family.

Yivan and the Healer arrived in the middle of a massacre. The wizards stood no chance. There may have been hundreds more of them than the dozen mages, but that did not matter.

Wizard spells took time to cast; they had to move their hands and say strange words. The mages, naturally, did not allow the wizards that chance.

The outer walls of the compound near the breach ran red with wizard blood, and the sands drank deeply of it. Yivan spotted his father singing an old Croatian song while roasting a wizard's face off with one hand, and summoning a Fire elemental with the other. Marko was in his element, and loving every second of it.

"These fools have no idea what real magic is!" he roared into the night. "They may have discovered how to conjure a few tricks, but they are no match for the wielders of the Ether; we who were chosen at birth to be a conduit for elemental power!"

As he roasted the head until it popped with a satisfying sizzle, Marko noticed two mages he never expected to see here in this fight – his son, Yivan, and his father, the Healer.

Maeris was near the breach, slicing men in half with her fiendish whip as they emerged from within the compound. Yivan watched in dismay, then added a layer of his own Rock magic onto his little sister, just in case. She felt the intrusion and turned to find the source, smiling as she saw Yivan standing amidst the carnage.

Beaming, she yelled, "Glad to see you joined us, big brother! Poppa will be very pleased!"

A wizard came running out of the broken wall, chanting and moving his hands in the shape of a pyramid. Maeris lashed out once, recoiled, and then once more. The man's arms fell away, one at a time. Unlike with Khalid and his hand, however, there was no Fire to cauterize the wounds. His screams and life's blood both leaped out into the night.

Seeing that she was doing quite well on her own, Yivan went in search of his parents. He had to warn them about the army on the other side of the compound. They were delayed, but it would not keep them away for long.

The Healer rushed off to assist injured mages, healing any wounds they had incurred during the fighting. There wasn't much he could do, though, as the wizards were being utterly destroyed. Everywhere he looked, they fell with gruesome deaths.

Ema was filling men with Water until they exploded into a shower of blood, bone, and offal. A Storm mage skirted the outer rim of the battle unseen, using a dark cloud to cover his entire body when a wizard found himself wandering alone. The hidden Storm mage cooked the wizard from the inside out with Storm power. The poor man's insides liquefied and ran out of every opening possible.

It was a scene from a nightmare, and death was pervasive. Yivan found his father, which wasn't overly difficult, as Marko was now a living inferno. There was no recognizable form of a man visible, only a raging tempest of Fire that gave instant death to any wizard foolish enough to come close.

"Father!" Yivan roared over the sound of destruction surrounding them. "Father, please listen to me!"

The creature of Fire turned its gaze upon Yivan, and the flames instantly vanished. Marko casually strolled over blood-soaked sand to greet his son with a warm embrace. "Yivan, I have never been prouder of you," Marko said. "I had assumed that you and the Healer would have fled this cursed land. Well done for coming to join in the fight for our birthright. We shall take our magic away from these filthy creatures!"

"Father, calm down and focus your thoughts on me for a moment," Yivan said coolly.

164

Marko barked a laugh and said, "I can tell you've been with the Healer. You sound just like him!"

"Grandfather is wise, and we would do well to listen to him, Poppa," Yivan replied. "But right now, you need to listen to me. There is an army of 10,000 men camped on the other side of this compound. They have one purpose, and that is to find and kill mages. Their weapons and training are designed to fight our kind. They will destroy every single mage here. I have delayed them, Father, but they will be coming soon. We must leave this place. Now."

"No," Marko flatly declared. "We will destroy this vile compound or die in the attempt. A mage must have convictions, son. I shall make a stand here and now. No ordinary man shall have magic while I live. I will murder every single wizard with my bare hands if I have to. They will not take this from us, Yivan."

"Father, it is hopeless. We cannot win. If we leave now, we can form our own army. We can travel the world and rally mages to our side. We can do this together, Poppa, as a family. I want to help you," Yivan said, begging for his father to listen.

"I know you do, my beautiful son. I know," Marko said as he grabbed Yivan by the back of the head and held him there and said, "But instead of that, why don't you help me now? Fight with me, right now. Die by my side if that is what it takes. Let us together show these wizards what actual power is. I know that you have it in you, Yivan."

A loud horn blared nearby, and all of the wizards still able began retreating into the compound. Yivan, fearing the worst, shakily replied, "It is too late, Father. They have come."

Father and son looked to the other side and found that the army had flanked them. They were surrounded. A man walked forth from the massive army straight towards Marko and

Yivan. Looking at the two magic users, the Rego General said, "Greetings to you, mages. I am the General of the Rego Army. We do not wish to kill you or your kin. It is better for all involved if you surrender yourselves to us now. We will take you inside the compound where you will be safe. The wizards will feed you, clothe you, and give you beds to sleep in. All they ask in exchange is the chance to study what you know, and how you use magic. Afterward, you will be free to go. If you do not stop this senseless attack and surrender to us now, however, we will be forced to fire arrows into your ranks. We have 10,000 men. You cannot stop them all. You will die."

The general of the Rego Army stood silently and waited for an answer. Someone would have to speak, but it couldn't be Marko. His temper would not allow him to converse calmly with an ordinary man. Yivan stepped forward to save his family; to save his little sister, whom he loved above all others.

"General of the Regos," Yivan began awkwardly.
"Please," the man said with kindness. "Our army is the Rego Army, but we prefer to call ourselves the Regs. What is your name, young mage?"

"My name is Yivan. I am pleased to meet you, reg."

From a short distance, Marko angrily watched the scene play out. "What is Yivan doing talking with that man? We should be slaying this army right now. We need not fear their weapons. We can withstand anything," Marko fumed while pacing. The thought of surrendering to these wizards and their pathetic army made him sick.

"My son, you have always been too quick to anger," the Healer said. "You never think before you act. Calm down, and focus your thoughts on a solution. Would you have your wife, son, and daughter murdered just so that you can stick to your ideals? Give these men what they desire, and then you can leave and go on with your life. Look at how many arrows would be coming for us at the first sign of attack."

Marko, ignoring his father's words, lit his hands with Fire and slapped them together. The shock wave knocked everyone within 500 feet to the ground. "Rise up, mages! Kill the army! Take their lives to spare our own!" he roared at his people. A resounding war cry went up from the remaining eleven mages as they rushed toward the Rego army. Eleven mages against 10,000 armed soldiers.

It was suicide.

The General jumped back to his feet and pulled his sword from its sheath. Pressing the blade to Yivan's throat, he said coldly, "Make it stop, boy."

"I… I can't," Yivan stammered in reply. "He's my father… he won't back down. I'm sorry."

The general pulled the sword back for a killing blow, but Yivan summoned a large slab of rock from deep within the ground beneath their feet. The Rock spears he conjured to cover its surface impaled the leader of the Rego Army, killing him instantly. There would be no escape from this, Yivan knew. The only thing he could do now was to protect his sister and help her get away safely.

Arrows began to rain down, and Yivan swept wave after wave of them away with his Storm winds. They flew wildly back where they came from, some going past the army, but many flying into the ranks of the soldiers. Being killed by their own projectiles slowed their rate of fire somewhat.

And then came the charge. Thousands of men brandishing an array of deadly weapons ran towards a tiny group of only eleven mages. Even though the Rego Army's weapons were distance weapons, they would still have to get close enough to use them, and that would prove to be quite a challenge.

Marko sent jets of killing Fire from both hands into the onslaught of regs. Men fell, roasted where they stood, the flames often spreading to nearby soldiers as well. A horseshoe-shaped dent in the advancing army formed around the Fire mage.

Another two mages among the remaining eleven were not entirely sure how to combat the oncoming mass of regs, and so they hesitated. It was unlucky that they did so, because instead of attacking with magic, they died filled with projectile weapons. Spears flew through the air, javelins soared in at the scared mages, and all the two of them could do was attempt to stop the rain of death. Unfortunately for them, neither of those two mages had the strength of Yivan's magic. Some of the projectiles got through their efforts at protection. The two mages fell, their bodies littered with protrusions, blood weeping into the desert sand.

Maeris and Ema stood together, doing as well or better than Marko. Maeris conjured the burning rain she had recently perfected. The Storm cloud rained droplets that set Fire to everything they touched; sand, swords, clothing, faces... it all burned. Ema created a globe of Water that surrounded Maeris and herself. It slowed any projectiles soaring towards them, trapping the missiles within the barrier. It worked very well until the regs reached the sphere of Water. They ran directly through it, only slightly slowed by the magic, and once inside, hundreds deep, they physically overpowered the two mages, capturing them alive.

The same was happening elsewhere. Whenever possible, the regs tried to take the mages alive. However, a few more mages had to be put down. Soon, it was all but over. The Rego Army had killed six mages and captured three others. The battle was almost won, except that two mages still fought on: Marko and his son.

Yivan saw the captive mages – Ema, Maeris, and the Healer – being dragged inside the compound, and abandoned his father's side, running to help them.

"Yivan, where are you going, son? We have them beaten! Together we can rid the world of these men! Help me, son," Marko pleaded.

"I cannot, Father! They have our family! They have Maeris! I have to save her!" Yivan yelled back over the sound of his father's raging, fiery devastation.

"Insolent child! Get back here!" Marko ordered his son, but Yivan ignored his father's calls and rushed to the entrance of the Wizards Guild compound. The army surged around the lone mage and overran Marko, temporarily incapacitating the powerful man. Yivan reached the inner courtyard and found his family staring in horror at him. From behind, the regs held blades to his family's throats. And behind the regs stood the wizards.

"Please, do not do this. We can all live in peace. It doesn't have to end in death. There does not have to be any more killing," Yivan begged. But, despite his pleas, none of the regs moved a muscle.

One of the wizards, however, stepped forward and said warmly, "Greetings, young mage. I speak for the Guild here in Cairo. My name is my own, but you may call me the Wizard Father. Now, I can assure you that we mean no harm to your three friends here. We only wish to study your kind and the astonishing spells that you mages use. If you are willing to make a bargain with us, we can protect you. Surrender yourself for study, and all four of you will be free to go in one year's time. It is as simple as that."

"How can we trust you, Wizard Father?" Yivan inquired.

"Says the mage who was just part of an attack on our home, killing countless members of our guild and the Rego Army that protects us," the Wizard Father snaps back.

"According to the regs," Yivan said, digging for the truth, "they do more than protect you. They govern you."

"Yes, well, for the time being their services are required," the Wizard Father growled in response, his demeanor instantly going cold.

This man was not old, nor was he young. The Wizard Father appeared to be in his late-thirties and had a sturdy physique. His beard was red, and his hair was receding. He did not look like a natural leader; he more closely resembled a laborer, with his calloused hands and scarred arms.

"If I agree, will you spare my father, too?" Yivan asked of man who looked out of place in such a high-ranking role. "He is still out there on the battlefield."

The Wizard Father looked curiously out into the night and said, "Ahh, the Fire mage. We can keep him safe as well, provided he wants our protection. That one seems the sort to bite the hand that feeds him."

"It is true. But please, you must try," Yivan said with resignation in his voice.

"Alright, young mage," the smiling Wizard Father said, "We will do all that we can. Now, if you will accompany your friends here, the soldiers will take you to the mage quarters."

Outside, the Rego Army struggled with the wild Fire mage. Marko set men ablaze with a thought, but no matter how many he burned, another always took his place. And his reactions were slowing. Marko was growing tired. His connection to the Ether was harder to maintain, which happened with spell fatigue. Soon he would need to rest for a time to recharge.

Marko slumped into the arms of the soldiers who surrounded him, his eyes closing against his will. "Ok, this one is done," a soldier remarked. "Let's take him inside with the others."

"Inside?" Marko mumbled with his eyes still shut tight. A memory fluttered through Marko's memory. Someone once told him mages go inside that compound, but never come back out. And his family had just gone inside. These wizards would not take Marko to the same fate.

The Fire mage violently erupted like a super-massive volcano. Anyone standing in the vicinity was instantly vaporized. The blaze immediately cleared a circle of 20 feet around him. Using this as his chance to escape, Marko fled to find more mages and later return to continue this fight.

"This is not over," he grunted with effort. "You may kill my family, but I will kill every last one of you." Marko fired streams of Fire as hard as he could from his hands and feet, the force of which propelled him upwards and out, away from the compound – and away from his family, who were more than likely already dead.

His flight was short-lived, only taking him about a mile away from the army of men. It would take them some time locate Marko. In the meantime, he made several more jumps to put more and more distance between them. But Marko swore to himself that he would come back sometime in the future.

And he would make the wizards pay dearly for their crimes.

TWENTY-FOUR
2015 AD
Shanghai, China

Standing behind the figure in black is that disgusting two-faced rat, Herod. Mian Mian needs to hurry her ass up; Herod may be weak, but taking on both of them by myself is not a wise idea. Unfortunately, the ghostly images of Rainbow, Liang, and Tian Yi appear in my mind and I quickly lose the patience required to wait for backup. Tapping into every connection I have with the Ether, I move towards the doorway. Rock magic hardens my skin while Fire surrounds my entire body in a moving curtain of dancing flames; Water rushes through my veins, leaving me energized and faster. I feel buffed up, and it's exhilarating.

Mian Mian's footsteps echo behind me, and a small sense of relief dances its way through my heart right before a wall of flames, filled with smoldering chunks of rock, flies forth from my body. The spell hits the figure in black with so much force that I get knocked backward a few steps and Mian Mian is made to hit the ground in a roll, expertly ending with her back on both feet.

The smoke begins to clear, and a Water spell leaps to the forefront of my mind, one that will silence Herod and keep him from casting. He has to be visible for accuracy, though, so I have to wait until I can see his face.

Luck is not on my side as the smoke dissipates enough for me to make out the person standing in the doorway. It is not Herod. The man in black still looms at the entrance to the basement, and I notice a red glow emanating from the door frame. Too late, I realize the entire entryway was covered in the barrier, not the door itself. Damn it.

"Please do not waste your energy, Mr. King," the mysterious man says. "As you can see, my barrier is still in place, and there is nothing you can do to bring it down."

"Well, that's great. Since we're now on speaking terms, why don't you tell me what it is you want from us, why you are holding us here, and who in the hell you really are, man?" I demand forcefully, my index finger jabbing his way.

A calm discussion is pretty much out of the question with this thing. The memories of holding Rainbow's dead body, seeing the tattered remains of Tian Yi, and of cradling a dying Liang fill me with fury as I stare down the person responsible for all three deaths.

His masked head turns from me to Mian Mian, and says curiously, "How is it that she is awake? The spell I put on her should be unbreakable. Only I could have woken her from that sleep."

"Apparently not, crammer," I growl through gritted teeth. His covered face turns back to me, head tilted, and says, "I am impressed. But how did you do it? Please, Mr. King, tell me. I am quite intrigued."

"It's a secret, champ. But I'll tell you what, you let us out of here, and I'll tell you how I did it. Hell, let my team go and I'll show you how to do it."

He tosses his head back, laughing deeply, then says, "No, I think not, Mr. King. It doesn't matter for now. We have other, more important things to discuss."

"Oh, do we?" I reply mockingly. "And what's that? How you have killed dozens of people in the past few days, three of those victims not only members of my team, but also my friends? Or is it that you want to admit to being the Maelstrom who killed thousands of people 25 years ago? Take off that mask, old man. I want to see the face of a mass murderer. Then you can dismiss this barrier and we'll see who's the real badass: you or me? I'm betting on the latter."

The horrible figure places both hands on his hips and shakes his head at me in disapproval. "All in good time, Jaret," he says. "May I call you Jaret?"

"Sure, you can call me Jaret. You can call me Puddin' Pop if you want," I answer instinctively. "Just let my team go, first. Then you and I can hang around all day and talk about whatever it is you have to get off of your chest."

The man in black shakes his head again and replies, "We do have much to talk about, Jaret, but with plenty of time to do it. At the moment, you are too agitated to have a proper discussion. For now, take this. I shall return shortly."

At the mysterious man's indication, Herod holds out some bags of food and a few big bottles of water. A small space in the magical barrier about the size a basketball opens long enough for him to toss it all through. No one used any hand gestures or words of magic to open or close the barrier.

The door stays open this time, and Herod lingers for a moment after the man in black retreats. He stands there and stares at the floor instead of looking me in the eyes.

Unwilling to let this traitor have the first word, I say, "Thanks for lying to me, Herod. I was really starting to like you. Now, of course, I'm going to turn you into a greasy mark on the floor as soon I get out of here."

He glances up and smiles crookedly, saying, "That might actually be a nice way to go at this point, matey boy." He then turns on his heels and strides away purposefully to join the mysterious man in black.

My team and I guzzle the water and quickly devour the food provided by the two criminals holding us captive, not worrying about poison. If they wanted us dead, we'd already be dead. No longer famished, we talk about my interaction with the evil wizard.

"Or is he a mage?" I ask. "I'm not sure what he is, to be honest."

"When he opened part of the barrier, he didn't use wizard magic," Mian Mian says. "There were no hand or finger movements and no incantation, Bossman. It looked like mage magic to me."

Aurora says, "Now that you mentioned it, when we were fighting in the warehouse I saw him cast spells with just a thought. No finger movements, and no incantations. But then again, I also saw him cast a few big spells where he did both of those things. It's not possible, though, is it? Wizards can't cast mage spells and vice versa."

Joyee chimes in and says, "He must be mimicking a mage's way of casting, maybe by wiggling his toes and mumbling words of power under his breath. We can't see his lips moving because he is wearing that creepy mask, after all."

"I think that rules don't apply to this guy," I say, "even the rules of magic. It sounds crazy, but maybe he can cast both types of magic," I add. In response, my team looks at me like I have a foot growing out of my forehead. "What?" I ask. "You don't think I could be right?"

In unison, they all reply, "No."

"Well, okay," I say, "you all can believe he is toe-casting like Joyee suggested, but I've never heard of that before. I choose to believe that he has found a way to cast wizard and mage magic. Both theories are far-fetched, but only yours is gross."

We all burst out laughing, and it's a much-needed moment of entertainment that helps ease our tension. What else can we do in here? Nothing. So, we wait. And wait. And wait.

At 6:00 am we finally reach our breaking point, and are all about to go stir-crazy. Kelly will be home in six hours and will be worried sick about me when Lilly tells her I haven't been home since yesterday. She'll probably think I'm dead and lying in a ditch somewhere. I don't want to put her through any of that, so I intend on being home when Kelly gets there. We are not going to die in here. There is a way to get us all out — a way to thrash him and make our escape. We'll have to be fast, but that shouldn't be a problem. I've got experience with speed.

Mian Mian suddenly points to something beyond the glowing red barrier, and I look to see what's happening. The man in black walks directly to the spell-protected doorway and he's holding two folding chairs in his murderous hands. *Bingo*.

I give Mian Mian a slight nod of the head and flick of the eyes and she responds with two taps on her leg, acknowledging her understanding of what to do and when.

Hands in my pockets, I lean against a cage near the barrier, and greet the man in black by saying, "So, you need two chairs? One for you, and one for the devil that lives inside of you?"

In times of high stress, I often find that I just don't know when to shut my damn mouth.

"Amusing, Jaret," the man in black says. "But I assure you that I am not evil. Once I explain my entire story, you will find I am only doing what is necessary; I am doing what must be done. Now, let us discuss the past, the present, and our future together."

He starts to move the chair towards the barrier, and my father's voice rings loudly in my ears saying, "Calm down. Focus your thoughts."

The barrier opens from the floor to his waist, and the man in black scoots the chair through. "Here we go," I say to myself "Think *fast*."

The instant that barrier opens, Mian Mian sends a jet of flame through, striking him on the legs, and instantly setting his cloak ablaze. Just as I had hoped, the mysterious figure did not have any magical protection on. Why would he when we are safely locked behind this barrier?

I conjure a shower of tiny gravel stones and toss them at his feet, causing the man to slip and fall on his back. Once he's down and covered in a blanket of gravel with one leg on fire, Mian Mian and I rush towards the door and dive through the hole he created in the barrier.

Or try to, at least.

We smash face first into the wall of protection magic, which is completely sealed. This monster chuckles mirthlessly while floating just above the loose gravel covering the ground. His leg is still on fire, but it doesn't seem to be bothering him.

Admonishing us with a wagging finger like we are naughty schoolchildren, the powerful magic user says, "Ingenious, Jaret. You almost got out of there. And I must say that I underestimated you, young woman. I knew that Jaret was incredibly fast, but you surprised me. I will have to remember that."

The man in black sits down in the chair on his side of the barrier. Then he points at Mian Mian and utters a bizarre magical phrase, his pinkies both zigzagging in the air. She falls to the floor, once again, fast asleep. Damn it. I don't want to have to wake her up with opposing forces again. My head still hurts from banging into that cage earlier.

He must have seen my expression change as I watched Mian Mian descend into unconsciousness, because the mysterious man says, "Don't worry, Jaret, I'll wake them all up after we're done here. Or maybe you could show me how to do your little trick, and we wake them up together."

What am I supposed to say to this creep? How am I expected to respond to the person who's been killing my friends for the past few days?

"Jaret, you must understand that I mean you no harm. We are allies."

"Wh...what are you talking about?" I stammer. "You've killed three of my friends, and you locked the rest of us down here in your gimp room. If you mean us no harm, you sure have a strange way of showing it."

The man in dark robes places his palms face down on his legs and leans toward me. "I said that I mean you no harm, Jaret. I said nothing of your pathetic friends. I must admit, however, that I do regret killing the other members of your team. I often forget how foolish people can be when it comes to love. I learned long ago that it would only cause pain to care for others. It is a weakness. One I hope to rid you of, if you are to become what I need, that is," he says. "In the meantime, I promise that no harm will come to you, or your team. Provided that you listen to my story, and show a modicum of restraint and intelligence. Do we have a deal?"

I honestly don't want to agree to anything with this guy, but I have to keep my team safe. Reluctantly, I nod in agreement and say, "Deal. Now tell me what you need so desperately to say."

Sitting up straight, the mysterious figure in black clears his throat and says, "Excellent. Let us begin. First, allow me to introduce myself."

The man then reaches up, with what I only now notice to be massively muscled arms, to remove the mask hiding his identity.

"My name is Yivan."

TWENTY-FIVE
1009 AD
Cairo, Egypt

The mages, led by the Wizard Father, ambled to a large building in the middle of the Guild compound. There was no door on the entryway to this building, and inside they could see many cages lining the walls, each with only a length of chain inside. Maeris began to struggle reflexively at the sight and summoned her StormWater whip.

Yivan grabbed her arm and shook his head saying, "Not now, my dear Maeris. Do not throw our lives away just yet."

"Why did you give up, Yivan? We could have killed the wizards and their weakling army," Maeris argued stubbornly.

"Do not be blind, sweet girl. They killed every mage except the four of us right here. Poppa is most likely dead. It is over. Let us serve our year of slavery, and then build a new life somewhere far from this terrible place," Yivan said, attempting to calm his sister and prevent her from making a fatal mistake.

Maeris released the whip, and the weapon made of Water and Storm magic disappeared as soon as it left the her hand.

As they passed into the building that housed the cages, a cold and dreadful feeling washed over the mage family. Suddenly, the four mages all had the same feelings and emotions running through their minds: abandonment, loneliness, and despair.

The Healer fell to his knees and vomited on the dirt floor. Maeris began crying and hugging her mother tightly. Ema held her daughter and looked at the man of the family, Yivan, for answers.

"Wizard Father, what have you done to us?" Yivan asked in a hollow voice.

The man smiled jovially, patted Yivan on the shoulder, and answered, "Do not worry, my young mage friend. This building is called the Hall of Study. There is no elemental magic allowed here. You have merely been cut off from the elemental Ether as long as you reside within these walls. Once you exit, it comes right back. Here, step out for a moment."

Yivan did so and felt the rush of contact with his old friends – Storm and Rock. Smiling at the reconnection, he opened and closed his hands. The moment of relief was cut short as two soldiers, not so gently, guided Yivan back into the Hall of Study.

"Why do this to us, Wizard Father? It is a vile and sad feeling. It... hurts," Yivan said.

"Oh, you will get used to it. It is a necessary precaution. Too many mages grew tired of their circumstances and began terrorizing our scholars trying to study their magic," the Wizard Father explained.

"But how? How can you so easily cut us off from the Ether?" Yivan asked.

"Well, it is not so easy as it seems, young mage. The spell to accomplish this task takes many wizards casting a steady stream of spells to keep the magical barrier up over this building. Ten wizards work together and chant an ongoing incantation while drawing and redrawing runes in the air. It is very tiring and can only be kept up for a couple of hours. We have to switch them out quite often. But it is for your safety and ours," the Wizard Father told Yivan.

Though he did not like the feeling, in fact, he quite despised it, Yivan felt there was nothing he could do about it. They were here now, and resisting would do no good.

The Wizard Father gave a guided tour as they moved through the building, saying, "These cages with chains should not frighten you. They are used only when mages cause trouble or resist study. As you can see, they are all empty now. All the mages currently contributing to our further understanding of magic are on the third level in the mage quarters. They are quite comfortable, I think you will find."

A wizard with a cart full of books walked past their group, and Yivan curiously asked, "What are all of those books for, Wizard Father?"

The man with the cart looked up in terror at the mention of the leader of his guild. He had not known mages were being brought in today, and tried to apologize for his indiscretion by saying, "Wizard Father...I... I apologize. I had no idea... we were expecting... uh, new arrivals. Please, Wizard Father, forgive me. I beg you."

The balding man who called himself the Wizard Father just laughed warmly and put his hand comfortingly on the younger wizard's shoulder.

"Calm yourself, Muharram. It is ok. Our friends have volunteered to help us create marvelous new spells." The terrified man breathed an immense sigh of relief and hurried off before the leader of the Guild could change his mind.

"In answer to your question, young man," the Wizard Father said, "those books are called spell tomes. They are where we wizards must store our spells. Whenever we want to use one, we first read it from the book, memorize the words and rune patterns to draw in the air, and then that spell is ours to cast. Once we use it, however, we must learn it all over again. It is a tedious process, but it is the only way we have found to access the Ether. Not like you mages! Your kind can just call upon magic anytime you want. This slow process is why we need your help."

"Spells from a book. How fascinating. Could a mage learn the magic from those books?" the Healer asked, clearly intrigued.

An annoyed look crossed the Wizard Father's features and he said, "I think it's quite impossible, old man. Either way, why would you want to do something like that? Magic flows through you like blood." For some reason, Yivan didn't quite believe the Wizard Father's answer to the Healer's question. Things in this place were not exactly as they seemed. There was something more going on, and Yivan planned on finding out what it was.

They soon arrived at the mage quarters and entered to find one large room, like a military barracks, with beds enough for nine people. There were currently already nine mages inside, some asleep in the beds and others having hushed converstaion. Yivan guessed that he and his family would be sleeping on the floor, as they were the newcomers. No one looked mistreated or unhappy, which Yivan took as a good sign.

The wizards and soldiers took their leave and locked the door behind them. Maeris looked longingly at the bolted and guarded door and muttered, "We're trapped."

"We may be trapped, little sister, but we are alive," Yivan answered solemnly, and added under his breath, "for now, at least."

One of the mages stood and rushed to greet the four new mages in the room. As he neared, his husky voice reverberated in the chamber. "Fresh meat for the slaughter, eh? Welcome, fellow mages. I am known as Mo the Fire Master."

The man was gangly, with skin the color of leather left too long in the sun, and had a head full short, wiry, black hair.

In answer, Yivan said, "Greetings, Mo. I am Yivan. This is my sister Maeris, my mother Ema, and my grandfather…"

"Oh, this man I know," Mo interrupted. "The Healer! How sad it is that you have come here to die, my friend. The world of mages is much diminished with your loss."

Yivan was caught off guard by this, and said, "To die? What do you mean, Mo? The Wizard Father told us it was to be one year of slavery, and then we would be set free!"

Mo stroked his pointy beard, made a "tsk" sound, and replied, "Lies, Yivan, used by the wizards to get mages surrendering peacefully. They know we are their betters, and so avoid fighting us whenever possible. Their intelligence is impressive, though, and they always find a way to bypass their weakness in battle. But that makes no matter to us now. We mages are all doomed in here, my friend."

"Why? What purpose does it serve to lure us here and then kill us? It makes no sense, Mo," the Healer said.

The dark-skinned man paced the walls, his arms held behind his back, and replied, "This I cannot say, Healer, for I do not know. They bring us in, ask us many questions about what

184

we can do, how does it feel to create this magic, can we tell them what it looks like in our minds as we access the Ether and more. Always the same questions they ask of us. The more information you can give them, the more you will be brought back here to rest before being examined again later. Once you run out of useful answers for them, you never come back to this room. I continue giving as many useful answers as I can think of. I arrived weeks ago, and have seen around sixteen other mages come and go."

"They kill you when you run out of answers to their questions?" Maeris asked.

"I assume so, young beauty. But I cannot say it is a complete truth; it is only what I believe," Mo answered.

Yivan gave a sigh of relief and said, "So they could be letting the mages go free once they have answered their questions."

Mo closed his eyes and shook his head. "After a few sessions," he murmured, "you will begin to understand why I believe this. They are never going to let us go. Ever."

"Why? What makes you say so?" Ema asked.

Mo raised his shirt and Maeris drew in a sudden breath. Ema stared at the earthen floor in silence, but the look on her face told a story of grim acceptance. Yivan's grandfather, the Healer, stepped closer to examine Mo's wounds and scars. Most looked as if the wizards removed chunks of his flesh, and then healed the wounds with magic. Others were long, thin cuts, still fresh and swollen.

"What have they done to you, Mo?" the Healer said sadly. A pale and weak mage lying on a bed answered in a monotone voice, "The wizards have done it to all of us. They open us up and they… they take things out."

Mo lowered his shirt and added, "Yes, they call it research."

Seeing the horrors underneath that shirt, Yivan knew he could not let this happen to himself, and especially not to his family. He had to find a way out.

A week later, Yivan and his family had yet to be taken for research. Some other mages went for questioning and never came back. Other than Mo, only four of the first mages, the ones present when Yivan and his family arrived, were still left. Mo sat gazing at the single window in the room. It was high, but not impossible to reach. For the millionth time, he considered climbing out and taking his chances.

"Why don't you do it?" Yivan's asked, bringing Mo out of his silent contemplation.

"Huh, what? Do what, Yivan?" Mo replied awkwardly.

Pointing to the window above them, Yivan said, "Escape. Jump to your death. Something like that."

Mo laughed and took Yivan by the hand. The self-proclaimed Master of Fire admitted, "Because I am afraid, young man. I do not want to die. Besides, we are only on the third level. A fall from this height would not kill me. Although I am sure there are some nasty wizard traps set around that window. There is no way they would leave it here unguarded for us to escape. That window is a temptation put there purposefully by our cruel captors. But it only offers a quick death and the chance to choose when you die, Yivan; not freedom."

"That seems like a form of freedom to me," Ema said, having been eavesdropping on their conversation.

"Do not speak like that, Mother. We will find a way to escape," Yivan said.

His mother was looking more sullen and bedraggled every day, and that worried Yivan. Ema merely shrugged and rolled over to fall back asleep. It was all she ever did anymore.

Maeris, on the other hand, was never idle. She trained physically all the time. When asked why she trained so often by one of the other mages, she had said, "I cannot use magic, so I will make myself strong enough to crush the wizards with my bare hands."

Yivan did not argue with this explanation because it kept his little sister busy. But he worried about her, too. He did not want his sister to die. Of all the people in the mage quarters, the one Yivan sincerely wished could escape the most was his little sister, Maeris. He had to think of a way to save her.

It was two days later, when Yivan and Maeris's mother, Ema, gave up all hope. In the early morning, she woke from her bed and went to the chamber pot. After emptying her bladder, she ate greedily for the first time in days. Ema drank deeply of the wine provided and gorged on dates and bread

Once she felt stuffed, Ema called to her children, "Yivan, Maeris – come to Momma." They obeyed the woman who had brought them into the world, and sat beside her, each holding one of her hands.

"You seem to be feeling well today, Momma," Maeris said.

"I am my child. I am," Ema said lovingly, kissing each of her children on their cheeks. "I have made a critical decision, and I wanted to tell you both that I love you very much. I am proud of the mages you have become. Your strength is more than your father and I could have ever dreamed of."

Yivan suddenly became more worried because of his mother's change in attitude that morning, and said, "Mother, thank you. We love you, too, but… why are you speaking like this?"

"I did not want to miss the chance to tell you both these things. That is all," Ema replied.

Yivan eyed her warily and said, "Alright, Mother. Please tell me if you need anything."

Maeris kissed her mother on the cheek and said, "I love you, too, Momma," then wandered off to eat some breakfast.

A few minutes later, Yivan was taking his turn with the chamber pot when he heard a scraping sound on the floor. Curious, he finished pissing and came out from behind the privacy partition. He saw that Ema had moved a cabinet in front of the only window in the mage quarters. She was now atop the wardrobe and standing before the opening in the wall.

"Mother! No! Do not do this! Please!" Yivan rushed over, screaming frantically.

Maeris watched the scene unfold without emotion and said, "Goodbye, Momma."

Mo and the Healer ran to help Yivan get Ema down before something bad could occur, but the other four mages only stood and watched, curious as to what would happen. Ema leaned forward to peer out of the window, and the stones forming the window frame began glowing purple the instant her head crossed through.

"Oh no, Mother, look out!" Yivan shouted, his warning coming seconds too late. He and the others watched as an invisible barrier crushed his mother's head, closing down upon it with lethal force. Her lifeless body fell half in and half out of the window. The wizard trap, a crushing barrier, repeated over and over, pulverizing Ema's body to a pulpy mess. The pounding only stopped once whatever remained of her fell out one side or the other of the window frame. The only sound that followed was Yivan softly whispering, "Why?" over and over again.

Later, once over the initial shock of his mother's suicide, Yivan climbed on top of the cabinet to toss the rest of his mother's messy corpse out of the treacherous window. He couldn't stand to look at it anymore.

Yivan was careful to make sure none of his body crossed the window sill as he performed the gruesome task. When finished, he noticed that a large portion of the remaining Rego Army was in sight through the window's field of view, and they led a group of nine captive people into the compound. The prisoners' arms were all chained together.

"Must be more mages," Yivan thought aloud. "Nine of them." A sudden idea suddenly struck the young mage, and Yivan looked back at the beds in the room. He remembered that there were nine mages when he and his family arrived. But then four went out and never came back... leaving nine mages in the room... eight, now that his mother had... left. Yivan had a bad feeling about this and asked, "Mo, has there ever been more than nine mages in these quarters during your time here?"

The dark-skinned mage considered for a moment before responding, "No, my friend. Well, once; when you and your family arrived, but then soon after four more were gone. It seems they like to keep us in small and manageable numbers, eh? Why do you ask?"

Yivan hopped down from the cabinet and said, "Because I think nine mages is all they can control, Mo. And because they are bringing nine new mages into the compound right now."

TWENTY-SIX
2015 AD
Shanghai, China

When I see his face, the recognition is immediate. "You? But... but you can't be the Maelstrom!"

The furious and heavily muscled metalhead I tried in vain to cheer up looks no older than 26. He was just being born when the first attacks were happening; he couldn't be the cause of them.

"Oh, but I am, Jaret," Yivan says. "I must confess to being quite shocked when you spoke to me in the street. I had hoped to go unnoticed by you until a time of my own choosing. May I ask why you are so surprised?"

"Well, I thought the Maelstrom would be older. I was ten years old back then, and you've got to be younger than me... so there's just no way. You can't be," I try to reason.

The murderer grins at me with amusement. "You must remember that some of us choose to lengthen our lives with magic, Jaret. I have done so to great effect — more so than any magic user in history, I think. I *am* the one responsible for all of those deaths, though my methods are now much simpler, and a good deal cleaner. As you can see, I no longer need to blow up hundreds of people to get what I need," he says, gesturing to the empty cages behind me.

"What methods?" I ask. "What are you two weirdos doing down here? Was Herod telling me the truth?"

"Yes, my little servant was instructed to tell you the truth. Mostly," the Maelstrom says vaguely.

"So, you actually are stealing unspent magical energy from dead wizards?" I ask. "Why? Is that how you can cast both mage and wizard magic?"

Yivan offers me a round of mock applause and replies, "Well done, Jaret. You are very observant. No one else has ever noticed that about me. But it does not enable me to cast both types of magic; all mages can cast wizard spells if they learn them properly," the monster known as Yivan explains. "And I am not stealing this energy, Jaret. I am taking it back. It was never theirs to begin with. My Spell of Reclamation recovers what was stolen from us, and also has the added benefit of enhancing my already significant level of power." Clapping his hands together, and looking as if we are discussing his favorite soccer team, Yivan continues, "Ah, but you are brilliant, Jaret. I knew that I chose wisely with you."

Still unsure what the hell is going on, I say, "Chose me for what? I...you...I just... I don't understand any of this."

Yivan nods and says, "Yes, I can see that you do not grasp it all quite yet. Do not worry, you will. Allow me to start at the beginning." He clears his throat again and settles back into his chair.

At that moment, Herod walks into the room holding another chair and a cup of tea. He hands a cup to the Maelstrom and then sits down beside the butcher.

"I am a mage," the Maelstrom begins. "I was born in Croatia and raised by two very loving and talented mages. My parents were thrilled the day I manifested my first school of magic…"

Yivan goes on to tell me of his nomadic childhood, and his family's chosen professions: murder and theft.

"Wait, how did the MOP never catch your family? Someone had to notice all of the murdered regs piling up?" I ask, interrupting the most dangerous person alive.

"There was no such thing as magical law enforcement in those days, Jaret. In today's world everyone is so soft and worthless, but when I was young, we were raised to be survivors. We were raised to rule the world," he says, pausing to sip his tea.

"Rule the world, huh?" I say. "Everybody wants to, I hear."

"Yes, well, by the time I reached the age of 18," Yivan continues, "I was an extremely talented mage and could access two types of elemental power: Storm and Rock…"

He tells me about his powerful sister, Maeris, and how much he loved her. He talks about his father, how Marko was firm but kind to him. Yivan mentions his mother, a caring parent, but always weighed down by her station in life.

"Yivan, they sound lovely. But you're not making any sense. The MOP has been around for longer than either of us."

"That is incorrect, boy. I am older than I look," he replies with a laugh. "My family and I lived like kings for years. But one day, everything changed for us. The regular people decided that enough was enough. They formed a guild, and called themselves wizards."

As he sips more of his tea, I snap at him, "What in the hell are you saying? I must have misheard you. You didn't just say that you were alive when the Wizards Guild started, did you?"

The Maelstrom ignores me and continues with his story. "The newly formed Wizards Guild began to capture mages for study and torture. This part of history you know: they learned their magic through our deaths."

"Yes, Yivan. All mages are taught magic history when they are assigned a tutor, as all wizard children learn it in spell school," I say. "The mages eventually fought back and started a long war. The result was the formation of the two High Councils. We have ours, and they have theirs. They work together to keep the peace and make sure a war never breaks out again. You're not telling me anything new."

"The mages fought back, indeed," he says with a far-off look in his eyes. "But even we are vulnerable to thousands of archers and soldiers. The one thing regular people have always had is plenty of numbers. We took many lives that night. Their army of 10,000 was cut nearly in half. Most of the mages with us died, arrows filling their bodies like a pincushion."

Yivan stops again to sip his tea and I say, "Ok, so you're telling me that you were alive when the Wizards Guild began and that you are over 1,000 years old? Impossible. Don't waste my time, Yivan. I knew you were crazy – you have to be to murder hundreds of people – but I had no idea how far your mental problems actually went."

His eyes regain the anger they held on the street days before, and he spits a furious answer, "I have murdered *thousands* of people, not hundreds. I will never lie to you, Jaret. What I say is true. I have walked this Earth for 1,029 years. I have seen empires form and fail. I have seen everyone I ever loved die. Compassion and love will always end with sorrow and pain."

Once again, I admit that knowing when to shut up is not one of my strengths. "Are you kidding me?" I say incredulously. "How am I supposed to believe this shit? And why? Huh? Why should I even believe you?"

"Ask yourself this, Jaret," he replies calmly. "Why would I lie about it? What could I possibly gain?"

For a brief moment our eyes meet, and surprisingly I find no madness there – only pain, heartbreak, and honesty. Seeing this written all over his face, I have a sudden and urgent feeling in my gut. This type of sensation is something I always try to listen to because it is almost always right. And right now that special sensation is saying one thing: Yivan is telling the truth.

TWENTY-SEVEN
1009 AD
Cairo, Egypt

Unfortunately for Yivan and the other captive mages, wizard magic still worked within the Hall of Study. The spell keeping mages closed off from the elemental Ether had no effect on their wizard spells. The door to the mage quarters slammed open, and dozens of soldiers rushed in with short swords, javelins, and bows and arrows all drawn and held at the ready.

Following the armed guard – or the armed masters; Yivan still wasn't sure what the truth was – the Wizard Father walked in with his hands clasped behind his back.

"Why the big show, wizard? You have taken our magic away. We can't fight back," Yivan said, not using the Wizard Father's preferred title. Only a small show of defiance, perhaps, but the leader of the Guild instantly noticed.

"I've learned it's never a bad idea to be overly cautious with your kind. How have you settled into your new quarters, mage?" the Wizard Father asked venomously, no longer with the pretense of friendliness.

"It is grotesque and empty of magic, just like the men who locked us in here," Yivan replied.

The Wizard Father's eyes grew smaller and his mouth twisted with fury as he growled, "You should watch your tongue, mage. You are the ones here without magic. Wizards in this building can still cast. For example," and with a quick chant, tracing the shape of a star in the air, the wizard sent a spray of colored lights into the nine mages standing before him. Instantly they all fell prone to the floor, unable to move.

Once immobilized, the Rego soldiers moved in and bound the mages by their hands and feet. They were each placed on a cart and wheeled out of the room.

"I apologize for this, mages," the Wizard Father said in his faux-friendly voice. "But it is time to make room for new volunteers, who will soon be arriving. Your services are no longer needed."

Yivan found that he could still talk, though the rest of him was frozen. He said, "But my family and I never gave you any assistance, and you said we would be here a year. Are we to be set free now?" Yivan asked, already knowing the answer, but needing to hear it for himself.

"Young man, you know as well as I do that this is the day you all die. Do not make it harder on yourselves than is necessary."

They entered a room Yivan had never seen before. Maeris was growling curses in three languages as the soldiers pushed Yivan in last. "Sister, calm down. It is all going to be ok," he said, attempting to keep her safe even here, even now.

"How, Yivan? How is it going to be ok?" Maeris said, sounding more like the elder sibling between the two. "We are about to die without ever feeling the Ether again. It is not ok, big brother. And it will never be."

196

Yivan knew she was right. He stared down at the floor and tried to think of any way to make an escape or, at least, to save his sister, but could think of nothing.

The Wizard Father strode purposefully into the chamber where they now found themselves and said, in a very straight-forward manner, "You nine are going to witness and be part of something truly astonishing today. You will be giving your lives and connection to the Ether over to the Wizards Guild. How, you may wonder? Let me show you."

The balding wizard brought forth a spell tome and walked around the room. Each mage sat in a chair with a small writing table in front of them. The soldiers had bound their hands in the front and connected their wrists to a ring at each table. The Wizard Father stopped at Mo's table and laid the spell tome under the mage's bound hands. The wizard then walked in a circle, around the mage and said strange words while moving his fingers in patterns up and down.

Mo's eyes suddenly opened wide, and he flashed a sparking white smile that stood at stark contrast with his dark skin. Fire surrounded Mo. His eyes turned red, and the chair beneath him began to smolder and smoke. His blazing hands clutched the spell tome in a victorious grasp.

"I am Mo the Fire Master!" he growled through that shining smile. "And you wizards shall all feel the…"

Yivan suddenly felt a strange pulling sensation, like the opposite of wind coming from Mo's direction. The tome in front of the self-proclaimed Fire Master glowed green, and his body began to shrink in on itself – his skin growing tight to his bones. Mo became as dry as an old scroll, his body devoid of both fluids and life.

As Mo fell over dead, his corpse looked as if it had been stranded in the desert for months – years even – baking in the sun. The spell tome glowed green for a moment more before reverting to its previous regular appearance… except that now the pages were full of flowing script: instructions on how to cast dozens of wizard spells.

The Healer, chained to a table, felt nauseous and moaned between labored breathing, "This… this horrid ritual is how wizards gain magic? It's an abomination!"

"No, mage," the Wizard Father snarled. "You are the abominations. All of this time you have killed innocent people and taken what you want, and yet have none of your kind has ever been brought to justice. Mages could do this because they alone had magic. But no longer. Through research and study, the Wizards Guild has found a way to take your connection to the Ether, and transfer it to one of our spell tomes."

Yivan struggled at his bonds, and said, "Then why does your magic seem so different?"

The Wizard Father could only shrug his shoulders. "We do not know," he answered mildly. "When a mage's lifeless husk falls away, we believe their essence becomes a part of the Ether, or perhaps all Ethers. The dead mage is believed to be the one who writes the spells into the tome. We do not know how it works. Sometimes the spells are the same as other tomes, and other times they are entirely new spells no one has ever seen before. One day, perhaps, we will find a way to communicate with the Ether and discover how or why. But, for the time being, we merely follow the instructions found within the tomes."

"There is more than just the elemental Ether?" Maeris said, having been silent until then.

"Yes, my dear child, of course. There are infinite Ethers, all with different types of power. We have only scratched the surface of what is possible in magic," the Wizard Father replied joyfully.

The Healer still didn't fully understand, and asked, "How did you discover the other Ethers?"

"First we theorized that they must exist. Then we set out to find them. Death was the key, you see," the Wizard Father said casually. "The link between all forms of magic seems to be death. Through trial and error..."

"By which you mean the torture and murder of countless mages, of course," Yivan hissed.

"Yes, of course, but please do not interrupt. Through *trial and error* we found Death has its own Ether; a conduit through which we could see, feel, and even control magic. The green glow you witnessed is direct contact with the Death Ether. So far, we've only been able to use it in crafting items that collect magic and to connect with other Ethers."

Silence filled the room. It was too much for the captive mages to handle. Except for young Maeris, who said, "Do we become part of all Ethers when we die naturally, or only when we join with one of your tomes?"

Once again, the Wizard Father shrugged nonchalantly, saying, "We do not know."

One of the other captive mages, Turk they called him, said, "I will not do this thing. I will not give you my magic. If I die, then I die with honor, and without helping you and your pathetic clan of thieves."

The Wizard Father called in a soldier and pointed to Turk, saying, "This one first. Start with the left foot, smallest toe."

The soldier nodded and pulled a dagger from his belt. A seemingly eternal few minutes later, the reg soldier reached the ankle of the second foot before Turk finally called a stop. Having no feet didn't bother the mage. He knew he was going to die, and would no longer need feet, but the pain was unbearable. He could have just passed out and bled to death: it was what he wanted to do, but the wizard would not let him. Every time Turk began to go unconscious, the Wizard Father kept him from doing so with a spell, and stopped the bleeding with his evil, stolen magic.

"You win, wizard… bastard… I cannot take any more. Let me die. I will do this thing for you," Turk said at last. "I will join the Ethers."

Once Turk's dried-out corpse fell to the floor, and a second tome created, the Wizard Father looked around to the gathered mages expectantly, and said, "Who is next? You have seen what will happen if you refuse, and we won't stop until you are nothing but a head and hands if we have to, and, believe me, that is not pleasant. Give yourself to the Ether. It has to be better than the alternative."

Maeris began to say something, but Yivan stopped her with a slight shake of his head. One by one, the other mages either volunteered or were slowly cut to pieces until they begged for mercy and an empty spell tome to hold.

All that now remained were the three family members: Maeris, the Healer, and Yivan. The Wizard Father looked from one to the other and said, "The day is growing late, and I am getting quite tired. Let us finish quickly. Do not linger here when the Ether calls for you. Who is next?"

"Take me, you abhorrent creature," said the Healer. "I have witneesed much, but I cannot bear the thought of watching these children die before my eyes. I volunteer."

"Very well, old man," the Wizard Father answered. "After you, it will be the girl, and then, finally, it will be your turn, Yivan. I will miss our banter. You're a very smart young man."

The Wizard Father placed a tome under the old Water mage's wrinkled and ancient hands. Before he could reconnect the Healer to the Ether, however, a loud, rumbling noise shook the building, causing dust to fall from the rafters and sending cracks along the walls of the room.

"What was that?" the wizard growled, disappointed to be interrupted. "Go and find out, now!" he shouted to several soldiers, who took off running instantly.

While they waited in the room, one wizard and three mages, no one said a word. All was completely still and quiet. The Wizard Father contemplated what he should do next. Meanwhile, Yivan stared hopelessly at his sister, and mouthed, "I'm sorry."

She ignored his apology and gazed into her open palms. The Healer listened intently to try and discover what was going on outside the walls. They all knew that, soon enough, the Wizard Father would start up again, and they would die. The mages gave up all hope.

That is... until Yivan felt his old friends return to him, flooding his body with buzzing energy. His eyes began to spark with tiny bolts of electricity, and the bonds exploded from his wrists. Using Wind, Yivan filled the Wizard Father's mouth with so much air that he could not speak, cast a spell, or even breathe.

Maeris froze her shackles until they shattered, and took the tome from beneath her grandfather's hands. She gave the book to Yivan, who laid it down on a table nearby. The Healer freed himself, swelling his arms until the iron bonds broke apart from the stress.

"Tell me how it works, wizard. I want to know everything about Death magic," Yivan demanded, his eyes still crackling with purple sparks.

The Wizard Father held up his chin and haughtily replied, "Never. I am not afraid of death, mage. I welcome it rather than live in fear of you and your kind. Do what you will to me, but I'll…uhhh!" The Wizard Father's heart burned a hole through his chest as it melted away, trailing rivers of molten skin, bone, and blood to the ground.

Yivan looked at Maeris with an annoyed expression. She shrugged and said, "He was not going to tell you anyway, big brother."

The three mages fled the Hall of Study as fast as they could. As they neared the ground floor and all of the cages, they finally encountered resistance. The room contained hundreds of wizards and soldiers; too many to fight. The three of them would surely die in the attempt, but what choice did they have.

Except that everyone in the room was facing the entrance and looking away from the three mages, as something outside the Hall of Study held their attention.

"The last of the attacking mages is still somewhere out there, general," one reg soldier said to a tall man in a very nice and clean outfit.

The new General of the Rego Army said, "The other eight have all been taken care of, then?"

"Yes, general," the soldier answered. "They all fell to the javelins and arrows you ordered. Though I feel the need to point out we could have taken them alive, sir."

"No, that was my predecessor's mistake," the tall man said, sounding thoughtful. "We will continue to hunt mages for spell tomes, as we have in the past. But if they come here to fight,

202

we must show no mercy. We must kill all agressive mages on sight. That is our new law. That is how we will win this war against the abominations."

"Yes, sir," the subordinate answered meekly.

Overhearing this exchange gave Yivan hope. There was a mage out there, a mage that came here to attack the wizards in their compound. "Could it be?" Yivan wondered.

"While their attention is elsewhere, it will be easy to kill them all," Yivan whispered to Maeris and the Healer.

His grandfather shook his head in disagreement and said, "No, that is what your father would do. We can escape quietly and be gone from here before they ever notice, Yivan."

"Is that what my father would do?" Yivan asked with anger in his voice. "Good. Then that is exactly what I shall do."

Yivan created an electrical eruption that began as a small ball of light and floated down from above. A lone soldier noticed the shining ball, and reached out to grasp it. As the orb descended into the man's outstretched palm, there in the midst of wizards and soldiers, the ball of light detonated. Yivan's enemies were decimated, 300 men instantly blown to pieces with a single spell. A few still lived, but they would not survive long from the looks of their torn and broken bodies.

Drawn by the thunderous electrical explosion, a mage with long, black hair held back with a band of pure Fire, strode into the Hall of Study, the flame tattoos covering his chest danced with actual Fire.

"Poppa!" Maeris cried out, as she ran to embrace her father, Marko.

"Father! You live!" Yivan said with an exuberant smile. "I knew it. I knew it was you attacking the compound again."

Marko embraced his children and breathed a sigh of relief, saying, "My little ones, how I have missed you. Where is your mother, children? I wish to hold her as well."

"She... she is... dead, Father," Yivan said haltingly, not wanting to tell Marko how Ema had given up and taken her own life. "The wizards killed her."

Marko asked no more questions after that. It did not matter to him the how of his love's death. Bringing revenge to every wizard still alive in this compound – and the ones all over the world, too – was all that filled Marko's dark thoughts. He set the Hall of Study ablaze and stalked away with a look of murder on his face.

TWENTY-EIGHT
2015 AD
Shanghai, China

As Yivan tells me of his time in the Wizards Guild compound, and of how spell tomes are made, all I can think is... bullshit.

"It's not possible; it can't be true. Everything I know about wizard magic can't be a lie, Yivan," I say, thinking of E.J., Aurora, and Joyee. Not to mention all the spell tomes I've ever held in my hands, like... "Every Network book is fuelled by a dead mage?" I say, feeling disgusted and avoiding eye contact with this dangerous man. "Do all wizards know about this, Yivan?"

"No, most wizards alive today have no idea how things are done. Your friends are not mage killers themselves, Jaret," Yivan says, easing my shock, even if only by a small amount.

"That's a relief," I mutter.

"However, they do contribute to mage deaths just by the mere fact of their existence. Spell tomes are still made in the same fashion as they were 1000 years ago. The Wizards Guild now has smarter, cleaner, and simpler ways of doing their dirty work. In fact, my current tactics are heavily inspired by them."

Yivan pauses, staring at a spot on the ceiling, lost in his memories. The Maelstrom sighs and rubs his face wearily. Reliving all of this horrible shit from his past must be wearing him down, which I may be able to use to our advantage. The weaker he is, the better for my team and me.

"I believe you, Yivan," I say stonefaced. "I do. What you went through must have been terrifying. But how can you use that awful experience to justify... all of this... becoming the Maelstrom and murdering thousands of people?"

Yivan looks at me flatly and emotionlessly. His eyes seem to never blink, and his chest neither rises nor falls for several heartbeats as his eyes bore into me. "I was born with this power, Jaret," he explains in a heartless timbre. "It is my birthright. It is every mage's birthright, and those weaklings found a way to steal it from us. Yet, they were still afraid of us, don't you see? They did not then, nor have they ever deserved magic."

Eyes locked with his, I see the torment hidden within; I feel the pain of his tragedy, even though it lies a thousand years in the past. "I'm sorry, Yivan. I can't imagine going through what you have," I tell him sincerely. "But that doesn't explain how or why you are still alive 1000 years later and killing all kinds of people without regard; mages, wizards, and regs. This is where my sympathy ends. I'm a cop, Yivan. I have to take you in front of the Mage High Council for judgment."

He nods and says, "I understand, Jaret. But do realize you are in no position to take me anywhere. I am your better and so you will have to do as I say. You will have to help me to finish what I started."

"And what is that, huh? What have you started, Yivan? Why do you need my help?" I blurt out, anxious for the end – for the real truth.

"I am getting to that part. You must be patient and listen, Jaret. That was our agreement, after all," the Maelstrom calmly reminds me.

"Alright, fine. I'm following your story so far, as impossible as it all sounds, and I'm trying not to judge you too harshly," I say. "You were a product of your environment, after all. Your parents were serial killers and they taught you and your sister to do the same thing." Again, sometimes I just don't know when to shut the hell up.

Yivan scowls at me, once more invoking a look of rage far beyond what a well-adjusted person would be capable of, and hisses, "It was a different time. My parents did as their parents taught them. It wasn't their fault, Jaret. They, too, were a product of their environment. It is how mages lived in those days."

"It's still no excuse, Yivan," I say, not willing to concede his point. "Evil is evil. You understood that, even back then from what you've told me. So why are you the one doing it now?"

"It is… all I know," Yivan softly admits. "I cannot change, Jaret. I will have justice for what happened to us. That is all that I care about now."

"Justice," I whisper. That's what this is all about for Yivan. But, to be honest, revenge is a more appropriate word. "I still don't understand how you've survived for so long," I tell him. "Magic can't keep you alive for 1000 years. If it could, the world would be full of ancient mages and wizards."

He raises a finger and says to me, "I will tell you that part later. It will be quite interesting to a student of spells, such as yourself."

Interesting? Yes. His story is interesting. It's tragic. It's heartbreaking. But none of that, no matter what else happened to him, is a reason for murdering one person, let alone the massive scale of killing for which this man is responsible. And while I'm sure it's all quite fascinating, I can't forget what he has done. The attacks when I was a child. Rainbow. Tian Yi. Liang. Thousands of people, all murdered by this one man.

Yes, what happened to him was awful, that's true. But it does not excuse what he has done since then... It does not excuse what he has become. I have to stop this maniac. All I need is a little time and his trust. Console him. Agree with him. Earn his confidence, and then? Take him down.

"Can we take a break, Yivan?" I say with a yawn. "I need something to drink, and a place to... um, relieve myself."

Yivan, surprised by my interruption, considers for a moment, and says, "Oh, yes. Forgive me. Please, go find a drain grate to relieve yourself. I will have Herod bring you some refreshments."

After a much-needed piss, I return to find a pitcher of ice water and a few sandwiches waiting for me. I dig in, and Yivan continues his long story.

"Now, as we left the Hall of Study, escape and the safety of my sister were the only things on my mind. My father had different plans, however. He wanted the blood of every wizard to stain the sands of Egypt."

"That is not a normal way to feel," I say. "You do know that, right?"

"Jaret, I thought by now you would understand. Wizards are the evil ones. We were the ones trying to stop them."

I raise my hands in surrender and remember that I am attempting to convince Yivan that I am on his side. "Sorry. Sorry, please continue," I say. "The wizards were using our stolen magic. I'm with you."

"Precisely," Yivan says with renewed vigor, "Magic is ours."

TWENTY-NINE
1009 AD
Cairo, Egypt

Marko, Maeris, Yivan, and the Healer all ran through the streets of the Wizards Guild compound, eradicating anyone who dared show their face.

"How will we get past the Rego Army, Father?" Yivan said between gasps for air, hands on his knees.

Marko smiled at his son, so happy to find him still alive. Maeris, like her father, wasn't even winded or sweating from the night's escape, and that made Marko even prouder.

Looking at his tired son, Marko said, "We go through them, my beautiful boy. My wife is dead. Today, I shall either avenge my sweet Ema or join her in death."

As they exited the front gate of the Wizards Guild compound, an army of thousands stood in their way. In a strange moment of déjà vu, Yivan noticed a lone man walking towards them, hands in the air.

"Please, let us talk peacefully for the time being. I am Captain Zahi of the Rego Army, you may call me Zahi, friend," the man said as he neared the mage family.

"You are not my friend, soldier," Marko replied.

"Ah, well, either way, mage, I have come to offer you a solution to our collective problem. As you can see, we outnumber you by thousands. You can kill many of us today, but you will fall eventually," Captain Zahi said icily.

Marko ignited his body in dancing flames, a wild look in his red eyes. He surged forward and let out an inhuman roar, saying, "PERHAPS, REG, BUT YOU DIE FIRST!"

"Son, please. Wait a moment before you get us all killed," the Healer said in a soothing manner. "What solution do you offer, captain?"

"A mage with some sense. Excellent," Captain Zahi said with a nervous laugh. "Well, old mage, I offer your family the chance to live forever… as a part of the Ether."

In the next heartbeat, four wizards appeared out of nowhere, each holding an empty spell tome. Yivan was expecting treachery and knew the wizards' plan as soon as he saw them step out of non-existence in front of him. He burst into action instantly. Using Storm winds, he knocked his three family members backward with one hand, and with the other arm sent lightning into the hearts of all five men standing before him. They fell to the sand void of life and blackened beyond recognition.

Yivan had been incredibly fast, he thought. His reflexes were quicker than anyone he knew of. But Yivan had not been quite fast enough. One of the men had time to throw the tome from his hands before the surge of electricity connected with his chest, stopping his heart from ever beating again. The airborne tome sailed directly towards Yivan's sister.

Maeris, oblivious to the danger, called forth her whip of frozen lightning to deal with these pathetic wizards and their foul reg soldier. The spell tome landed on her chest right as the conjured magical weapon appeared in her hand. There was a green glow, and a pulling sensation, which felt like the opposite of wind.

"MAERIS! NOOOOOOO!" Yivan howled into the night.

Marko, unaware of what happens to a mage using magic while holding an empty spell tome, had no idea anything was wrong. He was solely focused on the army surrounding his family. Still engulfed in flames, he began sending giant balls of Fire into the Rego Army, incinerating dozens of men at a time, and causing the night to smell of burned meat.

Maeris lay there on the warm desert floor, an unmoving and desiccated corpse. Her skin, as dry as the sand she lay on, pulled tight across her bones. Yivan fell to his knees and pulled the mummified body into his lap, hugging it and wailing in sorrow. The Healer joined Yivan to see what could be done. He connected with the Ether and pulled forth his healing Water. Magic fell through Maeris's empty shell like rain would a hole in a roof.

"Grandfather, bring her back! PLEASE!" Yivan begged the Healer.

"Yivan, I... I don't think it's possible. I am trying every spell I know, but there is nothing left of your sister in this husk," the elderly Water mage admitted. "She has left this plane of existence."

"SON!" roared Marko, his entire body flowing with wild Fire magic. "JOIN ME! LET US DEVOUR THESE WIZARDS WITH OUR COMBINED POWER!"

Marko continued standing in one spot while rotating and burning the Rego Army that surrounded them. Any soldier that ran towards the family of mages was turned to ash in mere seconds. Luckily, the three remaining mages were just outside of javelin and spear range. Unluckily, the archers had now moved to the front ranks, and their reach was quite a good bit longer than that of the spears and javelins.

The first volley came towards them, and Marko encased himself and his family in a globe of his hottest Fire. The arrows fell around them in the sand in the hundreds, but any that would have ended the mages' lives burned instantly as they fell through Marko's flaming barrier.

"Grandfather, please!" Yivan continued to beg.

The Healer was a man renowned in mage society as a marvelous and powerful healer going back hundreds of years. He should be able to bring Maeris back with his immense talents.

"It is no good, Yivan! Maeris is dead! I have no power over death," the Healer said with tears running down his cheeks.

Marko, for the first time, heard what was going on behind him. The Fire covering his body extinguished instantly, and his flaming barrier, too, disappeared.

"My daughter is… dead?" Marko asked haltingly, his throat somehow unable to draw enough breath.

Yivan turned to look at his father, tears streaming from his eyes, and moaned, "Yes, Poppa. She is gone. The wizards took her from us!"

Marko's eyes went to the dried-out corpse of his youngest child lying in the sand. His lip trembled as he gazed at the husk that was once his pride and joy.

Unable to hold back his sorrow, he tearfully asked, "How? What happened? She was…huhh!"

Following the sound of what seemed a short yet rapid bout of drumming, Marko's left eye came out of his face carried by the force of an arrow, interrupting his questions.

He fell over, lifeless and limp. As he tumbled to the sand, Yivan saw that many more arrows had found their way into his father's back. The Healer looked at the last of his sons now sprawled dead in the desert, and then he stared into Yivan's eyes and nodded acceptance.

"We are lost, child."

A black cloud suddenly fell over the two mages, a rain of arrows that would silence their magic for all of eternity. Rage filled Yivan as he felt the looming threat descend towards them. His mother, his father, and his little sister – all dead. The anger inside of him built until he felt it would kill him, leaving him unable to breathe.

Instead, Yivan tried to calm down and focus his thoughts, just as the Healer taught him to do during their time together.

"I am no child, grandfather," Yivan growled.

Gathering the air surrounding him and his grandfather, Yivan controlled it with his favored connection to the Ether: Storm magic. The arrows slowed their rapid descent and stopped in the air inches from Yivan and the Healer.

The Rego Army stood in stunned silence. They had never before seen magic this powerful. To stop a thousand arrows in the air and hold them still was an absolutely horrifying display of magic on its own, yet even more so as the arrows slowly turned around and pointed back at the army – the same men who first fired the arrows.

The Rego Army as one began to run in the other direction as fast as they could.

"Can you bring back my sister and my father, Healer?" Yivan asked his grandfather in a grim tone.

"No, Yivan. It is impossible," he replied. "I am sorry. They are dead. I cannot heal the dead. Using magic on a corpse is forbidden, and I've already broken that law just by trying."

Yivan looked to his father, filling the Egyptian sand with his lifeblood. He looked to his sister, his beloved Maeris, as dry as the winds Yivan controlled. The rage instantly returned to the young man in a flash of lightning and misery. He then looked to his elderly grandfather and said, "Then what good are you to me?"

A dozen of the arrows floating in the air flew quickly towards the Healer and pierced the old Water mage through his chest. He gasped once and then fell to the side, as lifeless as the rest of Yivan's family.

The last mage standing in Cairo that night, a powerful young Storm mage named Yivan, sent the rest of the arrows chasing after the fleeing soldiers. Cries of pain followed their attempted escape, and he knew that many were no longer running; they were dying. Yivan saw that many would escape; they would flee and tell of the actual power that mages could wield.

"Good," he said to himself. "Run away, little regs."

Yivan turned his gaze now to the Wizards Guild compound. The Hall of Study in the very center was still burning brightly from Marko's Fire. The rest of the buildings, however, stood untouched, and that made the youthful mage fume violently. His features became twisted with a fury that Yivan had never felt before in his life. He unleashed a guttural roar and began tearing the entire compound apart with his Rock magic. Walls exploded into dust, buildings crumbled to the ground, and the earth shook and swallowed whole sections of the large complex. A solitary wizard stumbled from the rubble, bleeding heavily from a multitude of wounds covering his body. He fell to the sand near Yivan, and began to die.

214

The young mage slowly made his way to the dying wizard, and said, "It is over, wizard. I have destroyed everything; all traces of your people. You will no longer trouble this world."

The dying man laughed at Yivan, bloody foam leaking from his smiling mouth as he gurgled through red teeth, "You have no idea of what you speak, mage. This is not everything. It is only one of many. Every day more and more compounds are made to house our growing numbers while your numbers slowly dwindle as we take your magic. You cannot win, mage. We are too many. And one day soon, our magic will be stronger than yours ever..."

Yivan grew tired of listening to the ramblings of a dying man, and dropped a large boulder on his face, ending their conversation once and for all. "So, there are more compounds," Yivan said to the headless corpse beside him. "More wizards. I shall enjoy destroying each and every one of them. All I need is more power."

As he walked away from the carnage, Yivan stooped to pick up the tome that held his sister's eternal connection to the Ether, and said, "Death magic. I must know more of this."

THIRTY
2005 AD
Birmingham, Alabama

"Are you sure you want to marry a reg, Jaret? With all of those silly secrecy rules you mages have?" E.J. asks. "You'll have to lie to her for the rest of your life about your job at the MOP. If your kids are mages, they'll have to lie to her. It's insane."

"You still don't get it," I say. "I can't breathe without saying her name. I can't sleep without dreaming about her. I'm sure, man. She's everything to me. I've been able to hide the truth from her for two years; I can keep it up."

E.J. shakes his head, bewildered, and looks me over from top to bottom with an appraising eye. "You look good, man," he says, and then strikes a pose and asks, "How's the better, I mean best man look?"

"You look like a stupid asshole to me," I say. "But I love you. Thanks for doing this."

E.J. hits me with a giant fist, and I instantly know it's bruised. "I'm honored you asked, Jaret. Really. But are you sure about this? Her parents seem to hate your fucking guts."

Rolling my eyes, I answer, "Hey, man, watch the language. We're in church, for Christ's sake. I mean… for goodness' sake. Yes, her parents aren't my biggest fans, and I don't even know why."

"Well, you can always change your mind," E.J. says with a smile, "and find a sweet wizard to settle down with."

"A wizard? Don't be gross," I say, pretending to gag. He hits me again, and I resist the urge to immediately seek medical attention.

E.J. points an enormous finger in my face and says, "One day, you'll wish you had married a magic user, Jaret. Mark my words, homie."

"Not a chance," I quip. "So what – I'm going to have to keep my magic a secret. Big deal. What could go wrong?"

Though I kept expecting something to go horribly wrong, and for someone to accidentally reveal magic to the regs in the family, everything was perfect. Our wedding ceremony was beautiful and, unexpectedly, went off without a hitch. My mother was in tears throughout, and I thought of my dad several times, wishing he were there.

"Your father would be so proud of you, Jaret," Aunt Janie says, bringing me out of my daze. She holds out two plates of food for me, urging me to take them.

"Thanks, Aunt Janie, but I'm not that hungry. One plate will be enough," I say with a wink.

"The other one is for your bride… I mean wife," Aunt Janie says. "You both need to take a minute and eat something. This day is going to fly by and if you don't eat, you won't have any energy left to consummate the marriage tonight."

Oh, dear God. Is my aunt talking to me about having sex with my wife? Change the subject… quickly!

"Thanks for the food, Aunt Janie," my wife Kelly says. "Don't worry, I'll make sure Jaret has plenty of energy for tonight."

"Oh dear Lord," I say. "Look, you're both embarrassing the crap out of me. Honey, let's sit down and eat so we can stop this horrifying conversation."

The two women look at each other and burst out with raunchy laughter. Kelly takes my hand and starts to lead me away to our table, but I hold back.

"You go on ahead, Kel. I'll be there in just a minute," I tell her.

"Alright, handsome. Don't make me wait too long," Kelly replies while pinching my ass before going to sit at our place of honor in the reception hall.

"Aunt Janie, I just wanted to thank you again for helping me get on with the MOP," I whisper. "Seriously, I can never thank you enough. It's everything I dreamed of."

"You're welcome, dearie," she says, waving my thanks away. "What does your wife, the reg, think you do?"

Almost all the magic users in my life believe I'm crazy for marrying a reg, but Aunt Janie has been the least vocal about it. This is the first time I've heard her refer to Kelly as a reg.

"She thinks I'm a freelance writer," I tell Aunt Janie. "I told her it's mainly ghostwriting, and so my name isn't on anything. I think that'll work."

I can tell Aunt Janie doesn't approve, but she doesn't say a word about it, only asking, "What does Kelly do again?"

"She has a Master's in Business, and works in corporate negotiations," I say. "Something about mediating conflicts, and helping find resolutions. She's apparently excellent; they just promoted Kelly to head up her own team. She's a boss now!"

"Well, Jaret, from what I hear, you will be a boss soon. In five years you've gone from an unpaid intern to Second in Command at your office. That's quite impressive," Aunt Janie says with pride.

"Thanks," I say, blushing a bit. "I'm sure that I've still got plenty to learn before I get my own team."

"Do people ever recognize you as you arrest them?" she asks.

"Sometimes. Not as often as a few years ago," I explain. "There are new Speedcasting heroes these days. No one thinks about the past much, I guess."

"Well, I do. I think about the past and I think about you and your father all the time," she says with watery eyes.

Why did she have to bring him up? I'm trying my absolute hardest not to break down today on this happy occasion. Of course, I think about him all the time, too; especially today... I just wish he was here.

"Yeah, well. Thanks again, Aunt Janie. I love you," I say hurriedly, trying to escape before getting into a longer conversation that will only make me sad.

She pulls me close for a hug and whispers, "You don't have to lie to her, you know. Plenty of regs marry into mage families and eventually learn the secret. But they also happen to learn the importance of it being kept a secret. Just something to think about, Jaret."

"Thanks, Aunt Janie, but I'm an officer of the law. It's my job to protect that secret at all costs. It would be irresponsible of me to break our most important rule."

She pats me on the back and walks away while saying, "Give it time, dearie. Give it time."

E.J., seeing my aunt leave, comes walking over to me in a rush, looking wide-eyed in shock.

"Jaret, you'll never believe what I just read on the Network," he says a little too loudly.

"Dude, you can't be on the Network here. There are regs around, man," I mutter sternly.

"Don't worry, I went upstairs and found an empty room," he explains. "Anyway, the reason I checked it was because I got an email from my department at the Wizards Guild. They announced that the WPS was joining forces with the MOP."

"That's not big news, E.J. We work together sometimes if the Guilds have intersecting interests in a crime or event," I say, exasperated. "Like a mage and a wizard were robbing banks recently. They were working together, and so I had to work with a WPS agent on the case. It happens."

"No, man. I mean they are joining forces! Like becoming one entity! That's why I checked the Network," he says too loudly, once again. This time, I don't care. There is no way they are becoming one police force. The Guilds pretty much hate each other!

"Show me," I say flatly.

We head upstairs to the empty room he had just used and access the Network via his pocket-sized tome. They're all the rage these days. No more carrying around a big dusty book. Now you can access the Network on the go more conveniently. Honestly, though, the little tomes are a real thorn in the side of the magical law enforcement community, as more and more magic users are starting to use them in public places while surrounded by regs.

E.J. goes straight to the primary magical news source, *Magicae est Potentia*, and finds the article.

It's the first of many steps towards more cooperation between the two Guilds. The Mage High Council and the Wizard High Council have created a dual division law enforcement office in Moscow.

The first of its kind in the world, this office will service all of Moscow for mage and wizard crime. Composed of a lead agent, a Second in Command and a mixed group of field agents, this department of mages and wizards all in the same office will be working together to keep our world a secret from the regs, and to stop unscrupulous magic users from taking advantage of others.

For more on this story, check back tomorrow when we will interview the first head of a dual division MOP / WPS office ever, a wizard by the name of Christopher "Blinky" Taylor, who is renowned for his skill with teleport spells.

"I can't believe it. This is huge, Eej!" I shout, using my nickname for the Jolly Giant. "This might be just what we need to bring our people closer together. I mean, you're really the only wizard I'm friends with. That's pretty sad. The agent I worked the bank robbing case with wouldn't even have a beer with me afterward."

"He didn't recognize you from Speedcasting?" E.J. asked.

"No! He had no idea that I was once a famous competitive sport Champion," I say.

"Well, that sport is more of a mage thing, I guess," E.J. admits. "Do you ever watch the Network show TomeTime? Where wizards compete to see who can hold the most within them from a set of never-before-seen spells?"

"NO! And that's my point, Eej. I should watch it. It's about magic, isn't it? That's something we all have in common. I'll be happy when mages and wizards can finally put the past behind us and come together. There is no reason for our two Guilds to be so distant," I say, all in a rush.

"You're right, man," E.J. replies with a sad smile, "but I just don't see it ever happening. It would be nice, but... we're just too different."

"That's just it. I don't think we're all that different, Eej. Our magic comes from the same place, right? We just find it in different ways," I say. "Come on, let's get back to the party."

THIRTY-ONE
1011 AD
Marseille, France

The two years following the loss of his family and escape from the Wizards Guild were full of sorrow and survival for Yivan. Other mages he encountered often told rumors of the wizards searching for a young mage going by the name of Yivan, so he decided the best way to survive was solitude.

Yivan stayed away from regs, wizards, and mages alike. He preferred the quiet calm of loneliness. Whenever he was around other people, Yivan became angry... furious at them for having the nerve to live their lives while his family were all dead.

Working with his magic constantly, Yivan gained strength in his spells. He became faster. He became more experienced with his two schools of magic, and many created new and destructive spells. But it wasn't enough. Yivan wanted revenge. He wanted to hurt the wizards. Every single one of them.

One night while somewhere in the freezing snows near the County of Flanders, an area between Northern France and Belgium, Yivan stared down the arrow shaft of his own mortality. It was cold; too cold, in fact. And Yivan was on the verge of starving, as his most recent meal was a distant memory. Yivan could always find water here, by putting snow in his waterskin and heating it with crackling Storm energy. It was this very process, the melting of the snow with lightning, that gave Yivan his most ingenious idea.

"I am…not…going…to…make it. It's… t-t-too c-c-c-old," Yivan chattered through his teeth to himself.

He warmed the snow in his waterskin past the melting point until the water was almost boiling. Yivan drank deeply, ignoring the burning pain in his mouth and throat. The magnificent heat filled him and spread outward. It felt wonderful but did not last.

The powerful young mage wept in despair at the state of his life. He was adrift, alone, and close to the end. Pulling out Maeris's spell tome, the book which held within its pages the lasting memory of his sister, Yivan spoke to it, as he often did.

"I wish… that you were h-h-here, sweet s-s-s-sister. I w-w-wish, too, that I was w-w-warm," Yivan said morosely to the spell tome. Suddenly, his mind became crystal-clear for a moment, and he thought, "Why can't I warm myself? It works on the snow, why not my blood?"

Yivan focused inwardly and calmed his thoughts, letting the Ether open to flood energy into his bloodstream. Storm power touched his veins and mingled with his circulating blood. The effect was immediate, as he quickly grew warm.

Yivan also no longer felt hungry. He had more energy than when his grandfather had filled him with Water magic and given him the strength to make it to Cairo after a long night of drinking. This felt tremendous. More than revived, and no longer knocking at death's door, Yivan became motivated once more to resume his hunt.

Months later he still pulsed with the same powerful spell, having cast it only that one time. Yivan was traversing the French countryside near the southern coast and came across the first Wizard Compound he had seen since his escape from the Egyptian desert. It was smaller, yet better fortified. Tall towers stood at every corner of the four-sided fortress. Wizards moved at the top of those towers, keeping watch for anyone approaching, ready to blast the trespassers with slow and pathetic wizard magic.

Here, too, they had a Rego Army. It was smaller by half than the one he had fought in Cairo, this one consisting of around 5,000 heavily armed men. There was no way Yivan could do this alone, though. If he dealt with the wizards first, the army would kill him. If he dealt with the regs first, the wizards would destroy him.

Yivan decided the best course of action would be to stay close, and wait for the right time. A single wizard would have to come out of the fortress sooner or later, and Yivan would be waiting. He had many questions that needed answering, and his parents had long ago taught him how to seek such answers.

His chance came a month later when a wizard emerged from the compound, all alone, and walked along a path heading east away from the Wizards Guild. Yivan plotted a course that would take him to the path farther along, to intercept the unsuspecting wizard. There, Yivan lay in wait for the man to show up.

As the hooded wizard walked along a path on the way to meet with a new group of nine mage volunteers, there lay a man in the road, unconscious. He was filthy and smelled as if he had not bathed for ages. The wizard approached and put a boot into the man's ribs. He stirred but did not awaken. Marie threw back her hood and kneeled next to the filthy man.

"Allo? Are you well, monsieur? Can you hear me?" she said with a decent amount of both genuine care and trepidation.

Yivan rolled over and, expecting a man, fumbled for words when he saw this woman. Her features were… shocking, to say the least. The wizard's nose was crooked and broken so that badly that it bore only a passing resemblance to a nose. Her hair was cut short and looked as though it felt like straw. She had one pupil colored purple, and the other was blood red. A puffy, pink scar ran from the left side of her top lip down to her throat. She also appeared to have only one ear.

Still, she *was* a woman and Yivan had been out of the company of other people for a long while. This wizard smelled of lavender and sage, and Yivan's pants grew tight at the curves in her cloak.

"Here now, monsieur. Stop staring. I know that I am quite ugly, I don't need to be stared at," Marie said, only mildly annoyed as she was used to constant stares.

"Madame, I think you are quite attractive," Yivan retorted. "I apologize for staring, however. Would you care to help me up? I would be grateful to you, and would gladly share some of my food."

"No offense," the woman said, "but if your food is in a similar state to the rest of you, then I shall politely decline."

Yivan took her offered hand and dusted himself off once standing, then said, "I can assure you the food is clean and safe to eat. Please, I have not seen another person in so long, I would love to have a conversation. Just for a little while."

He may have been road-dirty and a little disgusting, but beneath that, Marie could tell he was handsome and intelligent. It had been a long time since a handsome and intelligent man wanted anything to do with her.

Though she knew better, the loneliness of her life proved too powerful for Marie to turn down the company of this seemingly nice man, and so she replied, "Ok, monsieur. Let us get off the road and enjoy some lunch. I was going to wait until I got a little closer to my destination, but I would rather enjoy some pleasant conversation before the dreary work that lay ahead of me."

Yivan led the thuggish wizard to the lean-to where he had slept for the past month. He produced some fruit and dried meat from a bag and offered her choice pieces from each. They sat and discussed the weather of the day and past week, the beauty of the countryside, and the nice food that Yivan had been right about.

Marie pulled out a wineskin and offered some to Yivan. He gladly accepted and felt the warmth spread through his chest in a similar fashion to that of the boiling snow water that had given him a new lease on life.

"So, you are a wizard, madame," Yivan suddenly asked.

Marie's eyes grew suspicious as her lips pressed tightly together and her fingers moved to a practiced position, ready to cast. Quickly, she snapped, "Why would you say such a thing?"

"Well, you came from the direction of the Wizards Guild compound. I only assumed," Yivan answered innocently.

She appraised this man again, noting that he was not cold. He had no cloak to ward off the winter chill, and yet seemed quite comfortable.

"Monsieur, how was it that you came to be lying there in the road? What happened to you?" Marie asked carefully.

"I was waiting for *you*, my dear," Yivan said grimly, wrapping her in Storm wind, binding both arms to her side, and closing her hands into fists to prevent finger movements.

"Release me, mage! I am expected somewhere. They will be looking for me. Save yourself the trouble and flee while you can," Marie said with an edge of desperation in her trembling voice.

"I think not, mon ami," Yivan taunted. "You see, I am in need of some information, and only a wizard can provide the answers I seek. If your answers are to my satisfaction, I will release you alive. If they are not, I will hurt you. Very, very badly."

Marie suddenly became afraid for the first time since learning magic. The power of being a wizard had given her the ability to look those simple, taunting people in the eye and tell them exactly what they could do with their opinions of her physical appearance. It had given Marie some much-needed confidence. But now, that was all gone and she felt only fear.

"Tell me about Death magic," Yivan ordered without emotion. "How do I access the Death Ether? How does it work?"

Marie was shocked that this man knew anything about the Wizards Guild's biggest secret. She looked at this wild mage and reached a certain and fearful conclusion.

"You are the one," she sighed in fear. "The mage of Storm and Rock. The one who, by all accounts, destroyed an entire Guild compound without help. Are you not?"

"I am he," Yivan admitted. "Now speak, wizard. My patience grows thin."

Despite her loyalty to the Guild, Marie told Yivan everything she knew. She was terrified of what this mage could do to her, and so she explained as best she could.

"My name is Marie. I have been at this compound for one and a half years, but only the wizards who work in the Hall of Study have access to the knowledge of Death magic, monsieur. We all know of its existence and its use in crafting spell tomes, but we are not all taught how it is controlled. Wizards are brought in and taught magic from spell tomes, oui. If we show skill in a certain area, this is where we are assigned. Crafting, conjuration, necromancy, destruction, Ether walking…"

"Is this how wizards appear from out of nowhere?" Yivan interrupted. "Ether walking?"

"Oui. It is. I am… very unskilled in this area," she said, her cheeks turning red.

"What *is* your area of expertise, Marie?" Yivan asked.

"I am skilled in negotiations, using coercion spells and calming spells. It doesn't seem very powerful, but I can make people do whatever I want…" She paused and looked down at her balled-up fists and immobile arms. "As long as I have the full use of my appendages, that is. That is a very useful skill, no?"

Yivan laughed at the thought and said, "It is weak, Marie. I can make people do what I want as well. As I am right now, with you."

"Yes, but no one knows that I've done anything at all," Marie said slyly. "That is more dangerous, I'm thinking."

Yivan once again admired the curves beneath her cloak, but shook the thoughts from his mind and said, "So you know nothing of Death magic. Who does and where do I find them?"

"Well, it would be the wizards in the Hall of Study, as I told you," Marie explained. "But they never leave the compound. They are the most secretive of all our factions. Their knowledge is kept under lock and key."

Yivan, frustrated, released her bonds with a thought and growled in frustration, throwing his food into the grass nearby.

"Then you are of no use to me. Go, now. But know this, I will be long gone before you reach the compound. There is no use in telling anyone about our talk. I will come back if I find that you have lied to me, though. And you will be very sorry if I do."

Marie stood up and contemplated using her magic on Yivan before she remembered the reports of what he did in Cairo. Marie came to her senses and decided to leave. Yivan, in his stimulated yet repressed state, took her hesitation for something else entirely.

"If you wish to stay, remove your clothes. I find that I have a hunger for you. If not, please leave before I change my mind and fill your body with Storm energy until your organs flow out of your mouth, nose, and ears."

Marie considered for a moment. He smelled dreadful, but he was handsome. She had not been with a man for years. Perhaps it wouldn't be a bad idea to stay. She definitely couldn't tell anyone in the Guild about this if she did.

"We must be quick," Marie said as she dropped her cloak and other garments to the ground, her breath coming in exited gasps.

"Do not worry about that, wizard. I have never done this before. It will be quick."

Later, Yivan's lean-to was swallowed by the ground and buried under Rock. His Storm magic pulsed in his veins and sped his pace as he left the area in a mad dash.

"I should have killed that wizard," he thought aloud as he raced off. "They all deserve to die." But he couldn't bring himself to murder her after they had lain together. There were some lines he still wouldn't cross, no matter how much he hated the thieving bastards.

If he ever saw her again, then he would destroy her. That thought alleviated his guilt as he sped away in search of someone who could teach him about Death magic. If it took his whole life, he would find what he sought.

And with that pulse charging through his blood, keeping him from being tired and hungry, he felt that his life might actually be quite a good deal longer than he had ever imagined.

THIRTY-TWO
2015 AD
Shanghai, China

Yivan pauses from his retelling of the past and grins with a far-off look in his eye, probably thinking of something he's not telling me. Must be a good memory, too; he seems happy.

"Since I could not find a wizard that knew anything of Death magic, I began killing them," Yivan goes on to explain. "It felt good and I thought Death magic most likely came from death. Perhaps that is how the wizards discovered it in the first place. But, no matter how often I tried, I found it impossible to access the Death Ether in this way. Believe me, Jaret, I tried and tried. Killed hundreds of the creatures, but had nothing to show for it. This went on for what seemed an eternity."

"How much time did you spend aimlessly murdering people?"

"Until about 30 years ago. I've been through madness and sanity. I've spent an entire decade by myself on a mountain. I spent a century living on boats in the ocean. This whole time, for close to 950 years, I have killed wizards and tried to find the Death Ether. And then one day, I came across a study of dead wizards, an extremely intriguing subject for me, as you can imagine. The man who wrote it asked what came to be the most crucial question of all: What happens to unspent spells when wizards die?"

I know the man who wrote this particular article. He is sitting behind Yivan right now. "Herod, the lying piece of shit," I snarl.

"Aye, laddy. 'Twas I who wrote the article," Herod shamefully admitted.

"So that is when you sold your worthless soul to work for the Maelstrom?" I ask.

Yivan sits forward in the blink of an eye, glaring at me, and shouts, "Stop being so dramatic, Jaret! I am not the Devil! I am not evil!" Closing his eyes, and slowing his breathing, Yivan then adds, "I am not the villain in this story, Jaret."

"Okay, okay," I say to appease him. "So you sought out the author of this study on dead wizards?"

"Yes, I had to meet Herod. I knew that he was the key to finally finding the Death Ether. I had long since thought that if they can use the Ether to take our magic, we should be able to use the Ether to reclaim it. Dead wizards' unspent spells were the key. The story he told you about our first encounter was a lie. I contacted him on the Network, expressing interest in his theory."

"Oh, everything that comes out of his drunken, Scottish mouth is a lie, then. Nice to know," I say with my arms folded over my chest.

Herod can only stare at his feet with a frown on his face, too guilty to say a word to me. Yivan smiles and says, "Jaret, shame on you. You've embarrassed my servant."

"Fuck him, I don't care if he feels bad," I snap back.

Yivan gives a nonchalant shrug and continues. "Herod already had knowledge of the Death Ether, as he worked in the Library of Discovery, which is what they now call the Hall of Study. The wizards claim its purpose is to create new spells, but that is also a lie. We both know that wizards don't create spells, they only follow the orders written in a book by dead mages."

"So what did you actually do in the Library of Discovery, Herod?" I say with disgust.

"Research," Herod replies quietly.

"Exactly what you think he did, Jaret. Experimented with our magic," Yivan says.

"I never killed or tortured anyone, matey boy. I swear it," Herod says firmly. "I had no knowledge of Mage Farms. All of my work was theoretical. As usual, we were tryin' ta find a way for wizards to use magic without tomes."

"Yes, well," Yivan cuts in, just before I can ask what the fuck a Mage Farm is. He then says, "Once I revealed myself to Herod and expressed interest in his line of study, we formed – I would not call it friendship – more of a mutual interest in the truth."

Despite my better judgment, I say, "Herod, you teamed up with the Maelstrom. I hope you're at peace with all the deaths since then. Their blood is on your hands, too, pal."

"Jaret, my boy!" Yivan shouts. "Talk to me, not this little cretin. I thought you already understood that wizard deaths *do not matter*. They are the enemy."

Taking a deep breath, I say, "Yes, Yivan. I see what you mean."

"So, Herod told me something that led to my breakthrough with Death magic," he continues. "Every so often, a new spell will show up in an already created spell tome. No one knows how or why, but the theory is that the mage killed in that tome's creation maintains a connection with the book."

"So you can still communicate with these mages through the Ether?" I ask, my eyes wide with shock.

Yivan shrugs and says, "I honestly do not know, Jaret. I believe it is possible. I sat down with Maeris's spell tome after Herod told me of this phenomenon. I spoke to her, as I often do, though she never answers my questions. This time, however, I asked my sister how to access the Death Ether. The next day there was a new spell in her tome."

"That won't do you any good, it's wizard magic. We can't use their magic," I say.

Yivan shakes his head at comment. "That is a yet another lie spread by the wizards. Have you ever tried to learn a wizard spell, Jaret?"

"No, of course not," I reply.

"Have you ever used a Network tome?" Yivan asks. "The magic used in them is from an Ether called the Whispers. It is how beings all over the Etherverse communicate. Using any Network book is the same as using 'wizard magic'. The only difference in their magic and ours is that we were born with the skill to connect with the elemental Ether. They had to murder and steal to find a connection."

My heart starts to pound in my chest. My stomach feels like it might empty at any moment, and my vision goes fuzzy and dark around the edges. I know this feeling: I'm going to pass out.

"Stop, Yivan. Just… please. Stop. It's too much… I can't handle it all," I say, pulling at my shirt collar and breathing slowly. "Wizards murder mages to get their magic. You're 1000 years old. Mages can learn from tomes if they want to. What the hell is the Etherverse? I just… can I go home now? Can you let me and my team go back, please?"

Finally, after everything that has happened, I lose control of my emotions. After all the work I've done trying to convince Yivan that I am strong, that he should be afraid of me, and that I support his mission… I begin crying in front of the most powerful mage to ever walk the Earth.

"Soon, my boy. Soon. You have to hear the rest. But I promise it won't be long," Yivan says reassuringly.

I keep sobbing, and offer a nod to Yivan in acknowledgement as my throat closes tight. I can't speak if I want to.

"By using the spell Maeris's tome gave to me, I could recover our stolen magic," Yivan continues explaining. "It only works if the wizard is dead; trust me, I tried on living ones, too. It was not a pleasant sight and was quite ineffective. After I had discovered this power is when I began to kill as many wizards at once as I could. The more dead wizards together at one time, the more stolen magical energy I could reclaim, and the more powerful I could become."

"The Maelstrom," I say under my breath.

Yivan points a long, arching finger in my direction and says, "*Precisely*. Everyone thought it was about killing regs, as if I were some common terrorist. But I chose large crowds because I knew there would be a good number of wizards present, and no one would ever suspect my attacks were truly about them. The numbers of reg casualties would be so large that everyone would assume they were the targets."

He's right. As far as most people are still concerned, the attacks were all about killing regular, non-magic people. It is brilliant, yes, but also evil.

236

"So why did Herod agree to help you kill other wizards?" I ask, my body still feeling weak, but determined to reach the end of this.

Herod slumps down in his chair even more as Yivan answers, "I made a deal with him. Herod told me he was dying. His life-lengthening spell was equally as atrocious as the rest of his magic. A young, unskilled mage could have done better. So, I told him about my pulse, the spell that has lengthened my lifespan for a thousand years. Herod was desperate for it. I have never seen a man fear death as much as this worm. I have been casting it on him every so often to keep him alive, so Herod can avoid his well-earned and inevitable death. If I die, Herod dies. If I choose to stop giving him the pulse at my whim, he dies. His life is mine."

Yivan turns around to pat Herod on the shoulder as the pathetic wizard continues frowning at the floor. *Bingo.* Herod is just a scared old man who doesn't want to die yet. I get it. The whole picture is becoming clear in my mind, except for one thing.

"Ok, Yivan," I say, "but what is your endgame here, huh? What is it you need me to do?"

He rubs his hands together with a hungry look in his eyes and says, "For that, you'll need to know one more part of the story. I told you earlier that the wizards are still making tomes the same as they did long ago, except that they now have a cleaner way to do it?"

"Yeah, I've been wondering about that. How are they making tomes now?" I ask.

"For this, you have the two High Councils to thank. You see, to stop the war between us, which could only end in the eradication of all life on Earth, the two Guilds came together. They held a meeting. And they agreed to something horrible."

THIRTY-THREE
1991 AD
Rome, Italy

"Yes, but what are Mage Farms, Herod?" the Maelstrom asked.

Herod shrugged his shoulders and threw his hands in the air. "I told you I dunnae ken, Yivan. I only overheard a high-ranking wizard in the Council, when I still worked for the bastards, discussin' Mage Farms. Do ye mind that time I said to ye, 'The wizards are still gettin' new tomes made, and more than ever before'? Well, the mages are comin' from somewhere, ye ken. It's these farms, I'm sure of it, matey boy."

"I shall need to see one for myself then, Herod. Locate one for me. And be quick about it."

Over the next few months, as Herod searched, the Maelstrom plotted his next attack. The blast in Turin had provided quite a few dead wizards and a good amount of magical energy added to his strength. It was time to go somewhere new, and Yivan felt that South America seemed like a surprising departure from the rest of his attacks.

Herod spent all of his time on the prowl for the location of a Mage Farm. The name was ominous, and Herod was sure his new friend would be pleased with him if he found one. Yivan had been kind to Herod since they started working together. For a mage, the Maelstrom was very smart. Herod figured that must come with age. Being nearly 1,000 years old has its advantages, it would seem. Yivan wasn't the kindest person, though, and he *hated* wizards. And on top of that, Yivan was responsible for the deaths of thousands of innocents. Herod wasn't too keen on that fact, but the attacks furthered his research and fed Yivan's hunger for power.

And to be honest, what Yivan was doing was no worse than the murder of countless innocent mages going back 1,000 years. The wizards chose this path long ago, and Yivan was merely giving them some of their own medicine. Herod didn't mind, and only wanted to make Yivan happy. If he found a Mage Farm soon, Yivan might even provide an extra dose of the incredible Storm pulse, which made Herod feel so much younger and alive. He'd do anything to have more of that feeling, even sell out his own people and their secrets.

The Scottish wizard rang up the one contact he maintained within the Wizard High Council, a wonderful woman he had met the year before at the scene of one of Yivan's attacks. Herod had been performing some tests on the wizards' bodies after Yivan extracted their residual magical energy, when the WPS and MOP showed up, each with specialists in tow. The specialist for the Wizard Protection Services was an older Chinese woman named Mrs. Chang. Herod had fallen instantly in lust with her.

So far she had not responded to his interests, but Herod held out hope that she eventually would. Mrs. Chang had provided Herod with her card after discussing his thoughts on the

Maelstrom and said to call her if he had more information, or just needed her help with anything. Well, Herod needed her help now.

"Wei? Hello, this is Mrs. Chang," the feisty older woman answered.

"Hello, lass. This is yer favorite Scot, Herod the handsome."

"Ah, hello, Herod. How are you?"

"I'm a bit sad at the moment, Mrs. Chang. Who is this Wei fellow ye mentioned? Is that yer husband, lass?"

"My husband is long-dead, Herod. 'Wei' is how we answer the phone in China. How can I help you today? I'm actually quite busy."

Herod held his breath for a moment; he hated having to be dishonest with this woman. He really did like her. But he pushed on regardless of his reservations.

"Ye see, Mrs. Chang, I thought we could help each other, actually. I've made a breakthrough with what I think the Maelstrom has been up to, but eh, I was hopin' to trade it for some... sensitive information ye might have, bein' that you're so well respected by the Council and all."

"If it's sensitive, then I can't tell you about it, Herod. You should know this," Mrs. Chang scolded.

"Ok, lass. I'll just ring up someone else on the Maelstrom case about what those dried-out wizard corpses mean," Herod said to her, knowing she would be hooked.

Mrs. Chang didn't waste a millisecond before responding, "No! Um, I mean, yes. Let's have coffee today, Herod, shall we?"

"But dearie, aren't you in Shanghai?" Herod asked.
"Herod, I'm an Ether Walking specialist. I can be wherever you are in seconds," she said.

"Well, that's great! Meet me in Rome at the Piazza Fontana di Trevi. We can find a bite to eat and chat, then come back to my place and discuss biting each other, eh, lass?" he said in a suggestive tone.

"You... I... I'll be there at noon, Herod. Goodbye."

Yivan walked into the room, having overheard some of Herod's conversation, and asked, "Who was that, Herod?"

"Oh, jus' the love of my wee life is all," Herod dreamily responded. "She wants me, too. I can feel it."

"Be careful, wizard. Our working together has been very beneficial, and I still require inside information about your foul kind, which you have been kind enough to provide thus far. But if you begin to stray from what I desire, I will put an end to that 'wee life' of yours. Do you understand?"

Herod was once again reminded that this mage was not really his friend. He was not anyone's friend. He was a demon, hell-bent on one thing and one thing only: the destruction of the Wizards Guild and the Wizard High Council. His kindness to Herod was only a manipulation to get that which Yivan desired.

"Yes, Yivan. I do. I'm meetin' with her to find out if she knows the location of any Mage Farms, or what goes on at these places," Herod explained.

"Well then," Yivan said with a grin. "You better not be late for your rendezvous. Go. Find what I need and come back here as soon as you have the information." Yivan turned on his heels and headed back into his study, presumably to continue trying to access the Death Ether and speak with his sister.

After a delicious Italian meal al fresco, Mrs. Chang sat back in her chair and said, "That was a very nice lunch. Thank you, Herod."

"My pleasure, lass. Now, let's get down ta business. I have uncovered what I believe ta be the particular reason that the Maelstrom is blowin' wizards to hell with Storm magic," Herod whispered while looking around for spying ears.

"Ok, go on," she urged, leaning forward in her seat, anxious to hear a possible lead for her investigation. The WPS was all over her to provide more information, and no matter how many times she told them that she was just a historian, not a detective, they never let up. Relentless would describe them correctly, she thought.

"No, not now. First, you talk ta me about what I need ta know. Then I give you what ye're after."

"Yes, alright. What is it that you're looking into, Herod?" she asked.

Herod sat back in his seat and folded his hands over his chest. He heaved an enormous sigh and said, "Well, I want to know all about Mage Farms. What they are, and where can I find one?"

Her eyes went wide at the mention of the Wizard Guilds' darkest secret and she whispered, "How…"

"It does nae matter how, Mrs. Chang," Herod interrupted. "Tell me what you know, and I'll tell ye what I know. Even trade."

Mrs. Chang considered for a minute. She could get into serious trouble for this. On the other hand, she needed Herod's help. It was a tough spot to be in: the horny old Scot did have a point there. It didn't matter how he knew of their existence. It was none of her business, so she said, "Well, you are well aware of Death magic. And of how…"

She paused mid-sentence and cast her gaze around to make sure they weren't being spied on. Then Mrs. Chang said a few words of magic while moving her fingers in detailed patterns.

242

"Silenced the area around us, did ya, lass?" Herod coyly remarked.

"Can't be too careful. Anyway, you know how tomes are made?" she said, picking her story back up.

"I worked in the Library of Discovery, Mrs. Chang," Herod replied. "I'm aware of how we do what we do. I just don't know where the mages are coming from. They always seem so docile and ready ta die."

"I only know that my old boss was promoted to the position of Overseer of Mages," Mrs. Chang told him. "I had never heard that title before he gave me the news. I later heard him on a Network call discussing farms and how he would get them under control. He said there would be no problems with the mage crop under his management."

"Wow, lass. That's fucked. Proper fucked. Mage crop. Are ye sure that ye heard him, right?" Herod said with disgust. Yivan killing for power was bad enough, but raising people from birth for the sole reason to later kill them? That's positively cruel and monstrous.

"Yes, Herod, I heard right. I could then only, the same as now, come to the same conclusion you have," she said.

"Lass, even politicians are nae that evil."

"Herod, do you even know why the two High Councils were formed?" she asked the pervy old wizard.

"Yes, of course. It was ta stop the war. The damned mages and wizards were going to destroy the Earth with their idiotic fightin'. The Councils agreed to a peace treaty," he replied.

"Yes, but do you know under what conditions? What the wizards demanded, and the mages gave them?" Mrs. Chang, the detailed and brilliant historian asked.

"Well... no lass. I dunnae ken that much, ta be honest."

Mrs. Chang looked around once more, despite the barrier of silence guarding their conversation and making it entirely private, and whispered, "They asked to be allowed to raise their own families of mages, to strip them of their magic and use them to make spell tomes."

"The damn fool mages agreed, then? They allowed their own people ta be slaughtered like sheep? I cannae believe that, Mrs. Chang. I just… I just cannae."

"Believe it," she said. "It's the truth. The Wizards Guild farmed mages long ago, and it seems they still do."

Herod was silent. He worked for Yivan now – the Maelstrom – a man who did horrible things to wizards. He hated what Yivan was doing, but without the Maelstrom's Storm pulse, Herod would die. Thinking of his own situation in this way, Herod could now understand why the Mage High Council had agreed. He was no different from them.

"Ok, dear. I need to see one for meself. Where can I go?" Herod asked.

Mrs. Chang hesitated, and then thought about what Herod could tell her about the Maelstrom's intentions. She might be able to stop the madman from doing more harm to innocent people with this knowledge.

"My old boss, Patrick Odom, the new Overseer of Mages… moved to Taiwan. A little island off the coast called Xiǎo Liúqiú. There, that is all I know of it. Now, tell me, Herod. What do you know about the bodies?" the old woman asked.

"Lass, ye've read my theories about unspent spells. Ye know that somethin' is goin' on with these dead wizards," Herod explained. "But what if I told ye the Maelstrom was takin' the residual magical energy out of wizard corpses? Would ye believe me?"

Mrs. Chang's face suddenly went white. She did believe Herod. It made sense. But who would believe her, she thought sourly. And so, she decided right then to tell no one about this.

"There is no a chance we can get inside, Yivan. It's never gonnae happen," Herod said in hushed tones as they stared across the field at the wizards' fortress on the island called Xiǎo Liúqiú off the coast of Taiwan.

Yivan knew that the weak Scottish wizard was right. If only another mage as powerful as Yivan were there, together they could have breached the compound and freed the mages held inside, but alone he would have difficulty.

First, it was obviously spell-warded with magical traps on the field that lay between their vantage point on a hill nearby and the Mage Farm.

Second, in the thousand years since Yivan had been a captive, he had become very powerful. He had honed his magic and was more skilled than anyone else on Earth. Not to mention that, for the past two years, Yivan had added to his spell power by reclaiming stolen magical energy from dead wizards. But during all of that time, the wizards also honed their skills with magic. Every generation became more powerful than the last. The difference in skill level between the wizards of today, and the ones that he and his family had slaughtered in Cairo ages ago, was astonishing. The evolution of the thieving magic users was quite drastic.

Yivan could still destroy them with a thought, but the wizards could now also do the same for Yivan, especially with the kinds of numbers he saw inside the Mage Farm below them.

"I realize that, fool," Yivan spat from his angry grimace. "Though I have an idea. Long ago, I was in a similar situation. Instead of going in, I waited for one to come out alone. Then I took her."

"Ye want ta capture a wizard from inside the compound? Are ye bleedin' mad?" Herod said to the Maelstrom.

"No, Herod. I am not mad," Yivan said with calm determination, letting purple sparks jump from his menacing eyes, and said, "I am furious."

Two days later, their chance to learn more of Death magic strode out of the farm with a bag over her shoulder. "Another woman," Yivan said under his breath, with a laugh.

"Now what, Yivan?" Herod asked, intruding on Yivan's inner thoughts. "How do we take her? We cannae just leap out and blast her with spells! They'll see us, ye ken. Those towers are there for a reason."

Yivan came out of his reverie; the fond memory of his time with that unfortunate-looking woman, Marie, was still a warm spot in his cold heart. "Shut your mouth, wizard," he hissed. "I have a plan."

Sherri walked along a trail that led to her favorite spot on the island. The lighthouse offered a magnificent view of the surrounding countryside, and also of the peaceful ocean. It was the perfect place to practice the spells from her new spellbook. As she neared the tall structure, she noticed a man lying sprawled underneath a nearby tree. He lay face-down in the dirt and wasn't moving. Perhaps he was dead, she thought.

Sherri dropped her pack, and cautiously worked her way towards the mysterious figure on the ground, a spell already on her tongue and fingertips. She would not be caught unaware.

Prodding the seemingly lifeless body with the toe of her boot, she stepped back when it moaned. A sudden noise from behind caught Sherri's attention, and she spun around already casting the magic missiles previously prepared. They flew forth just as she saw the man standing behind her. The beams of purple light curved outward, then back in creating one large bolt just before slamming into his chest.

But instead of striking the man hard, the beam of light hit an invisible barrier, causing a red glow as they were absorbed. The well-protected man stood with his hands on his hips and stared at Sherri with a demonic visage. Feeling a knife suddenly at her throat, Sherri realized the man on the ground had been pretending after all. It was a good thing Sherri was well-versed in hand-to-hand combat, as well as magic.

The wizard stomped on the delicate bones of her attacker's foot, then reached up and grabbed his wrist that held the blade. Pulling the arm out in front of her, she spun around and twisted the offending arm behind the little man's back, applying pressure to his wrist until the knife dropped to the ground. A well-placed boot to the bend of his knee had the man kneeling in the field now, gasping in pain.

"Stranger, I have your companion at a disadvantage," Sherri said boldly. "Should you make any moves, I will break his arm." Yivan began to laugh. He bellowed mirthfully without moving a muscle.

"You are much more prepared than Marie was," he said, shaking his head slightly.

"Who the hell is Marie?" Sherri thought to say, but the little man whose arm she held beat her to it.

"Who in the blazes is Marie? And are ye going ta just stand there? Help me, man!"

Yivan lowered his hands from his hips and Sherri, without hesitation, snapped Herod's arm. He fell howling to the ground cursing the female wizard. Not wasting a movement, Sherri immediately began casting her own ward of protection around herself. Two could play at that game, she thought.

Unmoved by Herod's cries of pain, Yivan continued to smile as he said, "Wizard, there is no reason to fear us. I apologize for the ruse. We only wish to discuss the compound we saw you leave a short while ago. Could you tell us what it is?"

Sherri knew better than to reveal the truth about the Mage Farm, and so went with the prescribed lie they were taught to give out, saying, "It's a research facility, a branch of the Library of Discovery just looking for new spells."

Yivan took a step towards her, and Sherri readied another spell while saying, "Come no closer, stranger. Your barrier is exquisite, but I have more powerful spells in my arsenal. You do not wish to see them, I assure you."

The stranger laughed aloud once more, seeming genuinely amused by all of this. Yivan then called forth a gust of Storm wind so powerful that the trees around them uprooted and flew dozens of feet away. Sherri's barrier held, barely. However, she was blown to the ground, and the constant pressure of the wind on her barrier prevented her from getting to her feet.

The stranger stood over her and smiled that devilish grin. "You will not lie to me again, wizard. I will ask you once more to tell me the truth of that place. If you do not, I will hurt you very, very badly."

"Who are you?" Sherri asked. "Why do you want to know?" Yivan knelt closer, so that he was very near her ear, and whispered, "They call me... the Maelstrom."

Sherri knew real fear at that moment. She heard thunder pounding somewhere in the distance and looked for its source. Seeing nothing to indicate a storm rolling in, she realized that the thundering she heard was her own heartbeat in her ears.

"P... please. Don't k... kill me. I'll tell you whatever you want to know," she said, her body trembling uncontrollably.

Yivan stood tall once more and placed both hands on his hips again, saying, "Excellent choice. Now, for a little privacy, we can head over to the lighthouse nearby. It should serve as an exceptional place to have a talk. Herod, get up and carry this wizard."

Herod, still gasping in pain on the ground, sat up and shouted, "Yivan, my bloody arm is broken, lad. I cannae carry a thing." The powerful mage sighed in frustration. Without access to Water, he could not heal Herod. He sent a pulse of Storm through the Scot, just to stop the pain. It seemed to work, as Herod stood up right after the charge made its way through his system.

"Lass," Herod whispered to Sherri, "if ye have a healing spell in ye, might I suggest usin' it on me arm? I'll be much kinder ta ye than the Maelstrom, ye see? If I can't carry ye, he'll have ta do."

Sherri considered the man's words for a moment and then spoke a few words while tracing patterns in the air with one hand. Instantly, the bone knit and Herod's face showed immediate relief.

"Thank ye, lass," he said. "I promise it will all be over soon. Just tell the man what he wants ta know."

Herod bent to pick up the fellow wizard, but she said, "I can walk. I will not flee. I know what would happen if I did."

The old Scot looked to Yivan and shrugged, waiting for the Maelstrom's judgment on the matter.

"I do not care either way," Yivan said evenly. "Let us make our way to the lighthouse."

Once inside, Sherri began to try and save her life by telling the Maelstrom anything and everything she knew about the Mage Farm.

"This place, as you p… probably guessed, is where we m… make tomes," she said, still a little shaken. "We raise mage children from birth. Um, we have a boarding house where we keep the mothers. Th… they give us as many babies as they can, often becoming pregnant again directly after giving birth. Once their bodies give up and die, or they can no longer become pregnant, we… connect them with the Ether and make a spell tome. You're familiar with this process?"

Yivan glared at the horrible woman so calmly discussing these atrocious actions of the evil wizards, and growled, "I am quite familiar with the process, wizard. Go on."

"W… well, once the babies are born they move into the orphanage. In the orphanages, wizards raise the children until they reach magical maturity, at which point they are immediately connected with the Ether to create a tome. We feel it would be cruel to prolong their life and magical training."

Herod interrupts Sherri by saying, "Cruel? Ye daft bitch, everything about this is cruel. Ye're killing innocent children so that we can use magic? It's nae worth it, lass. It's vile, it is."

"Says the wizard working for the Maelstrom, a mage who has killed thousands of innocents in the past two years," Sherri said, her head held high.

Herod glowered at the floor and mumbled under his breath, "Arsehole."

"Enough, both of you. I will not have this drawn out longer than it needs to be. Her absence will be noticed. Let us continue," Yivan said before continuing his interrogation. "So, what happens to the children who never manifest a connection to the Ether - the children who will never become mages as they have no magic?"

Sherri looked away, hiding her face. This was the one part of her job that she hated. Honestly, though, she felt it was all the mages' fault. They started this fight thousands of years ago. They terrorized everyone without magic since the dawn of time! She had learned in Spell School about the history of the Councils and the Guilds. It was because of the mages' mistreatment of regular people that the Wizards Guild was formed in the first place. Everything that had happened since was their fault, not the wizards'.

But the children who never manifested any magic weren't mages. They were wholly innocent, and that is what made it hard for Sherri to sleep at night sometimes.

"We kill them," she shamefully admitted. "If they have no magic, they are of no use to us. They are killed and burned."

Yivan nodded. It was all as he had guessed: the purpose of Mage Farms, the fate of any child without magic. But he had needed to find out for himself. He wanted to know for sure. And now he did.

The wizards had always been a cancerous growth on the planet since the moment they came about. Wizards were not magical. They didn't have the right to use magic. They stole it and defiled the Ethers with their filthy touch. He enjoyed ridding the world of them and reclaiming the magic they had stolen. But it was not enough anymore. This… what they were doing… in these Mage Farms… it was wrong. No, it was worse than wrong. It was evil. He would stop it. Yivan would stop all of it.

And the only way Yivan could think of to do that was to destroy the Wizard High Council, then the Wizards Guild, and then all of the wizards on Earth. And to accomplish that, he must become utterly unstoppable.

Yivan would have to speed up his efforts. Doing so would draw more attention, though, and they would surely stop him eventually. He could not go on indefinitely like this, blowing up crowds of people just to get a few dozen wizards. The regs wouldn't stand for it, and that meant the mages and wizards would have to get involved. Mage Order and Protection and the Wizard Patrol Service would eventually catch on.

No, Yivan needed a new tactic; a new plan that was quieter, and only killed wizards. "Herod, pour the whisky in your pack down this woman's throat," Yivan ordered.

"But I was savin' that! Just ye blast her, and we'll be gone," Herod protested.

"No, please! I won't say a word to anyone, I swear it!" Sherri pleaded. But her begging fell on deaf ears. The two men's voices were raised over her cries for mercy as they discussed her fate.

"No. I do not want the wizards in the compound to find her body and think it was murder. It needs to be an accident. We are going underground, Herod. No more attacks," Yivan explained. "I need time to grow my power, and I cannot keep looking over my shoulder while doing it. Now, pour the whisky down her throat."

This time, Herod did as he was told, grumbling about the loss of a fine Scottish whisky while doing so, however. "It's a bloody fucking waste, Yivan. This is a special drink, lad." The Maelstrom only stared silently at the old Scot in reply.

Sherri sputtered and fought the flow of burning liquid as it coursed down her throat, but it did no good. Her shirt became soaked with the alcohol, even though she swallowed half of the bottle against her will. Feeling dizzy, unable to focus her thoughts, she began to feel strange. Sherri felt as if she were floating through the air. And she was.

The wizard floated right over the ledge of the lighthouse and dropped down the jagged cliffside. Her neck snapped on an outcrop of rocks, killing her instantly. Her body came to rest at the edge of the South China Sea. The waves lapped at her beautiful face, frozen forever in a look of drunken confusion.

252

THIRTY-FOUR
2015 AD
Shanghai, China

"The wizards are farming mages, Jaret. Today. Right now. Even as we speak, this is happening," Yivan says.

"And killing innocent children," I add, my chest feeling tight and my breathing coming in desperate gasps.

"It must stop," Yivan says coldly.

"So, what is it you want with me, Yivan? Where do I come into all of this? Why aren't my team and I dead?"

He stands and begins to pace the room on the other side of the barrier. "I have been watching you for quite a long time, Jaret," Yivan admits. "I know everything there is to know about you. I know you are one of 27 mages alive that can access three schools of magic and that, among those rare few, you are the fastest and most destructively powerful, all thanks to your days as a Speedcasting competitor. I chose you, Jaret because I felt that you had the power, skills, and attitude to be trusted with the responsibility of being my student."

"Student?" I say, confused. "Yivan, I'm an MOP officer. As much as what you've told me has… affected me… I am still the one leading the charge and trying to stop you. I am going to arrest you and take you to the Mage High Council. I'm not going to be your student, Yivan. I'm going to put an end to your plans, or die trying."

"Yes, yes. I know. I see my younger self in you, Jaret. Stubborn and stuck with a skewed sense of what is right and wrong, as I once was. I want to become your mentor; to act as a father to you, in a way," Yivan explained. "I want to teach you all that I know so that you can help me make the wizards pay for their crimes. Our goal is to stop them from killing our people, yes? Well, the Wizards Guild is not the only guilty party. We will make the Mage High Council pay for their crime – for allowing this to happen – as well."

"I have a father," I say coldly. "He may be dead, but you're not going to take his place. And how could you even expect the two of us would be able to stop the High Councils?"

"Jaret, together we are going to change the world of magic forever!" Yivan exclaimed. "With us attacking the different High Councils at the same time, they will not be able to warn each other. They will be taken completely by surprise, and we will wipe them out. Mages will then have a chance to start over. I need you to help me make this dream a reality."

I stare at him blankly, unsure of what to say to all of this.

Before I can come up with anything, Yivan says, "Don't answer right now, Jaret. I want you to return to your life, and take your team with you. Think about what I have said. Look at the world and realize what is happening out there. Every time you see a tome remember that a mage was murdered just so an average person could try to be like us. And who knows how many innocent children without magic were murdered before that one book could be made. Consider it all, and I'll find you in two days' time so that we can talk again."

My brain is fried from everything I've seen and heard over the past few days, but even through that mental fog, this shocks me – I can't believe the Maelstrom is really going to let us just walk out of here. But the detective in me is hungry for the whole story, and I can't let him slip out of my hands without it.

"One more thing before you let us go, Yivan," I say. "You never explained this new and more efficient way of reclaiming stolen magical energy from dead wizards."

"Look around you, my boy," Yivan says, motioning to the horrible dungeon behind me. "I took these cages from a Wizards Guild compound long ago. The wizards have their Mage Farms, yes? Well then, you might call this my Wizard Orchard. I take the unsuspecting fools, and then force them to expend their entire mental cache of spells. When the wizards are empty of magic, I force them to learn simple and harmless utility spells. After they have reached their unique spell capacity, I, shall we say, pluck the apples from the orchard... and juice them."

My mom always told me that two wrongs don't make a right, but that is exactly what Yivan is doing: attempting to pay back one horrible wrong by committing another. This makes him no better than the wizards at a Mage Farm. It must be terrifying to be stuck in those cages, tortured until you do as you're told, and then be murdered by this monster. He has to be stopped.

"Then why did you attack those people on the street the other day? Why did you kill those regs just for three wizards?" I ask him, hoping for something meaningful so I can know that Rainbow didn't die just for the sick thrills of a murderer.

But the butcher crushes my hopes by smiling, throwing his arms out to the sides, and shouting, "I had to get your attention somehow, Jaret!" The Maelstrom then turns around and walks away, cackling like a lunatic.

A few minutes later, Mian Mian opens her eyes and jumps to her feet. With one hand, she readies a Fireball to hurl at someone, or from the look in her eyes, at anyone. Including me.

"Calm down, Mian Mian," I say, holding my hands up in the air. "It's just me."

Mian Mian, looking confused, points to the doorway with the red glow and asks, "Where is he? He was just right there, Bossman."

"No," I tell my talented yet confused agent, "he put you and the others to sleep hours ago. He and I have been having a long chat. Come on, I'll tell you about it once we all get out of here."

"How are we going to do that, Bossman?" Mian Mian asks.

"The Maelstrom is letting us go," I admit, as much in disbelief as Mian Mian. She looks at me oddly for a moment before running off to check on the other two. I follow slowly behind her, turning back and checking a few times to make sure we aren't being tricked somehow. When I reach the others, Mian Mian has already started explaining. Aurora has a distrusting look on her face, as she should.

Joyee, on the other hand, is elated, and shouts, "I knew Jaret would get us out of this alive!"

Not wanting to burst his bubble just yet, I forego telling them all Yivan said to me. Instead, I just say, "Ok, team. Let's figure out a way to get out of here. If the Maelstrom said he was letting us go, then there must be a way to get out. You three go that way and…"

Aurora interrupts me and points to the rear entrance. There is no red glow anymore; the barrier is gone. We can just walk right out of the damn back door. So that is exactly what we do. As we stumble out into the light, I check the time. It's 11 am, which means I might make it home before Kelly… If I hurry.

Walking out to the company cars, I think of what Yivan revealed about the Councils. It's not sitting well with me. If any of it is even true. And one thought keeps floating to the surface and nagging at me… why would he lie about this?

Either way, though, the method Yivan uses to reach his goal is equally disturbing as what the wizards are doing. I'm with him when Yivan says it must stop, but he loses me with the whole "kill all wizards and reclaim our magical energy from their dead bodies" talk. There has to be a middle ground – some way to stop what they are doing, if they are actually doing it, but without mass murder.

All of that can wait a little longer, though. "First, find Jaysen. Then, get home to my family." I think.

When we reach the car, Jaysen is lying face-down on the sidewalk, still and unmoving.

"Not another one," I say through the tightening of my throat and chest.

Reaching down and rolling him over causes Jaysen's body to twitch hard as he shrieks, "Please don't kill me!"

It seems he ran into Yivan after all.

Luckily, however, it appears he has survived the encounter. Yivan was telling the truth about not killing any more of my team, at least. That's a relief, for the time being.

"It's ok, Jaysen. It's just us, your friends," Aurora says soothingly. "What happened?"

He sits up and regains his composure, clearing his throat gruffly a few times to fight off tears while glancing at Aurora.

"Jaysen," I whisper to him, "no one cares that you were scared. We all got our butts kicked. There's a lot to explain to you, but first why don't you tell me what went down out here?"

He sighs, wipes the moisture from his eyes, and says, "I was watching from the car to make sure the man in black didn't show up. Only... he did show up. He walked right up behind me and asked me for a lighter. As I turned, I did not see a cigarette needing a flame. I saw the black cloak... and the featureless black mask. And I freaked."

"That's ok, Jaysen," Aurora says.

"Jaret, I know you told me not to engage him, but... it was instinct. I... I couldn't help it. I cast a ball of Storm lightning right at that stupid black mask. But he shrugged off my magic like it was nothing... like I was nothing. Then he slammed me against the car with a gust of Storm wind and held me there... and he just... he just stared at me from behind his mask without making a sound. It was the most terrifying thing I've ever gone through." Jaysen pauses to choke back his emotions in an effort to control the fear still present in his mind.

"Then what happened, Jaysen?" I ask.

"Then... everything went black. The next thing I remember was lying on the sidewalk with someone touching my back. I thought it was him... and that he had come to kill me. I felt helpless against his magic, Jaret. He is... too powerful." Jaysen stops talking, hangs his head, and finally lets his tears spill out onto the filthy sidewalk.

"Yeah, Jaysen, he is too powerful," I say. "But you did well, and you have nothing to be ashamed of, do you understand?"

He nods, and Aurora helps him to his feet, supporting his weight as they walk to the car together.

Once we get back to the office, I tell my team, "Take the day off, everyone. I'm doing the same thing. We can all meet back here tomorrow morning and discuss what happened, then figure out what to do next. I promise you that there will be no more attacks between now and then. He's waiting for me. So go get some well-deserved sleep."

I grab my scooter and take off for home, thinking only of holding my family close and raining kisses down on their beautiful faces. I'm terrified of the fallout from me being gone for so long, but it'll be worth it no matter how mad she is because I am alive and so are they. I enter the house to an eerie silence. Dead silence. My heart stops… until I hear giggles coming from the back room.

Slowly pushing the door open, I find my gorgeous wife rolling around on the bed while tickling our boys. It is the most marvelous sight I have ever seen. I close the door, and then they notice me. "Daddy's home!" I say with a grimacing smile, hoping to ward off some of Kelly's anger.

"Oh thank God you're alright!" she exclaims with a hand on her chest. Maybe she won't be mad after all.

"Yeah, I…" is all I can get out before she goes off on me.

"Where the hell have you been, Jaret? I got home a little while ago, and Lilly said you've been gone since last night around 6! I thought you were dead, or worse, run off with some young Chinese woman! So talk, and it better be good. Like the best reason ever, or else… I don't know what."

Nope, she's pissed. Kelly breathes heavily with tears streaming down her face, and looks to me for answers, but I can't say a word. All I want right now is to tell her what a horrible night I just had, and how I don't know what to do next. But I can't tell her any of the truth. And it fucking sucks.

"WELL?" she shouts. "Where have you been? Why didn't you answer my calls or texts? What in the hell is going on?"

I had thought of what to tell her on the drive home, and after running through scenario after scenario eventually decided to go with as much truth as possible. So I tell her, "Don't freak out, Kel, ok? But I witnessed a man die last night. Not his actual murder, but the moment of his death. He was hit by something big and powerful – like a truck. I held him as he passed, and he… he died talking about his family, babe. It was the saddest and most awful experience of my entire life."

Telling her the truth about some of last night's events feels freeing. So much so that I almost tell her about being a mage, having magic, and that I am the Head Officer of the Shanghai Mage Order and Protection – Wizard Patrol Service Dual Division Office. But, as always, I decide to follow the law and keep my secret.

Kelly's glare softens as she hears about Liang dying in my arms. She holds one of my hands in both of hers and lets out a shuddering breath. In a trembling voice, she says, "Oh God, Jaret. I'm so sorry. That's awful. What did you do?"

And now I have to lie to my wife… again. Or maybe I don't. Maybe I should just tell her. What could go wrong? It won't matter if I get kicked out of the Mages Guild now. I kind of want to be fired at this point. That would mean no more dealing with Yivan. But he wouldn't let it go just because I was fired. Yivan would use that as more fuel to try and convince me to help him.

"I phoned for an ambulance and stayed with him, Kel," I lie. "The cops came and took me in for questioning. Even though I was only a witness, they needed to make sure that I wasn't responsible, and they needed lots of statements. You know how the red tape is here in China: one million forms

260

with one million stamps each. I would have called, but they took my cellphone and refused to let me use theirs. By the time I got it back, the battery was dead. The police said that they were taking precautions to avoid having details of the murder leaked to the press. They told me it would be easier to find the killer if he or she felt safe. If news about the hit-and-run reached the Internet or TV, the killer would probably take off and be much harder to find. So I spent all this time in jail, even though I did nothing wrong."

Kelly pulls me close and hugs my head to her body, whispering in my ear, "Oh love. That is so terrible. I'm so sorry that you had to go through it. I wish you could have called me, but I understand." Kelly suddenly gets up, pushes me towards the guest bedroom, and says, "Here, you look exhausted, Jaret. You can tell me more about it later, but right now you just lie down and sleep for as long as you need. I will take care of everything out there with the boys."

"Are you sure, babe?" I ask, feeling guilty but needing the sleep. "I don't mind helping."

She looks down her nose at me and scoldingly says, "Don't even think about it. You saw a man die and then got yourself locked up in jail! You're probably in shock, honey. I've got all of this out here, so don't you worry. Go sleep."

I smile and kiss her again and again and again. "Thanks, Kel. I love you more than you know."

She runs her hand down my cheek and whispers, "That's almost half as much as I love you."

I stumble off into the bed and fall into the deepest sleep of my life as soon as my head hits the pillow. All too soon, however, I wake to find that I am somewhere else: in the middle of what looks like an old stone fortress somewhere in a desert.

There are people in chains everywhere. Slaves. Mage slaves, I'm betting. I hear a noise and turn around to find its origin. A teenage Yivan is pointing right at me, and flying stones crush my body. As I lie broken on the ground, unable to speak or breath, this younger version of Yivan stands above me with a murderous glare in his Storm-filled eyes.

"Join me, son, or you and everyone you love will die." Yivan then snarls, and rams a knife into my forehead.

Dead silence. My eyes fly open, my heart is pounding, and my mind is racing. And then the sounds come crashing in like an F1 race car.

"Calm down," I whisper shakily. "Focus your thoughts." And then, realizing I am at home and safe for now, I breathe a sigh of relief and mutter, "Get up. You can do this."

We sit down and eat breakfast together. Kelly informs me that I slept from 3 pm all the way until just now, 6 am.

"Holy shit," I mumble groggily.

"Uh, language, sir. The boys are right here," Kelly says reproachfully.

"Sorry, babe," I groan.

The boys are eating fruit and tofu. Kelly made protein smoothies for the two of us, so we can keep fit. While sipping at it, my mind wanders, and I try desperately to keep it from thoughts of dead wizards and mages. If only I could manipulate my body with magic to lose some weight, I think to myself. I mean, if Yivan can live for a thousand years, then surely I can get rid of this softness and maybe sculpt some abs.

"What's that, Jaret?" Kelly asks, staring at me.

"Huh? What's what?" I say, confused.

Kelly offers a little huffing laugh. "You just mumbled something about Yivan and abs. Who is Yivan? Does he have nice abs, dear?" she says, attempting to make me smile.

Damn. "Actually yes," I tell her. "It's an ad I saw online for a workout routine called Abs by Yivan. I was thinking of ordering it. The ad says that it works just like magic."

Kelly says, "I don't think we need it, but if you order it I'll do the program with you, honey."

"Kel, I have to go back to the police station this afternoon," I lie, "so I might not be home for dinner. You just order some Melrose pizza and I'll be home as soon as I can."

She frowns faintly, and with a voice full of pity says, "Ok, dear. I'm sorry that you have more to do with all of this. It really is just awful. I can't even imagine."

At least I can be honest with her about this. "Don't worry, babe," I say. "I'm hoping it will all be over very soon."

THIRTY-FIVE
2014 AD
Shanghai, China

"Can we do this, sweetheart? Are we going to be ok?" Kelly says, her bottom lip trembling and with eyes that seem lost. My wife is looking for hope. She wants me to give that to her.

"Yes, Kel. Together we can do anything," I tell her. "We're strong. We're a team."

Our newborn twins add their own feelings on the subject as Luke, the one I'm holding, begins to wail like only a newborn can. Han, the one Kelly is holding, starts making "the face." Lots of parents tell us that newborn poop is a breeze compared to toddler poop, which they say is basically just like an adult shit. My response to that is this: getting burned by Fire is better than getting shocked by Storm, but they both really fucking suck.

An unbelievable amount of people stands up as soon as we land and are still taxiing to the gate. None of the flight attendants seems to notice or care.

"What the hell is going on?" Kelly asks. "The seat belt sign is still on, for crying out loud."

"I don't know, babe. Let's just wait. We can get our bags down when the pilot says it's ok," I tell her.

Once the seat belt light does go off, however, we are stuck in our seats until the plane empties. Everyone else is up early and ready to go, some people even moving forward quickly to position themselves closer to the exit, just to get off the plane one minute sooner. Neither Kelly nor I can believe it what we're witnessing.

"I've never seen people so eager to be first!" she shouts, thinking that no one would speak English.

"I know! It's crazy, Kel. I wonder if everything is like that here," I yell above the noisy passengers inching their way past our seats.

An older man standing in the aisle beside us, holding his bag and anxiously waiting for his turn to bolt off of the plane, looks over at us and explains in English, "I'm afraid it's like that everywhere in my country. If you can't be first, you can, at least, be ahead of everyone behind you. Welcome to China, laowai."

I push our luggage cart, piled high with bags, and Kelly has the double stroller. The arrivals area in the Pudong Airport is lined with locals holding signs, looking for a particular traveler, some written in Chinese, and some in English. I've done a lot of traveling over the years due to my family's involvement in mage sporting events, while Kelly, on the other hand, is new to international travel.

"I'm so nervous, Jaret," she admits shakily. "What if no one is here to get us? What'll we do? We don't speak the language, and we don't even know where we're living, and…"

"Don't worry, babe," I reassure her. "Someone will get us. I know it." Searching the signs along the long queue of people I see one that stands out. "*Bingo*," I say, "there's our guy."

A small, balding Chinese man with Aviator sunglasses and a long mustache is holding a piece of cardboard that reads:

KELLY KING
and family

"See?" I say, prodding my wife in the side. "No need to worry, Kel. We're going to be fine." I walk over to the man and stick out my hand then say, "Ni hao, er, hello. We're the King family. I'm Jaret and this is Kelly."

He smiles at me and shakes my hand vigorously and says rapidly, "Ni hao, ni hao. I am Lu Sun. Call me Lu. Come! Let me take your bags." Kelly pushes the stroller closer, and Lu puts his hands on his face in mock surprise, saying, "Oh my God. Are these your babies? Very beautiful! Boy or girl?"

"Both boys," I reply.

"Wah! So lucky," he exclaims before taking our luggage cart and guiding us to his van parked illegally near the exit. Lu Sun packs our suitcases into the van, and then drives us to our new apartment; about an hour and a half drive away.

One we arrive, Lu Sun dashes out and assists Kelly get the babies out and into the stroller, then helps me unload our luggage. Digging in my wallet, I find a bunch of monopoly-looking money and have no clue what to give him. So I just grab a couple of bills, I don't even know how much, and hand it to him.

Lu Sun pushes my hand away and shakes his head, saying, "No, no, no. No need, no need."

I shrug, a little embarrassed, and stuff the cash back in my pocket. Not wanting to insult him by insisting he take the money, I instead just tell him, "Ok, thank you so much, Lu."

"No problem, no problem. Here is my card. You call if you need a driver, ah? Ok. Bye-bye!"

Kelly waves to him as he drives away and says, "Well, he was nice. Maybe this place won't be too difficult to live in."

"Right?" I say. "I think we'll be fine, Kel. What could go wrong?"

A week later, the big moment arrives, and Kelly says, "Ok, Jaret. Are you sure you can handle the boys on your own?"

"For the last time, Kel," I say with mock aggravation, 'we'll be fine! Today is your first day. Calm down, and focus on that. I'll take care of the boys and clean the house. You go make that big ass paycheck."

She kisses me, and I want to pull her closer, but know she'll be late if I do. So I let her go. After she's gone, I get down to business myself. Taking my Network book out, and placing my hand on top, I release a touch of Fire into it, and say, "Contact Stephen DuFrane, Head of MOP. East Asian Division."

His face appears projected in front of me after a few moments, grinning from ear to ear. "Jaret! You made it to Shanghai!" he says warmly. "Welcome to China. You're going to love it here. I've only been in the area for about a month, but I've already got it all figured out. I can help you learn to live like a local. *Shee shee knee*! That's thank you in Chinese, you know. I don't even need to use a spell to say it."

"Uh, thank you, sir. I'm extraordinarily honored that you chose me to lead this office. I'm very excited to get started." I tell my new boss... or, well one of my new bosses. Having two bosses is sure to have its challenges, but knowing that they are from different Guilds is doubly nerve-racking. It's going to be strange working for a mage *and* a wizard in my new role.

"Excellent!" Stephen says, still full of excitement. "Of course, we chose you, Mr. King. You know, I was a big fan of your father's career years ago. He was a truly incredible Speedcaster. I still remember that match between the two of you. AMAZING. It's a shame he passed away. A real shame."

"Thank you, sir," I say awkwardly. "Yes, it is a shame. I… miss him. All the time."

"I'm sorry, Jaret. No use dwelling in the past, eh?" He says while wiping his sweaty forehead with a cloth, then adds, "I've arranged a housekeeper/nanny, what the locals call an *aiyo* or something, to come and help out around the apartment for you. She comes highly recommended, and her name is Lilly. She'll be there within the hour. When Lilly arrives you should go to your new office, a company car is already parked in the garage at space A-41. The keys are in the top drawer of your desk."

"Umm…sorry, Stephen, I… uh… don't drive," I tell him, embarrassed. "I'm sorry, I should have mentioned it in the interview, but it… it never came up. I'll be happy to use public transportation, or…"

Stephen cuts my explanation short and says, "Really? You don't drive? Why not?" When I don't immediately answer, the greasy Canadian says, "Oh, never mind. It's fine, Jaret. I'll just have your Second in Command come and pick you up. Give her the keys when she gets there, and she'll drive you. Her name is Aurora."

"Alright, sir, thank you," I say, happy that's over with. "Now, this being one of the newer dual division offices popping up in the past few years, I'm very excited to start cooperating as soon as possible. I'm just wondering if this Aurora is a mage or a wizard?"

"She is a wizard, and a damn good one, too. We almost gave her the job instead of you," Stephen admits, "but she's a little young and not as experienced as yourself. Treat her well, teach her how to run the place, and you can promote her to another office, or have her take this one over when you get promoted. It's a win-win for everyone."

"Yes, sir. Thank you for everything, Stephen," I say.

His eyes no longer looking at me through the Network projection, Stephen says, "Good luck, Mr. King," and dismisses the call.

Once the housekeeper arrives, I get ready to leave. Lilly is a lovely old Chinese woman, sweet as can be, and speaks absolutely no English. Luckily, I brushed up on language Water spells so we can understand each other perfectly, as long as Kelly isn't around. Lilly is a reg and was quite surprised at how good I can speak Mandarin. After some time with her and the boys, making sure she knows exactly what her duties are, I hear another knock at the door.

Standing there with a genuine yet silly grin on her face, her hand raised in mock salute, is an attractive young Chinese woman who says, "Greetings, Laoban, sir. Aurora, the crammer, reporting for duty."

Already I can see that we'll work well together. We're both complete weirdos with poor senses of humor.

"Jaret, the world's most bearded and brave caster is ready to be driven around by his Second in Command. Over and out." I reply.

After the short commute, she shows me to my office, and I meet my whole team, a seemingly awesome group of magic users. Aurora then offers to take me out for lunch so we can get to know one another a little better.

"Yeah, that would be great," I say. "I haven't eaten much local food. Kelly and I have been here a week and eaten McDonald's almost every day. We don't know anything about China or what's good. Plus, I'm not supposed to understand Chinese, so I have to pretend I don't know what people are saying."

"Why didn't you just marry a mage, or better yet a wizard, Laoban?" Aurora asks bluntly.

"A very forward question for someone I just met," I tell her.

"Chinese people tell it like it is, Laoban. If you're fat, we tell you that you are fat. If it is cold outside, we will tell you to put on a jacket. Even complete strangers will do this. Get used to it," she says with a smile.

"Well then, in answer to your question, mages are all way too strong and attractive, and I didn't want to marry someone just like me," I jokingly explain. "And wizards? I'd never stoop so low. Don't be gross."

A shocked look appears on her face when it dawns on me that I've taken our playfulness too far. "I'm so sorry, Aurora," I apologize. "It was just a joke. I didn't mean anything by it. I'm so used to working with mages and making stupid jokes about wizards. I know this is a dual division office and the whole point is to get us working together to create bonds between the guilds…. and all that. God, I already messed up. First day on the job, too."

"I'm sorry, Laoban. What did you say?" Aurora mutters in a monotone voice. "I was just mesmerized by how strong and attractive you are."

An awkward silence stretches out for a moment until I realize that she is just fucking with me. We both burst out laughing at the same time.

"Ok, we're going to work really well together," I say.

Aurora goes to fetch her jacket and one of the mages from my team, a man named Jaysen, approaches me and shyly says, "Hi, Jaret… boss. Um, I just wanted to say that I'm happy to have you here. I think having a laowai…um, I mean, a foreigner, to lead the team will be excellent. But… um, I see you and Aurora have…hit it off, as the Americans say. And I just wanted to tell you that there is no inter-office dating, according to the upper management, so… you know, uh…"

Cutting him off, I say, "Jaysen, buddy. It's ok. You don't have to be nervous around me. I'm just a mage that got a good job. I'm not some power-hungry politician trying to make a name for myself. I just want to stop some bad guys, you know? And for the record," I hold up my ring finger and show it as evidence, "I'm happily married with two newborn twins at home. So there will be no inter-office dating from me. Alright?"

His muscles visibly relax and his teeth show in a big grin for the first time. He replies, "Ok, Jaret, boss. Thanks. I'll see you around. Enjoy lunch!"

After we eat some hotpot at a small local shop, Aurora and I return to the office and gather the team in the conference room where a 3D map of Shanghai is projected on the wall through the magic of the Network.

"Thanks for meeting with me in here, everyone," I begin. "I just want to say that I'm incredibly grateful to be welcomed. Not just here in this office, but to your amazing country, as well. It's an honor to be a guest here, and to be treated so kindly by the citizens of China." This is met with a round of applause from the table. "Thank you for that," I say. "Also, I want to tell you all that I'm not a tyrant. I do not rule with an iron fist. All I ask is that you do your job well. If and when I ask you to do something, do it to the best of your abilities and we won't have any problems. I look forward to working alongside all of you as often as possible. That being said, I don't know how much of my situation has been explained to the team, but..."

A smartly dressed woman in a business suit sitting at the front raises her hand. Not wanting her to be left like that for long, I stop what I was saying and ask, "Um, yes... Rainbow, is it? Did I get that right?"

She stands, adjusts her suit, and says, "Yes, sir. Rainbow. You are correct. I just wanted to say that we have been made aware that you are married to a reg, and that according to the Mages Guild's rules you are not allowed to share your occupation or magical abilities with her. As a wizard, this seems very pointless, but I understand it is your people's law, and we must follow the rules set forth by the High Councils. That being said, could you please go over the protocol for when you are not able to be in the office?" She then sits down and folds her hands in her lap, and looks to me for an answer.

"Thank you, Rainbow," I reply. "I was just about to get there, but you said it all better than I could. Yes, I am married to a reg. No, I will not always be able to come to the office. I will be working from home using email and the Network. When I am not here, Aurora will be making assignments. Those orders will come from me in most cases unless there is an emergency. Let's hope that never happens."

One of the male members of my team stands up, and I try to recall his name. "Uh, Liang... right? You have something to add?" I ask.

He smiles and nods his head. "Yes, boss, it is Liang. Um, I was just wondering... you have twins? Are they boys or girls?"

A question out of left field, but it's time to roll with the punches. "Oh, uh, two boys, Liang. Luke and Han. Newborn twins, if you can believe it. That's one of the reasons I'll be working from home, as well," I answer.

"Wow, two boys! So lucky!" he says.

"Yes, well, xie xie ni! Thank you, Liang," I reply about as awkwardly as only a laowai can. "Now, I'm going to head home for the day. I know it's a bit early, but I need to be there when my reg wife returns. I will see you all tomorrow, and we'll begin our normal routine. Cross your fingers that no one breaks the law until then."

Once the team filters back to their desks, I ask Aurora, "How was that? Super-lame?"

"No, Laoban. Just lame enough. They like you. You're going to be fine here. Don't worry," she replies.

"I appreciate your help, Aurora. If there is anything I can do for you, just let me know," I tell her.

"Actually, I'd love to meet your babies soon," she says with a grin. "I love kids."

"I don't know," I say cautiously. "Don't wizards eat little children?"

"No, Laoban. You're thinking of witches. And those are not real," she says while rolling her eyes. "They need to teach you mages more about magic."

"We don't need to learn about magic, crammer," I say in reply. "We're born with it."

THIRTY-SIX
2015 AD
Shanghai, China

Opening the door marked MOP & WPS, I find the place has been straightened up since I left. It almost seems like a regular day at the office, until I look at my team and see things I never thought would show on those faces. Sadness. Exhaustion. Fear.

Aurora walks beside me and says, "I stayed at the office last night, Laoban. I spoke to Stephen and Jenny to let them know about the attack here, and I told them everything that went down in Minhang yesterday. They were both pretty pissed that you weren't the one making the call. They already sent a team to collect Tian Yi and take his body to the Hall of the Dead. Liang's mother and brother came to collect his body and take him to a funeral home… and… and I… helped… to clean the ladies' room after…" She stifles a sob, and I pull her close to me, squeezing her enough to let Aurora know that I appreciate all she's done.

"You didn't have to do all of that, Aurora," I tell her. "It's not your job. But thank you. I know it was difficult for you. Did you get any sleep at all? Did you cram any spells? I hate to say it, but I need you at your very best. You're smart, you're strong, and you're vital to this team."

"Thanks. We all need to be at our very best, Laoban. The Maelstrom comes back tomorrow. We need a good plan," Aurora says.

"No, Aurora. We need a great plan," I reply.

"Yeah. Well, you'll be happy to know that I slept on the couch here for a few hours. Then woke up and crammed like a good crammer should," Aurora explains. "I'm feeling great, Laoban. You don't have to worry about me. But I'm sorry to say that not everyone feels the same way," she adds meekly, pulling an envelope out of her pocket and handing it to me. I open it reluctantly and my heart drops upon seeing the contents. It's a letter of resignation from Jaysen. He was really shaken up by everything that happened over the past few days. I could tell it was affecting him, but I wasn't expecting this. I read through his letter and look up at Aurora.

"I can't believe he would do this right now," I say. "How can Jaysen expect us to stop Yivan without him? We're already down by three. I've gotta go talk to him, Aurora." Scanning the office, I spot Jaysen putting stuff from his desk into a box.

He notices me walking over and refuses to make eye contact. "I'm sorry, Jaret. I never thought I would quit on you. I love this job... but I wasn't trained for this kind of stuff. I'm just not cut out for it, you know? I don't have the skills. You all are so much braver than me, and I'll only be a burden. I'm... I'm scared, Jaret, and terrified of dying. I'm a coward."

I put a hand on his shoulder and say, "Jaysen, I'm terrified, too. We all are, and we have every right to be. MOP never prepared us for this and there is no shame in being scared. But we desperately need you. You've already shown your bravery."

He sniffs his running nose and snorts out a sad laugh. "How am I brave, boss?" he asks. "I'm quitting. I'm crying all over my last field report. I'm worthless."

"Remember when Yivan attacked Aurora in the warehouse? Did you run?" I ask him. "Yes, you did. You ran *towards* the danger. Jaysen, you have it in you to be better than the rest of us; you just need to believe in yourself like I believe in you."

He finally finds enough courage to look me in the eye and says, "Thank you, Jaret, but I can't stay. I wish I could. I'm so sorry to disappoint you like this. I admire you. I just wish that I were… good enough. Good enough for you, for the team… good enough for her." His lip quivers and he shuts his eyes tight.

I squeeze his shoulder with a firm grip and say, "Jaysen, you will never disappoint me. You've been a valuable member of this team and a good friend to all of us. If this is what you really want, then I won't stand in your way. But hear me out for just a minute. Okay?"

"Sure, Boss. Anything for you," Jaysen sniffles in response.

"Go ahead and go home," I tell him. "Go rest and think on this for a few hours. I need you here. We need you here. Aurora needs you here. You're never gonna impress her by giving up, man. If you really want to do something, then dig down deep and find the courage. You have it in you."

Jaysen looks up, red-eyed. "I'm so sorry," he mumbles, grabs the box of stuff, and walks out of the office. And then there were four.

Joyee, Aurora, and Mian Mian meet me in the map room, and I immediately ask, "Do you all know about Jaysen's decision to leave the team?"

Everyone confirms they know, but they all seem deflated like a raft desperately in need of a pump.

276

"Look," I tell them, "it's his choice to make. In fact, we all have that same decision in front of us. None of you has to be here. If you think that this isn't worth it, then please leave now. But I'm staying. Some madman bent on killing as many people as possible will not run me off. I plan on stopping him. Now, I could use all of your help doing that," I say, looking around at the three of them, and add, "So, what's it gonna be?"

No one moves a muscle or speaks for several breaths.

Finally, one of them chimes in. "I think I speak for all of us when I say that we are with you, Jaret. Just tell us what to do, Laoban," Aurora says.

"Thank you; all of you. We can do this together. We can stop him from killing anyone else," I say.

My team looks shaky on their feet. They look tired. They look beat-down. But, at least for now, they aren't going anywhere – and that's good enough for me.

"So, we know when Yivan and Herod will be back. They made the mistake of telling us because they think we are all too weak to do anything about it. But I believe we can surprise them," I explain. "Let's be ready. Let's find a place where we want to have this confrontation. Let us prepare the battlefield. But we've only got one day to set it up to our advantage, team." Pointing to my Second in Command, I say, "Aurora, you're in charge of finding the place. The rest of you go with her. Create one point of entry for Yivan and Herod. I don't want to be surprised by where they come in. I need magical barriers surrounding the area. I need traps. And I need places for us to hide. Once that is all done, we'll settle in and wait."

Joyee looks around, eyes full of doubt, and meekly asks, "Jaret, how do we know they will even come? They might not be able to find us."

"Joyee," I say with an arched eyebrow, "do you really think the Maelstrom, the most powerful magic user in the world, won't be able to find us? He's been a step ahead of us this whole time. He'll be there, Jo. I only hope he brings his shitty little sidekick, too, so we can bust them both."

Mian Mian smirks and says, "What about you? What will you be doing, Bossman?"

I'm not yet ready to tell my team about the Mage Farms and how tomes are made; not until I know its 100 percent true.

"I'm going to do some research into Yivan. I want to verify his story if I can. And if possible, try to find something to use against him. If he has a weakness, I want to know it."

There is only one wizard in this city that might have access to the information I need and would be willing to share it with a caster like me. So, I grab a taxi and head to the local Wizards Guild building. I've been to his office a bunch since he moved here a little over two months ago, just to have lunch and reminisce about the old days. So he probably won't think anything strange about me just showing up at his office for a chat.

The taxi driver pulls to a stop at the cross streets I gave him and tells me it's eighteen renminbi for the ride. I give him a twenty and tell him to keep the change. He refuses and tries to hand me 2 kuai back. I don't have time for the "Oh no I couldn't possibly…oh but you must, I insist" dance, so I just walk away.

The local Wizards Guild office is in an old French building located in the area of the Former French Concession, which is now called Xuhui. I see a magazine stand on the corner and, as luck would have it, they are selling some tea eggs. I buy two and scarf them down, as I know that lunch is probably out of the question for me.

The receptionist instantly recognizes me and doesn't give a second look as I stroll right past her with a wave. I poke my head into a nicely appointed office and find my friend deep in thought while reading something on the Network.

"Excuse me, is this where I file a complaint?" I say jokingly. "One of your employees, a man named E.J., has been harassing me to join his ska band for weeks."

E.J. looks up startled, and then a big smile spreads across his face. "You are such a nerd!" he shouts. "What are you doing here, Jaret?"

"I was in the neighborhood and just wanted to pop in and see if you'd like to grab a coffee, dude," I explain. "You up for it?"

He closes the Network book in a hurry and says, "Hell yeah. I need to get out of here and clear my head. You wouldn't believe the mess I'm having to deal with."

"Oh, I probably can," I think to myself. "Yeah, my past few days have been terrible as well, Eej," I say aloud. "It's why I was hoping we could hang out for a bit. I just really need to vent."

E.J. grabs his keys off the desk and stands up, and as he rises to his full height, I do a double take, as usual. I always forget how tall he is. The guy literally is a giant with hands the size of my head.

"Where to, man? Sumerian? Please say Sumerian," E.J. begs.

I can only nod and laugh, "Of course!" It is his favorite place in town, besides Yongkang Lu with its plethora of bars, so I knew we'd end up at Sumerian Coffee if E.J. agreed to go.

Sipping on our steaming hot drinks, E.J. and I talk about his week: paperwork, a new project scheduling gigs for a group of wizard trombone players coming to town, and a lot of people around the office calling in sick.

"But I gotta tell you, Jaret, I don't think they're sick," E.J. says, his eyes darting around the room. "I think something weird is going on."

"You might be on to something," I tell him, sounding impressed. Giving someone the power of feeling like the smartest person at the table will usually benefit you when trying to pry some information from them. I tell E.J. a little about the investigation I'm working, making sure not to reveal the secret stuff. I only say that Li Qiuan went missing and was found dead with some other wizards, then about the attack on a small crowd, including some wizard victims.

He seems genuinely surprised, and says, "Man, I haven't been keeping up with local news at all. Every day it's just Facebook with friends back home, and reading gossip on the Network. You got any leads yet? Is it a copycat of the Maelstrom or something?"

A copycat. I fucking wish. "A few leads, yeah," I admit. "I've got my team chasing some down today. I'm just superstressed out, you know? On top of all this, it's tough to keep Kelly in the dark about everything."

E.J. frowns and shakes his head, saying reproachfully, "Should have married a wizard, like I told you to!" He chuckles and adds, "Just kidding, bud. How are the kids and Kelly?"

"Good. Just wish I didn't have to lie," I say honestly.

"You could have Kelly train to be a wizard!" E.J. replies.

"Man, you know good and damn well that the Mages Guild would not be ok with that," I say. "Adding one more crammer to your already overflowing ranks! Not a chance. When the war comes, she'd kill me first." We both have a good snigger at that, but we both also understand that there is an uncomfortable truth in the dark humor.

"There will never be another war, Jaret. Don't even kid about it, man," E.J. says.

"Look, despite the peace having lasted this long," I reply, "there's still considerable tension between our Guilds."

"Like what, bro?" he asks.

"Well, for one, only a certain number of people are born to be a mage. Wizards can be taught, so there are tons more of you than there are of us, Eej. That makes the Mages Guild a little nervous," I calmly explain. "Think about it, if you guys decided to start the old conflict back up, which probably won't happen, but if it did, we would be hard-pressed to handle your massive numbers."

"Well then, my caster friend, as they say on the streets, 'don't start nothin' won't be nothin',' know what I'm sayin'?" E.J. says, smiling.

We both laugh again, but still know the joke holds some truth to it. A few more minutes of idle chat goes by before I just decide to just go for it, as time is growing short.

"E.J., do you know anything about the Wizard High Council running Mage Farms?" I blurt out.

My old college roommate spits his coffee all over the table, and between gasps, says, "What? I mean…how…uhh…no. No, I don't." *Bingo.*

"Look, E.J.," I say calmly, "we've been friends for a long time. I know you've got a new job with VIP access to sensitive information. I'm not trying to get you fired or anything, I just need to know a little information. Help me out."

He stares into his cup and finds it empty. I order another one for him, my treat, and gesture for him to start talking.

"Look, man. I don't know what you are talking about," E.J. says in an odd tone. "But if I did, I would be totally fired for telling you anything. If I knew anything about it, I would have only just found out like a week ago. And I would only know that it's a big secret which my level of access isn't really privy to."

"Stop fucking around, E.J." I tell him, growing angry. "People have died because of this. People I care about. And more people are going to die, so I need to know what you know. Yes, it's a big secret, which is why I came to you – because my friend E.J. would actually help me. Now spill it."

He lets out a sigh, sips his coffee while looking me in the eyes, and whispers, "Ok, ok. I'm sorry, man. I came across a memo about a week ago. It mentioned a job title I had never heard of before, the Overseer of Mages. I thought it was a little weird. I read the rest of the memo, which was not meant for my eyes, you know, and it mentioned Mage Farms. It didn't go into detail, but... it didn't seem to be on the level, Jaret. Something weird is going on there. I don't know. I'm scared to lose my job, though, man. This gig is a killer... sorry, poor choice of words. I mean... it's a great opportunity for me. And what can I do about this? Nothing."

I stare at my old friend with frustration written all over my face. "First of all, thank you for being honest, Eej. Second, I am seriously disappointed. You know what I do. You should have told me about this. Mages are being murdered."

He splutters into his coffee and coughs. "I don't know if anyone is actually dead! That memo could have just been hypothetical. I don't have a clue what's going on! I'm sorry, Jaret. I… uh…I have to get back to the office now. I'll… I'll talk to you later, bud." E.J. quickly stands up and hurries his massive frame out of the small door.

The good news, if you can call it that, is I'm pretty certain Yivan was telling the truth about Mage Farms. The bad news? It's just one more thing on my list of shit I have to fix. But number one on that list is still Yivan.

I leave Sumerian to find a public Network access point. They have them all over the city, but I head to a pretty seedy part of town where you can access the Network anonymously. I don't need anyone knowing that it's me doing these searches.

For 100 RMB you get a fake Network identity, and an hour to surf, which is perfect for what I need. First, a little digging around to find info on mages named Yivan. There isn't much to be found, but I do see a document from around 500 years ago that catches my interest. It talks about a Storm mage found breaking into a tome storage building. The article says the man had long, black hair and big muscles. When confronted for trespassing, he said his name was Yivan and that he was doing this "for Maeris." The wild mage then set the building on fire by igniting the dry pages of ancient tomes with a bolt of Storm lightning. During the confusion, he escaped.

While everything he told me is looking to be true, it still doesn't change anything. The question is still how to stop someone so much more powerful than I am. The answer is I'm going to need help. So, despite my reservations, I contact Stephen DuFrane, Head of MOP, East Asian Division.

Using my fake identity and the few minutes I have left on my hour of anonymous surfing, I make a Network call to his office using voice only. His assistant connects us and I see his face projected in front of me.

"Hello? Who is this? Why can't I see you?" his sweaty face asks, looking confused.

"Stephen, I'm making this call anonymously. I need to talk to you in person about some things. Can we meet?" I say in a voice deeper than my own, à la Christian Bale's Batman.

He stays quiet for a moment, and then Stephen says, "Jaret? Is that you?"

"No," I say in an even gruffer growl. "Can we meet?"

More silence from the floating head, and then: "Yes. Meet me at Yang's Fried Dumplings near my office in twenty minutes." He disconnects, and I look at the time. It'll be cutting it close, but I can make it. I just hope I can trust the unlikeable Canadian.

I find Stephen already sitting at a table with a big plate of fried dumplings in front of him as I enter Yang's eatery. The greasy mage in his mid-fifties with a head full of gray hair looks up at me uncomfortably. He always seems uncomfortable and out of place.

I grab a seat and a dumpling, and say, "I hope you don't mind if we share, boss. I'm starving."

Stephen smiles unconvincingly and pushes the plate closer to me and says, "I ordered them for you. I can't stand Chinese food anymore."

"Such a laowai thing to say, Steve," I tell him, popping another dumpling into my mouth.

"Oh who cares, Jaret?" Stephen replies, obviously annoyed. "Tell me, what did you find out? I need to know everything."

I put down the chopsticks and get serious. "Quite a lot, actually. I confirmed that wizards are the targets of the attacks. I confirmed that the assailant is the same man known as the Maelstrom, responsible for the attacks that ended 25 years ago."

Stephen's eyes shoot wide open and he says, "He must be somewhat old by now, eh?"

"You have *nooo* idea, Steve," I answer, snagging another dumpling.

My boss's demeanor shifts as he becomes fidgety, and speaks in a wild rush. "Why is he draining wizards dead bodies? What is the purpose? Is it for magical gain... for power??" The look of hunger in Stephen's eyes as he says this makes me uncomfortable.

"Why do you ask, Steve?" I say warily.

Stephen DuFrane, Head of MOP East Asian Division, growls through his teeth furiously at me, "Stop calling me that, Jaret. It's Stephen, not Steve or Stevey. And I ask because the Mage High Council wants to know. This information could be very useful to us. It's not something we are sharing with the crammers – if you catch my drift."

With apprehension, I drop the dumpling about to go in my mouth, lean forward, and whisper, "Are you saying that if this is magically beneficial for our people, the Mage High Council will do...what? Farm wizards like they farm us?"

Stephen's wormy mouth suddenly forms a frown. He picks up a dumpling and rolls it around in his already greasy hand, and says, "How did you find out about the farms? Did the, uh, Maelstrom tell you?"

"Yeah, *Stevie*," I say, now supremely pissed off. "He told me everything. I can't believe you know about this and are ok with the Wizard High Council killing innocent people."

Stephen rolls his eyes and replies casually, "Jaret, this is above your pay grade so you wouldn't understand. But if you must know, this is how we keep the peace. This is how things have been done for a very long time."

"Is this why you wanted me to dig deeper, and to do it off the books?" I ask. "So there would be no record on the Network about what the Maelstrom is doing, just in case it can benefit the Mages Guild?"

Stephen proudly answers, "The wizards will be caught completely off guard when we start farming them like they have us for so long."

"But why was your wizard counterpart, Jenny, so keen on all the secrecy as well?" I ask, confused.

Stephen looks at me with contempt and says, "Well, I assume it's because they don't want us to find a way to benefit from dead wizards. Politics can be very confusing for someone at your level, Jaret. Don't worry yourself about the specifics. Now, tell me how he is doing it, and what the benefits are."

This asshat is crazy if he thinks I am going to tell him anything now. I am not ok with any of this. "All I know is that he is more ruthless and magically powerful than anyone I have ever met, Stephen. And he has offered me an apprenticeship."

Stephen has never looked this happy in the whole year that I've worked for him. His eyes light up with wonder, and he foams at the bit. "Oh, that's superb. You must accept his offer, Jaret. Whatever he asks you to do, you must do it. We need his secrets. It's for the benefit of all mages."

"Ok, Stephen, I'll see what I can do," I tell him, deciding to play along for now.

He squishes the dumpling in his hand, burns it to a nugget of ash with Fire, and says, "Don't let us down, Jaret. You are a mage. Remember that. Or you could end up like your father."

THIRTY-SEVEN
2015 AD
Shanghai, China

Leaving the dumpling shop and Stephen behind, I am feeling absolutely disgusted. "What did he mean about my father?" I wonder. He wouldn't say any more when I asked, the bastard just walked out and left.

On top of that, I now know that the Wizard High Council is farming mages to create their tomes of power. The Mage High Council is aware, and is not only ok with it, but now they are also trying to find a way to farm wizards to become more powerful themselves. All the politicians say this is how we keep the peace, but it doesn't seem very peaceful to me. Yivan's methods may be equally horrible, but his vision of a world without the two Councils is starting to sound pretty damn great about now.

Or maybe he's right about wizards. Maybe it would be better if there were no wizards. We wouldn't be in this mess if it weren't for them. But I know that is total bullshit, too. Some of my best friends are wizards, and it's not their fault that wizard magic comes from dead mages. Most wizards have no clue about what is going on. And then you have people like Stephen who are despicable, know what is going on, and are mages. Honestly, all of this stems from the two Councils agreeing to this fucked-up spell tome creation deal in the distant past.

"Why do they even need more tomes anyway?" I think to myself. "Don't they have enough after all this time? Why don't they shut down the Mage Farms and stop tome production altogether?"

I can ask myself these questions all day long, but it doesn't do any good. I have other things to worry about in the meantime, namely: Herod and Yivan.

As I walk down the street having this brainstorming session, something strange catches my attention out of the corner of my eye. Jenny Yu, Head of WPS, East Asian Division – one of my two bosses – is standing ten feet away and looking right at me with a smirk on her lovely face. What the hell is she doing here?

"Hello, Jaret," Jenny says, waving pleasantly.

"Oh... hi there, Jenny. What, uh, what are you...? I mean, what's going on?" I say, trying to sound casual but failing miserably.

She walks over, takes me by the arm, and says, "As I understand it, you have something to report on the mission Stephen and I assigned you. I'm dying to hear what you found out."

"Actually," I lie, "I don't, Jenny. The investigation is still ongoing. I promise to let both of you know the minute we have something useful."

Jenny giggles and covers her mouth as she says, "Oh Jaret, you're funny. But I know you just spilled the beans to Stephen, and now you're going to do the same for us."

Suddenly, something buzzes toward me from behind and slams into my back. Damn it. And everything goes black.

288

I awake to a dead silence. My eyes fly open, my heart is beating like a drum, and my mind is racing. Then the sounds... *Blah blah blah*. I'm getting really fucking tired of waking up confused. Where the hell am I, anyway?

As my vision clears, Jenny Yu comes into focus. She is sitting right in front of me, her eyes glued to mine. Five dubious-looking men, probably crammers, surround us. Something strong is holding me in place. Magical constraints. Wizard magic.

"Let's start over, shall we, Jaret?" Jenny says. "Why don't you tell me everything you told my ignorant counterpart, Stephen DuFrane, and don't leave anything out." The smile Jenny offers me could not be less pleasant.

Using my confusion as a means to stall momentarily, I assess the magic holding me to the chair and find no elasticity; there is not an ounce of give on these suckers at all.

"These are some heavy-duty bonds you've got tying me to this chair, Jenny," I say. "Afraid I'll break free and kick your ass?"

"There are six of us and only one of you, Jaret; you poor little mage," Jenny replies.

"Let me out of these bonds and we'll see if six is enough, Jenny, my dear," I say menacingly.

"Shut your laowai mouth, *mage*," she snaps. "We have important things to discuss."

Déjà vu. She sounds exactly like Yivan. It seems like he's not the only power-crazed lunatic around. "Ok, Jenny. Let's get real, then, shall we?" I say. "The Wizard High Council is farming mages to create spell tomes. They have been for a thousand years or so. The mages are finally getting tired of it and are looking for a way to stick it to you guys while still keeping with the peace treaty. How am I doing so far?"

"Not bad," she says. "Go on, Jaret. Impress me with what you know."

"I will, you evil crammer. How's this; a terrorist comes along 27 years ago and starts doing something strange to wizards' bodies after he kills them. Now, both Councils get excited for different reasons. The mages want to know what it is and how to do it, and the wizards want to shut it down and keep it secret. But the funny thing is, neither side knows who is doing it or why, what benefits it offers, or how to stop him. Am I on the right track, Jenny?" I say angrily.

"You're doing just fine, caster. Please continue," Jenny replies calmly.

"So now, the Maelstrom is back and operating here in Shanghai. You and Stephen both want me to do all the dirty work and tell you the secret of his power. Well, Jenny, you may be a beautiful woman, but even that prick Stephen had a better approach than you, and I didn't tell him shit. Which means I'm definitely not telling you a damn thing after you've kidnapped me and held me hostage. Does that about sum it up, ma'am?" I say, ending with a "fuck off" kind of smile.

"Yes, Jaret, that about sums it up," Jenny says, and then gets up to walk out of the room, before suddenly spinning around and adding, "Oh but you forgot one thing. If you don't tell me everything you know about the Maelstrom right now, we're going to kill you and your family."

My breath catches in my throat for a moment. A mask of hatred falls over my face, and I say, "Don't threaten my family, Jenny. I can easily kill everyone in this room, should the need arise. Have you done anything to them?"

She walks behind me, and brushes her hand across the top of my head fondly, like an owner patting a dog. "No, don't worry. They are safe at home, still blissfully unaware of your predicament, and their own. Now, Jaret, if you cooperate and tell me what I want to know, we will still have to kill you, of course, to keep our secrets. But we will let your family live," Jenny explains.

"You'll leave my family alone? You swear?" I ask, buying a little more time.

"Your wife will be given access to the MOP financial account you've been saving for years. She'll quietly get another promotion at work, and your kids will be put on the fast track to spell school, all expenses paid. That way, they'll be trained as wizards," Jenny says, and then bends down to whisper in my ear, "just like their *mother*."

"What?" I say through a veil of disbelief and confusion. I've always felt there was something more to Kelly, something hidden, but I never once imagined that it was magic she was keeping from me. "What are you… what are you talking about?" I stammer, caught off guard. "I think you're mistaken, Jenny. My wife is not a wizard."

Jenny throws her head back and barks a sinister laugh. "Casters are such simpletons. Imagine the sense of humor fate must have, giving the gift of a natural connection with the Ether to the dumbest people on Earth. Of course she's a wizard, Jaret," Jenny says. "She's been one of us for a long time. Kelly has just been keeping it a secret, as you do. It's actually quite funny when you think about it. You lie to her, and she lies to you. A marriage based on dishonesty from both sides."

A sudden urge to vomit hits me as my mind spins in nauseating circles. My father's voice slides into my mind, though, telling me what I need to hear to get out of this alive.

"Calm down. Focus your thoughts."

Whatever this vile wizard is saying, true or not, does not matter. Nothing will matter if I die here and now. To save my family, to save the lives of countless innocents, I need to think clearly. Jenny looks down at me with pity, and my only thought as this horrible wizard waits for me to break the silence is to play along and get free.

I start to test the wizards' magical bonds holding me to the chair. As I initially felt, they are rigid and harsh, but not unbreakable. Given enough time, I should be able to pop them open; I just have to keep Jenny talking. Of course, once I'm free there'll be six crammers to deal with all at once, but one problem at a time, right?

"Ok, Jenny," I say in my most submissive voice, "I'll tell you everything you want to know. Just please leave my family alone."

"Agreed, mage. Speak, and leave nothing out," she says.

"It all started a thousand years ago," I say, beginning to weave a long and complicated story. Using this lie, I keep her and the others focused solely on my narrative. Jenny sits down opposite me once more and becomes enthralled by the tale, with the other five wizards paying very close attention to every syllable. "…And then, he discovered that wizard mummies can be used to fight each other for sport. Gambling took place. Much gambling."

Accessing Water through the Ether, I fill my body with it, making myself swell. The bonds start to tighten against my arms and chest; their stupid crammer spell didn't account for elasticity, making this an easily unbreakable bond. Slowly, my body becomes fatter and fatter, and I feel the first layer of their spell snap from the strain. "…Once the Maelstrom had established an underground wizard mummy fight club, he began to plot his most diabolical plan of all. You see…"

The second bond snaps as I tell a false tale of reanimated wizard corpses. The spell is thin now; almost insubstantial. I'm almost there. Unfortunately, however, the six crammers listening to my wild and ridiculous tale become aware that something is different about me. I look pretty massive, now, due to the swelling from the Water spell.

Despite my engaging and totally made-up story, I look like I've gained about 50 pounds in the telling. One of the crammers in the back nudges the one next to him and points in my direction. Jenny begins looking me up and down with a strange look before her mouth falls open in sudden understanding.

It's now or never.

I blast the last bond off with a massive force, mixing Fire and Water to create a cloud of steam that hides my next move. Hitting the floor, I feel magic missiles flying over my head. I'm not sure if those were meant to kill or stun, but I know they hit the wrong target. One of the thugs behind me drops to the ground, immobilized or dead.

Jenny's voice rises above the confusion uttering words of power, and the steam instantly disappears. The moment it's gone, I unleash a barrage of fist-sized stones in a 360-degree spray, which connects with the knees of every wizard in the room. Distracted by pain, the crammers offer the moment I need to silence them. My Speedcasting training kicks in, and I barely even consider how to accomplish this task. All mouths suddenly fill with boiling Water, scalding their tongues and throats, and making them incapable of saying a word.

I stand up calmly, dust myself off, and taunt, "No talking means no crammer spells. I gotta admit, Jenny, that was easier than I thought it would be. I'm disappointed." Sniggering at the stupid wizards, I let my guard down for a moment. They can't cast spells anymore, right? What could go wrong?

The remaining four very large men rush at me, swinging their ham-sized fists at my face.

"Oh shit," I sigh. "A fistfight." A left hook connects with my jaw, and a foot buries itself in my stomach. My breath rushes out, leaving me immobile momentarily. Both of my hands clutch at my mid-section as I hunch over in pain, gasping for one single breath. Stars are dancing around the edge of my vision. Luckily, though, I don't need words or hand gestures to use my magic.

A circle of Fire emerges from the ground to surround me, and straightaway flares all the way up to the ceiling. Two of the crammers get caught in the blaze, and they immediately stop, drop, and roll. Someone paid attention in kindergarten.

With three of six crammers now out of commission, and with the remaining three being unable to cast spells or get through my wall of Fire, the ones capable of doing so now turn tail and run away. Not wanting to let them go free, I dispel the fiery wall and chase the bastards.

My hopes for a peaceful resolution to this are completely shattered the moment I see Yivan standing at the far end of the hall. He waves at me like a little kid on the playground seeing his best friend for the first time in weeks. The Maelstrom then blasts Jenny Yu and her two companions with a barrage of Storm energy. Their charred bodies fall to the floor, utterly lifeless. Yivan casually strolls closer to them and kneels down beside the blackened bodies.

"I hate to waste unspent magic, Jaret," he says to me. "Would you care to join me in reclaiming our magical energy? I can show you how." The ominous green glow, signifying the use of Death magic, appears as I feel a tugging pull at my very core. The bodies of the dead wizards seem to shrink as the skin dries out and clings tightly to their lifeless skeletons.

Yivan guffaws maniacally and turns to walk away. As he leaves, the Maelstrom calls back over his shoulder, "See you tomorrow, Jaret. I hope you make the right decision."

And for the briefest moment, I consider chasing Yivan down, too. Of course, I realize that I won't be able to stop him; not alone, anyway. It would be foolish to throw my life away in the attempt. So, quickly leaving the scene behind, I hop into a taxi. On the way to my office, I can't help but think, "Why is this happening to me? Why am I at the center of all this?" I know that I chose this life: to chase down magical criminals and stop events like this from happening. And I did so because of the man who just killed those wizards: the Maelstrom.

I suddenly realize that this is the reason why I am at the center of everything. It is my responsibility to end this because of the oath I made long ago. I just hope that my team created a trap clever enough and powerful enough to stop this killer.

THIRTY-EIGHT
2015 AD
Shanghai, China

Aurora's cell goes straight to voicemail. "Great," I grumble in frustration. "How am I supposed to find them now?"

Nothing can be done about it for the moment, so I sit back to think about what has recently happened. My life has been completely turned on its end in just a few short days. Three of my friends are dead. Another has quit the team because of some misplaced lack of confidence. I found out some disturbing truths about wizard spells. I've been kidnapped twice. One of my bosses tried to kill me, but was instead murdered by a serial killer. Meanwhile, my other boss wants me to find out how to use dead wizards to benefit all mages.

Not to mention, I met the Maelstrom... the man whose violent actions inspired me to become an MOP agent... the man who almost killed my father and when I was ten years old... a one-thousand-year-old murderous mage who can also cast wizard spells and is determined to destroy both of the High Councils... Yivan.

Oh, and to top it all off? I found out my wife might actually be a wizard. That adds up to one hell of a stressful week on the job.

I arrive at the office to find it just as I left it, so I sit at my desk and put my head down for a bit, hoping to catch a few minutes of rest. In the midst of my body relaxing for a nap, I hear the door to the office open. One of my team must be here to take me to the trap they've set for Yivan. I lift my head to see who it is. Wrong again, Jaret.

A ball of Fire burns in my palm before I can even stand up. I sprint out of my office screaming a war cry that would make Braveheart forsake his freedom.

"Wait! Wait, laddy! Don't blast me to bits just yet! Please, hear me out!" Herod frantically begs.

I glare at the little wretch with streams of Fire flowing from my blood red eyes and snarl, "Tell me why I shouldn't just kill you right now, Herod."

He sits down on the couch and puts his head in his hands, muttering, "Honestly, matey boy, ye probably should. It would be a fair bit quicker than what he'll do ta me after he realizes that I've come ta help ye."

"Help me? Really?" I spit. "Why should I believe anything you say, Herod?"

The old Scot looks at me pathetically and says, "Because, lad, I think I ken how ta kill Yivan, and I'm goin' ta tell ye."

All at once, I release the Fire magic I've been holding, but not in a concentrated blast directed at Herod. Despite my desire to cause the old wizard a considerable amount of pain for all that he has done, I let the spell dissipate harmlessly into the air. The room becomes intensely hotter for an instant, and then I take a seat across from the old wizard. "Ok, Herod. Talk."

"Jaret, ye don't have ta believe what I say. It makes no difference ta me. My time is up, lad. Yivan hasn't given me any of that blasted pulse recently, and I'm startin' ta fade. I can feel my life slippin' thru the cracks. I dunnae think I'll be around much longer."

Herod creakily gets off the couch to get some water from the cooler. He drinks deeply and lets out a satisfied sigh. For the first time, I notice how terrible he looks. In fact, I can see Herod deteriorating before my eyes. He looks older every minute that passes.

"The First thing is, lad, he knows about the wee trap that ye've set for him," Herod admits. "In case ye have nae figured it out Jaret, he's been watching ye right close. That's how he was there today to murder those six wizards."

"He only killed three of them, Herod," I tell him. "I saw it. I left the other three perfectly alive in the back room."

Herod nods along, saying, "Right ye are, right ye are. Once you were gone, I killed the other three that ye left lyin' on the floor. But don't be upset much, I was ordered to do it by Yivan, *and* they were aimin' ta kill ye."

Before he can say more, I stand and punch Herod right in his face. He rolls off of the couch, onto the ground, and gives a hearty laugh.

"About time ye stopped relyin' on magic, matey boy," he lisps through a split lip. "There's just somethin' right satisfyin' about punchin' a man squarely in the face, no?" Herod sits back down and puts his hands in the air to hold me back, saying, "Look, I know that I've done wrong and that there is nae coming back from the evil I've committed at Yivan's behest, today's murders included. I only want to make amends in any way that I can. It's why I've come to ye. I no longer want to live forever, as he does. I want ta die, and I want ta die with dignity. I'll no longer use magic of any kind, lad. Those days are over. And I want Yivan to pay for what he's done. So hold off kickin' me arse for a few minutes, I beg ye."

The Fire inside me wants to come out and engulf this lying fucker. The fists at the ends of my arms want to continue their assault on his battered lips. But my father's Ethereal voice seems to whisper some good advice in my ear.

"Calm down, Jaret, and focus your thoughts."

Gaining control over myself, I motion for the old Scot to continue and he explains, "You see, Jaret, my boy, I figured it out a while back. Yivan will sometimes threaten to let me die by not givin' me any of his Storm pulse. And after a bit of time without it, I would start to fade rather quickly, as I am before yer eyes, right now. With my bein' less than 300 years of age and fadin' like a red shirt in the wash, imagine what would happen to him should he let go of the pulse? Imagine how fast he would fade with him being over 1000 years of age, eh?"

Rubbing my face harshly, I contemplate what Herod is saying. It is true, this would probably end Yivan rather quickly. But there's one fatal flaw in this plan.

"Yes, Herod," I snap, "but how would I convince him to let go of the pulse, huh? It's not like I can just ask the Maelstrom to turn off the spell, keeping him alive!"

Herod throws up his hands in frustration and says, "If I had the answer ta that, laddy, I would have bloody well done it already. I was hopin' that a man of your talents and magical stature would be able to puzzle it out."

Herod's breathing quickly begins to sound both wheezy and irregular. His skin goes grayer the more I watch. He looks like a fish bought at the market three days ago.

"Now, I'm not for livin' much longer," Herod says dryly, his voice like crumpling paper. "Do as I've told ye. Figure it out. And remember, he knows about that wee little trap."

Herod then coughs and motions for me to get him more water. I go to the cooler, still not sure if I can trust this little Scottish goblin, when the coughing from behind me suddenly stops. Spinning on my heels quickly, I find Herod, the old Scot, gone. In his place sits an old dried-out husk, not completely unlike the wizards drained by Yivan. Except Herod's body seems more peaceful than those created by Death magic. Looking at his lifeless body, I feel as if a coffin was opened to reveal a man who died around 300 years ago.

Maybe everything he said wasn't a lie, in the end.

My cell rings almost immediately, scaring the crap out of me. I answer, "Aurora, is everything alright? Is everyone ok?"

"Yeah, Laoban. Paranoid much?" she says jokingly. "We're all set here. Do you want me to tell you over the phone where we are, or should we just come get you?"

"No, don't say it over the phone. You'll definitely have to come get me. I'm not driving," I tell my Second in Command.

"Shocker," she says sarcastically. "We'll be there soon. Wait outside."

"Sure thing, smart-ass," I reply.

"Try to be serious, boss," she says. "People's lives are at stake."

A few minutes later, Joyee pulls up in a company car with Mian Mian riding shotgun.

"Where's Aurora?" I ask.

Mian Mian says, "She stayed behind to put some finishing touches on the location. You're going to love it, Bossman. We've made a dangerous work of art, crafted by magic. They'll never know what hit them."

Confused, I ask, "They?"

Mian Mian looks at me strangely and says, "Yes. They. Yivan and Herod. The two people responsible for all of this chaos and mayhem in our lives? Remember them?"

It only just happened, but everything is bleeding together into one large event in my head. I assume everyone already knows everything I know. Which, of course, they don't. I've got to tell my team about… everything. It's been unfair of me to keep it all a secret.

For now, I say, "Herod is dead. He came to see me and died in our office."

"Did you kill him, Bossman?" Mian Mian asks casually.

"No, but he told me how we might beat the Maelstrom," I reply. "And he said that Yivan already knows about our trap."

"Shit, should we just not worry about it then, Jaret?" Joyee says nervously. "I don't want to end up an empty wizard shell."

"No, Joyee. We move forward. It's too late to turn back," I reply. "Where is the location, by the way? Since Yivan already knows where we're going to spring the trap, I guess it's time that I know, too."

Joyee looks in the rear-view mirror and says, "Yu Garden. Aurora thought that would be a pretty epic place for a final showdown. Plus it's after hours right now so the place is deserted. We've also convinced the management to keep it closed all day tomorrow."

Yu Garden is one of the most recognizable places in Shanghai. Seems appropriate. I close my eyes to get a few winks in before we arrive at the famous Shanghai landmark.

A half-hour later, I stroll around and survey the scene, impressed with what they have done. The place is unrecognizable. There is a magically crafted tunnel shaped like a dragon's body leading from the entrance of Yu Garden directly to a large courtyard in the middle of the site. This courtyard, dotted with ponds full of koi fish and zigzagging stone bridges, is completely surrounded by a magical dome barrier, with a familiar red glow. It's just as spell-proof as Yivan's barrier, my team tells me. Of that, I am not so sure.

The courtyard is also littered with several spell enhanced walls for us to hide behind and cast at Yivan, should it come to that. There is nothing near the entrance so the Maelstrom will be completely out in the open when he arrives.

"Traps?" I ask.

"Yes, Laoban. Quite a few," Aurora says excitedly, "but the first one is the best. I made it myself."

"Well, tell me about it later. Right now I have to say that you've all done extraordinary work here. Really. But it's time for me to be honest with you. There are some things I should have already told you all but have neglected to do so for some dumb reason. I'm sorry about that. You need to know this stuff before we move forward. Please, sit down, this is going to take a little while."

For the first time since leaving Herod and Yivan's dungeon full of cages, I lay out the entire story for my team from start to finish: every last detail, leaving nothing out, all the way up until Herod's death on our office couch.

Stunned silence is my team's initial response. They stare at each other, and me, as if having just woken from a nightmare. Eyes watery, Joyee says, "Mian Mian…Jaret…I had… I had no idea our spells came from dead mages. I swear it. I…I'm so sorry…so sorry to both of you."

"I know you didn't, Joyee," I reassure him. "Believe me. Not many people do know about this." He nods and wipes the dampness from his eyes with shaking hands.

Aurora looks stunned but composed as she says, "I always knew that our spells were linked to mage magic. I mean, they teach us that much in spell school, but I never imagined it was like this. I swear to you both that I will never learn another spell from a tome as long as I live."

"Look," I say calmly, "the tomes that are already created have done their evil. There's no harm in learning from them at this point. You've done it a million times, and it won't hurt anyone except Yivan, which right now is priority one."

Mian Mian looks suspiciously at the two wizards on our team and says, "Do you think that Yivan could be convinced to help us, Jaret? You know, stop the Mage Farms without killing innocent people?"

"And are wizards considered innocent to you, Mian Mian?" Joyee asks.

Mian Mian looks at her Doc Martens and replies, "I'm… not sure who is innocent anymore, Jo."

Joyee's eyes grow wild with desperation as he pleads with the beautiful punk rock mage, "We didn't know! Don't shut us all out because of this, Mian Mian, please."

"I know this is hard to hear as a mage," I tell Mian Mian. "Believe me, I know. But Joyee is right. Most wizards have no idea what is going on. It's not their fault."

"Yeah, I guess you're right," she mumbles in response.

"And as far as Yivan helping us peacefully," I add, "I'm afraid he probably won't. But I have to try and talk to him about it. I can't just kill him as soon as he walks into our trap. We need to do the right thing here. If we have to kill him, we will, but I would rather convince him to help us, or if that fails, take him into custody."

Aurora smirks at me skeptically and says, "You don't actually think we can hold the Maelstrom, do you? Our only chance is to hit him hard and fast so he doesn't know what's coming, Laoban. Kill him, I say."

Joyee agrees vigorously with Aurora, nodding his head and saying, "It's our only chance of survival."

Mian Mian grows irritated again and shouts, "Imagine that: two wizards trying to immediately kill the one man on Earth attempting to stop their kind from slaughtering innocent mages."

"Stop it, Mian Mian," I say. "You're not helping. We're not going to fight amongst ourselves and let Yivan win. These are your friends and you will treat them that way, not as enemies. Do you understand?"

"Yeah, Bossman. Sorry," she says, ashamed. "I'm just… confused… and pissed as hell."

Aurora hugs Mian Mian and whispers, "We know. It's ok."

Joyee nods, putting his hand on Mian Mian's elbow and says, "I'd never do anything to hurt… mages."

"Anyway, I'm sorry, Joyee and Aurora, but I'm in charge here and I say we have to be better than Yivan. If not, then why are we even stopping him? If we are willing to kill him just to get our way, then what makes us any different from the Maelstrom?" I ask them.

They both look away, not wanting to make eye contact.

"You're right, Jaret. It's just…" Aurora trails off and for the first time ever… I see her cry, but only one single tear runs down her soft features.

"I know," I tell her. "Listen, Yivan won't come until tomorrow, so let's take the rest of the night off and go get some sleep. We'll need to be well rested for this confrontation tomorrow. Plus, I need to get home and talk with my wife… the wizard."

THIRTY-NINE
2015 AD
Shanghai, China

I put my key into the lock, trying to be silent. Kelly is still awake, lying in bed with her laptop open and watching some streaming show.

"You're such a Netflix junkie," I say, edging into the room. Sticking her tongue out, Kelly says, "Shows what you know! The VPN isn't working right now, so I'm watching stuff on Youku." I stare at her lying there with two thoughts running through my mind… she is so incredibly beautiful, and what I'm about to do is going to freak her out so much.

Remembering all the times I've lied to her and she's lied right back to me breaks my heart. Nervous doesn't even begin to explain how I feel about this. So, I run through my routine.

"Calm down," I think to myself. "Focus your thoughts."

My connection to the elemental Ether opens; Fire and Water collide within me, causing a gust of steam to rush out, blowing Kelly's laptop closed. Rock energy channels through my feet and into the floor, creating a small earthquake beneath the bed, making it jostle back and forth.

Kelly looks at me with wild astonishment on her gorgeous face and whispers, "Jaret, you're a mage? Since… since when?"

"Since I was a teenager, Kel. I heard a rumor today that you're a wizard. If that's true, then our marriage just got a lot more politically complicated, didn't it?"

We spend the rest of the night talking, holding each other, and enjoying being completely honest for the first time in our marriage. I should have slept. I should have rested. But instead, Kelly and I stayed up and discussed our secret lives.

"You work for the MOP? You're a cop? How did I miss that?" Kelly asks. "I always knew you were away more than you said, but I figured you were just out having beers with friends!"

"Yeah, I've been a cop for years. Since we met, actually. Once you got the job offer here, I applied to the local office. Turns out they needed someone to head up a dual division office. It's MOP and WPS. I've got wizards working for me, too. It's insane, Kel. All this time we could have been honest with each other."

"I know. It sucks we lost all that time," Kelly murmurs, before adding, "But we can start now! What's the crime like here in Shanghai, Jaret?"

"Well, I'm sure you've seen the news on the Network," I begin to say.

Kelly cuts me off. "I don't like the Network. I don't even own a Network tome. To be honest, Jaret, I'm not a very skilled wizard. I only have one spell tome, and its mostly calming and coercion spells. Stuff I use at work for negotiating deals, and keeping the peace. I really don't enjoy magic or other wizards. It's just something I do to help make money, it's not who I am."

"Wow. I just wish you had admitted it when we met, Kel. Then I could have told you about being a mage."

"Oh my God. That's why you never told me!" she said, "Mages aren't allowed to say anything about magic to regs! And as far as you knew..."

"*Bingo*," I say. "You were just a reg. I caught so much shit from people over the years about marrying one, too. But I didn't care. You're perfect to me, with or without spells."

"I'm so sorry, Jaret," she says, "I thought it would freak you out at first, and then later that you'd leave me if you found out."

"I'll never leave you, Kelly. The only way I could ever leave you and the boys would be if I were doing it to save you. Other than that, get used to me because I'm here for the long haul," I say while running my hands through her hair. And then I scrunch up my face and say, "Even though you're a yucky wizard."

I wink at Kelly, and she slaps the hell out of my arm, saying, "You're the abomination that can touch the Ether without a spell tome!" As she says this, even though I know it's a joke, an urge to know the truth hits me.

"Kel," I say, suddenly serious, "do you know how spell tomes are made?" My heart beats faster than I ever thought possible, and my palms begin to sweat. I'm sure she doesn't know. But if she does... if she's ok with it... or a part of it... how can I... I'm just not sure how we could...

"No," she says innocently. "I never went to spell school. I learned about magic in college. I've never been trained, actually. A boy once showed me some magic to impress me and get into my pants. I asked him to get me a tome. So he did. It's still the only one I have."

"I guess that's how you were able to keep it from almost everyone, then, huh?" I ask.

"Yeah, you're the first person I've ever talked to about it."

"I wonder how Jenny knew about it," I say.

"Jenny? Jenny Yu?"

My eyes dart to Kelly's face to look for any signs of lying. Cop habit. I ask my wife, "How do you know her, Kelly?"

"She came into my office last week and was asking about my negotiation services. She was interested in hiring me out to do some work on the side. My bosses were ok with it. We're going to start next week on her project," Kelly explains.

"No, I don't think you will be, Kel. She's dead," I say.

"What?" Kelly says, astonished. "Tell me more."

"I'll tell you what I can, babe. But for your and the boys' safety, I can't tell you everything right now."

I enter the office the next morning, still exhausted from my lack of sleep from the night before. Everyone else on the team seems to have taken my advice, though. They all look very well rested this morning. Good for them. I, however, am going to need a gallon of coffee right away or I will die.

"Aurora, please tell me we have coffee," I say, struggling to form words. "Lots and lots of coffee."

Holding up an empty pot, she says, "Fresh out, Laoban. Want me to make some more?"

Keeping the tears and rage at bay, I tell her, "No, no. I'll do it. Thank you, though. I barely got any sleep. I had a long talk with the wife about magic last night."

The smile that spreads across her face is telling before she even makes the joke. "Is that what the kids are calling it these days?" Aurora asks while raising her eyebrows up and down.

"I hate you, Aurora. I'm too tired and worried to laugh. How dare you try and make me feel better."

Joyee walks in with half a cup of coffee and drinks it right beside me. I've never wanted to hit a man so much.

"Have a good night of rest, Joyee? How's that coffee?" I ask, reaching for it with both hands.

His eyes look about as bad as mine, and Joyee shakes his head while answering, "No, Jaret. I had terrible nightmares. I don't think this is going to work. There's no way we can stop him. The Maelstrom…Yivan…he is just too powerful."

"That's the spirit, Joyee," I reply sarcastically. "Listen, we're going to win. We have to. There is no other option. Now, no more talking from you, unless it's something positive. Things like 'we'll win' or 'we can do it' or 'have my coffee, Jaret' will all be acceptable."

Aurora laughs, and Mian Mian walks into the room with two coffees from Starbucks. She looks right at me and says the most magical words I've ever heard… and that is coming from a mage cop who works with wizards.

"I got you a coffee, Bossman. Black as my heart," Mian Mian says.

"Holy mother of goats. Mian Mian is now my favorite person in the universe. You hear that, team? Mian Mian is now the favorite."

Coffee in hand, a fresh pot brewing, and everyone gathered around the conference table, ready to brainstorm. "Alright, I figure we'll head over to the gardens in about an hour," I say in a much better mood. "We don't know when he'll come to find me, but I assume it will be around midday. Of course, you know what they say about making assumptions."

Joyee raises his hand to catch my attention, and replies, "No, Jaret, I don't."

I heave a sigh, and say, "Don't what, Joyee?"

He slouches down in his chair and quietly answers, "I, uh, don't know what they say about making assumptions."

Mian Mian puts her hand on his and says, "They say don't do it, Jo." Their eyes lock as they trade silly smirks with each other.

"Anyway," I say, getting back on track, "Yivan knows where the trap is set, so he will most likely wait until we are all there. He'll want to make a grand show of this."

Joyee has more wisdom to add, and says, "Either that or he'll walk in right now and kill us all."

"Joyee, didn't I say no more talking from you?" I fire back with a raised eyebrow. The laughter that fills the room calms all of our nerves just a little bit. Making jokes seems idiotic when faced with this kind of danger, but if it softens the mood a little bit, I'm going for it. The more we can ease the tension, the better. The four of us pass some time with idle chat before Aurora finally asks the big question.

"What are we going to do about the two Councils, Laoban?" she asks, more serious than I've ever seen her. "We can't let the Wizards Guild continue murdering innocent people now that we know. And we can't let the mages get a hold of Yivan's knowledge on unspent spells."

No one says anything right away. Joyee opens his mouth to say something but then closes it without uttering a syllable. Probably remembering that he isn't supposed to talk unless to say something positive, which he is all but incapable of doing.

Mian Mian says it for him, though. She stands and says, "I'm sorry, but I think this is all too much for the four of us to handle, Bossman."

"No, Aurora, we can't let it continue, and yes, Mian Mian, it probably is too big for us to handle. But that won't stop me from trying," I answer both of them. "No one is going to attempt to stop Yivan except for us. We are it. Keep that in mind. We can't fail because there is no backup team. There is

310

no plan B. I believe in all of you. I am putting my life in your hands because of how much I trust this team."

Aurora gives me her little mock salute, but her words have no silliness in them. In fact, they are the most honest and heartfelt words I've ever heard her say.

"I wouldn't follow anyone into this situation other than you, Jaret." Mian Mian nods in agreement with Aurora's vote of confidence, and Joyee gives two thumbs-up accompanied by a weak grin.

"If you all keep this up," I say, "we'll be singing camp songs and holding each other ever so tightly." They all laugh a little more, and I add, "Okay, it's time. Let's get out of here. Grab your gear and meet me down by the car. One of you is driving."

FORTY
2015 AD
Shanghai, China

Footsteps echo towards us. The sound of someone walking down the newly constructed dragon hallway my team created in Yu Garden fills our ears. Inside the gardens, foliage and water lay in late-night shadows, but inside the magically constructed dome my team has created, everything is pitch-black. So I can't see Yivan, but I can hear every single step. This is it.

Earlier, while waiting, Aurora filled me in on her clever trap that, hopefully, will ensnare Yivan as he enters the courtyard. "First his feet will become trapped within the ground, immobilizing him. Next, his fingers and lips will become stuck together to stop him from casting wizard spells. Lastly, his eyes will be completely shielded to keep him from targeting us with mage spells. It's the best trap I've ever seen, Laoban," Aurora said without a hint of modesty.

"Nice work, Aurora," I replied. "Let's just hope he actually steps in the area of effect."

"He will, Laoban. He will," Aurora assured me, before adding, "Are you sure you don't want me to add something lethal? It would be much easier if we just killed Yivan here and now."

"No. The fewer lives lost, the better. And that does include Yivan's life, Aurora," I answered.

As the footsteps draw nearer, Yivan's breathing becomes audible. He's exiting the corridor, and entering the wide-open space beneath the magically created dome. I can hear the blood flowing through my body.

"Guys? Are you in here?" a shaky voice asks from the dark and shaded courtyard. Fuck. I know that voice...and it's not Yivan.

"Jaysen!" Aurora shouts.

Trying to stop him from ruining our chances with Yivan, I yell, "Don't come any closer, Jaysen! There's a..." A muffled shout of surprise cuts me off, and then there is only dead silence. "...trap," I finish saying. "Shit."

The elemental Ether opens to me at my call, and I fill the courtyard with the light from a dozen globes of Fire. Jaysen is standing in the middle of the open courtyard. His feet are encased in stone, keeping him from moving. His fingers are completely stuck together and he is waving his arms around. His mouth is stuck shut, and he is yelling as best he can with sealed lips. And there is also a black cloud covering his eyes.

Despite him ruining our well-planned-out trap, it's a pretty funny sight. My team and I begin to laugh nervously. After long hours of waiting, none of us quite expected this. Aurora begins walking to Jaysen so she can undo all the different layers of her spell trap. She never makes it, though.

Yivan descends from the sky and lands directly beside Jaysen before Aurora can take two steps in that direction. Following his descent, I notice a hole in my team's "spellproof barrier dome." Yivan's open palm is crackling with immensely powerful Storm lightning. He can kill Jaysen with one bolt right to his temple. Everyone freezes as Yivan casts his gaze around the courtyard and mockingly says, "Well done team. We got him." An oppressive and sinister laugh then bellows from between Yivan's lips.

I motion for everyone to stay where they are, then raise my hands in a show of surrender and say, "Ok, Yivan. I'm all yours. Let's talk." The Maelstrom says nothing, but the look on his face is quite familiar. He is really pissed off. Attempting to defuse his anger somewhat, I start yammering, "I've dug around and confirmed just about everything you told me, Yivan. I'm not ok with what the Wizard High Council is doing, or with the Mage High Council letting them get away with it. In fact, my boss told me to learn what you know so that we can start farming wizards to be more powerful. I figure you and me? We can do something about all of this together. But we have to do it my way. No more innocent people need to die. With you and me working as a team, we can come up with a plan that makes us both happy. What do you say?"

Yivan merely shakes his head, and icily replies, "Jaret, stay where you are. If you take one more step, I will melt this poor fool's brainstem and you'll be cleaning another team member's remains off of the floor."

I immediately stop moving and put my hands down. "Please don't, Yivan. You're in charge. Just tell me what to do to keep everyone safe," I say.

The corners of his mouth twist upward wickedly as he surveys the room. "You should have never brought these people here if you wanted them to be safe, Jaret," Yivan says in a dark voice. "What happens next is your fault for trying to stop me."

314

The next few seconds become a blur. On instinct, I summon a Rock barrier around myself. An instant later, a lightning bolt slams into my chest and it hurts like a mother. But the barrier holds and I don't die. Well, not yet, anyway. I do, however, get tossed like a rag doll thrown by a bored toddler, landing about 20 feet away.

As I sail through the air, Yivan creates a 10-foot-long whip made of Storm power that flashes with purple sparks of energy. By the time I land and hop back to my feet, he is terrorizing the courtyard with this demonic weapon. Stones shatter at its touch. Every wall of shelter is obliterated in mere seconds, leaving my team entirely exposed.

They spread out anyway, as per one of our contingency plans, and begin to fire spells back at Yivan. He focuses his attention on Mian Mian for the time being, so Joyee, Aurora, and myself begin to circle to Yivan's sides and back. He sends the whip in her direction, but Mian Mian dodges every blow. The problem is that his attacks come so fast she has no time to retaliate. That's where we come in.

Joyee calls forth an ice golem by muttering exotic words of power and using both hands to draw shapes in the air. He directs his creation to attack Yivan from behind and then prepares another spell. Aurora also thinks to distract Yivan with magical creations, and summons a swarm of firebees to attack his face and arms.

Leaving distraction to my team, I choose destruction. One hand hurls a missile of roiling magma at Yivan, by combining Fire and Rock. My other hand sends a comet-like mixture of frozen Water and Rock towards the Maelstrom. The time that passes from Joyee's first cast until all of our spells hit can be counted in mere seconds, but it seems like an eternity.

Mian Mian finally manages to fire off a spell that melts the ground beneath Yivan's feet, tripping him for an only an instant, but long enough for our spells to reach the Maelstrom. The ice golem slams both fists into Yivan's back, but a glowing red magical barrier protects Yivan from the full force of its blow. He does stumble forward with a sudden rush, and unfortunately, this forward motion causes Yivan's arm to fly backward. His fearsome whip inadvertently reaches out to slice the ice golem across the chest.

The golem detonates in a shower of ice and freezing rain just as the firebee swarm hits the Maelstrom full in the chest and face. Instinctively, Yivan begins swatting them away with his hands, before coming to his senses and using magic. He swirls his free hand around and around creating a chilled whirlpool in the air with Storm wind. The entire swarm is swallowed and frozen by his magical tempest. Every one of the tiny, magical creations falls to the floor and shatters. Yivan's face is covered with welts from the firebees, and an expression of pure hatred and evil.

Luckily, my two magical projectiles reach Yivan before he can unleash more of his insidious magic on us. The magma missile hits him in the ribs, and the comet slams into his lower back just breaths apart from each other, the first spinning him one way, and the second knocking Yivan face first to the ground. As he falls, the Storm whip drops from his hand and immediately disappears.

Joyee's second spell is ready just in time for Yivan's fall. A glowing blue net shoots forth, holding the Maelstrom tightly to the ground while slowly constricting. Growing tighter and tighter, the net only stops when Yivan is curled into a fetal position with only one eye visible. That one single eye glares up at each of us in turn.

Everyone stops casting for the moment but holds their hands at the ready. "We did it," I say in shock. "We captured the most powerful magic user to ever live. And it was actually pretty easy." I look around at my team, who all hold a similar look of happy surprise on their faces.

"Don't dismiss your protection spells just yet, everyone. Let's play this safe," I say before kneeling at Yivan's side and saying, "Yivan, are you willing to talk about this peacefully? Or should we just take you to the High Council now and see what they'll do to you?"

The Maelstrom begins to sob. Harder and harder he weeps, until his cries start to sound... fake. The moans change suddenly into something else: laughter... raucous, mocking laughter. The Maelstrom is laughing at us. Yivan rolls his one visible eye over to lock stares with me.

"Oh shit," I mutter under my breath.

The blue net explodes in a shower of Storm-fed lightning and wind. Yivan rises into the air six feet above our heads, and his booming voice fills the courtyard.

"Do you pitiful creatures believe that I can be stopped so quickly? You are ignorant and weak fools, whereas I am immortal. I am no simple mage, and I am not some revolting wizard. I am a GOD. The Maelstrom can do things that no other being has ever been able to accomplish, and yet you fools think to finish me with your pathetic magic? I am insulted and disgusted!" he screams.

"Yivan," I begin to say, but he interrupts me and I feel spell power in his words.

"Jaret, I am going to murder you slowly," he says without emotion. "I am going to kill your entire team before your eyes. I am going to slay your wife. But your children – I won't kill them... not yet, at least. I will wait, and watch them grow up.

Once they have young ones of their own, only then will I kill your boys and their spouses… but not their children. I will repeat this for all of eternity because you were too blind to see the truth; too blind to follow me. Too blind and too ignorant!"

I suddenly realize that my team and I don't have what it takes for this – we never did. I finally understand that no matter what we do, Yivan is going to win. There is only one chance to save both my team and my family.

"Yivan, please. I'll…" I begin to say.

Before I can finish the thought, however, the Maelstrom casts his arms out and flattens us all to the ground. Using his Storm wind as weight, Yivan presses down and begins crushing the life out of us. I can hear the gasps and gurgled cries of despair from my team.

"Yivan, I'll do it. I join you," a voice calls out.

My vision fades to black around the edges from the loss of oxygen as I hear it. Who said that? Then I hear it again, but weaker this time.

"Yivan, please… I'll do it…join your… crusade," the voice says breathlessly.

It's then that I realize… the meek and surrendering voice is coming from my own mouth. Feeling separated from my body, I seem to watch myself being crushed while pleading with Yivan to free me so that I can join his vicious campaign of murder. The pressure eases a little.

"How can I trust you, Jaret?" he asks. "How can I be sure you won't try and reunite with your pathetic squad of imbeciles to once again fail in stopping me? I have no more patience for this. The time will soon be at hand, and I need total obedience. I need an apprentice. I need loyalty. I need… a son."

Though my skin crawls at the thought of it, I nod my head, and say, "I'll learn everything you have to teach, Yivan. I'll be your apprentice and your son. Please, just let them go and I'll never see them or my family again. I'll be yours and yours alone."

The weight on my chest is instantly gone, and air rushes into my lungs, cold and shocking. What have I done?

FORTY-ONE
2015 AD
Shanghai, China

I've done the one and only thing I can think of to stop this maniac from killing everyone I love; the only thing that makes any sense. I gave up. Whatever he asks, I will do it to keep my family from harm.

Now that I am free, I notice my team is still restrained on the ground. Thankfully, though, they are no longer being crushed to death by Yivan's powerful Storm magic. Instead, they are forced to lie on the ground and stare unbelievingly up at me. Tears stream from Joyee's eyes as he looks away. Jaysen's mouth gapes open, but nothing comes out. He shakes his head and his eyes tell me not to do this, but I have to. Mian Mian offers only a stone-cold stare, lacking any discernible emotion.

Aurora is the only one to speak. "Jaret, do what you have to do. We'll be okay. Don't forget about your family, or us... but don't ever come back. I'll make sure they are all taken care of."

My throat tightens as if a hand is grasping it tightly, and my only response is in the form of a curt nod. Turning my attention to Yivan, I say, "Ok, I'm yours. Now what?"

Yivan doesn't move a muscle but says, "Your first lesson begins here and now. Follow me."

The Maelstrom leads me to the entrance of the courtyard. As we approach, he picks up a satchel leaning against the wall and motions with his hand. The ground begins to move and rises up, forming a table and two seats. We sit down; Yivan looks into my eyes and begins the first of many lessons.

"This is a spell tome, and just like every other tome that exists, a mage had to die to create this one. My sister Maeris bonded with this one as she passed from this plane of existence. She was robbed of her future, but her connection to the Ether resides within these pages. Until now, no one, save for me, has ever read from this tome. You will now learn a spell from it. A very useful spell, Jaret."

A look of confusion crosses my face and I say, "But... I'm a mage, Yivan. I don't need tomes."

He sighs and chidingly says, "It is time for you to stop thinking like that, Jaret. Use your detective intuition, Lead Agent of the Shanghai MOP and WPS Dual Division Office, and tell me what spell it is that I want you to learn from this tome."

I already know. Of course, I do. I knew the instant Yivan said it was his sister Maeris's spell tome. "It's the spell used to reclaim unspent magic from dead wizards. Death magic.' I tell him.

Yivan's face lights up with pride. "Indeed. Well done, Jaret. I call it, quite simply, the Spell of Reclamation. For us to be successful in destroying the two High Councils, you must become as I am. You must become immortal. You must become unstoppable. The first step towards that goal is to learn to connect with the Death Ether and draw more power into your being. First there were mages. Next came wizards. Last of all there will be you and me."

I open the tome, and turn to the page that holds the instructions for the Spell of Reclamation. I read the words of power, mimicking the hand gestures as I do, and… nothing happens.

I look up confused, and Yivan is glaring angrily at me. "You're not concentrating, Jaret. Try again."

Once again, I read the incantation, and copy the hand movements simultaneously. The magic, sudden and cold, flows into me from the tome. As it does so, I understand that I will never have to use the book again. The power surges through me. It's like… drinking a 5-hour Energy made of pure magical essence. The feeling lasts for only a second, but I can now access the Spell of Reclamation like any other spell I've ever known.

That's not all that happened in the transfer, though. As I connected with the Death Ether for that split second, and the power rushed into my body, I felt a presence. Someone was there, sending images to me through the connection. Flashes of the things Yivan has already told me, and more that he never did. A wizard woman with very… unique and brutish features… she was naked and… well, it was a very private moment for the Maelstrom. But after they made love, Yivan let her go, refusing to kill the wizard. I saw the Mage Farm in Taiwan, and the French woman Herod and Yivan murdered there.

This presence is Maeris; I know it's her. She is telling me things through the Death Ether, but why?

Maeris showed me Stephen DuFrane kneeling on the ground. Yivan pulled his heart out with Storm wind. The Earth opened and swallowed Stephen's lifeless body at the Maelstrom's command. I didn't actually want the bastard to die. But truthfully, after our meeting yesterday, I can't say that I'm entirely sorry Stephen is gone. The same can be said of Jenny Yu, to be honest.

"So you killed both of my bosses, Yivan?" I mumble. "That's one way to make me available for freelance work."

Yivan looks at me strangely for a moment, then laughs and slaps me jovially on the back. "Come, let us go and seal the deal, as they say. You will now need to cast this spell on a dead wizard to take back their unspent spells. Then I shall know you are worthy of my trust and teachings."

This is what I was afraid of. I can't possibly kill an innocent person. If I do, then I am no different than Yivan, and will deserve to die. This line that I cannot cross, however, becomes more vague and harder to define as I picture my wife and children dying horribly by the Maelstrom's hands. And I suddenly realize that I'll do anything to keep them safe. Even murder. I stuff Maeris's tome back into the satchel and start to walk out of the courtyard down the long dragon corridor. Halfway down, I realize Yivan is not walking beside me, and turning back I see him standing in the gardens with hands on his hips.

"Wrong way, son," Yivan says gravely. "The wizards are over here." At this, the Maelstrom motions to my team, still helplessly restrained on the ground.

"Yivan, no. Please. I've said that I'll go with you and do whatever you ask, but I'm begging you: don't make me do this." But he ignores my pleas and takes me by the arm, leading me to stand over my powerless team.

"Do not be a child, Jaret. All wizards will eventually die if we succeed. Just pick one and be done with it."

Joyee and Aurora are the only wizards in the courtyard. He wants me to choose one of my team... one of my friends... and kill them. Joyee is weeping harder than ever, and I wonder for a moment if I should choose him. Aurora and I are so close...

But no. I can't do this. If I had to kill a stranger to save my family, fine. It would haunt me until my dying day, but I would do it. Asking me to kill someone I love... to protect someone else I love... is monstrous. I won't do it. I *can't*.

I tense my muscles, summon my most powerful magic, and prepare to throw myself at Yivan, who notices something wrong, and looks at me with a puzzled expression.

Suddenly, before I can foolishly throw all of our lives away, my dear friend says, "Jaret, it's alright. I volunteer." Aurora has a peaceful expression on her face as she gladly accepts this fate.

"Aurora, no. No. I can't..." I begin to say.

"Ever since you told me the truth of how wizard spells are created," she says, interrupting me. "I've been appalled at myself. I feel as if I was responsible for killing all of those mages. I don't want to cast magic anymore, Jaret. I don't want to die, but I also don't want anyone else here to die. I definitely don't want your family to suffer because I didn't volunteer. Please... don't say anything else. Just get on with it. I love you like a brother, Jaret King. I forgive you."

Tears fall from her eyes as she speaks, and Jaysen begins screaming, "Aurora, you can't do this! I love you. I've been too afraid to tell you for years, but I'm in love with you. I want to marry you and have a family with you. We can move to my parents' house in Wuhan. We can live in the country. We can move to America. Whatever you want! Please just... don't do this. I love you! I need you!"

Aurora looks at him with warmth in her eyes and a knowing smile on her face. "I know you do. I always thought you would eventually get the courage to tell me. I would have said yes if you'd asked me out, you know. Office dating policy or not… I think that I love you, too, Jaysen. We would have been happy together. But I have to do this. Would you have it be Joyee instead? If one of us has to die, let it be me. I could not live the rest of my life knowing Joyee died and I could have saved him."

Jaysen, sobbing and wailing, answers, "Yes! Let Joyee be the one! I'm sorry, Joyee. I'm sorry! I really am, but are you actually going to let Aurora die for you? Man up! Don't let her do this!"

Joyee, still lying flat on the ground, held tight by Yivan's Storm magic, tries to ball up and cover his face, where his shame shows plainly. Joyee closes his eyes and shakes his head back and forth.

Aurora looks at him and says, "Don't listen to Jaysen. I know you've never been the bravest, and I don't hold that against you. You are a great person, Jo. You don't have to 'man up' because I have decided to 'woman up.' Don't let my death haunt you, and don't waste your life. Be something. Do something. Tell her how you feel, Joyee. Don't wait like Jaysen did."

Aurora looks at me now and murmurs, "Ok, Laoban. I'm ready. Over and out."

Looking at my friend lying there unmoving and ready to die to save the rest of us, I whirl around to face the Maelstrom directly and tell him, "Yivan, I can't do what you ask. I can't kill my friend. I won't."

He merely shrugs and says flatly, "That is not a problem. You do not have to kill her, Jaret."

Silence fills the courtyard as he says this. Relief washes over me like the freezing cold water on the log flume ride at Six Flags, and my muscles relax.

"Thank you, Yivan… thank you," I say. "We can go find someone else, anyone else. I promise… I'll do it then."

Yivan smiles, places his hand on my shoulder warmly, and says, "Do not worry about it, Jaret. I never needed you to kill a wizard. I just need you to prove that you will take their spells. It is fine. I shall kill her." The Maelstrom extends his hand towards Aurora, and a spike made out of rock flies into her heart. Her back arches and she gasps loudly.

As the light fades from her eyes forever, Aurora whispers, "It's… o… kay…"

Jaysen roars incoherently and struggles at his magical bonds, trying to break free.

"Do it now, Jaret. We must leave this place soon," Yivan says coldly. There is absolutely no time to process what happened. Following his orders is the only way to keep everyone else in the courtyard from suffering Aurora's fate. I can't even say goodbye to her. The only thing I can do is to make the correct finger movements and say the right incantation.

As I do, a green glow surrounds me, and there is a feeling of being pulled forward by some force. Inside my mind, body, and soul, the feeling is much different. If learning a tome of power felt like drinking a magical Red Bull, then this is like being electrocuted with power and pleasure all at once. It's intoxicating and makes me feel unstoppable. If everyone knew how casting this Death magic felt, I feel sure there would be a lot more murdered wizards in the world. It's like I can, and will, do anything. My magical energy grows stronger, like a balloon filling with helium.

Aurora had at least eighty unspent spells within her: I know because I can taste each and every one of them. And all of that power is now added to my own. It's strange, but I know for a fact that every spell I cast from this moment forward will be more powerful than ever before. I can see how Yivan has become addicted to this.

Suddenly, despite the euphoric wave of invincibility washing over me, the memory of this power's source hits me. One of my dearest friends was murdered; someone I admire and respect died for me to have this power. I puke all over the floor.

Wiping the vomit from my mouth, I come to the conclusion that I never want to feel this way again. It's magnificent, but at what cost? I can't justify it. I am not like Yivan and don't want this kind of power.

My new boss - or master - leads me away, while my team watches in dead silence. My *former* team, I should say. There is no way I can continue to be their leader after this. Mian Mian stares up at the magical dome barrier with a hole in it and refuses to look at me. Joyee's watery eyes find mine and seem to say, "Thanks," while condemning me at the same time. Jaysen howls in despair, and screams, "NOOOOOOOO!" over and over. My heart wants to break, but I know that I can't let it; I stumble along after Yivan, mindlessly.

"We have so much planning to do before we can move on the two High Councils," he explains. "I have a safe house we can use in the meantime since Herod's shop will be crawling with reg police by now. It is good that he is dead."

"How do you know Herod is dead?" I ask.

"I told you, Jaret. I have been watching you," Yivan says with a wicked grin. "I saw the weakling go to your office. He was most likely trying to convince you to help him find a way to save his pathetic life. I had refused to give him the pulse any longer, now that I was so close to having you by my side. Herod was relatively useless anyway. We do not need him for the next part of my plan."

Yivan doesn't know that Herod turned against him and told me how to possibly kill the thousand-year-old devil. And I damn sure ain't telling him.

"Yes, Father," I reluctantly say, "he asked me to save his life but I let him die. Too bad I couldn't reclaim his spells at that time." From now on, I will do my best to play the part of the villain, since that is what he wants. It's necessary.

"That's the spirit, my son. But don't worry. In time," the Maelstrom says, "We shall take them back. We'll take them all back."

Yivan waves his hand, and a chariot made out of rock erupts from the ground as we exit the gardens and reach the road. There are no horses to lead it, but that doesn't seem to matter. Once we are inside, the elemental creation takes off at blazing speeds.

Yivan says, "I hope you don't mind, but I find this form of transportation much more to my satisfaction than modern vehicles. I can't stand riding in cars, and I hate to drive them."

Well, at least Yivan and I can agree on that.

FORTY-TWO
2015 AD
Shanghai, China

The next few weeks pass in a blur. The days are spent cramming spell tomes into my head while Yivan waxes poetically about how amazing the world is going to be once we rule it. The nights are full of terrible nightmares or lying awake with an aching pain in my gut, the feeling of something missing. I just don't have the power, will, or desire to try and stop Yivan anymore.

He has a few anonymous Network accounts and a couple of Network tomes at his safe house. In the rare bits of free time he grants me, I comb the news looking for anything about us, my old team... my family. One article mentions Jenny and Stephen's deaths. They were reported as a murder/suicide as a result of a lover's feud. Ridiculous. Anyone who knew them would never believe that crap.

There was also mention of Aurora and me: the Lead Agent and Second in Command of the local MOP and WPS office were reported missing. The author speculated that we had run off to be together on some South-East Asian island, citing the frequent occurrence of white men running off with Chinese women as proof. An interview with my wife showed that she didn't believe it for a second. Thank God.

She was quoted as saying, "I only found out recently that my husband was a mage. He didn't know I was a wizard either. We lived for years lying to each other; that's true. But I know he loves me, and that he is missing for a good reason. Jaret told me he was working on a politically sensitive and serious case for MOP and WPS. I trust him completely. He'll be back soon."

But I won't be back, ever.

If I do go back, Yivan will make good on his threat to haunt my family until the end of time. I have to stay away for the sake of my family and friends. That doesn't make me miss them any less, of course. This hole inside of me, this awful empty feeling, is caused by not being able to see them every day; to hold my boys, kiss my wife, and tell them all how much I love them. It hurts worse than any pain I can imagine, except for one thing: the pain of losing them to the Maelstrom. That's why I have to do whatever Yivan tells me to do. Up until now, though, I've been putting off absorbing more unspent spells from dead wizards.

"I want to learn as many spell tomes as I can, Father. The more spells I know, the better it will be for us when we attack," I told him.

"Alright, my son. I have countless tomes here at your disposal. Take what you want, it is your right as a mage to do so," he replied.

Most of the tomes he owns are full of defensive and attack spells; all battle magic. I've learned how to conjure golems, summon swarms of insects, create barriers like the ones he had in his dungeon. I studied a paralysis spell, an amnesia spell, and an unbelievable healing spell... If only I'd known this one on that day in the ladies' room, Liang would still be alive.

The problem is I'm running out of tomes to cram, and soon we'll have to go out into the Shanghai streets... hunting for wizards. The only comforting thought is that my soul is already damned to Hell for absorbing Aurora's energy. If I keep it doing it, then maybe one day I'll be powerful enough to kill Yivan all by myself. A mage can dream, can't he?

"Jaret, my son, I have a special treat for you," Yivan says to me.

"What is it, Father?" I reply, internalizing the shudder that always coincides with calling this murderer my father.

Yivan throws his arms out wide and tells me his "good" news. "There is a music festival at Century Park in Pudong. Thousands of people will be in attendance, and three of the bands playing consist solely of magic users. They are quite popular among young mages and wizards."

"I'm not really into pop music," I tell him, "but thanks. I like old punk bands."

Yivan strokes my head like a dog, and says, "Oh we're not going for the music. We're going hunting, Jaret. You need more power and the only way to get it is to kill wizards and take back our magic."

This is what I was afraid of; what I've been avoiding. "But we don't want to draw attention from the two High Councils just yet, do we, Father?" I say.

"Which is exactly why we won't be using the old tactics from my days as the Maelstrom. I have a more devious plan, something more along the lines of how I have been operating in the years since."

Giving in and agreeing to do this makes me just as evil as Yivan. So, I should sacrifice myself right now to stop him. Right? But I can't. I have my family to think of, after all.

"Sounds great. When do we leave?" I say.

"Shortly. But there is one problem," he says. "Though I know you are loath to do so, you will have to drive the bus."

Somehow, after what I've already done, and what I'll be forced to do next, the thought of driving a car no longer seems to bother me, so I tell my captor, "If I can murder people and suck the unspent spells out of dead wizards, I should be comfortable behind the wheel. It won't be a problem, Father."

He firmly places a hand on my shoulder and says, "That is good. We'll have to do much worse before this is over, but it is *all* for our benefit. We are stronger than them, and we deserve to rule. Not the Councils. And wizards? They will not even be a memory when we are done. The world will be ours. The strong will survive, and the weak will not. What could be better?"

"Not being held captive by you, forced to do evil shit, for starters," I think to myself.

A while later, I stare down one of my worst fears for the past 20 years. A cold sweat breaks out over my entire body, and I hear screams of pain inside my mind. I see a blinding white light and a terrifying wave of blood and body parts rushing towards me.

"Calm down," I whisper. "Focus your thoughts."

The key turns in the ignition and the bus roars to life. After the first few tense minutes, I find a profound sense of freedom comes with driving for the first time in years. The window rolls down, and the breeze on my face provides a feeling of serenity I never thought to find again as long as I lived.

332

As we cross the Nanpu Bridge, the city that has been my home for the past year spreads out to my left. Images of my family and friends float before my eyes. I hope they are all well, and that none of them ever has to find out what I had to become to keep them safe.

Using fake passes bought on the street, we wander around Century Park munching on festival food and drinking beer. For a few minutes, I actually start to enjoy myself – until Yivan kills my buzz.

"Oh, Jaret. One day, all of these fools will either be dead or bowing down and groveling at our feet, begging for their lives. We won't need to pay for filth like this," he says, motioning to his beer and meat on a stick. "We will take what we want and order slaves to bring us food and drink. We will be kings. And it cannot happen soon enough."

"Well, Father, you've waited this long," I reply. "I guess a little longer won't kill you. Nothing can kill you, right?"

"Indeed," he exclaims. "We need to make you immortal, just as I am. Come, let us find magical fuel with which to fill you with power."

The Main Stage is where the all of the magical bands will play later, or so we hear. So, we find a spot to recline and watch the audience, picking out those we think may be of any use to us. After two reg bands go through their sets, Round Eye and XXYY, a group of all magic users takes the stage.

"This is the all-wizard band we are here for," Yivan says, indicating the people onstage. "Hei Xin Ren, they call themselves," he adds.

"So what is the plan, Father?" I ask.

"We wait until they are finished playing their vile excuse for music, then invite people to an after-party with the band," Yivan replies. "I will use a coercion spell to make them more susceptible to suggestion, and get them on the bus. Our goal is to only get the wizards among them."

His mention of a coercion spell reminds me of Kelly for an instant. What would she think of me doing this? We watch the band, but more so the audience as they slam into each other and jump from the stage into the waiting arms of their fellow fans. Yivan gestures happily to an unusually large and loud group of fans singing along to every word of Hei Xin Ren's last song, "Laowai for Lunch."

We start passing out fliers for the fake Hei Xin Ren after-party to this group. The flier says that the bus leaves as soon as this set is over and indicates the gate where the bus will be waiting. Yivan's finger movements and incantation go unnoticed to all but me, and the effects of his coercion spell are immediately evident. The fans all suddenly grow very excited about the after-party and the chance to party with the band. Everyone in this group wants to attend. There are about 40 of them, but the bus can only seat 18-20 people.

At Yivan's order, I pull the bus around to the closest exit to the Main Stage. Yivan leads the crowd of 40 people over and explains to them about the limited room on-board.

"To attend this secret after-party and meet Hei Xin Ren, you must perform some magic for me," Yivan says, explaining the selection process.

The regs in the group all laugh and call him crazy, and are then immediately not allowed on the bus. The mages and wizards each discreetly show Yivan a spell to prove they are magical. It's a foolproof plan. Yivan can see how they cast, and only let the wizards on the bus. The thought of draining the magical energy from the corpses of these wizards causes Kelly's face to appear in my mind, and guilt races through me like Ricky Bobby. I can't go through with this.

Next to the bus a man is holding an enormous number of balloons for sale, and next to him is a drink vendor with a cart full of bottles and cans. "A distraction or spectacle might shock these people out of their coercion stupor, and send them back into the festival," I think to myself.

Saying a silent apology to these poor vendors, I set the balloons and drink cart ablaze with a thought. People begin screaming and running away. The groups of fans under the coercion spell near the bus begin to awaken from the magic and notice the intense situation.

Yivan glares at me suspiciously for a moment, before saying, "Start the bus." A group of wizards file into the idling bus and take their seats; fifteen in all. "Drive, Jaret. Now," Yivan orders. I press the gas pedal, but the bus barely moves. Pressing harder only makes the bus scrape forward with a horrible sound. "What is the problem, Jaret?" Yivan snarls.

"I have no idea, Father," I say. "Want me to get out and check?"

The Maelstrom looks at me suspiciously again, and says, "No need. I shall go. Keep the bus running; I will only be a moment." He exits and does a full circuit of the bus while shaking his head. He calls forth some elemental magic, and the bus rattles with a new addition. Yivan looks massively pissed again as enters and sits down. "The tires were all melted off, Jaret," Yivan says menacingly. "Did you have anything to do with that? I sure hope not...for your family's sake, and your own."

"No, Father. I swear it wasn't me," I reply honestly. I have no idea what happened to the tires.

"It makes no matter. I have crafted some replacements that will do just fine. Please drive to the… after-party."

The bus edges forward shakily on the Rock wheels Yivan created. Unfortunately, the bus is still drivable. However, we only make it one block before facing the next hurdle. The engine hisses loudly and water pours out onto the muddy road. All of the wizards on the bus start complaining loudly, the coercion spell now completely broken, as they demand to be let off the bus.

"Forget this party, man, I want to see Rolling Bowling play!"

"Yeah, open the fucking doors! We're out of here!"

"Let us out of the bus, or I'll blow a hole in the side of it, man!"

"You can't do that, Eddie! WPS will lock your ass up!"

Yivan tries to calm the mutinous passengers, and as I listen, slumped forward on the steering wheel, I notice someone standing directly in front of our broken-down transport. A joyous and welcome greeting catches in my throat before it escapes. I'm not so sure she is too happy to see me. Mian Mian looks pissed, and there's a white-hot ball of Fire in her palm.

FORTY-THREE
2015 AD
Shanghai, China

Yivan stops trying to convince the wizards to stay on the bus once he notices Mian Mian. Growling an inhuman string of sounds and whipping his hand in vicious circles, Yivan rips the back of the bus off. The wizards are all blown out like an airlock being opened on a spaceship in the movies. Every one of them hits the ground and runs away screaming in search of safety.

Mian Mian looks dead at me now, and not Yivan. Suddenly a Fire dragon is flying directly towards my face from her hand. Dropping to the floor of the bus, I wrap myself in a globe of frozen Water. The fire dragon explodes through the windshield, sending fragments of safety glass spraying in every direction. It continues onward and slams into Yivan. The full force of the blast catches him in the chest and sends the violent maniac sailing out of the gaping hole at the rear of the bus.

"Was she trying to hit him...or me?" I wonder aloud. Army crawling to the back of the bus as quickly as I can, I find Yivan standing upright and fuming with anger. His shirt has a giant hole scorched into the front, and his skin is severely burned. He waves a hand in front of the wound, tracing intricate patterns and chanting a short phrase, and his skin knits back together before my eyes. Immediately, I recognize the healing spell I learned while in Yivan's safe house. When I said it might come in handy down the line, this isn't quite what I had in mind.

Yivan glowers down at me while I still lie flat on the floor of the bus. "If I find out that you contacted this worthless mage to come and rescue you, I will strip the meat from your bones and feed it to your family," he mutters almost incoherently.

A sudden and overwhelming fear makes my blood run cold, and I tell him, "Father, I had nothing to do with this. You saw her! She was aiming that spell at me!"

Yivan nods and begins to float above the bus in search of Mian Mian. I run around the bus to warn her or flank her, I'm not sure which at this point, but find my old friend has vanished. There is no sign of her at all.

"Good," I mumble under my breath, glad that Mian Mian is wise enough to escape before Yivan can regroup and obliterate her.

The Maelstrom touches down beside me, all the while scanning the street for any signs of Mian Mian. "The coward has fled," he concludes dramatically, as he does with everything. "Come, Jaret. We shall return home and forget about going hunting for the night. With that mage on the loose after us, it would be difficult to finish this in secrecy."

"Thank you, Mian Mian," I think to myself, "Even if you were aiming at me." To Yivan, I say, "The bus is trashed, Father. How are we going to get back home?"

338

Yivan sighs heavily and replies, "If only you had access to Storm magic, we could just fly home. As it is, you could hold onto me, but I would be too worried about my student falling to his death. We cannot risk it. We shall have to take the Rock chariot, once more, and risk being seen." He summons the chariot from the Earth, and we head back to his safe house.

On the ride back home, Yivan is as silent as the dead. The calming quiet gives me time to think about what just happened. Was Mian Mian really aiming that spell at me? If so, why? It might be that she blames me for what happened to Aurora. And why shouldn't she blame me? It was all my fault. I could have said no to Yivan; I could have fought. I should have died rather than learn his dreadful Death magic, and I should never have used it on Aurora… my friend. But I chose to be a coward in order to save my family. So, Mian Mian probably *was* aiming that Fire dragon at me, and I probably deserve it.

Tonight's hunt may be canceled, thanks to Mian Mian's stupidly brave act of heroism, but it's just postponing the inevitable. Yivan wants me stronger to take down the two High Councils, and for that, I will eventually have to go through with the Spell of Reclamation again. The thought of doing so makes me feel sick again. I lean over the side of the chariot and puke my guts out as we race along, too fast for most regs to notice, thanks to Yivan's Storm winds.

The Maelstrom glances at me curiously, and I wave off his concern. "Those lamb sticks are not sitting well with me. Don't worry, Father, I'll be fine."

Seeming satisfied with this explanation, Yivan even touches his own stomach with a questioning hand, as he had eaten his fair share of the festival food, too. It wouldn't be the first time a couple of laowais got sick from street food in Shanghai.

Later, back at his safe house, Yivan sits down beside me on the couch. "Jaret, we must talk, my son," he says. "I have noticed your attempts to forestall the inevitable. Don't deny it, I can see through your lies. You have to be more powerful, my son, and there is only one method with which to do so. I can understand your reluctance, based on your first experience with the Spell of Reclamation. It was my fault the experience was so traumatic, and I fully accept this truth. I did it what I felt would ensure some distance between you and your former team. I realize now that maybe it would have been better had we just chosen a stranger for your first time."

I nod along in agreement, not really wanting to talk to Yivan about this.

"I have made a decision," he suddenly exclaims, his eyes racing back and forth as if searching for something only he can see. "We will begin our mission to eradicate the two High Councils in one week's time. If you wish to die in the attempt, as I assume you do, please know that I will fulfill my promise of tormenting your family until the end of time, should you perish. There is no way out of this, my son. You will do as I say. You will absorb unspent spells, and you will take down the Wizard High Council by yourself while I will attack the Mage High Council at the exact same moment."

"I know, Father. I'm sorry," I lie to his face. "Will we be attacking the local offices here in Shanghai, then?"

"No. That will do nothing," Yivan explains. "We will be traveling to Egypt where both of the Head Councils are housed. If you think that you can take on the entire Wizard High Council all by yourself and prevail with your current level of power, you are mistaken. If you fail, you know what I will do. So the question you must now answer is this: Are you ready to become more powerful?"

I'm stuck. This insane, powerful, ancient asshole has me trapped. I have no choice. "Bring me some wizards then, you old, evil bastard." I snarl, all pretenses dropped. "I need more power. I'll do this with you, but when it's over," I say, pointing a steady hand at his disgusting heart, "I'm going to kill you.'

Yivan regards me for a moment in thoughtful silence, then replies, "Very well, Jaret King. Together we destroy the High Councils. After that, we test each other and find out who is more deserving of life and power. The other will die. It seems rather fitting. My father would approve." He stands up and as he steps out of the room says, "Prepare yourself, Jaret. Now the fun really begins."

I am not proud of what came next, of what I had to do to keep my family safe forever. Yivan made it as easy for me as he could, though. I didn't actually have to murder anyone. The Maelstrom took care of that part of our bloody business.

"It doesn't matter how they die," he said while an ominous green glow surrounded my body, and an odd pulling sensation filled the room. "It only matters that you take back what was ours to begin with, Jaret."

And so I did. I took it back from their cold, dead bodies – many, many times over. I lost count of how many, to be honest. It must have been over a hundred, at the very least. The Network sites must all be going crazy with the rise of missing wizards in Shanghai. Is this all worth it? I don't know I do know that I despise what I have become. Draining unspent spells and continually growing in power is rotting my soul from the inside out, and the worst part is that every time I do it... the feeling is incredible. I exalt in the effects of the Spell of Reclamation. I bathe in the green glow of Death magic and emerge more formidable each time.

My only consolation is the belief that a tiny spark of who I once was is still alive inside of me. Every time I finish the Spell of Reclamation, and the dried-out remains of innocent wizards stare back at me, I become violently ill and vomit everything I've eaten recently. Because after that intoxicating feeling of invulnerability fades away, the realization of what I have done always settles in, and puking is the only way my conscience can cleanse itself.

Now, with only three more days until we fly to Egypt, Yivan seems satisfied with how powerful I have become. "At this point, Jaret," the Maelstrom says, "the only person in the entire world who can defeat you in battle would be me. Taking on the entire Wizard Head Council will pose no problem to you now. Like me, you breathe, sleep, and eat magical power, son. You have become a God."

The Maelstrom has found a happy medium between granting me enough power to destroy the Wizard High Council by myself, but not enough power to defeat *him*. I can tell that Yivan is holding back on me, you see. But the good news? I think that means Yivan is scared he might lose to me. Knowing that he feels fear gives me hope. And with that hope comes an understanding.

"Do I really need to follow through with his plan if I am powerful enough to defeat him now?" I wonder. Why should I do his bidding if I have the power to fight him and win, here and now?

What the High Councils have both agreed to is horribly wrong. What the wizards are doing with the Mage Farms is vile and evil. But there has to be a better way to stop it all other than killing everything and everyone involved. Yivan will never agree with that, though, because he is still filled with hatred over what happened to him a thousand years ago.

After that long, his grudge has festered and grown into something more. It's no longer about Maeris or his parents. It's all about power. Yivan wants more and more and more. His desire will never be satisfied, even if he controls the entire planet with a magical iron fist. The Maelstrom will always want more power.

So, I will not go to Egypt. Instead, I will risk everything to stop Yivan from killing more innocent people. But to pull this off, I'm going to need some help. Even with all this new power, I know that I can't do it alone. Yivan won't let me use the phone, so I have thought of another way to call for backup.

"Yivan, I am going to take a cruise along the Huangpu River," I tell him. "I want to say goodbye to this city. I don't care if you approve or not. You're welcome to join me, though."

He regards me calmly, shrugs his shoulders, and says, "Fine. I shall accompany you, Jaret. But remember this; I have given you massive amounts of power. I have provided you with a whole new world of ability, and I have given you the truth about wizards. I did all of this because I need your help to take down the High Councils and the guilds. You were strong before. You were fast before. Now, you are almost unstoppable. No one on this planet can defeat you in single combat, other than me. I want your help, but I *will* kill you in a heartbeat if you betray me in anyway… like contacting your family or pathetic friends."

I give him a mocking smile and say, "But you're my only family and friend now, Father."

"You laugh, Jaret," he snaps back, "but it is truer than you realize. Do you think they will take you back and accept what you have done here, within these walls? They will not. As you saw in the park, your old team blames you for what happened. They hate you. Your wife and children will think you a monster now. You are like me, son, and we are better than all of them. We are strong and they are weak. Remember that. After we kill the Councils, and you challenge me, there is a chance you could win – a slight chance, to be sure, but stranger things have happened. I want you to remember what I am saying now, just in case that comes to pass. You are better than everyone else. You deserve to sit high above these mortals and be revered. Never forget that, my son."

I will not listen to this demon anymore. It's time to bring him down or die trying. "Yes, Father," I say. "I will remember every single word that you have said to me. After lunch, let's head down to the river together for one last visit. I'll drive."

FORTY-FOUR
2015 AD
Shanghai, China

We pull up to the pier in a stolen car and park it on the curb. After coming this far and doing so many terrible things, taking a car is pretty meaningless at this point. The area is relatively deserted, as is usual for this time of day.

"I've always wanted to ride this gaudy dragon cruise ship," I admit, being completely honest with Yivan. "I've seen tourists riding up and down the Huangpu River on it a million times. Well, today I'm going to take it."

"You finally begin to see," Yivan says predictably. "We can take whatever we want. Regs cannot stop us. Wizards cannot stop us. This is what life should be like."

Strolling leisurely to the ugly, golden-embossed boat with dragon heads on either side, Yivan and I find it completely unmanned. We board the tourist trap and walk the stairs all the way to the top deck.

"Who is going to drive this dreadful thing for us?" Yivan asks, his eyes scanning the deck disdainfully.

Raising both hands into the air, I tap into the Water energy flowing through the Elemental Ether. The boat lurches forward and slowly pulls away from the pier. "Just call me Captain Jaret," I answer.

Yivan laughs gruffly and grunts out a half-hearted "Aye, aye."

The boat pushes out into the middle of the river and then heads downstream at my command. The Maelstrom and I both watch the Shanghai skyline pass in silence. It's peaceful here. The air pollution is not bad today, so the sky is a lovely shade of blue. Every building is clearly visible, and the breeze is pleasant. However, the calm tranquility of the moment is not destined to last much longer.

Once we reach the far end of the usual tourist cruise route, I turn the boat around and catch Yivan's attention with a mischievous smirk. "What do you say we crank it up a little bit?" I say.

Gripping the rails with white knuckles, my body floods with more exuberant Water magic. The dragon ship surges forward like a high-powered speedboat, and the wake we leave behind us has water rushing over the banks of the Huangpu. My fist flies into the air, and I unleash a roar of excitement at the giant buildings surrounding us. Yivan adds his voice to mine, and we howl like wild animals flying down the river at ridiculous speeds in a big clunky passenger ship covered in dragons.

"It's now or never," I say under my breath. "Time to call the cavalry." More Water magic courses through my connection to the Ether and a massive wave in the dirty waters of the Huangpu River begins to rise. Forming beneath our fat little cruise ship, the wave raises us to the height of nearby skyscrapers. Inside the top ball of the Pearl Tower, tourists look on in

346

shocked amazement. The flash from dozens of smartphones and digital cameras taking pictures of us captures Yivan's attention.

His eyes go wild as Yivan says, "What do you think you're doing, Jaret?"

Shrugging my shoulders and wearing my most uncaring facial expression, I try to emulate Yivan while saying, "Who cares if they find out about magic now? Pretty soon it won't matter. They will know about it because we will use it to crush them under our thumbs and rule over them forever like kings – like GODS."

Yivan, still looking worried, says, "Yes… but we don't want their eyes on us so soon, my boy. This will draw too much unwanted attention. Take us down. Immediately."

Sighing heavily, I lower the wave back into the river. "You're right, Yivan. I'm sorry. I just got carried away with the thought of our new life."

Calling this monster father is an insult to Christopher King's memory, and I won't do it anymore. By the look in his eye, I think he noticed the switch in terminology.

"Oh, it is fine, *my son*," the Maelstrom says. "Don't worry too much about it. We must be cautious, though. There is already too much attention from the High Councils on this city due to my recent activity here. Your big wave will probably cause more of their attention to be drawn to Shanghai. However," he says, stroking his chin, "I believe that might just be to our benefit. Once we leave this place, the Councils will both have their gazes focused on China. They will never expect what we are bringing to Egypt: death and destruction, and the birth of a new world!"

I laugh along with his maniacal blathering, and Yivan embraces me. My skin crawls at his touch, but it's almost over... for one of us, at least.

"I grow weary of this scenery, Jaret," Yivan says after a few minutes of silence with the wind blowing across his face. "Let us take our leave and return home."

"You'll never see that safe house again, Maelstrom," I think to myself. To Yivan, I say aloud, "Sure thing. I just want to go around one more time and really take it all in."

He accepts this and sits on the deck, closes his eyes, and begins to rest in a meditative state. As we slowly travel upriver and back around one final time, I feel calm and resolute. Everything up to this point doesn't matter. I may have done terrible things, but I did them for what I consider to be a good reason. I can't justify it any more than that.

Yes, many wizards had to die. I didn't kill them, but I was the reason for their deaths. But wizards have been killing mages for a thousand years to create spell tomes, so what I've done in the past few days is just a drop in the bucket. Does the end justify the means, though? I don't really know. What I do know is that without the extra spell power provided by those dead wizards, I would never have the courage or ability to stop Yivan.

Searching the shore thoroughly as we drift by, I look for the final piece I need to put an end to the Maelstrom, and mumble to myself, "Come on, please let them have been there. Please let them have seen it on the map."

Bingo. Two figures stand on the shoreline watching the dragon boat sail past. I would recognize Mian Mian and Joyee from their body language alone, but the fact that one of them is glowing with magical fire surely helps.

"Why isn't Jaysen with them?" I wonder. Hopefully, he is just staying hidden. We're going to need all the help we can get in the next few minutes if we hope to stop this murderer. The boat suddenly shudders to a stop, and not at my bidding. "Here we go," I say with a smile. "Things are about to get a little crazy." Saying a little prayer to whoever may be listening, I beg for the will to succeed and for the safety of my family. Kelly, Luke, and Han...I love you all.

"Why have we stopped, Jaret?" Yivan asks, concerned.

"I'm ready to go *home*, Yivan. Very ready," I tell him, completely honest for the second time today.

The Maelstrom looks up at me in a way that seems to say he and I have been friends for years. He looks lovingly at me like a father looks at his son. But, like I said before, he is not my dad. He is not Christopher King. Yivan is just an old, crazy man who wants to rule the world. And I will not have that. No fucking way.

Yivan, still looking at me with what whatever form of love he could possibly be capable of feeling, smiles as I gather my strength. A huge fist made of solid Rock catches Yivan completely unaware and knocks him down, crashing him through the deck to the level below us. I follow, hopping down through the hole, not wanting to lose the momentum my surprise attack has given me.

Any hopes that he would be unconscious or confused when I see him are lost. Yivan is dazed, but very much awake. And he is furious. Before he can cast, I send a vast stream of the dirty Huangpu River tearing through the floor of the boat. It crushes his entire body in a tidal force. Yivan is blown out of the side of the ship, and carried by the strength of the deluge all the way to shore. I quickly follow on a controlled stream of Water that rises under my feet.

Behind us, the boat begins to sink into the river. I set down just behind Yivan, as he crashes into the stone wall of the embankment on the Bund. There are tourists everywhere – so much for no innocent bystanders at this time of day.

With a magically augmented voice carrying the length of the Bund Promenade, I weave a wizard coercion spell into my words and shout, "Run away! Do not look back! Get to safety now!" Said in both English and Chinese, the spell works instantly, and regs flee the scene without hesitation. This care for the innocent, however, costs me time and focus.

By the time I find Yivan, he is on his feet with that deadly Storm whip in his hands once more. His seemingly infinite anger is focused solely on me, and thankfully he doesn't notice my two friends standing nearby. I call forth a shield and sword made of pure molten lava, woven with Fire and Rock magic. They bubble and spit fire in constant motion. Every protection spell that I know covers me from tip to toe, and I crouch in a low stance ready to settle the score with the Maelstrom. We circle each other as I try to make sure his back is to Mian Mian and Joyee. His attention has to stay on me. They are not strong enough to handle him alone. I need to soften him up first.

"Jaret King, you have made an error in judgment. If you thought to catch me off guard and kill me quickly, you were sorely mistaken. While I admit to being surprised by your attack, I have been expecting it. You took a lot longer to defy me than I gave you credit for. Now, we can go around in circles with this dual or you can just let down your guard and we will call it even. I will forgive your indiscretions, and we will return to the truly important work that we must complete. What do you say, my son?"

Fire leaps forward from my sword as it swings in his direction. Yivan rolls to the side and lashes out with his fiendish whip made of Storm lightning, but I catch the full blow on my shield and turn it aside.

"I AM NOT YOUR SON, YIVAN!" I roar so forcefully that the taste of blood enters my mouth as my throat tears. "I will not go along with you anymore. You will not win. You will not kill anyone else. Do you hear me?"

Yivan merely shakes his head, and looks down his nose at me, saying, "What a pity. You could have been something wonderful, Jaret. You could have done amazing things. Instead, you will only die. And everyone you love will die, too. I will erase your memory from history, boy. Once I rule this world, I will write a new history that curses your family line for eternity. I will hold true to my previous threat and continue to plague your descendants for the rest of my never-ending life. Do *you* hear *me*, you fool?" As he says, "fool," Yivan strikes out with his Storm whip, except this time the blow is directed at my legs. It catches me off guard and I am dragged to the ground. Luckily my whole body is shielded. Otherwise, I would be an amputee below both knees.

From the concrete sidewalk, I see him raise the whip again for a final and deadly strike. I roll to the side and fling my shield at his chest. While on its way to connect with Yivan, I change the shape into that of an elongated spear aimed right for the Maelstrom's black heart. It strikes him, and my spirits soar momentarily... until I notice the spear did not pierce his flesh. It struck Yivan, knocking him back a few strides, but he caught the missile with his free hand before it could penetrate his chest. Yivan squeezes the Fire spear, filling it with freezing Storm wind, and the magical weapon dissipates in his hands. Despite the burn marks on his hands and chest, his lips peel back as he shows his teeth to me in a feral snarl. There is murder in Yivan's eyes, and lightning, too. Purple sparks leap from his pupils.

The Maelstrom ignores the pain from his burns and swings his whip once more. It flies towards me and wraps around my Fire sword. He snaps his wrist, and my blade goes tumbling away onto the ground, where it vanishes.

"Two can play at that game," I mumble, trying to keep up with this madman's frantic pace. I call on the Water of the Huangpu once again and douse his whip. The Water instantly washes over the magically charged weapon, leaving Yivan holding nothing but air.

Again, we begin to circle one another, and I risk a glance in the direction of my friends. For the moment, they still bide their time but seem to be growing impatient. Pretty soon one of them may do something stupid, like attack Yivan. I can't let that happen yet. Not until the right moment.

I open myself up to the full force of Fire magic and send jets of flames forth from the ends of my arms. Yivan quickly counters by creating a Rock wall in front of him. The Rock begins to turn molten and melt away almost immediately, but by the time it does he is no longer behind it. I look about frantically to find him, only to see Yivan floating directly above my head. He drops right on top of me, and we fall to the ground punching, kicking, scratching, biting, and trying to inflict as much physical damage as possible before breaking apart.

Yivan rubs his chin where I caught him with a right hook. He smirks at me and says, "With the two most powerful magic users on Earth having a spellfight on the Bund in Shanghai, who would have thought the most painful blow landed so far would have been a simple punch to the face?"

Taking the hint, I summon my Rock magic and encase myself in armor harder than any metal on Earth. "As Herod once told me, 'There's just something right satisfying about punching a man squarely in the face.' And at this moment, I couldn't agree more," I say.

I wade in and begin to pummel Yivan with my Rock-enhanced fists. He roars a bestial sound and copies my armor spell, encasing himself in a blackened ash shell, equally impenetrable as my own Rock barrier. We clash to the sounds of an earthquake.

I hit him solidly in the armored solar plexus, and he clips me on the Rock-covered chin. We break apart and come forward again, throwing haymakers with abandon. I kick the Maelstrom in the mid-section, forcing him back a step, causing him to pause for a split second. Not wanting to waste the opportunity, I dive headlong into Yivan, taking him at the knees. Once down, I realize that this brawl is going nowhere. His armor has to go if I want to crush Yivan. I decide to try something different, but familiar – something I have now sworn twice to never use again. I guess I'm a liar.

Just as I did with Mian Mian and my old tutor Lee, I reach out with a tendril of magic, except this time I use Rock. Once I find Yivan's Rock essence, I brush against it with my own. To Yivan's, and my own, surprise… his armor is dispelled instantly. The look of shock and horror on Yivan's face is priceless.

"So, opposing forces cause a violent reaction, but like forces cancel each other out. Nice to know," I think to myself.

Both of my hands rush down to crush his head and end this once and for all. Unfortunately, they never make contact with his cranium, as the Maelstrom raises both of his hands to my chest and blasts me with an absurd amount of Storm energy. Wind and lightning are woven together expertly and split open my armor, sending me flying back into a statue of a bull near-by, which shatters on contact. My Rock armor crumbles off of me in small pieces that instantly turn to dust. I ache all over and feel like a city bus just plowed into me. Gasping for breath, I remember how truly powerful Yivan is.

"That was a very nice trick you pulled back there, Jaret," the Maelstrom says with an approving look on his evil face. "How did you dispel my armor? What is it that you aren't telling me?"

A chance to recover after he fried my eggs like that would be very welcome, so I take this opportunity to stall. "I ain't tel-lin' you shit!" I shout, channeling my Southern roots. "Any help I give to you is only hurting other people, and I refuse to do that ever again, Yivan."

The Maelstrom places both hands on his hips and shakes his head at me as if I was a petulant child. "Jaret, you know that I cannot be defeated. Why do you continue with this folly? I admit that it has been great fun, but we should end this, put it behind us, and get back to work! Can you not see that we are better than everyone else? Look at what we can do! Even now you surprise me with new talents. I admire you, Jaret. I wish to learn from you as you have learned from me. Please, let us work together. Stop this ridiculous fight so we can move forward!"

I flex my hands to test them out and discover that I'll need to filibuster a little bit longer to regain my full strength. "I've already told you how I feel, Yivan," I explain. "I do believe that something must be done about these Mage Farms. What was done to your family and countless others by the Wizards Guild and High Council is nothing short of evil. But to fight evil with evil is wrong. There has to be a better way to stop all of this. The Mage High Council is trying to do exactly what you are doing, and they are wrong, too. I will find a way."

"Yes, Jaret. We will," Yivan says smiling.

"*I* will, Yivan. Not you. I once thought to convince you that working together to find a better solution was possible. Now I see that it's not feasible. You only crave power, not peaceful resolution. If I could somehow bring your parents and Maeris back to life right now, you'd kill them in a heartbeat for the chance to sit on a throne and rule over the Earth. This is what you have become over the past 1000 years, and I will not follow you down that path. I refuse!"

Yivan's mouth twists tightly with rage. His hands clench so forcefully that blood drips from his palms, and the Maelstrom stares at me with only desire in his eyes – the desire to kill.

FORTY-FIVE
2015 AD
Shanghai, China

"HOW DARE YOU SAY HER NAME?" Yivan rages savagely, saliva flying from his mouth. "If Maeris were alive now, I would teach her as I have taught you, Jaret. She would be by my side and help me to reclaim all that is rightfully ours. WIZARDS STOLE EVERYTHING FROM US! They stole everything from me, Jaret. Wizards do not deserve magic. It is ours by right of birth! Why can you not understand that?"

Yivan punctuates the word "that" with a bolt of lightning right at my chest. Fortunately, I was ready for one of his slick tricks and cast a Rock wall directly into the path of Yivan's lightning. The stone barrier explodes into a million shards as it connects with the deadly bolt of Storm energy, sending shards soaring in every direction. My body would be filled with hundreds of tiny stone spears right now if not for the red glow of my wizard barrier.

Yivan, however, is not so lucky. He neglected to cast any protective spells on his body. The Maelstrom's hands and chest remain scorched from the Fire spear, and his entire body is full of Rock shards, blood weeping from tiny wounds all over.

Without moving or saying a word, Storm wind surrounds Yivan as he pulls all of the rock fragments out of his body. Then, saying words of power and tracing patterns in the air, Yivan casts the wizard spell of healing.

I don't waste his distraction by being idle. Using my connection with Water, I freeze a section of the Huangpu and then hurl giant chunks of the frozen river at him. I don't expect them to hit Yivan; I only need to keep his attention elsewhere for another breath or two.

"Now!" I shout to Mian Mian and Joyee.

Yivan sees the chunks of ice coming his way and lashes out with Storm lightning to destroy them. One single bolt emerges from his hand before branching out into several others, matching the number of ice blocks flying his way. Upon contact, the sections of frozen dirty river water rip apart with a resounding crack. As they shatter, a searing hot spray of Fire from Mian Mian's hands surprises Yivan. Caught off guard, he whirls towards the source of the painful intrusion. At the same moment, Joyee creates a shower of stinging, poison rain over the Maelstrom.

He spins again, now towards Joyee, to assess this newest threat. Still staring daggers at Jo, Yivan blindly creates a temporary shield against Mian Mian's intense barrage using the broken ice all around him. Knitting it together, he forms an ice wall. It instantly starts to melt, but gives the Maelstrom all the time he needs to defend against the terrible pain of Joyee's wizard spell. Using his left hand, Yivan creates a cyclone of air around himself. The acid rainstorm Joyee created is torn apart by the power of the violent Storm winds.

While Yivan is dealing with my team and their magic, I begin chanting an incantation and trace intricate shapes in the air with my hands. Now, I have complained before about the lack of creativity involved with wizard spells, it's true. You know, the spell is just there in a tome and can be cast in only one way, whereas my elemental magic requires an artist's touch. Mage spells are open to interpretation and easily changed in any way the caster can imagine. I can shoot a ball of Fire and change it into a spear mid-flight, or add Rock to make it slam into my target with more force. A mage's options are unlimited with spellcasting. A wizard spell just...is. You can't adapt it.

That being said, I am very thankful for this wizard spell I was forced to learn while captive in Yivan's safe house. A confusion spell, as Yivan explained it, afflicts the recipient with amnesia for a short period, making them confused and lost. Yivan's eyes find mine just in time to see the completion of this confusion spell on my lips. His scream echoes over the river, "Nooooo!"

The Maelstrom's hands reach out to me just as the bright blue beam of light hits him in the forehead, knocking him around in a circle. When I see his face look up, there is no anger in his eyes anymore. It has been replaced with fear.

"Where am I? Who are you? What's going on?" he says with a shaky voice. As I look at Yivan's confused and frightened face, I remember what he told me about this particular spell in the safe house...

"Any pain suffered by a person under the confusion spell will nullify its effects, causing them to remember everything. So strike hard at that moment. Make sure they never recover. Kill them, Jaret. Do not hesitate."

Remembering those words and watching the Maelstrom fidget around in this way makes me suddenly question what I want to do next. That is when I realize the flaw in this plan.

"Hey, Bossman. Nice moves out there," Mian Mian says from behind me.

"Thanks," I reply.

She points to Yivan and adds, "So, what are we going to do with him?"

Joyee edges around my other side, opposite from Yivan, keeping my body between him and the Maelstrom. "Kill him. Kill him now before he snaps out of it, Jaret. It's the right thing to do. After all he has done, he deserves to die," Joyee says, looking more frightened than usual.

Letting Rock magic flow from my hand into the ground, a long, slender knife rises out of the Earth, its edge as sharp as any blade ever made. Grasping it by the handle, I look over at Yivan, who is now kneeling on the ground poking an empty noodle container.

"What is this? Is it alive?" Yivan asks fearfully.

I raise the knife above my head and bring it down swiftly...

...then gently place the razor-sharp stone blade into Joyee's hands. "If you want him dead so badly," I say, "you do it, Jo. I have been forced to see and do some terrible things by this man. But right now he is just confused and scared. I can't kill him in cold blood like that. Can you?"

Joyee looks from the knife to the long-haired, muscular man holding an empty noodle container and examining the cardboard cup – looking at it from every angle. As Joyee sees the innocence found in those lost eyes, he loosens his grip on the knife, and it falls to the ground, where the blade vanishes.

Mian Mian shakes her head in dismay and says, "What are we supposed to do then, Bossman?"

I stare at Yivan, searching for the answer. The Maelstrom… my adoptive "father" over the past month, just sits there with eyes darting at every movement. Everything surrounding Yivan at the moment terrifies him. "I don't know," I admit. "I'm at a loss. But, since we're all here, and have a minute to rest, can I ask you something, Mian Mian? Were you aiming that Fire dragon at Yivan… or at *me* in Century Park? And how did you find us?"

Mian Mian smirks and answers, "Well, I figured that if he were still attacking large crowds of people, then a music festival would be a good start to find you. And finding you was all we've been trying to do since he took you, Bossman. I just happened to be walking by an exit when I saw the balloons and drink cart go up in flames. That was when I noticed you behind the wheel of a bus. As far as which one of you I was aiming at, I think it was a little bit of both. I…" She hesitates. "I can't get what you did out of my head. How could you do that to her, Jaret?"

"I know you won't understand, and I don't expect either of you ever to forgive me," I tell them. "I did what I had to do to stop this madman from killing all of us… from killing my family…from killing thousands more people. She was already dead; I couldn't help her… but I could help everyone else. I'm sorry." I look both of them in the eyes, no longer ashamed of what I did, yet, not proud, either. "Listen, you didn't have to come, I know that. I want to thank you both for being at the office and for coming when you saw the map light up today."

Joyee puts his arm around Mian Mian and pulls her close. "It's our job, Jaret. With you gone, this amazing woman decided that someone had to keep running things. So she stepped up and took charge."

"I'm proud of both you," I say, beaming. "But... where's Jaysen? Why isn't he here with you?"

They glance at each other, and then back at me. "He isn't coming," Mian Mian answers curtly.

"He... you have to understand that Jaysen was madly in love with Aurora, Jaret. I know that you didn't kill her. You didn't have any choice in what you did. I see that, even if Mian Mian is struggling with the truth," Joyee says, squeezing her shoulder. "You saved us. You absolutely did. But... Jaysen... he blames you for everything. He thinks it's your fault she's dead. Jaysen said... well, he said that he never wants to see you again, Jaret. And that, if he does, you'll die... screaming." Joyee looks away as he stutters through the disturbing part at the end.

It's like a blow to the gut, honestly. I love Jaysen like a brother; he's a great friend and an amazing person. I knew he loved Aurora, but... to now find out that Jaysen wants me dead? It sucks.

Joyee hugs Mian Mian closer, and their eyes both stray to the frightened mage sitting on the ground. Yivan. We still have to deal with him.

"Well, we better finish this now." I say. "I can't kill him like this, though. It's not right. So, I'm going to wake him up, and then we'll all strike together before he can cast. The moment you see recognition in his eyes, strike and don't hold back."

Three new items appear before us, made of pure magical energy. I thought it was a strange spell to learn back at the safe house, summoning these astral weapons. But Yivan assured me, with a guarantee based on his past experience, they can be *quite* dangerous. Mian Mian takes the knife while Joyee takes the sword, which leaves me with the spear. These astral weapons should put an end to him once and for all. It'll be faster than a spell with them in close combat, and they'll pass right through any magic barrier. What could go wrong?

I shift my attention to the long-haired, heavily muscled and tattooed mage kneeling on the ground holding a noodle container. I reach out as if to help him to his feet. Yivan takes my hand with a smile… and then I kick the Maelstrom in his chest as hard as I can. He falls backward, landing on the ground.

"*Hey*, why did…you…?" he begins to say before his eyes go cloudy, and the fear disappears. Yivan comes back to himself, seeing us standing over him holding deadly spell-made weapons. As quickly as possible, I plunge the spear towards his chest while the other two begin to swing their astral armaments at Yivan's head. Just as the tip of my spear makes contact with his skin, the world suddenly goes upside down.

Intense, hurricane-strength Storm winds have lifted Joyee, Mian Mian, and me off of the ground, leaving us dangling in mid-air. The wind blows around us so fast that it is hard to breathe. Yivan has created an isolated and intensely violent storm directly over the four of us standing on the Bund.

"You have erred for the final time, Jaret King. It would have been wise to kill me while I was confused and lost," Yivan says with death in his voice.

"I couldn't do it, Yivan," I admit. "I refuse to be as cold and heartless as you are."

"Cold and heartless, am I?" he says. "So be it. First I shall kill your two friends very slowly in front of you, one at a time. They will feel more pain than humanly possible, and then they will die. You will be unable to help them, Jaret. In your despair, you will realize that you are next, followed by your family. I regret that you will not be able to assist me further, but I see now that I cannot trust you. I must do this alone as I have done for so long."

Yivan casts a sleep spell on Mian Mian and tosses her unconscious body to the side. She has such shitty luck with sleep spells. Yivan wraps me in a binding of Storm wind that barely allows me room to breathe. I try to break out of it the same way I did with Jenny Yu's magical bonds, but Yivan is not a fool. He accounted for elasticity in this spell. It moves and stretches, but always keeps me locked down tight.

Next, Yivan removes Joyee's shoes with a flick of his wrist. Tiny fingers of electricity stretch out from Yivan's hand and make contact with Joyee's bare feet. His screams echo off the French colonial buildings lining the Bund. There is nothing I can do to stop this from happening. I can't help them. Mian Mian lies there sleeping soundly, and I suddenly remember the first time she was under one of his sleep spells. I woke her from it with my tendril of Water – opposing forces cause a violent reaction. It was similar to how I dispelled Yivan's rock armor earlier; using a tendril of Rock magic – like-kind forces cancel each other out. And just like that, I have a cunning plan.

The ancient texts I read as a teenager said it was possible to control all four elemental magics. You just had to find them, and take control. The wizards did this, in a way, with Death magic. It's possible that I could find something new in my time of need. Maybe I can take control of a new Ether. All I have to do is reach out and look for it, right?

My father's face appears in my mind's eye, as he so often does when I'm stressed out. He smiles and puts his hand on my shoulder. As always, my real dad tells me the two things I need to hear to get things done. "Calm down, Jaret. Focus your thoughts, son."

Reaching out with a tendril of Water magic to connect with Mian Mian's Fire for the second time, I brace for the impact. The violent reaction is a distraction that could buy me some time. My power extends outward, and suddenly I become hyperaware of everything magical around me. I can feel the Storm winds that Yivan is using to hold me in place, and the Storm lightning causing Joyee incredible amounts of burning pain. I detect all of this magic strand by strand, in a strange and unusual way that I've never experienced before.

Yivan's connection with the Elemental Ether is enormous; a massive tendril of Storm magic flowing into his being that pulses with power. More power than I have ever felt before, in fact. It is both awesome and awful at the same time. How can one man carry so much?

And why can I now suddenly feel it?

The Spell of Reclamation is the answer, I immediately realize. As with Yivan, but to a much lesser degree, all of the reclaimed spells have made my magic more potent. And now I'm experiencing something entirely new. Yivan's Storm energy continues to draw my attention for some reason. It is the most powerful magic I have ever felt. His Storm pulse is there, thrumming with life-extending power, making the Maelstrom immortal. I can feel it like a heartbeat surging through his body. And just like that, the memory of Herod's advice fills my mind.

"... *imagine what would happen to him should he let go of that pulse of his? Imagine how fast he would fade at over 1000 years of age, eh?*"

"Not bad, old man," I mutter. "Not bad at all." I calm my mind and focus my thoughts, extending all three of my connections with the Ether together; Rock, Water, and Fire. As they reach out, I weave them into a braided tendril containing every bit of power I possess. This has to work; I'm out of options. Joyee roars in pain as Yivan rakes his body with larger and stronger lightning strikes. "Don't rush," I whisper to the wind.

"Stay calm. Stay focused." My combined magical tendrils inch closer and closer to Yivan. I can feel his Storm pulse more and more the closer my magic gets to him. I can almost touch it. This close, it's less like a heartbeat and more like a thundering drum keeping a constant rhythm.

My magic makes contact. And then... nothing.

Now, when I say nothing, I really mean it. There was nothing. Nothing left at all. Every one of Yivan's spells immediately shut down. The Storm wind holding me, the Storm lightning tormenting Joyee, and even the Maelstrom's infamous Storm pulse, too.

The moment everything stops, Yivan's face becomes a mask of pure terror, a mask that suddenly looks older. Very much older. In the blink of an eye, Yivan is no longer in his mid-twenties. Instead, he looks to be in his mid-fifties now. Graying hair, wrinkled skin, with a leaner frame that is less muscled. There's no time for me to revel in the fact that this worked, unfortunately, because I fall to the ground and erupt with agonizing pain criss-crossing my entire body.

The blood boils in my veins, and my skin bubbles all over as if being melted. As I try to take a breath, I find it impossible. Foam pours from my mouth like a rabid dog. I begin to convulse, and the pain intensifies tenfold. "I'm being electrocuted," I realize and think to myself.

Lightning pours from my face as I scream and writhe in agony. Somehow, amidst all of the pain, I notice that something is vastly different inside of me; my magic has changed.
The convulsions continue unabated, though, and my skin begins smoking. Electrical sparks are coming out of parts of me I'd rather not mention. And yet, I am more worried about my inability to sort out my connection with the Ether. Everything is jumbled in my mind. It feels like my brains are packed tight-

er than a clown car. There is something new there, inside my mind. It feels like a raging *storm*.

And just like that, as quickly as it started, the pain stops and I gain full control over this new power. My heartbeat thunders, and I feel complete… like I was always meant to be this way. Storm winds lift me back to my feet, and Yivan stares at me with awe. His rapid aging has stopped, and I feel that his pulse has been put back in place.

Yivan looks to be in his sixties now, resembling a grandfather hippie with long, white hair with a big, gray beard. "Greetings, GRANDfather," I say as lightning arcs between my hands.

"How is this possible, Jaret? How did you cut off my connection to the Ether? How did you take Storm for yourself?" Yivan asks in a rush. "This cannot be possible."

"But it can be, Yivan. AND IT IS," I reply, calling forth every bit of Storm magic available to me, and creating a storm that covers Shanghai. Violent winds howl. Torrential rains flood the streets of this magnificent city. And enough thunder and lightning to scare the devil himself follow, as well.

"It's over, Yivan," I add. "I am the stronger between us now. So *you* will now have to do as *I* say."

The Maelstrom's face contorts and twists with pure hatred. Joyee lies motionless on the ground behind Yivan, but his chest rises and falls, as does Mian Mian's; both are alive but out of the fight. Good. They would only get in my way.

Yivan brings forth his electrical whip once again and whirls it around to lash out at my chest. I catch it in one hand and dispel the terrible weapon with a tendril of Storm. The horror on his face is worth all of the tea in China… And there is a lot of tea in China. Trust me. Yivan tries changing tactics and starts casting a wizard spell. Before he can finish, though, I surround both of his hands with heavy Storm winds. Weaving Rock magic into those two little windstorms and contracting them, both of his hands are crushed into a mess of broken fingers. He won't be casting any crammer spells for quite a while.

"Your reign of terror is over, Yivan," I begin to explain. "There will be no more murdering from you. There will be no destruction of the High Councils in your future. There will be a change in the way things are done, but I'll see that it's done peacefully."

The old man looks at me with wetness rimming his eyelids, and begs, "You cannot take this from me, Jaret. I have spent a thousand years preparing for my revenge. There is no peaceful resolution, but you and I... we can stop them together!"

"I will not let the wizards continue to breed and murder mages for the sake of spell tomes. I will also not let the mages learn your foul Death magic and farm wizards for their own gain," I tell him. "But I will not murder innocent people to reach that end. I won't kill anyone if I can help it... including you, Yivan."

The Maelstrom, Yivan, looks utterly exhausted as he realizes I won't kill him. He sits down on a bench nearby and puts both broken hands in his lap. "So, you're going to let me live then?" he asks without looking up. "I will be forced to live forever as an old man... I guess I deserve it. I am a thousand years old, after all. It just might be time to experience what old age is really like. Maybe a change like this will be right for me. Thank you, Jaret. I...I'm sorry for all that I've done to you."

"Yivan," I utter in total disbelief, "understand me; letting you live doesn't mean you get to go unpunished. I will see you charged for your crimes and brought to justice. I am going to block your magic and take you before the Mage High Council, where you will be tried and executed. Just not by me."

Nodding his head slowly, Yivan stays silent for a moment and then heaves a big sigh. "I thought you might say that, boy," the Maelstrom mutters quietly. Sparks shoot from Yivan's eyes as he raises his broken hands into the air and calls upon the Ether. Two enormous chunks of Rock emerge from the ground and soar towards Joyee and Mian Mian's helpless bodies.

The Maelstrom leaps at me, biting at my face and neck, Storm lightning arcing over his entire body with the hopes he can fry me into a crispy husk. It would have to any other person in the world. Hell, it would have worked on me if he had done it a few minutes ago. But now that I am stronger than he could ever hope to be, I am not afraid of Yivan the Maelstrom or his magic any longer.

Reaching out with all four of my magics combined into a large, braided tendril, I grab a hold of his connection to the Ether. But this time, I don't dispel his magic. Instead, on instinct I take full control of his spells somehow. By combining all four elemental magics, it seems that I have found something new. There are no elemental properties to this new magic, like Fire, Water, Storm, or Rock. It is just pure ethereal power; possibly even a connection to some new Ether. It is what I was born to control.

My newfound magic shuts off Mian Mian's spell sleep, and she sits up immediately, looking confused. Searching within myself for a particular spell, I discover all of my wizard magic no longer requires incantations or gestures. The spell of healing revives Joyee with just a thought, and his wounds completely heal in a matter of seconds. He sits up looking dazed as well.

The chunks of Rock hurtling towards my two friends now hover in mid-air, stopped by my will alone. They crush to dust at my command. I let Yivan keep his little net of electricity surrounding his body, but it does me no harm. He rises into the air on a gust of Storm wind against his will and settles back down on the bench. Realizing he is indeed beaten, Yivan tries to dismiss the Storm-powered lightning web, but finds that he cannot.

"It's mine now," I say, "all of it." Condensing the web into a ball of electricity, I hold it directly in front of Yivan's face. He stares in wonder as I close my hand over the sparking blue ball and dismiss it.

"This is impossible, Jaret," he says in an empty voice. "How are you doing these things, my son?"

"I am not your damn son, Yivan," I spit madly. "Don't ever say that to me again." Mian Mian and Joyee watch intently from the side, but wisely stay back.

"I've created something new... or maybe rediscovered something ancient. It might be a connection to another Ether. I feel like I can do anything with it." This revelation is met with dead silence. It always starts like that.

The sounds come rushing in like a thousand tigers snarling simultaneously. Yivan lets loose a guttural roar and leaps for Mian Mian, who in her interest, has moved too close to the Maelstrom. She screams in terror and Joyee grabs her, casting a barrier over the two of them. Yivan never reaches my friends, though. I wrap him in a bond made of Storm wind and squeeze it just enough to make him hurt.

He glares at me in pain and fury, and growls, "You will never stop me from trying. I will never back down. The wizards will all die. The mages who help them will all die as well. I will discover your new magic, and I will reverse my aging. I will rule over all of you one day. You will be my son once more. I swear all of this to you now, Jaret King. Listen to my words, *boy*."

I stare in cold silence at this man I used to fear. This legend that terrorized the world... This monster that has killed thousands of people; this magic user that taught me to be more than just a mage; a man who has lived for more than a thousand years; but most of all… a stubborn old fool that will never stop killing. Our eyes meet and a moment of understanding passes between us.

"No, you won't do any of that, Yivan," I say, reaching out with my newly found power and shutting down his Storm pulse once and for all.

As his pulse is cut off, Yivan wears a look of peace on his features, accepting this death, and maybe even welcoming it, in the end. In another blink of the eye, the Maelstrom goes from looking like a man in his early sixties to an ancient and withered creature. His hair falls out. His teeth rot in his mouth, and they fall out as well. His eyes go milky white and sink into his face. He becomes nothing but taut skin over frail bones.

In his very last moment, Yivan whispers to me in a dry, dusty, and rasping voice, "You're welcome, boy. I led you to this. You truly are better than the rest of us. Don't waste this power. Stop… them… Jaret." His flesh falls away in dried strips, and his bones turn to dust.

Yivan… the Maelstrom… is dead.

FORTY-SIX
2015 AD
Shanghai, China

"What now?" Mian Mian asks, yawning away the rest of her spell sleep.

"I don't really know," I answer honestly. "First of all, are you both alright? Are you hurt?"

Mian Mian nods and says, "Yeah, Bossman. I'm alright."

Joyee does a full body-check, including a pat down. Finding no wounds, he looks shocked and says, "Surprisingly, I feel fantastic. How is that even possible?"

"I, uh, learned a healing spell," I answer, not wanting to go into how I came about such magic.

"That's one hell of a healing spell, Jaret," Joyee adds with a hand on his stomach. "I think you cured my acid reflux, too."

Quickly changing the subject, I say, "Well, since we're all good, let's get the hell out of here before the regs all return. We have a lot of explaining to do to the home office, and I'd rather not be listed as part of an international terrorist attack on The Bund in Shanghai."

Mian Mian gives a stretch and another yawn, saying, "Yeah, good call, Bossman." Waving goodbye to me, she takes Joyee by the hand and begins to walk away.

Joyee, however, looks around at the violent tempest still raging throughout our city and says, "I've never seen a storm this bad in Shanghai before."

Realizing that I'm still holding onto the enormously devastating Storm magic, I immediately release the spell, and the tempest dissipates instantly. Joyee and Mian Mian appear startled at the suddenness of the storm's retreat.

"How did that happen?" Joyee asks, looking at me suspiciously.

I shrug and reply, "I turned it off, Jo."

"Turned it off?" he asks. "How, Jaret?"

"Well… I…uh," I stutter, hesitant once again to admit the truth, "I created the storm in Shanghai," I say, clenching my fists tightly as this new power courses through my body like a maelstrom. "I *am* the Storm in Shanghai," I mutter to myself.

Joyee and Mian Mian hurriedly rush off together, leaving me alone with the remnants of Yivan lying at my feet. Unsure as to why, I reach down and pick up the pile of clothes that remain. An immediate humming energy catches my attention as I pilfer through his garments, and a bright green amulet falls out of his cloak and tumbles to the ground. I see it flash as if reflecting sunlight off its Emerald façade. Reaching out, I pick up the strange amulet, and find it freezing cold to the touch. The necklace pulses with magical power as I hold it in my hand. Knowing Yivan, this amulet is dangerous. I better not leave it here for any regs to find.

As I put the necklace around my neck, there is a strange, yet familiar, pulling sensation for just a moment…I look around for a telltale green glow but see nothing. It has been a very long day. I'm starving, dehydrated, and almost falling asleep on my feet. My mind is more than likely playing tricks on me. So I ignore the feeling and walk away from this place; the site of one of the most incredible moments in magical history.

Yawning, I mumble, "I've never been so tired in my entire life." And it's true. Every muscle in my body aches and my mind is exhausted. "This must be spell fatigue," I say, guessing. My tutor, Lee, used to talk about spell fatigue all the time, warning me of the dangers involved with overactive casting. I've never used enough magic at once to feel it before, though. I gotta say – spell fatigue? I'm not a fan.

Grabbing some street noodles and a can of soda from a vendor nearby, I hop into a taxi and head for home. Scarfing down the noodles in seconds and draining the drink in two gulps leaves me feeling slightly better. My mind seems clearer, at least. So I play back what just went down on the Bund.

Will the Mages Guild kick me out for using that much magic in public? Will the Wizards Guild blame me for everything, including all the dead wizards? What am I going to tell them both? I'm not saying anything about my new magic, that's for damn sure. I won't become a weapon for the casters or the crammers. The only plan I can form in my mind right now is to go home and be with my family.

The cab pulls up to my compound and stops, dragging me out of my deep thoughts. I sling the driver some cash and stumble out of his car. The local kids are all playing in the fish pond in front of my building, taking the loose gravel from nearby and creating a little rock bridge to cross the pond. I've seen them at this before. The custodial staff who work for the compound always show up and wreck the bridge, for some strange reason, as soon as the kids go back home. All of that hard work put in by these kids, and the adults just tear it down. It always bums me out. Well, not this time, damn it.

I wait until the kids leave to get more gravel, and I tap into my Rock magic. The bridge suddenly extends all the way across, and even forms handrails for the kids to hold onto. They come running back with a bucket full of rocks, which they immediately drop as they see their new bridge.

"Tai bang le!" they all shout. It's kind of the equivalent of "awesome" in Mandarin. The children all run across the bridge, stopping in the middle. They scream and cheer, and yell at each other about who gets to rule the bridge first. As they argue, I suddenly feel a strange pulling sensation again, more insistent this time. I look around once more for the source, thinking to see the ominous green glow of Death magic... but again there's nothing. I must still be spell-fatigued.

Exiting the elevator on the ninth floor, I open the front door to my apartment and find it deserted and silent. There is nothing to indicate anyone lives here; there is no furniture, no clothes, and no personal effects whatsoever. There is nothing at all... except for a duffel bag and a Network tome on the floor.

Terrified, I run through every room in search of some clue as to where my family has gone. Did Yivan have a backup plan that I didn't know about? Did he get his revenge on me in the end somehow? My thoughts immediately go to the darkest possibilities and I become frantic. In the kitchen, though, I find a note on the refrigerator. It reads:

Jaret King: Lead Agent
Shanghai MOP & WPS Dual Division Office,

Due to the danger involved with your current investigation, along with the recent deaths of both your staff and management, my colleagues and I at the Council felt it best if your family was placed under maximum protection for the time being. We know that you will be pleased with our foresight and proactive action in this, and will agree with our decisions. We in the Mage High Council hold you, Jaret King, in high regard, and feel that you are a valuable asset to the continuance of our people. As soon as you are ready to see your wife and children, please contact me via the Network.

Best Regards,
Faye Minter, 3rd Seat Mage High Council
Cairo, Egypt

"They have my family," I say aloud, knowing exactly what this is all about. The Mage High Council will want me to fill them in on how Yivan – the Maelstrom – was reclaiming spells from dead wizards. They will want me to tell them everything, and help build them an army of powerful casters to start a war with the Wizards Guild. I know it, without question.

Well (and this may sound cliché as hell), if it's a war they want, then it's a war they'll get. But not with the wizards… they'll have to deal with my newly found power.

The problem is… I can't put my wife and boys in danger. If the Council has my family, then I'm at their mercy for the time being. I mean, I could show up and just waste everyone with my new powers, sure, but I have no desire to be like Yivan. I won't take innocent lives, and I won't risk my family.

No, I'm going to play along for a little while to save my family, and find out just how deep the corruption goes. And then I'll take care of business. Placing my hand on the Network tome, I say, "Faye Minter, High Council of Mages, Cairo."

Waiting for the connection, I realize this is absolutely the highest-ranking government official I've ever talked with. Speaking with a person actually on the Mage High Council? I'm moving up in the world. Hell, a month ago, I would have been out of my mind with excitement. Now, though, I'm only filled with dread.

The Network joins our two tomes, and I find myself looking at a slender woman with dark skin and shoulder-length dreadlocks. She has a large, toothy grin as she greets me.

"Hello, Mr. King. It's wonderful to finally speak with you. I have been following your exploits in the MOP for years. Those are quite some achievements you have in your file, I must say. But all of that is nothing compared to the stuff we aren't allowed to put in there from the past week, am I right?"

376

Just how much does she know about the events of the past week, I wonder. "Yeah, it's been hectic around here for sure," I say. "I could use a vacation, no doubt. I'd love to bring my family with me, though…"

Faye's demeanor changes instantly, and she snaps, "Don't take this situation too lightly, Mr. King. It is no laughing matter. People are dead. Good people. Both of your direct supervisors were found not far from each other, murdered. Jenny, along with several other high-ranking members of the WPS were found drained of their magical essence, presumably by the man known as the Maelstrom. Stephen's body was hard to locate, but… well let's just say it was a closed casket funeral, Mr. King. Most of your team is also deceased. So let us be candid, any attempt at humor will not go over well with me."

Fuck. She's intense. "Yes, ma'am. I do apologize," I reply in a remorseful tone. "I'm spell-fatigued, and my mind is not right at the moment. Please forgive me. Now, about my family?"

Faye changes back to her big toothy grin and replies, "Yes, yes. That is some beautiful family you have, Jaret. They are all safe, so don't worry. You and I will need to meet in person to discuss all that occurred in Shanghai, though. As you can see, all of your belongings have already been moved to your new apartment, which is located in the city of your new assignment. Your family has arrived well ahead of you and is settling in quite nicely. The kids are already in a great day care. We have taken care of everything for you, Jaret. All you need to do is wash up, put on the fresh clothes we've provided for you, and head to the airport. The tickets are in the overnight bag we packed. First-class tickets, too. You're welcome." Faye Minter winks at me, but it feels… predatory… not friendly.

"Ma'am, if you don't mind my asking," I say, "just where am I going and what is my new job?"

She reveals her wicked, toothy grin again and says, "Mr. King, your efforts in the Asian region have been so successful that we can't imagine sending you elsewhere. In fact, you are being promoted to Stephen DuFrane's old position. Since his and Jenny's passing, there is a void to fill in the region. My counterparts in the Wizard High Council and I agree that you will make a fine choice to fill both positions. We've consolidated the roles, you see. Jaret, you will be the brand new Head of Magical Patrol and Protection for all of Asia, or Head of MPP Asia."

My head spins as I try to fully grasp what Faye is telling me. "Ma'am, what is Magical Patrol and Protection? Am I not working for MOP anymore? What about WPS? Will they be involved? I'm sorry, I'm just a little lost."

Her reply has an edge of anger to it as Faye says, "Yes, as I've just stated, Mr. King, we have consolidated Stephen and Jenny's roles and also their respective departments. We've given it a new name to highlight the cooperation between our two Guilds. Do you understand, now?"

"I, uh, think I do," I answer. What I really understand is that both sides are trying to use me. They both want to be able to claim Jaret King as their champion when they find out what I know. The crammers don't want me working solely for the mages, and the casters don't want me working only with the wizards. And neither of them knows about my new magic! They both only want to know about Yivan's Spell of Reclamation; the wizards want to keep it secret while the mages want to spread the knowledge far and wide. Well, I won't be telling either side a damn thing. "Ma'am?" I ask, stiffly.

She flashes her teeth again. "Please, Jaret, call me Faye."

As I stare at those fangs, I begin to grow more suspicious of this mage. "Ok. Faye," I say cautiously, "who will I answer to in this new position, and where is my office? Where will I be living? WHERE IS MY FAMILY?" I finish loudly, desperate for some information about the three people I love most in the world.

She glances down at something I can't see and clears her throat. Faye sounds quite unhappy as she says, "Some of that is… currently being discussed between the two High Councils, Jaret. For the time being, you will report to no one. You will be a self-sufficient department."

"Nice," I say with a smile. I bet the Councils both hate that. For me, though, it's perfect. With access to both sides and no boss to control me, I will have freedom to investigate Mage Farms and find out more about the truth. Plus, it will make taking down the current government system a little bit easier. "And my new location, Faye, where is it?" I ask again.

Every single time I see her crocodilian grin, I get the shivers. But this time she finally answers my question. "Oh, yes. You've been assigned to Penang, Malaysia … for now at least. Your wife has secured employment with a school there. We looked for something in the corporate negotiations sector, much as with her previous jobs, but Kelly told us she was tired of working in that world. She wants to make a difference that matters. It pays a good bit less than her last career, but with the bump in salary you will receive as Head of MPP, it all evens out."

"Ok, Faye. That sounds excellent," I tell her. "I just have one last question before I go. How many Magical Patrol and Protection – MPP – offices are there?"

She pauses, looks me dead in the eye, and says, "Yours is the first, Mr. King. Do not make us regret it." Faye Minter, 3rd Seat of the Mage High Council, then ends the connection without saying goodbye.

"She's a little bit scary," I think to myself. But being on the High Council is probably stressful enough to drive anyone crazy. "You know what, though?" I say aloud, "It's going to get a lot more stressful once I start cleaning house."

And trust me, cleaning out both of the High Councils is definitely high on my To-Do List. But first, I need to take a shower and get ready to fly out. Before I leave China, though, I should probably make a couple of calls. I mean, seeing as how I'm in charge of the division with no one to answer to and all – I must also be in charge of hiring. And I know a couple of good agents that might want a fresh start somewhere in a new office. I'll surely need their help for what is next.

What is next, though? Well, the way I see it, I will have to reunite with my family, stop a war from breaking out between the casters and crammers, build a new magical government from the ground up – including finding a new way to create spell tomes – and basically make the world a safer place. Sounds easy enough, right?

What could go wrong?

TO BE CONTINUED IN BOOK TWO OF
THE MAGE FATHER SERIES...